Case Studies in Contemporary Criticism

NATHANIEL HAWTHORNE

The Scarlet Letter

Case Studies in Contemporary Criticism

SERIES EDITOR: Ross C Murfin

Emily Brontë, *Wuthering Heights*
EDITED BY Linda H. Peterson, Yale University

Kate Chopin, *The Awakening*
EDITED BY Nancy A. Walker, Vanderbilt University

Joseph Conrad, *Heart of Darkness*
EDITED BY Ross C Murfin, University of Miami

Nathaniel Hawthorne, *The Scarlet Letter*
EDITED BY Ross C Murfin, University of Miami

Henry James, *The Turn of the Screw*
EDITED BY Peter G. Beidler, Lehigh University

James Joyce, *The Dead*
EDITED BY Daniel R. Schwarz, Cornell University

James Joyce, *A Portrait of the Artist as a Young Man*
EDITED BY R. B. Kershner, University of Florida

William Shakespeare, *Hamlet*
EDITED BY Susanne L. Wofford, University of Wisconsin–Madison

Mary Shelley, *Frankenstein*
EDITED BY Johanna M. Smith, University of Texas at Arlington

Jonathan Swift, *Gulliver's Travels*
EDITED BY Christopher Fox, University of Notre Dame

Henry David Thoreau, *Walden*
EDITED BY Michael Meyer, University of Connecticut

Edith Wharton, *The House of Mirth*
EDITED BY Shari Benstock, University of Miami

Case Studies in Contemporary Criticism

NATHANIEL HAWTHORNE
The Scarlet Letter

Complete, Authoritative Text with Biographical Background and Critical History plus Essays from Five Contemporary Critical Perspectives with Introductions and Bibliographies

EDITED BY

Ross C Murfin

Southern Methodist University

Bedford/St. Martin's

BOSTON • NEW YORK

For Bedford/St. Martin's
Publisher: Charles H. Christensen
Associate Publisher: Joan E. Feinberg
Managing Editor: Elizabeth M. Schaaf
Developmental Editor: Stephen A. Scipione
Production Editor: Lori Chong
Copyeditor: Kathryn Blatt
Text Design: Sandra Rigney, The Book Department
Cover Design: Richard Emery Design, Inc.
Cover Art: Quilt, fans patterns. Amish, artist unknown, initialed "P.M." Indiana. 1931. Cotton, 83 × 73¼ inches. Collection of the Museum of American Folk Art, New York; Gift of David Pottinger. 1980.37.86

Library of Congress Catalog Card Number: 89-63918

Manufactured in the United States of America.

4 3 2
p o n

For information, write: Bedford/St. Martin's
75 Arlington Street, Boston, MA 02116 (617-399-4000)

ISBN: 0-312-06024-6 (hardcover)
ISBN: 0-312-03546-2 (paperback)

Published and distributed outside North America by:

MACMILLAN PRESS LTD.
Houndmills, Basingstoke, Hampshire RG21 2XS and London
Companies and representatives throughout the world.

ISBN: 0-333-57560-1

Acknowledgments

The text of *The Scarlet Letter,* Volume I of the Centenary Edition of the Works of Nathaniel Hawthorne, is copyright © 1962 by the Ohio State University Press. All rights reserved. It is an approved text of the Center for Editions of American Authors and the Modern Language Association.

Acknowledgments and copyrights are continued at the back of the book on page 371, which constitutes an extension of the copyright page.

Preface

A Word about the Series

The *Case Studies in Contemporary Criticism* series provides college students with an entrée into the current critical and theoretical ferment in literary studies. Each volume in the series reprints the complete text of a classic literary work, together with critical essays that approach the work from different theoretical perspectives and editorial material that introduces the work and the critical essays.

A Word about This Volume

Part One reprints the Centenary Edition of Nathaniel Hawthorne's *The Scarlet Letter.* Established by the Ohio State University Center for Textual Studies and the Ohio State University Press, the Centenary Edition is a critical unmodernized reconstruction of *The Scarlet Letter* that has been certified as an approved text by the Center for Editions of American Authors and the Modern Language Association. In short, it is the most authoritative version of Hawthorne's most famous novel.

Part Two includes five exemplary critical essays, prepared especially for a student audience, that examine the work from five contemporary and influential theoretical perspectives: psychoanalytic, reader-response, feminist, deconstructive, and new historicist. (Other volumes in the series introduce different perspectives.) Each critical essay is preceded by an editorial introduction to its theoretical perspective, history, and principles and by a bibliography that promotes further exploration within that perspective.

The text of *The Scarlet Letter* and the critical essays with their introductions and bibliographies are complemented by additional editorial material. In Part One, the text of the work is preceded by a general introduction that provides biographical and historical information about Hawthorne and *The Scarlet Letter*. Part Two opens with a history of the critical reception of the work, tracing important arguments that have arisen since its initial publication. This interpretive history not only shows how critics have read the work but also reveals how they have read one another and suggests the theoretical implications for modern readings of the work. Finally, a glossary includes succinct definitions and discussions of key terms that recur in the volume and in the literature of contemporary theory and criticism.

Acknowledgments

I am greatly indebted to all of the contributors to this volume. Joanne Feit Diehl, David Leverenz, Michael Ragussis, and Sacvan Bercovitch revised their published essays with remarkable sensitivity to the capabilities and needs of student readers. Shari Benstock, whose enthusiasm for rereading Hawthorne regularly rekindled my own, devised an original essay that seems likely to lead feminist studies of Hawthorne into the 1990s even as it leads students into feminist theory. I would also like to thank Johanna M. Smith, without whose help the introduction to feminist criticism and accompanying bibliography would have been less than comprehensive; Frank Palmieri, who substantially improved my introduction to the new historicism; and Peter Bellis, who shared not only his knowledge of Hawthorne, but also numerous library volumes.

William E. Cain, John Limon, and Charles N. Watson served as readers for Bedford Books and provided very helpful suggestions for final revisions. Of the people at Bedford, I would like to thank Charles H. Christensen, Joan Feinberg, Elizabeth Schaaf, Ellen Kuhl, Lori Chong, Kathryn Blatt, and, in particular, the indefatigable Steve Scipione.

Finally, I would like to express my appreciation to two wonderful assistants without whom this book could not have been completed: Elaine Koch, of the College of Arts and Sciences at the University of

Miami, and Suzanne Klekotka, of the provost's office. They have been ready with wit and wisdom—as well as assistance—at times when there simply weren't enough hours in the day.

Ross C Murfin
Southern Methodist University

Contents

PART ONE

The Scarlet Letter: The Complete Text

Introduction: The Biographical and Historical Background

Nathaniel Hawthorne, born Nathaniel Hathorne, Jr., was the son of Elizabeth Manning Hathorne of Salem, Massachusetts, and a man he hardly ever saw: Nathaniel Hathorne, also of Salem.

The senior Nathaniel, a sea captain, had no sooner married than he headed off to sea, leaving a pregnant young bride of twenty-one behind in the house he and his brother shared with their rigidly Puritanical mother and three equally sharp and stern unmarried sisters. When the baby, christened Elizabeth but to be known all her life as "Ebe," was born seven months after the wedding, Nathaniel Hathorne, Sr., was off at sea.

As Nina Baym has suggested in an article entitled "Nathaniel Hawthorne and His Mother" (1982), life with three pious, stern, and eccentric women must not have been very pleasant for Elizabeth Hathorne, a young woman who had become pregnant before getting married. And yet Elizabeth was to stay with the Hathornes for seven years, a period in which she bore two more children, both of them conceived during her husband's brief shore leaves. The first of these was Nathaniel Jr., later to become the author of *The Scarlet Letter;* the second was Maria Louisa, known simply as Louisa.

Nathaniel Sr. was, as usual, at sea when his only son was born, and he set forth on what was to be his final voyage just two weeks before the birth of his second daughter. Not long after sailing, he became ill with a fever and died, in Surinam in South America, far from the Salem where he had rarely lived — and from the wife and children he had hardly known.

Nina Baym succinctly characterizes a man, a marriage that was hardly a marriage, and, consequently, a young mother's predicament: "He left Elizabeth a widow at the age of twenty-eight, with children aged six and four and an infant of a few months. In seven years of married life he had spent little more than seven months in Salem, and had been absent from home at the births of all his children" (Baym 9). It is little wonder that Elizabeth, given what we know about her in-laws, returned to her own family, the Mannings, shortly after learning of her husband's death.

The Mannings were prosperous, middle-class people who had established and developed a stagecoach line connecting Marblehead, Newbury, and Boston. The family was a large and seemingly affectionate one; certainly, we know that Nathaniel and his two sisters were doted on, especially by their numerous unmarried aunts and uncles.

Thanks to the Mannings, young Nathaniel received a solid education. When he seriously injured his foot while playing ball, the head of his school in Salem — the famous lexicographer, J. E. Worcester — continued to provide the injured student with his lessons at home. This long period of confinement proved critically important to the development of Hawthorne as a writer; while recuperating, he read not only allegories like Spenser's *The Faerie Queene* and Bunyan's *The Pilgrim's Progress* but also plays by Shakespeare, historical novels by Sir Walter Scott, and popular Gothic romances. Allegorical, dramatic, historical, and supernatural, or Gothic, elements can be found in abundance throughout *The Scarlet Letter*.

When he was about thirteen years old, Hawthorne was to receive an education different from the kind available from schoolmasters and books. His mother took an opportunity to move herself and her two children out of the busy family compound in Salem and into a house adjacent to the one where her brother Richard lived, near Sebago Lake in Raymond, Maine. Although Hawthorne was only in Raymond sporadically over the next two years and consistently for two years after that, his time there was as important to his development as the period of convalescence in Salem.

In rural Maine, Hawthorne developed a deep appreciation of nature. He became enamored of hunting and fishing, of walking and skating, of paths leading deep into forests. Because of this experience, the world of the woods held a powerful fascination for Hawthorne which resurfaced within the characters he created in his fiction. In *The Scarlet Letter,* Hester Prynne and Arthur Dimmesdale hope to find in a forest beyond the outskirts of Boston some chance for freedom or, at least, relief from their tragic predicament.

The Maine years drew to an inevitable end; in 1819, the day after his fifteenth birthday, Nathaniel was sent back to Salem. There, as a student in Mr. Archer's "New School," he prepared for entrance into college. There, too, he began to prepare for a career beyond his college career by beginning to work at the craft of writing. He wrote mainly satiric, parodic pieces, interspersed with similarly disrespectful poetical compositions. His models were *The Spectator* papers of Addison and Steele; his audience was at first composed only of his family.

Hawthorne continued to write during his years at Bowdoin College, back in Maine, but he also developed new interests. He had met Franklin Pierce, later to become the fourteenth American president, on his first trip by coach to Bowdoin, and, during his undergraduate years, he came to share Pierce's enthusiasm for Democratic party politics. Like Pierce, he was also active in the Athenean Literary Society. And, like Pierce, he was known for enjoying other activities that were less sanctioned by college officials.

The president of Bowdoin, who took an active interest in students' behavior, fined Hawthorne several times during his student days for gambling at cards, among other things. "When the President asked what we played for," Hawthorne wrote home during his freshman year, "I thought it proper to inform him it was 50 cts. although it happened to be a Quart of Wine, but if I had told him of that he would probably have fined me for having a blow." Those critics who find in *The Scarlet Letter* more approval than disapproval for the deeply conservative ways of seventeenth-century Puritan society might do well to reread this frank communication between a twenty-year-old Hawthorne and his mother.

Following college, Hawthorne returned to Salem, to which his family had gone to live several years earlier. The next twelve years, spent mainly with his family, were among the worst of his life. His letters to Sophia Peabody, the woman who was to become his wife, refer to his mother's house as "Castle Dismal" and to himself as a "prisoner" in a "lonely chamber." A notebook that came to light in the 1970s suggests that these letters accurately represent Hawthorne's state of mind at the time. Before the notebook's rediscovery, biographers had speculated that the letters were highly imaginative and even literary in character — that they greatly exaggerated, in other words, the gloom and depression the writer felt.

After all, Hawthorne was writing Gothic fiction during these years back at home, as well as reading histories, especially of New England. Along with *Fanshawe* (1828), a novel with strong Gothic elements that he published anonymously and tried to suppress, Hawthorne wrote tales for magazines using pen names such as "Oberon," "Ashley Allan Royce," or "The Reverend A. A. Royce." He set many of these stories and sketches in the historical past that he found so fascinating. Literature, he once explained, "is a plant which thrives best in spots where blood has been spilt long ago."

Eventually, Hawthorne began publishing sketches and stories in his own name, some of them powerful works that were to be collected in a successful volume entitled *Twice-Told Tales*. Henry Wadsworth Longfellow, a former Bowdoin classmate whose reputation as a writer had developed more quickly than Hawthorne's, wrote a favorable review imploring Hawthorne to "tell us more." Even good press, though, failed to make writing profitable as an occupation, so Hawthorne decided, after becoming secretly engaged to Sophia in 1838, to accept a political appointment in 1839 as Measurer of Coal and Salt in the Boston Custom-House.

Hawthorne wrote relatively little during the years he spent in the dusty hulls of ships. For that reason and others he eventually resigned and moved, on New Year's Day, 1841, to Brook Farm, an experimental Utopian community. Technically an Institute of Agriculture and Education, Brook Farm was in fact designed as a haven for intellectuals. The short-range goal of its founder, George Ripley, was to provide its residents with a place to think and write while they worked only to supply life's basic necessities. But the ultimate philosophical goal of the place was that of most, if not all, Utopian communities: the regeneration of society.

Hawthorne had moved to Brook Farm thinking that, after a few years of living, working, and writing, he would marry Sophia and have her join him there. Unfortunately, the Farm proved a disappointment. Hawthorne rather quickly decided it was no place for Sophia. He didn't care for the work and found himself suddenly unable to write. Hawthorne was also less than impressed with the idealists who lived and visited at the Farm. From the Brook Farm days on, he was skeptical of people who believe that all social ills are ultimately curable. In his later *Life of Franklin Pierce,* he wrote that "there is no instance, in all history, of the human will and intellect having perfected any great moral reform by methods which it adapted to that end" (113–14).

In "The Custom-House," his preface to *The Scarlet Letter,* he refers to the "impracticable schemes" of "the dreamy brethren of Brook Farm" (38). And in the novel that follows, an essentially skeptical attitude toward the possibility of moral or social perfectibility is everywhere implicit. Puritan society, for all its efforts, has been unable to prevent the Reverend Arthur Dimmesdale from "sinning." The most good is done by his partner, Hester, who finally lives alone at the edge of the city and accomplishes what she does slowly, painfully, partly by talking, but mainly by listening, to the people who "brought all their sorrows and perplexities" to her, "as one who had herself gone through a mighty trouble"(200–01).

Hawthorne married in 1842, the year after his sojourn at Brook Farm. His new residence was the Old Manse in Concord, where he and Sophia were to live for several years. Originally a parsonage, the Old Manse had been home to several writers before Hawthorne. The late Dr. Ezra Ripley had written over 3000 sermons in the house, and more recently Ralph Waldo Emerson had composed "Nature" there, an essay that had helped galvanize the American Transcendental movement.

In general, Hawthorne remained unconvinced by the views of the Transcendentalists, whose writings were regularly published by Margaret Fuller, first editor of *The Dial,* a Transcendentalist organ. Their vision was far too hopeful, even idealistic, to satisfy a skeptic holding an essentially tragic view of the human condition. But, perhaps because Sophia and her sister were sympathetic to the movement, Hawthorne was cordial with his Transcendentalist neighbors when they called at his house to visit. He was especially friendly with Emerson and Thoreau, with whom he took long walks and conversed.

The years at the Old Manse were productive ones for Hawthorne: he published *Grandfather's Chair,* a child's history of New England; a second edition of *Twice-Told Tales;* and a new volume of stories, entitled *Mosses from an Old Manse,* that was favorably reviewed by Herman Melville. And these were pleasant domestic years for Hawthorne as well: he and Sophia were happy together and their happiness was compounded, in 1843, by the birth of their first child, Una. But, pleasant and productive as the times were, they certainly were not prosperous; the family became so poor, in fact, that at one point in 1844 Sophia and Una had to go and live with the Peabodys while Hawthorne returned, briefly, to live with his mother — just to enable him to pay the bills.

In his biography *Nathaniel Hawthorne in His Times* (1980), James R. Mellow relates that "for months, Hawthorne's friends had been making a concerted effort to get him a political appointment" (255). John L. O'Sullivan, the editor of the *Democratic Review,* put pressure on President Polk's Democratic administration, as did Franklin Pierce, a former U.S. senator who within half a dozen years would be running for president. (Pierce made Hawthorne's case to the historian George Bancroft, an old Bowdoin classmate, who happened to be Secretary of the Navy at the time.) As a result of his friends' efforts, Hawthorne found himself offered a job as Inspector of the Revenue for the Port of Salem in April of 1846. It was a position he could hardly turn down, since he was supporting not only a wife and child but also his mother and his sisters, who had by this point moved in with him.

For the second time in a decade, Hawthorne found himself working in a Custom-House. At first, he found the job "beneficially distracting," and it allowed him time for consorting with his fellow-writers as well as for staying close to his family, which grew by one when a son, Julian, was born. Finally, though, the business of managing subordinates — of collecting imposts, signing documents, and confirming that his name was stamped on paid-up cargo — became more than a little tedious. "The Custom-House," which follows this introduction and precedes the text of *The Scarlet Letter,* describes Hawthorne's boredom and frustration with the job. It also tells how he unexpectedly lost the position in 1849, after the Whigs had come to power in 1848 and General Zachary Taylor had succeeded Polk as president.

The loss of his post, combined with the death of his mother, was devastating for Hawthorne, but ultimately liberating as well. He plunged into writing with almost maniacal dedication. Had Hawthorne stayed on, year after year, as Surveyor of the Salem Custom-House, he probably never would have written *The Scarlet Letter*. With this novel, he not only earned for himself and for his family the comfortable living as a writer that had eluded him for decades, but he also established himself as one of America's foremost literary talents.

"The Custom-House," of course, does more than merely recount Hawthorne's job as Surveyor and how he lost it. It also tells us about his relation to that same Puritan past that he presents in *The Scarlet Letter*. Like Hester, Hawthorne feels somewhat alienated from and intimidated by "stern and black-browed Puritans" (27). And yet they are his very own ancestors — the progenitors of the pious eccentrics his mother had had to endure for seven years. "What is he?" Hawthorne imagines one of his forefathers murmuring to another from a shadow world beyond the grave. "A writer of story-books! What kind of a business in life, — what mode of glorifying God, or being serviceable to mankind in his day and generation, — may that be? Why, the degenerate fellow might as well have been a fiddler!" (27). Hawthorne, we realize, took on the Surveyor's job not only to alleviate his financial burdens but also to prove himself to his forebears — or, at least, to that conservative and old-fashioned side of himself that he allows to speak through imagined ancestral voices.

"The Custom-House" makes us realize that Hawthorne was descended from New England Puritans not unlike those he describes in the first pages of *The Scarlet Letter*. In the novel's first chapter, he speaks of "bearded men, in sad-colored garments and gray, steeple-crowned hats, intermixed with women, some wearing hoods" (53), and a chapter later he says that these early Boston settlers were "people amongst whom religion and law were almost identical" (55). In "The Custom-House," he speaks of his own "first ancestor," who came to Massachusetts from England as a "grave, bearded, sable-cloaked, and steeple-crowned progenitor" (26).

This ancestor, William Hathorne — "who came so early [in 1630], with his Bible and his sword" — is presented as a man for whom "religion and law" must have been " almost identical":

> He was a soldier, legislator, judge; he was a ruler in the Church; he had all the Puritanic traits, both good and evil. He was likewise a bitter persecutor; as witness the Quakers, who have remembered him in their histories, and relate an incident of his hard severity towards a woman of their sect. (27)

For those who have read *The Scarlet Letter,* it is difficult not to wonder if Hawthorne had that Puritan woman in mind when he created his heroine, Hester Prynne. No Puritan, she is nonetheless the victim of Puritan judges who have acted toward her with "hard severity" at best.

Next in line among Hawthorne's ancestors stood another Puritan judge. This one, John Hathorne, was involved in the now-infamous Salem witch trials of 1692. According to "the histories that Nathaniel Hawthorne read" as a young man, John Hathorne was a "stern, relentless prosecutor" who believed that "Satan enticed followers into his service and used them in his special warfare against New England." Thus, as Arlin Turner explains in *Nathaniel Hawthorne: A Biography* (1980), John Hathorne "saw it his duty to discover any who had joined the devil's band and to extract a confession, . . . evidence that could be introduced at the [witchcraft] trials later" (Turner 64). Unlike one of the other two judges, Samuel Sewall, John Hathorne never repented of his part in one of the worst atrocities committed by an early North American colonist.

As readers of *The Scarlet Letter,* we may be tempted once again to make connections amongst history, Hawthorne's family history, and his most famous work of fiction. We may be tempted as well to wonder if the novel itself is not some belated act of repentance, an expression of regret by Nathaniel Hawthorne for the sins of an ancestor. To be sure, Hester Prynne has not been accused of witchcraft; rather, she has borne a child fathered by someone other than her elderly — and long-absent — husband. But the sympathetically portrayed heroine of *The Scarlet Letter* is the victim of magistrates who act with "hard severity," even when they believe that they are acting mercifully.

That severity is evident even from the words of a minor character in the novel who, a Puritan himself, does not see the magistrates' judgment as harsh. "Now, good Sir," a "townsman" explains to the "stranger," who turns out to be Hester's long-lost husband:

> "Our Massachusetts magistracy, bethinking themselves that this woman is youthful and fair, and doubtless was strongly tempted to her fall; — and that, moreover, as is most likely, her husband may be at the bottom of the sea; — they have not been bold to put in force the extremity of our righteous law against her. The penalty thereof is death. But, in their great mercy and tenderness of heart, they have doomed Mistress Prynne to stand only a space of three hours on the platform of the pillory, and then and thereafter, for the remainder of her natural life, to wear a mark of shame upon her bosom." (64)

Hester, unlike alleged witches judged in the Salem witchcraft trials, utters no curse against her judges while standing on the pillory platform, wearing her mark of shame. In fact, she speaks only the following words — "I will not speak!" (68) when exhorted to confess the name of her sexual partner before Governor Bellingham and the assembled multitude. But her silence itself is an indication of her tragic alienation from a harsh society whose religion and law are almost identical. And so, too, is the scarlet A on her breast: "It had the effect of a spell, taking her out of the ordinary relations with humanity, and inclosing her in a sphere by herself" (58). She is no less isolated than an accused witch — or a Quaker among Puritans.

Of course, in "The Custom-House," several pages after that on which we read about Hawthorne's stern first American ancestor, we are told that the source, or historical prototype, for Hester Prynne was neither a Quaker woman harshly dealt with by William Hathorne nor a woman prosecuted as a witch by his son John. We are told, rather, that the source for Hester Prynne was Hester Prynne herself. Hawthorne writes that "one idle and rainy day," while he was "poking and burrowing into the heaped-up rubbish in the corner" of the Salem Custom-House, where he served as Surveyor, he came upon "a small package, carefully done up in a piece of ancient yellow parchment" (41) containing the papers of a long-dead predecessor, an "ancient Surveyor" named Jonathan Pue.

> But the object that most drew my attention, in the mysterious package, was a certain affair of fine red cloth, much worn and faded. There were traces about it of gold embroidery, which, however, was greatly frayed and defaced. . . . This rag of scarlet cloth, — for time, and wear, and a sacrilegious moth, had reduced it to little other than a rag, — on careful examination, assumed the shape of a letter. It was the capital letter A. By an accurate measurement, each limb proved to be precisely three inches and a quarter in length. (42–43)

Shortly after discovering the letter, Hawthorne claims, he learned the story behind the letter by reading the papers of Surveyor Pue.

In these "foolscap sheets, containing many particulars respecting the life and conversation of one Hester Prynne" (43), Hawthorne claims that he

> found the record of [the] doings and sufferings of this singular woman, for most of which the reader is referred to the story entitled "The Scarlet Letter"; and it should be borne carefully in mind, that the main facts of that story are authorized and authenticated by the document of Mr. Surveyor Pue. The original papers, together with the scarlet letter itself, — a most curious relic, — are still in my possession, and shall be freely exhibited to whomsoever . . . may desire a sight of them. (43–44)

Much of what Hawthorne has to tell us in "The Custom-House" is undeniably true. "The election of General Taylor to the Presidency" (49), like Hawthorne's subsequent dismissal from his position as Surveyor, is historical fact. Even Hawthorne's depiction of a fellow-Custom-House worker, the "permanent Inspector" (32) who "possessed no higher attribute" than the "ability to recollect the good dinners" he had enjoyed (33), must have seemed realistic to Hawthorne's contemporaries. Indeed, it prompted a cry of foul from the editor of the Salem *Register*, who wrote that the "chapter" about the "venerable gentleman" whose "chief crime seems to be that he loves a good dinner" managed to "obliterate . . . whatever sympathy was felt for Hawthorne's removal from office."

But the business about finding the "package, carefully done up in . . . ancient yellow parchment" is altogether a different story. It is, we may assume, just that: a fictional story with the semblance of biographical and historical truth. Hawthorne's mid-nineteenth-century audience was a practical one not entirely accustomed to the "imaginings" of a "romance-writer," yet even among these early readers there must have been those who saw through Hawthorne's account of finding the scarlet letter and the story of the "real" Hester Prynne. In "The Custom-House," Hawthorne describes the half-real, half-unreal world of a familiar room lit by moonlight: "the floor of our familiar room," he points out, "become[s] a neutral territory, somewhere between the real world and fairy-land, where the Actual and the Imaginary may meet, and each imbue itself with the nature of the other" (46). The story of finding Surveyor Pue's package is a kind of frame story that brings about that meeting, bridging the gap between fact and fiction by imbuing a biographical introduction with a touch of fantasy — and the fiction that follows with the air of fact.

This is not to say that Hawthorne entirely made up the idea of a woman sentenced to wear a scarlet letter, only that he didn't find such a letter in the Custom-House where he worked nor did he come upon any historical account of a real woman named Hester Prynne. Instead, what he may well have discovered, either while working at the Custom-House or earlier, in the solitary decade following his graduation from college, was Joseph B. Felt's 1827 volume *The Annals of Salem*. There he would have read that, in 1694, a law was passed requiring adulterers to wear a two-inch-high capital A, colored to stand out against the background of the wearer's clothes.

As Charles Boewe and Murray G. Murphey point out in their essay "Hester Prynne in History" (1960), Hawthorne may also have read the story of Goodwife Mendame of Duxbury in old historical annals of the region (Goodwife Mendame was found guilty of adultery, whipped, and forced "to weare a badge with the capital letters AD cut in the cloth upon her left sleeve"). Finally, he may even have come across the following entry in the records of the Salem Quarterly Court for November 1688: "Hester Craford, for fornication with John Wedg, as she confessed, was ordered to be severely whipped and that security be given to save the town from the charge of keeping the child" (Boewe and Murphey, 202–03). There would seem to be, then, no end of sources for Hester Prynne in the annals of the period of Hawthorne's first (and second) ancestor.

Among those historical models not yet discussed and deserving of particular attention is the famous seventeenth-century antinomian Anne Hutchinson. Antinomians rejected the Puritan concept of religion as the observance of institutionalized precepts; rather than stressing God's will as something taught and enforced by a church, they believed that God reveals Himself through the inner experience of the individual. Instead of believing that good actions prove the doer to be predestined for salvation, antinomians argued that faith alone is necessary. Anne Hutchinson argued that she did not need Puritan elders to teach her true from false and right from wrong, because divine guidance and inspiration could be attained through intuition and faith. Nor did she accept the authority of the Puritan elders. As Michael Colacurcio puts it in his ground-breaking article, "Footsteps of Ann Hutchinson" (1972), her "proclamation — variously worded at various times . . . — that 'the chosen of man' are not necessarily 'the sealed of heaven,'" brought about "a state of near civil war in Boston" (471).

In the opening scene of *The Scarlet Letter* Hawthorne describes, next to the prison door from which Hester Prynne steps with her three-month-old baby, "a wild rose-bush" contrasting sharply with the "beetle-browed and gloomy front" of the prison and the rusty "ponderous iron-work" of its door. "Whether it had merely survived out of the stern old wilderness, . . . or whether . . . it had sprung up under the footsteps of the sainted Ann Hutchinson, as she entered the prison-door, — we shall not take upon us to determine" (54), the narrator adds. What Hawthorne *has* determined through these remarks about the rose bush and the imprisoned (but saintly) Anne Hutchinson is that we regard Anne Hutchinson and Hester Prynne in the same light.

Hester's "crime" against society is sexual, not theological as was Mrs. Hutchinson's. And yet, on a deeper level, the two women are much the same. In her thinking, Hester, like Anne Hutchinson, questions the authority and desirability of her Puritan society, wondering at one point whether "the whole system of society" (134) shouldn't be torn down and rebuilt, and deciding at another that "in Heaven's own time, a new truth would be revealed, in order to establish the whole relation between man and woman on a surer ground" (201). And, of course, by her one antisocial act, Hester, like Anne Hutchinson, has disregarded, and implicitly denied the authority of, the Puritan moral law. "The world's law was no law for her mind," we read of Hester (133). What the narrator gives us in those nine words is a short definition of antinomianism.

Using essays Hawthorne himself wrote about Anne Hutchinson's life and times, Colacurcio draws still more parallels between the literary character and the historical figure. He points out, for instance, that although Hutchinson's transgression was not sexual, it was often spoken of in such terms: her influence was seen as "seductive," her ideas as illegitimate children and even monstrous births. Colacurcio also suggests an interesting link between Hester's secret accomplice, Arthur Dimmesdale, and John Cotton, the great Boston minister and scholar. As Hawthorne himself points out in his own historical sketches, Cotton ultimately sat in judgment of Anne Hutchinson, even though she, who had been his parishioner both in England and in New England, always believed him to be a partner in, and to some extent even a source for, her alleged heresies. (And yet "Cotton alone, Hawthorne reports, is excepted from her final denunciations.") Cotton was historically the theological partner of John Wilson; together those two are known to have urged public confessions not unlike the one Wilson and Dimmesdale try to pry from Hester Prynne. "Like Ann Hutchinson," Colacurcio observes, "Hester Prynne is an extraordinary woman who falls afoul of a theocratic and male-dominated society; and the problems which cause them to be singled out for exemplary punishment both begin in a special sort of relationship with a pastor who is one of the acknowledged intellectual and spiritual leaders of that society" (461).

Hawthorne obviously absorbed a great deal of history during his years of reading in his "Castle Dismal," and he reworked that history into his novels and tales. In an essay entitled "The New England Sources of *The Scarlet Letter*" (1959), Charles Ryskamp goes far beyond indicating the possible historical sources for Prynne, Dimmesdale, and Wilson. He shows that particular histories of New England, especially Caleb Snow's *History of Boston,* the best available in Hawthorne's day, were followed closely by the novelist as he fashioned the world of his most famous novel.

Snow's *History* provided a precise description of the houses and streets of Boston as they existed in the mid-seventeenth century; Hawthorne follows these descriptions in detail in setting his own story. He has placed the homes of the Governor and of the Reverend John Wilson in the proper locations, and he even uses historical names for persons who are not central characters in his story. It is also Snow's *History* that Hawthorne usually relies on when there is any doubt about the facts. Snow is the only historian Hawthorne could have read who says that the Boston jailer of the period was named Brackett; every other historian mentions a jailer named Parker. Hawthorne, however, follows Snow's lead, referring, in Chapter 4 of *The Scarlet Letter,* to "Master Brackett, the jailer" (69).

Even some of the bizarre events in the novel are grounded in Snow's *History*. The great letter A that appears in the sky on the night of John Winthrop's death is based loosely on Snow's account of the night after John Cotton died, a night when "Strange and alarming signs appeared in the heavens." As for the more ordinary details of Hawthorne's story, many are even more closely based on the *History*.

Perhaps the most impressive example Ryskamp gives of Hawthorne's attention to historical detail and reliance on Snow is the comparison he makes between Snow's description of a great, early Boston house and Hawthorne's description of Governor Bellingham's mansion, to which, in the seventh chapter, Hester takes a pair of gloves she has fringed and embroidered. To indicate "what was considered elegance of architecture . . . a century and a half ago," Snow refers to a "wooden building," the outside "covered with plastering" in which the "broken glass" of "common junk bottles" had been used to "make a hard surface on the mortar. . . . This surface was also variegated with ornamental squares, diamonds, and flowers-de-luce" (Ryskamp 264–65). And how does Hawthorne describe the Governor's house? As a "large wooden house, . . . the walls being overspread with a kind of stucco, in which fragments of broken glass were plentifully intermixed. . . . It was further decorated with strange and seemingly cabalistic figures and diagrams" (91).

What is most interesting about Ryskamp's article, though, is that, in addition to showing how often Hawthorne tells the historian's version of the truth in writing *The Scarlet Letter,* it also recounts how often Hawthorne distorts the truth as represented by Snow, Cotton Mather, and others. Governor Winthrop actually died in March 1649; Hawthorne's novel says he died in May. Governor Bellingham would not have been governor at the novel's opening — not, that is, if seven years were to pass between Hester's day and Dimmesdale's night on the scaffold, as the novel indicates. Mistress Ann Hibbins, the self-styled witch of the novel, is a historical figure Hawthorne would have read about in Snow. (She was condemned and executed for witchcraft in 1655.) But she was *not,* according to Snow, Governor Bellingham's sister. As for the Reverend John Wilson, in some ways accurately described by Hawthorne, he would not have been an old man with "a border of grizzled locks beneath his skull-cap" (65).

Why would Hawthorne so carefully follow history in some instances only to violate it in others? Because, as Ryskamp reminds us, the novel is a place where — to use the language of "The Custom-House" — "the Actual and the Imaginary . . . meet." By having Winthrop die in March, not May, Hawthorne makes his novel more effective by compressing its action. By putting Dimmesdale on a balcony with "the eldest clergyman of Boston" (65), a balcony from which the two men will attempt to pry a confession from a determinedly taciturn young woman, Hawthorne highlights the youthful confusion of Dimmesdale and darkly underscores the inappropriateness of his position.

As a work of fiction, then, *The Scarlet Letter* has its *own* reality, and that reality has a special form; like all historical novels and romances, it is itself an artifact of history, the history of a complex nineteenth-century culture, as well as a representation of the history of a previous culture. The very truths of the novel are sometimes conveyed by what are historical inaccuracies. By making Bellingham governor at the book's beginning, when Hester stands on the scaffold, and by transforming Mistress Hibbins into Bellingham's sister Hawthorne forges connections that throw into question his own, perhaps our own, distinctions between legitimate and illegitimate, good and bad.

Finally, *The Scarlet Letter* is a composite. The story it tells of seventeenth-century New England is a mixture of fact and fancy, of history and imagination. As we have seen, the novel's main character is a blend of the "sainted Ann Hutchinson," adulteress Hester Craford, Goodwife Mendame of Duxbury, as well as the Quaker woman harshly judged by William Hathorne and the accused witches prosecuted by John. She is also, of course, as Nina Baym suggests, Hawthorne's own mother, who became pregnant out of wedlock, who suffered the stern disapproval of the Puritanical Hathornes, and whose first child, Ebe, according to Baym, "grew up into a strikingly independent, only partially socialized woman, much as though she had been exempted from normal social expectations by those entrusted with rearing her" (9).

But to some extent, Hester is also Margaret Fuller, the feminist founder of *The Dial,* toward whom Hawthorne had always had mixed feelings. As critics have long pointed out, she is partially Hawthorne himself. Like Hester, Hawthorne was an artist who felt significantly alienated from a family and a society of sober pragmatists. A history embroidered by fancy, *The Scarlet Letter* outraged Puritanical readers of Hawthorne's day because of its treatment of adultery, much as Hester's act of adultery had outraged *her* society. As for Pearl, she is as much Hawthorne's daughter, Una, as she is his sister, Ebe; this much we know from Hawthorne's notebooks, in which Una is described in words later used to describe Pearl.

Similarly, the period of history Hawthorne represents in the novel is as much his own period as it is any earlier one, as Larry J. Reynolds points out in "*The Scarlet Letter* and Revolutions Abroad" (1985). Eighteen hundred forty-eight, the year before Hawthorne began his novel, was a year of revolutions in Europe, revolutions that had been applauded by intellectuals of Hawthorne's day, including Margaret Fuller. Even Hawthorne's wife, an admirer of Fuller's, had thought the 1848 French revolution "good news" (Reynolds 47). Hawthorne himself, however, was skeptical. Like many Americans, he viewed the victory of Taylor and his Whig party as an American manifestation of the spirit of 1848. But that Whig revolution cost him his job. By the time he started working on the novel, which he, being jobless, now had time to write, it had become clear that revolutionary efforts in Europe were doomed to failure.

So, in *The Scarlet Letter,* Hawthorne quietly and indirectly cautions against revolutionary fervor by writing the novel the way he does — and by setting it where and when he does. "The opening scenes . . . take place in May 1642 and the closing ones in May 1649," Reynolds explains in his essay. "These dates coincide almost exactly with those of the English Civil war fought between King Charles I and his Puritan Parliament. . . . By the final scenes of the novel, when Arthur is deciding to die as a martyr, Charles I has just been beheaded" (52–53). Additionally, the scaffold so prominently featured in the novel's opening is, according to Reynolds, a "historical inaccuracy intentionally used by Hawthorne to develop the theme of revolution. . . . With increasing frequency during the first French Revolution," the word scaffold had "served as a synecdoche for a public beheading — by the executioner's axe or the guillotine" (51). (Note that Hawthorne, in "The Custom-House," connects his own mistreatment by the victorious Whigs with French revolutionary activity, referring to himself as "A DECAPITATED SURVEYOR," 52.)

Reynolds suggests that Hawthorne, because of his distrust of revolution, presents Hester and Arthur sympathetically as long as they are trying to "regain their rightful place in the social or spiritual order," but unsympathetically "when they become revolutionary instead and attempt to overthrow an established order" (58). As Reynolds describes, at the beginning of the novel Hester is the almost regal-seeming martyr, a martyr antagonized by the Puritan mob. Later, she becomes the revolutionary, thinking thoughts about the overturning of society and dreaming dreams of "a revolution in the sphere of thought and feeling." At this point Hawthorne's narrator becomes less sympathetic. Still later, when Dimmesdale conforms to the social order by repenting of his sin, that act is viewed by the narrator with approval. The narrator equally approves Hester's final return to New England, where she reattaches the scarlet letter to her breast and counsels wretched people in her cottage. It is better to accept than to revolt, the ending of the novel suggests, delivering a mid-nineteenth-century message to a mid-nineteenth-century audience, while seeming to be about the mid-seventeenth century.

In the pages that follow, you will find interpretations of *The Scarlet Letter* written since Baym wrote "Nathaniel Hawthorne and His Mother," Colacurcio wrote "Footsteps of Ann Hutchinson," Ryskamp wrote "The New England Sources of *The Scarlet Letter,*" and Reynolds wrote "*The Scarlet Letter* and Revolutions Abroad."

Some of these essayists go further than Reynolds in suggesting that *The Scarlet Letter* was a reflection by Hawthorne on the history of his own day. In his new-historicist reading of the novel, Sacvan Bercovitch argues that Hawthorne was warning against not only the dangers of the European revolutions but also of the developing feminist revolution and the radicalism of the abolitionists.

Other critics whose work is found in the pages ahead would have it that, when we read *The Scarlet Letter,* our own historical period and its concerns become implicated as well, turning the text into one in which we end up reading about our own times as well as those of Hawthorne and Hester, of Polk and the Puritans.

But before that composite of critical material comes the text itself, a complicated mix of biography and history, of seventeenth- and nineteenth-century history, and, most important, of history and the imagination that brings it to life. It is to that text that you should now turn.

WORKS CITED

Baym, Nina. "Nathaniel Hawthorne and His Mother: A Biographical Speculation." *American Literature* 54 (1982): 1–27.

Boewe, Charles, and Murray G. Murphey. "Hester Prynne in History." *American Literature* 32 (1960): 202–04.

Colacurcio, Michael. "Footsteps of Ann Hutchinson: The Context of *The Scarlet Letter.*" *ELH* 39 (1972): 459–94.

Hawthorne, Nathaniel. *Life of Franklin Pierce*. Boston: Ticknor, Reed, and Fields, 1852.

Mellow, James R. *Nathaniel Hawthorne in His Times*. Boston: Houghton, 1980. One of the two standard biographies of Hawthorne.

Reynolds, Larry J. "*The Scarlet Letter* and Revolutions Abroad." *American Literature* 57 (1985): 44–67.

Ryskamp, Charles. "The New England Sources of *The Scarlet Letter.*" *American Literature* 31 (1959): 257–72.

Turner, Arlin. *Nathaniel Hawthorne: A Biography*. New York: Oxford UP, 1980. One of the two standard biographies of Hawthorne.

The Scarlet Letter

PREFACE

To the Second Edition

Much to the author's surprise, and (if he may say so without additional offence) considerably to his amusement, he finds that his sketch of official life, introductory to THE SCARLET LETTER, has created an unprecedented excitement in the respectable community immediately around him. It could hardly have been more violent, indeed, had he burned down the Custom-House, and quenched its last smoking ember in the blood of a certain venerable personage, against whom he is supposed to cherish a peculiar malevolence. As the public disapprobation would weigh very heavily on him, were he conscious of deserving it, the author begs leave to say, that he has carefully read over the introductory pages, with a purpose to alter or expunge whatever might be found amiss, and to make the best reparation in his power for the atrocities of which he has been adjudged guilty. But it appears to him, that the only remarkable features of the sketch are its frank and genuine good-humor, and the general accuracy with which he has conveyed his sincere impressions of the characters therein described. As to enmity, or ill-feeling of any kind, personal or political, he utterly disclaims such motives. The sketch might, perhaps, have been wholly omitted, without loss to the public, or detriment to the book; but, having undertaken to write it, he conceives that it could not have been done in a better or kindlier spirit, nor, so far as his abilities availed, with a livelier effect of truth.

The author is constrained, therefore, to republish his introductory sketch without the change of a word.

SALEM, *March* 30, 1850.

THE CUSTOM-HOUSE

Introductory to "The Scarlet Letter"

It is a little remarkable, that — though disinclined to talk overmuch of myself and my affairs at the fireside, and to my personal friends — an autobiographical impulse should twice in my life have taken possession of me, in addressing the public. The first time was three or four years since, when I favored the reader — inexcusably, and for no earthly reason, that either the indulgent reader or the intrusive author could imagine — with a description of my way of life in the deep quietude of an Old Manse. And now — because, beyond my deserts, I was happy enough to find a listener or two on the former occasion — I again seize the public by the button, and talk of my three years' experience in a Custom-House. The example of the famous "P. P., Clerk of this Parish," was never more faithfully followed. The truth seems to be, however, that, when he casts his leaves forth upon the wind, the author addresses, not the many who will fling aside his volume, or never take it up, but the few who will understand him, better than most of his schoolmates and lifemates. Some authors, indeed, do far more than this, and indulge themselves in such confidential depths of revelation as could fittingly be addressed, only and exclusively, to the one heart and mind of perfect sympathy; as if the printed book, thrown at large on the wide world, were certain to find out the divided segment of the writer's own nature, and complete his circle of existence by bringing him into communion with it. It is scarcely decorous, however, to speak all, even where we speak impersonally. But — as thoughts are frozen and utterance benumbed, unless the speaker stand in some true relation with his audience — it may be pardonable to imagine that a friend, a kind and apprehensive, though not the closest friend, is listening to our talk; and then, a native reserve being thawed by this genial consciousness, we may prate of the circumstances that lie around us, and even of ourself, but still keep the inmost Me behind its veil. To this extent and within these limits, an author, methinks, may be autobiographical, without violating either the reader's rights or his own.

It will be seen, likewise, that this Custom-House sketch has a certain propriety, of a kind always recognized in literature, as explaining how a large portion of the following pages came into my possession, and as offering proofs of the authenticity of a narrative therein contained. This, in fact, — a desire to put myself in my true position as editor, or very little more, of the most prolix among the tales that make up my volume, — this, and no other, is my true reason for assuming a personal relation with the public. In accomplishing the main purpose, it has appeared allowable, by a few extra touches, to give a faint representation of a mode of life not heretofore described, together with some of the characters that move in it, among whom the author happened to make one.

In my native town of Salem, at the head of what, half a century ago, in the days of old King Derby, was a bustling wharf, — but which is now burdened with decayed wooden warehouses, and exhibits few or no symptoms of commercial life; except, perhaps, a bark or brig, half-way down its melancholy length, discharging hides; or, nearer at hand, a Nova Scotia schooner, pitching out her cargo of firewood, — at the head, I say, of this dilapidated wharf, which the tide often overflows, and along which, at the base and in the rear of the row of buildings, the track of many languid years is seen in a border of unthrifty grass, — here, with a view from its front windows adown this not very enlivening prospect, and thence across the harbour, stands a spacious edifice of brick. From the loftiest point of its roof, during precisely three and a half hours of each forenoon, floats or droops, in breeze or calm, the banner of the republic; but with the thirteen stripes turned vertically, instead of horizontally, and thus indicating that a civil, and not a military post of Uncle Sam's government, is here established. Its front is ornamented with a portico of half a dozen wooden pillars, supporting a balcony, beneath which a flight of wide granite steps descends towards the street. Over the entrance hovers an enormous specimen of the American eagle, with outspread wings, a shield before her breast, and, if I recollect aright, a bunch of intermingled thunderbolts and barbed arrows in each claw. With the customary infirmity of temper that characterizes this unhappy fowl, she appears, by the fierceness of her beak and eye and the general truculency of her attitude, to threaten mischief to the inoffensive community; and especially to warn all citizens, careful of their safety, against intruding on the premises which she overshadows with her wings. Nevertheless, vixenly as she looks, many people are seeking, at this very moment, to shelter themselves under the wing of the federal eagle; imagining, I presume, that her bosom has all the softness and snugness of an eider-down pillow. But she has no great tenderness, even in her best of moods, and, sooner or later, — oftener soon than late, — is apt to fling off her nestlings with a scratch of her claw, a dab of her beak, or a rangling wound from her barbed arrows.

The pavement round about the above-described edifice — which we may as well name at once as the Custom-House of the port — has grass enough growing in its chinks to show that it has not, of late days, been worn by any multitudinous resort of business. In some months of the year, however, there often chances a forenoon when affairs move onward with a livelier tread. Such occasions might remind the elderly citizen of that period, before the last war with England, when Salem was a port by itself; not scorned, as she is now, by her own merchants and ship-owners, who permit her wharves to crumble to ruin, while their ventures go to swell, needlessly and imperceptibly, the mighty flood of commerce at New York or Boston. On some such morning, when three or four vessels happen to have arrived at once, — usually from Africa or South America, — or to be on the verge of their departure thitherward, there is a sound of frequent feet, passing briskly up and down the granite steps. Here, before his own wife has greeted him, you may greet the sea-flushed ship-master, just in port, with his vessel's papers under his arm in a tarnished tin box. Here, too, comes his owner, cheerful or sombre, gracious or in the sulks, accordingly as his scheme of the now accomplished voyage has been realized in merchandise that will readily be turned to gold, or has buried him under a bulk of incommodities, such as nobody will care to rid him of. Here, likewise, — the germ of the wrinkle-browed, grizzly-bearded, careworn merchant, — we have the smart young clerk, who gets the taste of traffic as a wolf-cub does of blood, and already sends adventures in his master's ships, when he had better be sailing mimic boats upon a mill-pond. Another figure in the scene is the outward-bound sailor, in quest of a protection; or the recently arrived one, pale and feeble, seeking a passport to the hospital. Nor must we forget the captains of the rusty little schooners that bring firewood from the British provinces; a rough-looking set of tarpaulins, without the alertness of the Yankee aspect, but contributing an item of no slight importance to our decaying trade.

Cluster all these individuals together, as they sometimes were, with other miscellaneous ones to diversify the group, and, for the time being, it made the Custom-House a stirring scene. More frequently, however, on ascending the steps, you would discern — in the entry, if it were summer time, or in their appropriate rooms, if wintry or inclement weather — a row of venerable figures, sitting in old-fashioned chairs, which were tipped on their hind legs back against the wall. Oftentimes they were asleep, but occasionally might be heard talking together, in voices between speech and a snore, and with that lack of energy that distinguishes the occupants of alms-houses, and all other human beings who depend for subsistence on charity, on monopolized labor, or any thing else but their own independent exertions. These old gentlemen — seated, like Matthew, at the receipt of custom, but not very liable to be summoned thence, like him, for apostolic errands — were Custom-House officers.

Furthermore, on the left hand as you enter the front door, is a certain room or office, about fifteen feet square, and of a lofty height; with two of its arched windows commanding a view of the aforesaid dilapidated wharf, and the third looking across a narrow lane, and along a portion of Derby Street. All three give glimpses of the shops of grocers, block-makers, slop-sellers, and ship-chandlers; around the doors of which are generally to be seen, laughing and gossiping, clusters of old salts, and such other wharf-rats as haunt the Wapping of a seaport. The room itself is cobwebbed, and dingy with old paint; its floor is strewn with gray sand, in a fashion that has elsewhere fallen into long disuse; and it is easy to conclude, from the general slovenliness of the place, that this is a sanctuary into which womankind, with her tools of magic, the broom and mop, has very infrequent access. In the way of furniture, there is a stove with a voluminous funnel; an old pine desk, with a three-legged stool beside it; two or three wooden-bottom chairs, exceedingly decrepit and infirm; and, — not to forget the library, — on some shelves, a score or two of volumes of the Acts of Congress, and a bulky Digest of the Revenue Laws. A tin pipe ascends through the ceiling, and forms a medium of vocal communication with other parts of the edifice. And here, some six months ago, — pacing from corner to corner, or lounging on the long-legged stool, with his elbow on the desk, and his eyes wandering up and down the columns of the morning newspaper, — you might have recognized, honored reader, the same individual who welcomed you into his cheery little study, where the sunshine glimmered so pleasantly through the willow branches, on the western side of the Old Manse. But now, should you go thither to seek him, you would inquire in vain for the Loco-foco Surveyor. The besom of reform has swept him out of office; and a worthier successor wears his dignity and pockets his emoluments.

This old town of Salem — my native place, though I have dwelt much away from it, both in boyhood and maturer years — possesses, or did possess, a hold on my affections, the force of which I have never realized during my seasons of actual residence here. Indeed, so far as its physical aspect is concerned, with its flat, unvaried surface, covered chiefly with wooden houses, few or none of which pretend to architectural beauty, — its irregularity, which is neither picturesque nor quaint, but only tame, — its long and lazy street, lounging wearisomely through the whole extent of the peninsula, with Gallows Hill and New Guinea at one end, and a view of the alms-house at the other, — such being the features of my native town, it would be quite as reasonable to form a sentimental attachment to a disarranged checkerboard. And yet, though invariably happiest elsewhere, there is within me a feeling for old Salem, which, in lack of a better phrase, I must be content to call affection. The sentiment is probably assignable to the deep and aged roots which my family has struck into the soil. It is now nearly two centuries and a quarter since the original Briton, the earliest emigrant of my name, made his appearance in the wild and forest-bordered settlement, which has since become a city. And here his descendants have been born and died, and have mingled their earthy substance with the soil; until no small portion of it must necessarily be akin to the mortal frame wherewith, for a little while, I walk the streets. In part, therefore, the attachment which I speak of is the mere sensuous sympathy of dust for dust. Few of my countrymen can know what it is; nor, as frequent transplantation is perhaps better for the stock, need they consider it desirable to know.

But the sentiment has likewise its moral quality. The figure of that first ancestor, invested by family tradition with a dim and dusky grandeur, was present to my boyish imagination, as far back as I can remember. It still haunts me, and induces a sort of home-feeling with the past, which I scarcely claim in reference to the present phase of the town. I seem to have a stronger claim to a residence here on account of this grave, bearded, sable-cloaked, and steeple-crowned progenitor, — who came so early, with his Bible and his sword, and trode the unworn street with such a stately port, and made so large a figure, as a man of war and peace, — a stronger claim than for myself, whose name is seldom heard and my face hardly known. He was a soldier, legislator, judge; he was a ruler in the Church; he had all the Puritanic traits, both good and evil. He was likewise a bitter persecutor; as witness the Quakers, who have remembered him in their histories, and relate an incident of his hard severity towards a woman of their sect, which will last longer, it is to be feared, than any record of his better deeds, although these were many. His son, too, inherited the persecuting spirit, and made himself so conspicuous in the martyrdom of the witches, that their blood may fairly be said to have left a stain upon him. So deep a stain, indeed, that his old dry bones, in the Charter Street burial-ground, must still retain it, if they have not crumbled utterly to dust! I know not whether these ancestors of mine bethought themselves to repent, and ask pardon of Heaven for their cruelties; or whether they are now groaning under the heavy consequences of them, in another state of being. At all events, I, the present writer, as their representative, hereby take shame upon myself for their sakes, and pray that any curse incurred by them — as I have heard, and as the dreary and unprosperous condition of the race, for many a long year back, would argue to exist — may be now and henceforth removed.

Doubtless, however, either of these stern and black-browed Puritans would have thought it quite a sufficient retribution for his sins, that, after so long a lapse of years, the old trunk of the family tree, with so much venerable moss upon it, should have borne, as its topmost bough, an idler like myself. No aim, that I have ever cherished, would they recognize as laudable; no success of mine — if my life, beyond its domestic scope, had ever been brightened by success — would they deem otherwise than worthless, if not positively disgraceful. "What is he?" murmurs one gray shadow of my forefathers to the other. "A writer of story-books! What kind of a business in life, — what mode of glorifying God, or being serviceable to mankind in his day and generation, — may that be? Why, the degenerate fellow might as well have been a fiddler!" Such are the compliments bandied between my great-grandsires and myself, across the gulf of time! And yet, let them scorn me as they will, strong traits of their nature have intertwined themselves with mine.

Planted deep, in the town's earliest infancy and childhood, by these two earnest and energetic men, the race has ever since subsisted here; always, too, in respectability; never, so far as I have known, disgraced by a single unworthy member; but seldom or never, on the other hand, after the first two generations, performing any memorable deed, or so much as putting forward a claim to public notice. Gradually, they have sunk almost out of sight; as old houses, here and there about the streets, get covered half-way to the eaves by the accumulation of new soil. From father to son, for above a hundred years, they followed the sea; a gray-headed shipmaster, in each generation, retiring from the quarter-deck to the homestead, while a boy of fourteen took the hereditary place before the mast, confronting the salt spray and the gale, which had blustered against his sire and grandsire. The boy, also, in due time, passed from the forecastle to the cabin, spent a tempestuous manhood, and returned from his world-wanderings, to grow old, and die, and mingle his dust with the natal earth. This long connection of a family with one spot, as its place of birth and burial, creates a kindred between the human being and the locality, quite independent of any charm in the scenery or moral circumstances that surround him. It is not love, but instinct. The new inhabitant — who came himself from a foreign land, or whose father or grandfather came — has little claim to be called a Salemite; he has no conception of the oyster-like tenacity with which an old settler, over whom his third century is creeping, clings to the spot where his successive generations have been imbedded. It is no matter that the place is joyless for him; that he is weary of the old wooden houses, the mud and dust, the dead level of site and sentiment, the chill east wind, and the chillest of social atmospheres; — all these, and whatever faults besides he may see or imagine, are nothing to the purpose. The spell survives, and just as powerfully as if the natal spot were an earthly paradise. So has it been in my case. I felt it almost as a destiny to make Salem my home; so that the mould of features and cast of character which had all along been familiar here — ever, as one representative of the race lay down in his grave, another assuming, as it were, his sentry-march along the Main Street — might still in my little day be seen and recognized in the old town. Nevertheless, this very sentiment is an evidence that the connection, which has become an unhealthy one, should at last be severed. Human nature will not flourish, any more than a potato, if it be planted and replanted, for too long a series of generations, in the same worn-out soil. My children have had other birthplaces, and, so far as their fortunes may be within my control, shall strike their roots into unaccustomed earth.

On emerging from the Old Manse, it was chiefly this strange, indolent, unjoyous attachment for my native town, that brought me to fill a place in Uncle Sam's brick edifice, when I might as well, or better, have gone somewhere else. My doom was on me. It was not the first time, nor the second, that I had gone away, — as it seemed, permanently, — but yet returned, like the bad half-penny; or as if Salem were for me the inevitable centre of the universe. So, one fine morning, I ascended the flight of granite steps, with the President's commission in my pocket, and was introduced to the corps of gentlemen who were to aid me in my weighty responsibility, as chief executive officer of the Custom-House.

I doubt greatly — or rather, I do not doubt at all — whether any public functionary of the United States, either in the civil or military line, has ever had such a patriarchal body of veterans under his orders as myself. The whereabouts of the Oldest Inhabitant was at once settled, when I looked at them. For upwards of twenty years before this epoch, the independent position of the Collector had kept the Salem Custom-House out of the whirlpool of political vicissitude, which makes the tenure of office generally so fragile. A soldier, — New England's most distinguished soldier, — he stood firmly on the pedestal of his gallant services; and, himself secure in the wise liberality of the successive administrations through which he had held office, he had been the safety of his subordinates in many an hour of danger and heart-quake. General Miller was radically conservative; a man over whose kindly nature habit had no slight influence; attaching himself strongly to familiar faces, and with difficulty moved to change, even when change might have brought unquestionable improvement. Thus, on taking charge of my department, I found few but aged men. They were ancient sea-captains, for the most part, who, after being tost on every sea, and standing up sturdily against life's tempestuous blast, had finally drifted into this quiet nook; where, with little to disturb them, except the periodical terrors of a Presidential election, they one and all acquired a new lease of existence. Though by no means less liable than their fellow-men to age and infirmity, they had evidently some talisman or other that kept death at bay. Two or three of their number, as I was assured, being gouty and rheumatic, or perhaps bed-ridden, never dreamed of making their appearance at the Custom-House, during a large part of the year; but, after a torpid winter, would creep out into the warm sunshine of May or June, go lazily about what they termed duty, and, at their own leisure and convenience, betake themselves to bed again. I must plead guilty to the charge of abbreviating the official breath of more than one of these venerable servants of the republic. They were allowed, on my representation, to rest from their arduous labors, and soon afterwards — as if their sole principle of life had been zeal for their country's service; as I verily believe it was — withdrew to a better world. It is a pious consolation to me, that, through my interference, a sufficient space was allowed them for repentance of the evil and corrupt practices, into which, as a matter of course, every Custom-House officer must be supposed to fall. Neither the front nor the back entrance of the Custom-House opens on the road to Paradise.

The greater part of my officers were Whigs. It was well for their venerable brotherhood, that the new Surveyor was not a politician, and, though a faithful Democrat in principle, neither received nor held his office with any reference to political services. Had it been otherwise, — had an active politician been put into this influential post, to assume the easy task of making head against a Whig Collector, whose infirmities withheld him from the personal administration of his office, — hardly a man of the old corps would have drawn the breath of official life, within a month after the exterminating angel had come up the Custom-House steps. According to the received code in such matters, it would have been nothing short of duty, in a politician, to bring every one of those white heads under the axe of the guillotine. It was plain enough to discern, that the old fellows dreaded some such discourtesy at my hands. It pained, and at the same time amused me, to behold the terrors that attended my advent; to see a furrowed cheek, weather-beaten by half a century of storm, turn ashy pale at the glance of so harmless an individual as myself; to detect, as one or another addressed me, the tremor of a voice, which, in long-past days, had been wont to bellow through a speaking-trumpet, hoarsely enough to frighten Boreas himself to silence. They knew, these excellent old persons, that, by all established rule, — and, as regarded some of them, weighed by their own lack of efficiency for business, — they ought to have given place to younger men, more orthodox in politics, and altogether fitter than themselves to serve our common Uncle. I knew it too, but could never quite find in my heart to act upon the knowledge. Much and deservedly to my own discredit, therefore, and considerably to the detriment of my official conscience, they continued, during my incumbency, to creep about the wharves, and loiter up and down the Custom-House steps. They spent a good deal of time, also, asleep in their accustomed corners, with their chairs tilted back against the wall; awaking, however, once or twice in a forenoon, to bore one another with the several thousandth repetition of old sea-stories, and mouldy jokes, that had grown to be pass-words and countersigns among them.

The discovery was soon made, I imagine, that the new Surveyor had no great harm in him. So, with lightsome hearts, and the happy consciousness of being usefully employed, — in their own behalf, at least, if not for our beloved country, — these good old gentlemen went through the various formalities of office. Sagaciously, under their spectacles, did they peep into the holds of vessels! Mighty was their fuss about little matters, and marvellous, sometimes, the obtuseness that allowed greater ones to slip between their fingers! Whenever such a mischance occurred, — when a wagon-load of valuable merchandise had been smuggled ashore, at noonday, perhaps, and directly beneath their unsuspicious noses, — nothing could exceed the vigilance and alacrity with which they proceeded to lock, and double-lock, and secure with tape and sealing-wax, all the avenues of the delinquent vessel. Instead of a reprimand for their previous negligence, the case seemed rather to require an eulogium on their praiseworthy caution, after the mischief had happened; a grateful recognition of the promptitude of their zeal, the moment that there was no longer any remedy!

Unless people are more than commonly disagreeable, it is my foolish habit to contract a kindness for them. The better part of my companion's character, if it have a better part, is that which usually comes uppermost in my regard, and forms the type whereby I recognize the man. As most of these old Custom-House officers had good traits, and as my position in reference to them, being paternal and protective, was favorable to the growth of friendly sentiments, I soon grew to like them all. It was pleasant, in the summer forenoons, — when the fervent heat, that almost liquefied the rest of the human family, merely communicated a genial warmth to their half-torpid systems, — it was pleasant to hear them chatting in the back entry, a row of them all tipped against the wall, as usual; while the frozen witticisms of past generations were thawed out, and came bubbling with laughter from their lips. Externally, the jollity of aged men has much in common with the mirth of children; the intellect, any more than a deep sense of humor, has little to do with the matter; it is, with both, a gleam that plays upon the surface, and imparts a sunny and cheery aspect alike to the green branch, and gray, mouldering trunk. In one case, however, it is real sunshine; in the other, it more resembles the phosphorescent glow of decaying wood.

It would be sad injustice, the reader must understand, to represent all my excellent old friends as in their dotage. In the first place, my coadjutors were not invariably old; there were men among them in their strength and prime, of marked ability and energy, and altogether superior to the sluggish and dependent mode of life on which their evil stars had cast them. Then, moreover, the white locks of age were sometimes found to be the thatch of an intellectual tenement in good repair. But, as respects the majority of my corps of veterans, there will be no wrong done, if I characterize them generally as a set of wearisome old souls, who had gathered nothing worth preservation from their varied experience of life. They seemed to have flung away all the golden grain of practical wisdom, which they had enjoyed so many opportunities of harvesting, and most carefully to have stored their memories with the husks. They spoke with far more interest and unction of their morning's breakfast, or yesterday's, to-day's, or to-morrow's dinner, than of the shipwreck of forty or fifty years ago, and all the world's wonders which they had witnessed with their youthful eyes.

The father of the Custom-House — the patriarch, not only of this little squad of officials, but, I am bold to say, of the respectable body of tide-waiters all over the United States — was a certain permanent Inspector. He might truly be termed a legitimate son of the revenue system, dyed in the wool, or rather, born in the purple; since his sire, a Revolutionary colonel, and formerly collector of the port, had created an office for him, and appointed him to fill it, at a period of the early ages which few living men can now remember. This Inspector, when I first knew him, was a man of fourscore years, or thereabouts, and certainly one of the most wonderful specimens of winter-green that you would be likely to discover in a lifetime's search. With his florid cheek, his compact figure, smartly arrayed in a bright-buttoned blue coat, his brisk and vigorous step, and his hale and hearty aspect, altogether, he seemed — not young, indeed — but a kind of new contrivance of Mother Nature in the shape of man, whom age and infirmity had no business to touch. His voice and laugh, which perpetually reëchoed through the Custom-House, had nothing of the tremulous quaver and cackle of an old man's utterance; they came strutting out of his lungs, like the crow of a cock, or the blast of a clarion. Looking at him merely as an animal, — and there was very little else to look at, — he was a most satisfactory object, from the thorough healthfulness and wholesomeness of his system, and his capacity, at that extreme age, to enjoy all, or nearly all, the delights which he had ever aimed at, or conceived of. The careless security of his life in the Custom-House, on a regular income, and with but slight and infrequent apprehensions of removal, had no doubt contributed to make time pass lightly over him. The original and more potent causes, however, lay in the rare perfection of his animal nature, the moderate proportion of intellect, and the very trifling admixture of moral and spiritual ingredients; these latter qualities, indeed, being in barely enough measure to keep the old gentleman from walking on all-fours. He possessed no power of thought, no depth of feeling, no troublesome sensibilities; nothing, in short, but a few commonplace instincts, which, aided by the cheerful temper that grew inevitably out of his physical well-being, did duty very respectably, and to general acceptance, in lieu of a heart. He had been the husband of three wives, all long since dead; the father of twenty children, most of whom, at every age of childhood or maturity, had likewise returned to dust. Here, one would suppose, might have been sorrow enough to imbue the sunniest disposition, through and through, with a sable tinge. Not so with our old Inspector! One brief sigh sufficed to carry off the entire burden of these dismal reminiscences. The next moment, he was as ready for sport as any unbreeched infant; far readier than the Collector's junior clerk, who, at nineteen years, was much the elder and graver man of the two.

I used to watch and study this patriarchal personage with, I think, livelier curiosity than any other form of humanity there presented to my notice. He was, in truth, a rare phenomenon; so perfect in one point of view; so shallow, so delusive, so impalpable, such an absolute nonentity, in every other. My conclusion was that he had no soul, no heart, no mind; nothing, as I have already said, but instincts; and yet, withal, so cunningly had the few materials of his character been put together, that there was no painful perception of deficiency, but, on my part, an entire contentment with what I found in him. It might be difficult — and it was so — to conceive how he should exist hereafter, so earthy and sensuous did he seem; but surely his existence here, admitting that it was to terminate with his last breath, had been not unkindly given; with no higher moral responsibilities than the beasts of the field, but with a larger scope of enjoyment than theirs, and with all their blessed immunity from the dreariness and duskiness of age.

One point, in which he had vastly the advantage over his four-footed brethren, was his ability to recollect the good dinners which it had made no small portion of the happiness of his life to eat. His gourmandism was a highly agreeable trait; and to hear him talk of roast-meat was as appetizing as a pickle or an oyster. As he possessed no higher attribute, and neither sacrificed nor vitiated any spiritual endowment by devoting all his energies and ingenuities to subserve the delight and profit of his maw, it always pleased and satisfied me to hear him expatiate on fish, poultry, and butcher's meat, and the most eligible methods of preparing them for the table. His reminiscences of good cheer, however ancient the date of the actual banquet, seemed to bring the savor of pig or turkey under one's very nostrils. There were flavors on his palate, that had lingered there not less than sixty or seventy years, and were still apparently as fresh as that of the muttonchop which he had just devoured for his breakfast. I have heard him smack his lips over dinners, every guest at which, except himself, had long been food for worms. It was marvellous to observe how the ghosts of bygone meals were continually rising up before him; not in anger or retribution, but as if grateful for his former appreciation, and seeking to reduplicate an endless series of enjoyment, at once shadowy and sensual. A tenderloin of beef, a hind-quarter of veal, a spare-rib of pork, a particular chicken, or a remarkably praiseworthy turkey, which had perhaps adorned his board in the days of the elder Adams, would be remembered; while all the subsequent experience of our race, and all the events that brightened or darkened his individual career, had gone over him with as little permanent effect as the passing breeze. The chief tragic event of the old man's life, so far as I could judge, was his mishap with a certain goose, which lived and died some twenty or forty years ago; a goose of most promising figure, but which, at table, proved so inveterately tough that the carving-knife would make no impression on its carcass; and it could only be divided with an axe and handsaw.

But it is time to quit this sketch; on which, however, I should be glad to dwell at considerably more length, because, of all men whom I have ever known, this individual was fittest to be a Custom-House officer. Most persons, owing to causes which I may not have space to hint at, suffer moral detriment from this peculiar mode of life. The old Inspector was incapable of it, and, were he to continue in office to the end of time, would be just as good as he was then, and sit down to dinner with just as good an appetite.

There is one likeness, without which my gallery of Custom-House portraits would be strangely incomplete; but which my comparatively few opportunities for observation enable me to sketch only in the merest outline. It is that of the Collector, our gallant old General, who, after his brilliant military service, subsequently to which he had ruled over a wild Western territory, had come hither, twenty years before, to spend the decline of his varied and honorable life. The brave soldier had already numbered, nearly or quite, his threescore years and ten, and was pursuing the remainder of his earthly march, burdened with infirmities which even the martial music of his own spirit-stirring recollections could do little towards lightening. The step was palsied now, that had been foremost in the charge. It was only with the assistance of a servant, and by leaning his hand heavily on the iron balustrade, that he could slowly and painfully ascend the Custom-House steps, and, with a toilsome progress across the floor, attain his customary chair beside the fireplace. There he used to sit, gazing with a somewhat dim serenity of aspect at the figures that came and went; amid the rustle of papers, the administering of oaths, the discussion of business, and the casual talk of the office; all which sounds and circumstances seemed but indistinctly to impress his senses, and hardly to make their way into his inner sphere of contemplation. His countenance, in this repose, was mild and kindly. If his notice was sought, an expression of courtesy and interest gleamed out upon his features; proving that there was light within him, and that it was only the outward medium of the intellectual lamp that obstructed the rays in their passage. The closer you penetrated to the substance of his mind, the sounder it appeared. When no longer called upon to speak, or listen, either of which operations cost him an evident effort, his face would briefly subside into its former not uncheerful quietude. It was not painful to behold this look; for, though dim, it had not the imbecility of decaying age. The framework of his nature, originally strong and massive, was not yet crumbled into ruin.

To observe and define his character, however, under such disadvantages, was as difficult a task as to trace out and build up anew, in imagination, an old fortress, like Ticonderoga, from a view of its gray and broken ruins. Here and there, perchance, the walls may remain almost complete; but elsewhere may be only a shapeless mound, cumbrous with its very strength, and overgrown, through long years of peace and neglect, with grass and alien weeds.

Nevertheless, looking at the old warrior with affection, — for, slight as was the communication between us, my feeling towards him, like that of all bipeds and quadrupeds who knew him, might not improperly be termed so, — I could discern the main points of his portrait. It was marked with the noble and heroic qualities which showed it to be not by a mere accident, but of good right, that he had won a distinguished name. His spirit could never, I conceive, have been characterized by an uneasy activity; it must, at any period of his life, have required an impulse to set him in motion; but, once stirred up, with obstacles to overcome, and an adequate object to be attained, it was not in the man to give out or fail. The heat that had formerly pervaded his nature, and which was not yet extinct, was never of the kind that flashes and flickers in a blaze, but, rather, a deep, red glow, as of iron in a furnace. Weight, solidity, firmness; this was the expression of his repose, even in such decay as had crept untimely over him, at the period of which I speak. But I could imagine, even then, that, under some excitement which should go deeply into his consciousness, — roused by a trumpet-peal, loud enough to awaken all of his energies that were not dead, but only slumbering, — he was yet capable of flinging off his infirmities like a sick man's gown, dropping the staff of age to seize a battle-sword, and starting up once more a warrior. And, in so intense a moment, his demeanour would have still been calm. Such an exhibition, however, was but to be pictured in fancy; not to be anticipated, nor desired. What I saw in him — as evidently as the indestructible ramparts of Old Ticonderoga, already cited as the most appropriate simile — were the features of stubborn and ponderous endurance, which might well have amounted to obstinacy in his earlier days; of integrity, that, like most of his other endowments, lay in a somewhat heavy mass, and was just as unmalleable and unmanageable as a ton of iron ore; and of benevolence, which, fiercely as he led the bayonets on at Chippewa or Fort Erie, I take to be of quite as genuine a stamp as what actuates any or all the polemical philanthropists of the age. He had slain men with his own hand, for aught I know; — certainly, they had fallen, like blades of grass at the sweep of the scythe, before the charge to which his spirit imparted its triumphant energy; — but, be that as it might, there was never in his heart so much cruelty as would have brushed the down off a butterfly's wing. I have not known the man, to whose innate kindliness I would more confidently make an appeal.

Many characteristics — and those, too, which contribute not the least forcibly to impart resemblance in a sketch — must have vanished, or been obscured, before I met the General. All merely graceful attributes are usually the most evanescent; nor does Nature adorn the human ruin with blossoms of new beauty, that have their roots and proper nutriment only in the chinks and crevices of decay, as she sows wall-flowers over the ruined fortress of Ticonderoga. Still, even in respect of grace and beauty, there were points well worth noting. A ray of humor, now and then, would make its way through the veil of dim obstruction, and glimmer pleasantly upon our faces. A trait of native elegance, seldom seen in the masculine character after childhood or early youth, was shown in the General's fondness for the sight and fragrance of flowers. An old soldier might be supposed to prize only the bloody laurel on his brow; but here was one, who seemed to have a young girl's appreciation of the floral tribe.

There, beside the fireplace, the brave old General used to sit; while the Surveyor — though seldom, when it could be avoided, taking upon himself the difficult task of engaging him in conversation — was fond of standing at a distance, and watching his quiet and almost slumberous countenance. He seemed away from us, although we saw him but a few yards off; remote, though we passed close beside his chair; unattainable, though we might have stretched forth our hands and touched his own. It might be, that he lived a more real life within his thoughts, than amid the unappropriate environment of the Collector's office. The evolutions of the parade; the tumult of the battle; the flourish of old, heroic music, heard thirty years before; — such scenes and sounds, perhaps, were all alive before his intellectual sense. Meanwhile, the merchants and ship-masters, the spruce clerks, and uncouth sailors, entered and departed; the bustle of this commercial and Custom-House life kept up its little murmur roundabout him; and neither with the men nor their affairs did the General appear to sustain the most distant relation. He was as much out of place as an old sword — now rusty, but which had flashed once in the battle's front, and showed still a bright gleam along its blade — would have been, among the inkstands, paper-folders, and mahogany rulers, on the Deputy Collector's desk.

There was one thing that much aided me in renewing and re-creating the stalwart soldier of the Niagara frontier, — the man of true and simple energy. It was the recollection of those memorable words of his, — "I'll try, Sir!" — spoken on the very verge of a desperate and heroic enterprise, and breathing the soul and spirit of New England hardihood, comprehending all perils, and encountering all. If, in our country, valor were rewarded by heraldic honor, this phrase — which it seems so easy to speak, but which only he, with such a task of danger and glory before him, has ever spoken — would be the best and fittest of all mottoes for the General's shield of arms.

It contributes greatly towards a man's moral and intellectual health, to be brought into habits of companionship with individuals unlike himself, who care little for his pursuits, and whose sphere and abilities he must go out of himself to appreciate. The accidents of my life have often afforded me this advantage, but never with more fulness and variety than during my continuance in office. There was one man, especially, the observation of whose character gave me a new idea of talent. His gifts were emphatically those of a man of business; prompt, acute, clear-minded; with an eye that saw through all perplexities, and a faculty of arrangement that made them vanish, as by the waving of an enchanter's wand. Bred up from boyhood in the Custom-House, it was his proper field of activity; and the many intricacies of business, so harassing to the interloper, presented themselves before him with the regularity of a perfectly comprehended system. In my contemplation, he stood as the ideal of his class. He was, indeed, the Custom-House in himself; or, at all events, the main-spring that kept its variously revolving wheels in motion; for, in an institution like this, where its officers are appointed to subserve their own profit and convenience, and seldom with a leading reference to their fitness for the duty to be performed, they must perforce seek elsewhere the dexterity which is not in them. Thus, by an inevitable necessity, as a magnet attracts steel-filings, so did our man of business draw to himself the difficulties which everybody met with. With an easy condescension, and kind forbearance towards our stupidity, — which, to his order of mind, must have seemed little short of crime, — would he forthwith, by the merest touch of his finger, make the incomprehensible as clear as daylight. The merchants valued him not less than we, his esoteric friends. His integrity was perfect; it was a law of nature with him, rather than a choice or a principle; nor can it be otherwise than the main condition of an intellect so remarkably clear and accurate as his, to be honest and regular in the administration of affairs. A stain on his conscience, as to any thing that came within the range of his vocation, would trouble such a man very much in the same way, though to a far greater degree, than an error in the balance of an account, or an ink-blot on the fair page of a book of record. Here, in a word, — and it is a rare instance in my life, — I had met with a person thoroughly adapted to the situation which he held.

Such were some of the people with whom I now found myself connected. I took it in good part at the hands of Providence, that I was thrown into a position so little akin to my past habits; and set myself seriously to gather from it whatever profit was to be had. After my fellowship of toil and impracticable schemes, with the dreamy brethren of Brook Farm; after living for three years within the subtile influence of an intellect like Emerson's; after those wild, free days on the Assabeth, indulging fantastic speculations beside our fire of fallen boughs, with Ellery Channing; after talking with Thoreau about pine-trees and Indian relics, in his hermitage at Walden; after growing fastidious by sympathy with the classic refinement of Hillard's culture; after becoming imbued with poetic sentiment at Longfellow's hearth-stone; — it was time, at length, that I should exercise other faculties of my nature, and nourish myself with food for which I had hitherto had little appetite. Even the old Inspector was desirable, as a change of diet, to a man who had known Alcott. I looked upon it as an evidence, in some measure, of a system naturally well balanced, and lacking no essential part of a thorough organization, that, with such associates to remember, I could mingle at once with men of altogether different qualities, and never murmur at the change.

Literature, its exertions and objects, were now of little moment in my regard. I cared not, at this period, for books; they were apart from me. Nature, — except it were human nature, — the nature that is developed in earth and sky, was, in one sense, hidden from me; and all the imaginative delight, wherewith it had been spiritualized, passed away out of my mind. A gift, a faculty, if it had not departed, was suspended and inanimate within me. There would have been something sad, unutterably dreary, in all this, had I not been conscious that it lay at my own option to recall whatever was valuable in the past. It might be true, indeed, that this was a life which could not, with impunity, be lived too long; else, it might make me permanently other than I had been, without transforming me into any shape which it would be worth my while to take. But I never considered it as other than a transitory life. There was always a prophetic instinct, a low whisper in my ear, that, within no long period, and whenever a new change of custom should be essential to my good, a change would come.

Meanwhile, there I was, a Surveyor of the Revenue, and, so far as I have been able to understand, as good a Surveyor as need be. A man of thought, fancy, and sensibility, (had he ten times the Surveyor's proportion of those qualities,) may, at any time, be a man of affairs, if he will only choose to give himself the trouble. My fellow-officers, and the merchants and sea-captains with whom my official duties brought me into any manner of connection, viewed me in no other light, and probably knew me in no other character. None of them, I presume, had ever read a page of my inditing, or would have cared a fig the more for me, if they had read them all; nor would it have mended the matter, in the least, had those same unprofitable pages been written with a pen like that of Burns or of Chaucer, each of whom was a Custom-House officer in his day, as well as I. It is a good lesson — though it may often be a hard one — for a man who has dreamed of literary fame, and of making for himself a rank among the world's dignitaries by such means, to step aside out of the narrow circle in which his claims are recognized, and to find how utterly devoid of significance, beyond that circle, is all that he achieves, and all he aims at. I know not that I especially needed the lesson, either in the way of warning or rebuke; but, at any rate, I learned it thoroughly; nor, it gives me pleasure to reflect, did the truth, as it came home to my perception, ever cost me a pang, or require to be thrown off in a sigh. In the way of literary talk, it is true, the Naval Officer — an excellent fellow, who came into office with me, and went out only a little later — would often engage me in a discussion about one or the other of his favorite topics, Napoleon or Shakspeare. The Collector's junior clerk, too, — a young gentleman who, it was whispered, occasionally covered a sheet of Uncle Sam's letter-paper with what, (at the distance of a few yards,) looked very much like poetry, — used now and then to speak to me of books, as matters with which I might possibly be conversant. This was my all of lettered intercourse; and it was quite sufficient for my necessities.

No longer seeking nor caring that my name should be blazoned abroad on title-pages, I smiled to think that it had now another kind of vogue. The Custom-House marker imprinted it, with a stencil and black paint, on pepper-bags, and baskets of anatto, and cigar-boxes, and bales of all kinds of dutiable merchandise, in testimony that these commodities had paid the impost, and gone regularly through the office. Borne on such queer vehicle of fame, a knowledge of my existence, so far as a name conveys it, was carried where it had never been before, and, I hope, will never go again.

But the past was not dead. Once in a great while, the thoughts, that had seemed so vital and so active, yet had been put to rest so quietly, revived again. One of the most remarkable occasions, when the habit of bygone days awoke in me, was that which brings it within the law of literary propriety to offer the public the sketch which I am now writing.

In the second story of the Custom-House, there is a large room, in which the brick-work and naked rafters have never been covered with panelling and plaster. The edifice — originally projected on a scale adapted to the old commercial enterprise of the port, and with an idea of subsequent prosperity destined never to be realized — contains far more space than its occupants know what to do with. This airy hall, therefore, over the Collector's apartments, remains unfinished to this day, and, in spite of the aged cobwebs that festoon its dusky beams, appears still to await the labor of the carpenter and mason. At one end of the room, in a recess, were a number of barrels, piled one upon another, containing bundles of official documents. Large quantities of similar rubbish lay lumbering the floor. It was sorrowful to think how many days, and weeks, and months, and years of toil, had been wasted on these musty papers, which were now only an encumbrance on earth, and were hidden away in this forgotten corner, never more to be glanced at by human eyes. But, then, what reams of other manuscripts — filled, not with the dulness of official formalities, but with the thought of inventive brains and the rich effusion of deep hearts — had gone equally to oblivion; and that, moreover, without serving a purpose in their days, as these heaped-up papers had, and — saddest of all — without purchasing for their writers the comfortable livelihood which the clerks of the Custom-House had gained by these worthless scratchings of the pen! Yet not altogether worthless, perhaps, as materials of local history. Here, no doubt, statistics of the former commerce of Salem might be discovered, and memorials of her princely merchants, — old King

Derby, — old Billy Gray, — old Simon Forrester, — and many another magnate in his day; whose powdered head, however, was scarcely in the tomb, before his mountain-pile of wealth began to dwindle. The founders of the greater part of the families which now compose the aristocracy of Salem might here be traced, from the petty and obscure beginnings of their traffic, at periods generally much posterior to the Revolution, upward to what their children look upon as long-established rank.

Prior to the Revolution, there is a dearth of records; the earlier documents and archives of the Custom-House having, probably, been carried off to Halifax, when all the King's officials accompanied the British army in its flight from Boston. It has often been a matter of regret with me; for, going back, perhaps, to the days of the Protectorate, those papers must have contained many references to forgotten or remembered men, and to antique customs, which would have affected me with the same pleasure as when I used to pick up Indian arrow-heads in the field near the Old Manse.

But, one idle and rainy day, it was my fortune to make a discovery of some little interest. Poking and burrowing into the heaped-up rubbish in the corner; unfolding one and another document, and reading the names of vessels that had long ago foundered at sea or rotted at the wharves, and those of merchants, never heard of now on 'Change, nor very readily decipherable on their mossy tombstones; glancing at such matters with the saddened, weary, half-reluctant interest which we bestow on the corpse of dead activity, — and exerting my fancy, sluggish with little use, to raise up from these dry bones an image of the old town's brighter aspect, when India was a new region, and only Salem knew the way thither, — I chanced to lay my hand on a small package, carefully done up in a piece of ancient yellow parchment. This envelope had the air of an official record of some period long past, when clerks engrossed their stiff and formal chirography on more substantial materials than at present. There was something about it that quickened an instinctive curiosity, and made me undo the faded red tape, that tied up the package, with the sense that a treasure would here be brought to light. Unbending the rigid folds of the parchment cover, I found it to be a commission, under the hand and seal of Governor Shirley, in favor of one Jonathan Pue, as Surveyor of his Majesty's Customs for the port of Salem, in the Province of Massachusetts Bay. I remembered to have read (probably in Felt's Annals) a notice of the decease of Mr. Surveyor Pue, about fourscore years ago; and likewise, in a newspaper of recent times, an account of the digging up of his remains in the little grave-yard of St.

Peter's Church, during the renewal of that edifice. Nothing, if I rightly call to mind, was left of my respected predecessor, save an imperfect skeleton, and some fragments of apparel, and a wig of majestic frizzle; which, unlike the head that it once adorned, was in very satisfactory preservation. But, on examining the papers which the parchment commission served to envelop, I found more traces of Mr. Pue's mental part, and the internal operations of his head, than the frizzled wig had contained of the venerable skull itself.

They were documents, in short, not official, but of a private nature, or, at least, written in his private capacity, and apparently with his own hand. I could account for their being included in the heap of Custom-House lumber only by the fact, that Mr. Pue's death had happened suddenly; and that these papers, which he probably kept in his official desk, had never come to the knowledge of his heirs, or were supposed to relate to the business of the revenue. On the transfer of the archives to Halifax, this package, proving to be of no public concern, was left behind, and had remained ever since unopened.

The ancient Surveyor — being little molested, I suppose, at that early day, with business pertaining to his office — seems to have devoted some of his many leisure hours to researches as a local antiquarian, and other inquisitions of a similar nature. These supplied material for petty activity to a mind that would otherwise have been eaten up with rust. A portion of his facts, by the by, did me good service in the preparation of the article entitled "MAIN STREET," included in the present volume. The remainder may perhaps be applied to purposes equally valuable, hereafter; or not impossibly may be worked up, so far as they go, into a regular history of Salem, should my veneration for the natal soil ever impel me to so pious a task. Meanwhile, they shall be at the command of any gentleman, inclined, and competent, to take the unprofitable labor off my hands. As a final disposition, I contemplate depositing them with the Essex Historical Society.

But the object that most drew my attention, in the mysterious package, was a certain affair of fine red cloth, much worn and faded. There were traces about it of gold embroidery, which, however, was greatly frayed and defaced; so that none, or very little, of the glitter was left. It had been wrought, as was easy to perceive, with wonderful skill of needlework; and the stitch (as I am assured by ladies conversant with such mysteries) gives evidence of a now forgotten art, not to be recovered even by the process of picking out the threads. This rag of scarlet cloth, — for time, and wear, and a sacrilegious moth, had reduced it to little other than a rag, — on careful examination, assumed the shape of a letter. It was the capital letter A. By an accurate measurement, each limb proved to be precisely three inches and a quarter in length. It had been intended, there could be no doubt, as an ornamental article of dress; but how it was to be worn, or what rank, honor, and dignity, in by-past times, were signified by it, was a riddle which (so evanescent are the fashions of the world in these particulars) I saw little hope of solving. And yet it strangely interested me. My eyes fastened themselves upon the old scarlet letter, and would not be turned aside. Certainly, there was some deep meaning in it, most worthy of interpretation, and which, as it were, streamed forth from the mystic symbol, subtly communicating itself to my sensibilities, but evading the analysis of my mind.

While thus perplexed, — and cogitating, among other hypotheses, whether the letter might not have been one of those decorations which the white men used to contrive, in order to take the eyes of Indians, — I happened to place it on my breast. It seemed to me, — the reader may smile, but must not doubt my word, — it seemed to me, then, that I experienced a sensation not altogether physical, yet almost so, as of burning heat; and as if the letter were not of red cloth, but red-hot iron. I shuddered, and involuntarily let it fall upon the floor.

In the absorbing contemplation of the scarlet letter, I had hitherto neglected to examine a small roll of dingy paper, around which it had been twisted. This I now opened, and had the satisfaction to find, recorded by the old Surveyor's pen, a reasonably complete explanation of the whole affair. There were several foolscap sheets, containing many particulars respecting the life and conversation of one Hester Prynne, who appeared to have been rather a noteworthy personage in the view of our ancestors. She had flourished during a period between the early days of Massachusetts and the close of the seventeenth century. Aged persons, alive in the time of Mr. Surveyor Pue, and from whose oral testimony he had made up his narrative, remembered her, in their youth, as a very old, but not decrepit woman, of a stately and solemn aspect. It had been her habit, from an almost immemorial date, to go about the country as a kind of voluntary nurse, and doing whatever miscellaneous good she might; taking upon herself, likewise, to give advice in all matters, especially those of the heart; by which means, as a person of such propensities inevitably must, she gained from many people the reverence due to an angel, but, I should imagine, was looked upon by others as an intruder and a nuisance. Prying farther into the manuscript, I found the record of other doings and sufferings of this singular woman, for most of which the reader is referred to the story entitled "THE SCARLET LETTER"; and it should be borne carefully in mind, that the main facts of that story are authorized and authenticated by the document of Mr. Surveyor Pue. The original papers, together with the scarlet letter itself, — a most curious relic, — are still in my possession, and shall be freely exhibited to whomsoever, induced by the great interest of the narrative, may desire a sight of them. I must not be understood as affirming, that, in the dressing up of the tale, and imagining the motives and modes of passion that influenced the characters who figure in it, I have invariably confined myself within the limits of the old Surveyor's half a dozen sheets of foolscap. On the contrary, I have allowed myself, as to such points, nearly or altogether as much license as if the facts had been entirely of my own invention. What I contend for is the authenticity of the outline.

This incident recalled my mind, in some degree, to its old track. There seemed to be here the groundwork of a tale. It impressed me as if the ancient Surveyor, in his garb of a hundred years gone by, and wearing his immortal wig, — which was buried with him, but did not perish in the grave, — had met me in the deserted chamber of the Custom-House. In his port was the dignity of one who had borne his Majesty's commission, and who was therefore illuminated by a ray of the splendor that shone so dazzlingly about the throne. How unlike, alas! the hang-dog look of a republican official, who, as the servant of the people, feels himself less than the least, and below the lowest, of his masters. With his own ghostly hand, the obscurely seen, but majestic, figure had imparted to me the scarlet symbol, and the little roll of explanatory manuscript. With his own ghostly voice, he had exhorted me, on the sacred consideration of my filial duty and reverence towards him, — who might reasonably regard himself as my official ancestor, — to bring his mouldy and moth-eaten lucubrations before the public. "Do this," said the ghost of Mr. Surveyor Pue, emphatically nodding the head that looked so imposing within its memorable wig, "do this, and the profit shall be all your own! You will shortly need it; for it is not in your days as it was in mine, when a man's office was a life-lease, and oftentimes an heirloom. But, I charge you, in this matter of old Mistress Prynne, give to your predecessor's memory the credit which will be rightfully its due!" And I said to the ghost of Mr. Surveyor Pue, — "I will!"

On Hester Prynne's story, therefore, I bestowed much thought. It was the subject of my meditations for many an hour, while pacing to and fro across my room, or traversing, with a hundredfold repetition, the long extent from the front-door of the Custom-House to the side-entrance, and back again. Great were the weariness and annoyance of the old Inspector and the Weighers and Gaugers, whose slumbers were disturbed by the unmercifully lengthened tramp of my passing and returning footsteps. Remembering their own former habits, they used to say that the Surveyor was walking the quarter-deck. They probably fancied that my sole object — and, indeed, the sole object for which a sane man could ever put himself into voluntary motion — was, to get an appetite for dinner. And to say the truth, an appetite, sharpened by the east-wind that generally blew along the passage, was the only valuable result of so much indefatigable exercise. So little adapted is the atmosphere of a Custom-House to the delicate harvest of fancy and sensibility, that, had I remained there through ten Presidencies yet to come, I doubt whether the tale of "The Scarlet Letter" would ever have been brought before the public eye. My imagination was a tarnished mirror. It would not reflect, or only with miserable dimness, the figures with which I did my best to people it. The characters of the narrative would not be warmed and rendered malleable, by any heat that I could kindle at my intellectual forge. They would take neither the glow of passion nor the tenderness of sentiment, but retained all the rigidity of dead corpses, and stared me in the face with a fixed and ghastly grin of contemptuous defiance. "What have you to do with us?" that expression seemed to say. "The little power you might once have possessed over the tribe of unrealities is gone! You have bartered it for a pittance of the public gold. Go, then, and earn your wages!" In short, the almost torpid creatures of my own fancy twitted me with imbecility, and not without fair occasion.

It was not merely during the three hours and a half which Uncle Sam claimed as his share of my daily life, that this wretched numbness held possession of me. It went with me on my sea-shore walks and rambles into the country, whenever — which was seldom and reluctantly — I bestirred myself to seek that invigorating charm of Nature, which used to give me such freshness and activity of thought, the moment that I stepped across the threshold of the Old Manse. The same torpor, as regarded the capacity for intellectual effort, accompanied me home, and weighed upon me in the chamber which I most absurdly termed my study. Nor did it quit me, when, late at night, I sat in the deserted parlour, lighted only by the glimmering coal-fire and the moon, striving to picture forth imaginary scenes, which, the next day, might flow out on the brightening page in many-hued description.

If the imaginative faculty refused to act at such an hour, it might well be deemed a hopeless case. Moonlight, in a familiar room, falling so white upon the carpet, and showing all its figures so distinctly,—making every object so minutely visible, yet so unlike a morning or noontide visibility,—is a medium the most suitable for a romance-writer to get acquainted with his illusive guests. There is the little domestic scenery of the well-known apartment; the chairs, with each its separate individuality; the centre-table, sustaining a work-basket, a volume or two, and an extinguished lamp; the sofa; the book-case; the picture on the wall;—all these details, so completely seen, are so spiritualized by the unusual light, that they seem to lose their actual substance, and become things of intellect. Nothing is too small or too trifling to undergo this change, and acquire dignity thereby. A child's shoe; the doll, seated in her little wicker carriage; the hobby-horse;—whatever, in a word, has been used or played with, during the day, is now invested with a quality of strangeness and remoteness, though still almost as vividly present as by daylight. Thus, therefore, the floor of our familiar room has become a neutral territory, somewhere between the real world and fairy-land, where the Actual and the Imaginary may meet, and each imbue itself with the nature of the other. Ghosts might enter here, without affrighting us. It would be too much in keeping with the scene to excite surprise, were we to look about us and discover a form, beloved, but gone hence, now sitting quietly in a streak of this magic moonshine, with an aspect that would make us doubt whether it had returned from afar, or had never once stirred from our fireside.

The somewhat dim coal-fire has an essential influence in producing the effect which I would describe. It throws its unobtrusive tinge throughout the room, with a faint ruddiness upon the walls and ceiling, and a reflected gleam from the polish of the furniture. This warmer light mingles itself with the cold spirituality of the moonbeams, and communicates, as it were, a heart and sensibilities of human tenderness to the forms which fancy summons up. It converts them from snow-images into men and women. Glancing at the looking-glass, we behold—deep within its haunted verge—the smouldering glow of the half-extinguished anthracite, the white moonbeams on the floor, and a repetition of all the gleam and shadow of the picture, with one remove farther from the actual, and nearer to the imaginative. Then, at such an hour, and with this scene before him, if a man, sitting all alone, cannot dream strange things, and make them look like truth, he need never try to write romances.

But, for myself, during the whole of my Custom-House experience, moonlight and sunshine, and the glow of firelight, were just alike in my regard; and neither of them was of one whit more avail than the twinkle of a tallow-candle. An entire class of susceptibilities, and a gift connected with them, — of no great richness or value, but the best I had, — was gone from me.

It is my belief, however, that, had I attempted a different order of composition, my faculties would not have been found so pointless and inefficacious. I might, for instance, have contented myself with writing out the narratives of a veteran shipmaster, one of the Inspectors, whom I should be most ungrateful not to mention; since scarcely a day passed that he did not stir me to laughter and admiration by his marvellous gifts as a story-teller. Could I have preserved the picturesque force of his style, and the humorous coloring which nature taught him how to throw over his descriptions, the result, I honestly believe, would have been something new in literature. Or I might readily have found a more serious task. It was a folly, with the materiality of this daily life pressing so intrusively upon me, to attempt to fling myself back into another age; or to insist on creating the semblance of a world out of airy matter, when, at every moment, the impalpable beauty of my soap-bubble was broken by the rude contact of some actual circumstance. The wiser effort would have been, to diffuse thought and imagination through the opaque substance of to-day, and thus to make it a bright transparency; to spiritualize the burden that began to weigh so heavily; to seek, resolutely, the true and indestructible value that lay hidden in the petty and wearisome incidents, and ordinary characters, with which I was now conversant. The fault was mine. The page of life that was spread out before me seemed dull and commonplace, only because I had not fathomed its deeper import. A better book than I shall ever write was there; leaf after leaf presenting itself to me, just as it was written out by the reality of the flitting hour, and vanishing as fast as written, only because my brain wanted the insight and my hand the cunning to transcribe it. At some future day, it may be, I shall remember a few scattered fragments and broken paragraphs, and write them down, and find the letters turn to gold upon the page.

These perceptions have come too late. At the instant, I was only conscious that what would have been a pleasure once was now a hopeless toil. There was no occasion to make much moan about this state of affairs. I had ceased to be a writer of tolerably poor tales and essays, and had become a tolerably good Surveyor of the Customs. That was all. But, nevertheless, it is any thing but agreeable to be haunted by a suspicion that one's intellect is dwindling away; or exhaling, without your consciousness, like ether out of a phial; so that, at every glance, you find a smaller and less volatile residuum. Of the fact, there could be no doubt; and, examining myself and others, I was led to conclusions in reference to the effect of public office on the character, not very favorable to the mode of life in question. In some other form, perhaps, I may hereafter develop these effects. Suffice it here to say, that a Custom-House officer, of long continuance, can hardly be a very praiseworthy or respectable personage, for many reasons; one of them, the tenure by which he holds his situation, and another, the very nature of his business, which — though, I trust, an honest one — is of such a sort that he does not share in the united effort of mankind.

An effect — which I believe to be observable, more or less, in every individual who has occupied the position — is, that, while he leans on the mighty arm of the Republic, his own proper strength departs from him. He loses, in an extent proportioned to the weakness or force of his original nature, the capability of self-support. If he possess an unusual share of native energy, or the enervating magic of place do not operate too long upon him, his forfeited powers may be redeemable. The ejected officer — fortunate in the unkindly shove that sends him forth betimes, to struggle amid a struggling world — may return to himself, and become all that he has ever been. But this seldom happens. He usually keeps his ground just long enough for his own ruin, and is then thrust out, with sinews all unstrung, to totter along the difficult foot-path of life as he best may. Conscious of his own infirmity, — that his tempered steel and elasticity are lost, — he for ever afterwards looks wistfully about him in quest of support external to himself. His pervading and continual hope — a hallucination, which, in the face of all discouragement, and making light of impossibilities, haunts him while he lives, and, I fancy, like the convulsive throes of the cholera, torments him for a brief space after death — is, that, finally, and in no long time, by some happy coincidence of circumstances, he shall be restored to office. This faith, more than any thing else, steals the pith and availability out of whatever enterprise he may dream of undertaking. Why should he toil and moil, and be at so much trouble to pick himself up out of the mud, when, in a little while hence, the strong arm of his Uncle will raise and support him? Why should he work for his living here, or go to dig gold in California, when he is so soon to be made happy, at monthly intervals, with a little pile of glittering coin out of his Uncle's pocket? It is sadly curious to observe how slight a taste of office suffices to infect a poor fellow with this singular disease. Uncle Sam's gold — meaning no disrespect to the worthy old gentleman — has, in this respect, a quality of enchantment like that of the Devil's wages. Whoever touches it should look well to himself, or he may find the bargain to go hard against him, involving, if not his soul, yet many of its better attributes; its sturdy force, its courage and constancy, its truth, its self-reliance, and all that gives the emphasis to manly character.

Here was a fine prospect in the distance! Not that the Surveyor brought the lesson home to himself, or admitted that he could be so utterly undone, either by continuance in office, or ejectment. Yet my reflections were not the most comfortable. I began to grow melancholy and restless; continually prying into my mind, to discover which of its poor properties were gone, and what degree of detriment had already accrued to the remainder. I endeavoured to calculate how much longer I could stay in the Custom-House, and yet go forth a man. To confess the truth, it was my greatest apprehension, — as it would never be a measure of policy to turn out so quiet an individual as myself, and it being hardly in the nature of a public officer to resign, — it was my chief trouble, therefore, that I was likely to grow gray and decrepit in the Surveyorship, and become much such another animal as the old Inspector. Might it not, in the tedious lapse of official life that lay before me, finally be with me as it was with this venerable friend, — to make the dinner-hour the nucleus of the day, and to spend the rest of it, as an old dog spends it, asleep in the sunshine or the shade? A dreary look-forward this, for a man who felt it to be the best definition of happiness to live throughout the whole range of his faculties and sensibilities! But, all this while, I was giving myself very unnecessary alarm. Providence had meditated better things for me than I could possibly imagine for myself.

A remarkable event of the third year of my Surveyorship — to adopt the tone of "P.P." — was the election of General Taylor to the Presidency. It is essential, in order to form a complete estimate of the advantages of official life, to view the incumbent at the in-coming of a hostile administration. His position is then one of the most singularly irksome, and, in every contingency, disagreeable, that a wretched mortal can possibly occupy; with seldom an alternative of good, on either hand, although what presents itself to him as the worst event may very probably be the best. But it is a strange experience, to a man of pride and sensibility, to know that his interests are within the control of individuals who neither love nor understand him, and by whom, since one or the other must needs happen, he would rather be injured than obliged. Strange, too, for one who has kept his calmness throughout the contest, to observe the bloodthirstiness that is developed in the hour of triumph, and to be conscious that he is himself among its objects! There are few uglier traits of human nature than this tendency — which I now witnessed in men no worse than their neighbours — to grow cruel, merely because they possessed the power of inflicting harm. If the guillotine, as applied to office-holders, were a literal fact, instead of one of the most apt of metaphors, it is my sincere belief, that the active members of the victorious party were sufficiently excited to have chopped off all our heads, and have thanked Heaven for the opportunity! It appears to me — who have been a calm and curious observer, as well in victory as defeat — that this fierce and bitter spirit of malice and revenge has never distinguished the many triumphs of my own party as it now did that of the Whigs. The Democrats take the offices, as a general rule, because they need them, and because the practice of many years has made it the law of political warfare, which, unless a different system be proclaimed, it were weakness and cowardice to murmur at. But the long habit of victory has made them generous. They know how to spare, when they see occasion; and when they strike, the axe may be sharp, indeed, but its edge is seldom poisoned with ill-will; nor is it their custom ignominiously to kick the head which they have just struck off.

In short, unpleasant as was my predicament, at best, I saw much reason to congratulate myself that I was on the losing side, rather than the triumphant one. If, heretofore, I had been none of the warmest of partisans, I began now, at this season of peril and adversity, to be pretty acutely sensible with which party my predilections lay; nor was it without something like regret and shame, that, according to a reasonable calculation of chances, I saw my own prospect of retaining office to be better than those of my Democratic brethren. But who can see an inch into futurity, beyond his nose? My own head was the first that fell!

The moment when a man's head drops off is seldom or never, I am inclined to think, precisely the most agreeable of his life. Nevertheless, like the greater part of our misfortunes, even so serious a contingency brings its remedy and consolation with it, if the sufferer will but make the best, rather than the worst, of the accident which has befallen him. In my particular case, the consolatory topics were close at hand, and, indeed, had suggested themselves to my meditations a considerable time before it was requisite to use them. In view of my previous weariness of office, and vague thoughts of resignation, my fortune somewhat resembled that of a person who should entertain an idea of committing suicide, and, altogether beyond his hopes, meet with the good hap to be murdered. In the Custom-House, as before in the Old Manse, I had spent three years; a term long enough to rest a weary brain; long enough to break off old intellectual habits, and make room for new ones; long enough, and too long, to have lived in an unnatural state, doing what was really of no advantage nor delight to any human being, and withholding myself from toil that would, at least, have stilled an unquiet impulse in me. Then, moreover, as regarded his unceremonious ejectment, the late Surveyor was not altogether ill-pleased to be recognized by the Whigs as an enemy; since his inactivity in political affairs, — his tendency to roam, at will, in that broad and quiet field where all mankind may meet, rather than confine himself to those narrow paths where brethren of the same household must diverge from one another, — had sometimes made it questionable with his brother Democrats whether he was a friend. Now, after he had won the crown of martyrdom, (though with no longer a head to wear it on,) the point might be looked upon as settled. Finally, little heroic as he was, it seemed more decorous to be overthrown in the downfall of the party with which he had been content to stand, than to remain a forlorn survivor, when so many worthier men were falling; and, at last, after subsisting for four years on the mercy of a hostile administration, to be compelled then to define his position anew, and claim the yet more humiliating mercy of a friendly one.

Meanwhile, the press had taken up my affair, and kept me, for a week or two, careering through the public prints, in my decapitated state, like Irving's Headless Horseman; ghastly and grim, and longing to be buried, as a politically dead man ought. So much for my figurative self. The real human being, all this time, with his head safely on his shoulders, had brought himself to the comfortable conclusion, that every thing was for the best; and, making an investment in ink, paper, and steel-pens, had opened his long-disused writing-desk, and was again a literary man.

Now it was, that the lucubrations of my ancient predecessor, Mr. Surveyor Pue, came into play. Rusty through long idleness, some little space was requisite before my intellectual machinery could be brought to work upon the tale, with an effect in any degree satisfactory. Even yet, though my thoughts were ultimately much absorbed in the task, it wears, to my eye, a stern and sombre aspect; too much ungladdened by genial sunshine; too little relieved by the tender and familiar influences which soften almost every scene of nature and real life, and, undoubtedly, should soften every picture of them. This uncaptivating effect is perhaps due to the period of hardly accomplished revolution, and still seething turmoil, in which the story shaped itself. It is no indication, however, of a lack of cheerfulness in the writer's mind; for he was happier, while straying through the gloom of these sunless fantasies, than at any time since he had quitted the Old Manse. Some of the briefer articles, which contribute to make up the volume, have likewise been written since my involuntary withdrawal from the toils and honors of public life, and the remainder are gleaned from annuals and magazines, of such antique date that they have gone round the circle, and come back to novelty again.* Keeping up the metaphor of the political guillotine, the whole may be considered as the POSTHUMOUS PAPERS OF A DECAPITATED SURVEYOR; and the sketch which I am now bringing to a close, if too autobiographical for a modest person to publish in his lifetime, will readily be excused in a gentleman who writes from beyond the grave. Peace be with all the world! My blessing on my friends! My forgiveness to my enemies! For I am in the realm of quiet!

The life of the Custom-House lies like a dream behind me. The old Inspector, — who, by the by, I regret to say, was overthrown and killed by a horse, some time ago; else he would certainly have lived for ever, — he, and all those other venerable personages who sat with him at the receipt of custom, are but shadows in my view; white-headed and wrinkled images, which my fancy used to sport with, and has now flung aside for ever. The merchants, — Pingree, Phillips, Shepard, Upton, Kimball, Bertram, Hunt, — these, and many other names, which had such a classic familiarity for my ear six months ago, — these men of traffic, who seemed to occupy so important a position in the world, — how little time has it required to disconnect me from them all, not merely in act, but recollection! It is with an effort that I recall the figures and appellations of these few. Soon, likewise, my old native town will loom upon me through the haze of memory, a mist brooding over and around it; as if it were no portion of the real earth, but an overgrown village in cloud-land, with only imaginary inhabitants to people its wooden houses, and walk its homely lanes, and the unpicturesque prolixity of its main street. Henceforth, it ceases to be a reality of my life. I am a citizen of somewhere else. My good townspeople will not much regret me; for — though it has been as dear an object as any, in my literary efforts, to be of some importance in their eyes, and to win myself a pleasant memory in this abode and burial-place of so many of my

*At the time of writing this article, the author intended to publish, along with "The Scarlet Letter," several shorter tales and sketches. These it has been thought advisable to defer.

forefathers — there has never been, for me, the genial atmosphere which a literary man requires, in order to ripen the best harvest of his mind. I shall do better amongst other faces; and these familiar ones, it need hardly be said, will do just as well without me.

It may be, however, — O, transporting and triumphant thought! — that the great-grandchildren of the present race may sometimes think kindly of the scribbler of bygone days, when the antiquary of days to come, among the sites memorable in the town's history, shall point out the locality of THE TOWN-PUMP!

THE SCARLET LETTER

I. The Prison-Door

A throng of bearded men, in sad-colored garments and gray, steeple-crowned hats, intermixed with women, some wearing hoods, and others bareheaded, was assembled in front of a wooden edifice, the door of which was heavily timbered with oak, and studded with iron spikes.

The founders of a new colony, whatever Utopia of human virtue and happiness they might originally project, have invariably recognized it among their earliest practical necessities to allot a portion of the virgin soil as a cemetery, and another portion as the site of a prison. In accordance with this rule, it may safely be assumed that the forefathers of Boston had built the first prison-house, somewhere in the vicinity of Cornhill, almost as seasonably as they marked out the first burial-ground, on Isaac Johnson's lot, and round about his grave, which subsequently became the nucleus of all the congregated sepulchres in the old church-yard of King's Chapel. Certain it is, that, some fifteen or twenty years after the settlement of the town, the wooden jail was already marked with weather-stains and other indications of age, which gave a yet darker aspect to its beetle-browed and gloomy front. The rust on the ponderous iron-work of its oaken door looked more antique than any thing else in the new world. Like all that pertains to crime, it seemed never to have known a youthful era. Before this ugly edifice, and between it and the wheel-track of the street, was a grass-plot, much overgrown with burdock, pig-weed, apple-peru, and such unsightly vegetation, which evidently found something congenial in the soil that had so early borne the black flower of civilized society, a prison. But, on one side of the portal, and rooted almost at the threshold, was a wild rose-bush, covered, in this month of June, with its delicate gems, which might be imagined to offer their fragrance and fragile beauty to the prisoner as he went in, and to the condemned criminal as he came forth to his doom, in token that the deep heart of Nature could pity and be kind to him.

This rose-bush, by a strange chance, has been kept alive in history; but whether it had merely survived out of the stern old wilderness, so long after the fall of the gigantic pines and oaks that originally overshadowed it, — or whether, as there is fair authority for believing, it had sprung up under the footsteps of the sainted Ann Hutchinson, as she entered the prison-door, — we shall not take upon us to determine. Finding it so directly on the threshold of our narrative, which is now about to issue from that inauspicious portal, we could hardly do otherwise than pluck one of its flowers and present it to the reader. It may serve, let us hope, to symbolize some sweet moral blossom, that may be found along the track, or relieve the darkening close of a tale of human frailty and sorrow.

II. The Market-Place

The grass-plot before the jail, in Prison Lane, on a certain summer morning, not less than two centuries ago, was occupied by a pretty large number of the inhabitants of Boston; all with their eyes intently fastened on the iron-clamped oaken door. Amongst any other population, or at a later period in the history of New England, the grim rigidity that petrified the bearded physiognomies of these good people would have augured some awful business in hand. It could have betokened nothing short of the anticipated execution of some noted culprit, on whom the sentence of a legal tribunal had but confirmed the verdict of public sentiment. But, in that early severity of the Puritan character, an inference of this kind could not so indubitably be drawn. It might be that a sluggish bond-servant, or an undutiful child, whom his parents had given over to the civil authority, was to be corrected at the whipping-post. It might be, that an Antinomian, a Quaker, or other heterodox religionist, was to be scourged out of the town, or an idle and vagrant Indian, whom the white man's fire-water had made riotous about the streets, was to be driven with stripes into the shadow of the forest. It might be, too, that a witch, like old Mistress Hibbins, the bitter-tempered widow of the magistrate, was to die upon the gallows. In either case, there was very much the same solemnity of demeanour on the part of the spectators; as befitted a people amongst whom religion and law were almost identical, and in whose character both were so thoroughly interfused, that the mildest and the severest acts of public discipline were alike made venerable and awful. Meagre, indeed, and cold, was the sympathy that a transgressor might look for, from such bystanders at the scaffold. On the other hand, a penalty which, in our days, would infer a degree of mocking infamy and ridicule, might then be invested with almost as stern a dignity as the punishment of death itself.

It was a circumstance to be noted, on the summer morning when our story begins its course, that the women, of whom there were several in the crowd, appeared to take a peculiar interest in whatever penal infliction might be expected to ensue. The age had not so much refinement, that any sense of impropriety restrained the wearers of petticoat and farthingale from stepping forth into the public ways, and wedging their not unsubstantial persons, if occasion were, into the throng nearest to the scaffold at an execution. Morally, as well as materially, there was a coarser fibre in those wives and maidens of old English birth and breeding, than in their fair descendants, separated from them by a series of six or seven generations; for, throughout that chain of ancestry, every successive mother has transmitted to her child a fainter bloom, a more delicate and briefer beauty, and a slighter physical frame, if not a character of less force and solidity, than her own. The women, who were now standing about the prison-door, stood within less than half a century of the period when the man-like Elizabeth had been the not altogether unsuitable representative of the sex. They were her countrywomen; and the beef and ale of their native land, with a moral diet not a whit more refined, entered largely into their composition. The bright morning sun, therefore, shone on broad shoulders and well-developed busts, and on round and ruddy cheeks, that had ripened in the far-off island, and had hardly yet grown paler or thinner in the atmosphere of New England. There was, moreover, a boldness and rotundity of speech among these matrons, as most of them seemed to be, that would startle us at the present day, whether in respect to its purport or its volume of tone.

"Goodwives," said a hard-featured dame of fifty, "I'll tell ye a piece of my mind. It would be greatly for the public behoof, if we women, being of mature age and church-members in good repute, should have the handling of such malefactresses as this Hester Prynne. What think ye, gossips? If the hussy stood up for judgment before us five, that are now here in a knot together, would she come off with such a sentence as the worshipful magistrates have awarded? Marry, I trow not!"

"People say," said another, "that the Reverend Master Dimmesdale, her godly pastor, takes it very grievously to heart that such a scandal should have come upon his congregation."

"The magistrates are God-fearing gentlemen, but merciful overmuch, — that is a truth," added a third autumnal matron. "At the very least, they should have put the brand of a hot iron on Hester Prynne's forehead. Madam Hester would have winced at that, I warrant me. But she, — the naughty baggage, — little will she care what they put upon the bodice of her gown! Why, look you, she may cover it with a brooch, or such like heathenish adornment, and so walk the streets as brave as ever!"

"Ah, but," interposed, more softly, a young wife, holding a child by the hand, "let her cover the mark as she will, the pang of it will be always in her heart."

"What do we talk of marks and brands, whether on the bodice of her gown, or the flesh of her forehead?" cried another female, the ugliest as well as the most pitiless of these self-constituted judges. "This woman has brought shame upon us all, and ought to die. Is there not law for it? Truly there is, both in the Scripture and the statute-book. Then let the magistrates, who have made it of no effect, thank themselves if their own wives and daughters go astray!"

"Mercy on us, goodwife," exclaimed a man in the crowd, "is there no virtue in woman, save what springs from a wholesome fear of the gallows? That is the hardest word yet! Hush, now, gossips; for the lock is turning in the prison-door, and here comes Mistress Prynne herself."

The door of the jail being flung open from within, there appeared, in the first place, like a black shadow emerging into the sunshine, the grim and grisly presence of the town-beadle, with a sword by his side and his staff of office in his hand. This personage prefigured and represented in his aspect the whole dismal severity of the Puritanic code of law, which it was his business to administer in its final and closest application to the offender. Stretching forth the official staff in his left hand, he laid his right upon the shoulder of a young woman, whom he thus drew forward; until, on the threshold of the prison-door, she repelled him, by an action marked with natural dignity and force of character, and stepped into the open air, as if by her own free-will. She bore in her arms a child, a baby of some three months old, who winked and turned aside its little face from the too vivid light of day; because its existence, heretofore, had brought it acquainted only with the gray twilight of a dungeon, or other darksome apartment of the prison.

When the young woman — the mother of this child — stood fully revealed before the crowd, it seemed to be her first impulse to clasp the infant closely to her bosom; not so much by an impulse of motherly affection, as that she might thereby conceal a certain token, which was wrought or fastened into her dress. In a moment, however, wisely judging that one token of her shame would but poorly serve to hide another, she took the baby on her arm, and, with a burning blush, and yet a haughty smile, and a glance that would not be abashed, looked around at her townspeople and neighbours. On the breast of her gown, in fine red cloth, surrounded with an elaborate embroidery and fantastic flourishes of gold thread, appeared the letter A. It was so artistically done, and with so much fertility and gorgeous luxuriance of fancy, that it had all the effect of a last and fitting decoration to the apparel which she wore; and which was of a splendor in accordance with the taste of the age, but greatly beyond what was allowed by the sumptuary regulations of the colony.

The young woman was tall, with a figure of perfect elegance, on a large scale. She had dark and abundant hair, so glossy that it threw off the sunshine with a gleam, and a face which, besides being beautiful from regularity of feature and richness of complexion, had the impressiveness belonging to a marked brow and deep black eyes. She was lady-like, too, after the manner of the feminine gentility of those days; characterized by a certain state and dignity, rather than by the delicate, evanescent, and indescribable grace, which is now recognized as its indication. And never had Hester Prynne appeared more lady-like, in the antique interpretation of the term, than as she issued from the prison. Those who had before known her, and had expected to behold her dimmed and obscured by a disastrous cloud, were astonished, and even startled, to perceive how her beauty shone out, and made a halo of the misfortune and ignominy in which she was enveloped. It may be true, that, to a sensitive observer, there was something exquisitely painful in it. Her attire, which, indeed, she had wrought for the occasion, in prison, and had modelled much after her own fancy, seemed to express the attitude of her spirit, the desperate recklessness of her mood, by its wild and picturesque peculiarity. But the point which drew all eyes, and, as it were, transfigured the wearer, — so that both men and women, who had been familiarly acquainted with Hester Prynne, were now impressed as if they beheld her for the first time, — was that SCARLET LETTER, so fantastically embroidered and illuminated upon her bosom. It had the effect of a spell, taking her out of the ordinary relations with humanity, and inclosing her in a sphere by herself.

"She hath good skill at her needle, that's certain," remarked one of the female spectators; "but did ever a woman, before this brazen hussy, contrive such a way of showing it! Why, gossips, what is it but to laugh in the faces of our godly magistrates, and make a pride out of what they, worthy gentlemen, meant for a punishment?"

"It were well," muttered the most iron-visaged of the old dames, "if we stripped Madam Hester's rich gown off her dainty shoulders; and as for the red letter, which she hath stitched so curiously, I'll bestow a rag of mine own rheumatic flannel, to make a fitter one!"

"O, peace, neighbours, peace!" whispered their youngest companion. "Do not let her hear you! Not a stitch in that embroidered letter, but she has felt it in her heart."

The grim beadle now made a gesture with his staff.

"Make way, good people, make way, in the King's name," cried he. "Open a passage; and, I promise ye, Mistress Prynne shall be set where man, woman, and child may have a fair sight of her brave apparel, from this time till an hour past meridian. A blessing on the righteous Colony of the Massachusetts, where iniquity is dragged out into the sunshine! Come along, Madam Hester, and show your scarlet letter in the market-place!"

A lane was forthwith opened through the crowd of spectators. Preceded by the beadle, and attended by an irregular procession of stern-browed men and unkindly-visaged women, Hester Prynne set forth towards the place appointed for her punishment. A crowd of eager and curious schoolboys, understanding little of the matter in hand, except that it gave them a half-holiday, ran before her progress, turning their heads continually to stare into her face, and at the winking baby in her arms, and at the ignominious letter on her breast. It was no great distance, in those days, from the prison-door to the market-place. Measured by the prisoner's experience, however, it might be reckoned a journey of some length; for, haughty as her demeanour was, she perchance underwent an agony from every footstep of those that thronged to see her, as if her heart had been flung into the street for them all to spurn and trample upon. In our nature, however, there is a provision, alike marvellous and merciful, that the sufferer should never know the intensity of what he endures by its present torture, but chiefly by the pang that rankles after it. With almost a serene deportment, therefore, Hester Prynne passed through this portion of her ordeal, and came to a sort of scaffold, at the western extremity of the market-place. It stood nearly beneath the eaves of Boston's earliest church, and appeared to be a fixture there.

In fact, this scaffold constituted a portion of a penal machine, which now, for two or three generations past, has been merely historical and traditionary among us, but was held, in the old time, to be as effectual an agent in the promotion of good citizenship, as ever was the guillotine among the terrorists of France. It was, in short, the platform of the pillory; and above it rose the framework of that instrument of discipline, so fashioned as to confine the human head in its tight grasp, and thus hold it up to the public gaze. The very ideal of ignominy was embodied and made manifest in this contrivance of wood and iron. There can be no outrage, methinks, against our common nature, — whatever be the delinquencies of the individual, — no outrage more flagrant than to forbid the culprit to hide his face for shame; as it was the essence of this punishment to do. In Hester Prynne's instance, however, as not unfrequently in other cases, her sentence bore, that she should stand a certain time upon the platform, but without undergoing that gripe about the neck and confinement of the head, the proneness to which was the most devilish characteristic of this ugly engine. Knowing well her part, she ascended a flight of wooden steps, and was thus displayed to the surrounding multitude, at about the height of a man's shoulders above the street.

Had there been a Papist among the crowd of Puritans, he might have seen in this beautiful woman, so picturesque in her attire and mien, and with the infant at her bosom, an object to remind him of the image of Divine Maternity, which so many illustrious painters have vied with one another to represent; something which should remind him, indeed, but only by contrast, of that sacred image of sinless motherhood, whose infant was to redeem the world. Here, there was the taint of deepest sin in the most sacred quality of human life, working such effect, that the world was only the darker for this woman's beauty, and the more lost for the infant that she had borne.

The scene was not without a mixture of awe, such as must always invest the spectacle of guilt and shame in a fellow-creature, before society shall have grown corrupt enough to smile, instead of shuddering, at it. The witnesses of Hester Prynne's disgrace had not yet passed beyond their simplicity. They were stern enough to look upon her death, had that been the sentence, without a murmur at its severity, but had none of the heartlessness of another social state, which would find only a theme for jest in an exhibition like the present. Even had there been a disposition to turn the matter into ridicule, it must have been repressed and overpowered by the solemn presence of men no less dignified than the Governor, and several of his counsellors, a judge, a general, and the ministers of the town; all of whom sat or stood in a balcony of the meeting-house, looking down upon the platform. When such personages could constitute a part of the spectacle, without risking the majesty or reverence of rank and office, it was safely to be inferred that the infliction of a legal sentence would have an earnest and effectual meaning. Accordingly, the crowd was sombre and grave. The unhappy culprit sustained herself as best a woman might, under the heavy weight of a thousand unrelenting eyes, all fastened upon her, and concentred at her bosom. It was almost intolerable to be borne. Of an impulsive and passionate nature, she had fortified herself to encounter the stings and venomous stabs of public contumely, wreaking itself in every variety of insult; but there was a quality so much more terrible in the solemn mood of the popular mind, that she longed rather to behold all those rigid countenances contorted with scornful merriment, and herself the object. Had a roar of laughter burst from the multitude, — each man, each woman, each little shrill-voiced child, contributing their individual parts, — Hester Prynne might have repaid them all with a bitter and disdainful smile. But, under the leaden infliction which it was her doom to endure, she felt, at moments, as if she must needs shriek out with the full power of her lungs, and cast herself from the scaffold down upon the ground, or else go mad at once.

Yet there were intervals when the whole scene, in which she was the most conspicuous object, seemed to vanish from her eyes, or, at least, glimmered indistinctly before them, like a mass of imperfectly shaped and spectral images. Her mind, and especially her memory, was preternaturally active, and kept bringing up other scenes than this roughly hewn street of a little town, on the edge of the Western wilderness; other faces than were lowering upon her from beneath the brims of those steeple-crowned hats. Reminiscences, the most trifling and immaterial, passages of infancy and school-days, sports, childish quarrels, and the little domestic traits of her maiden years, came swarming back upon her, intermingled with recollections of whatever was gravest in her subsequent life; one picture precisely as vivid as another; as if all were of similar importance, or all alike a play. Possibly, it was an instinctive device of her spirit, to relieve itself, by the exhibition of these phantasmagoric forms, from the cruel weight and hardness of the reality.

Be that as it might, the scaffold of the pillory was a point of view that revealed to Hester Prynne the entire track along which she had been treading, since her happy infancy. Standing on that miserable eminence, she saw again her native village, in Old England, and her paternal home; a decayed house of gray stone, with a poverty-stricken aspect, but retaining a half-obliterated shield of arms over the portal, in token of antique gentility. She saw her father's face, with its bald brow, and reverend white beard, that flowed over the old-fashioned Elizabethan ruff; her mother's, too, with the look of heedful and anxious love which it always wore in her remembrance, and which, even since her death, had so often laid the impediment of a gentle remonstrance in her daughter's pathway. She saw her own face, glowing with girlish beauty, and illuminating all the interior of the dusky mirror in which she had been wont to gaze at it. There she beheld another countenance, of a man well stricken in years, a pale, thin, scholar-like visage, with eyes dim and bleared by the lamp-light that had served them to pore over many ponderous books. Yet those same bleared optics had a strange, penetrating power, when it was their owner's purpose to read the human soul. This figure of the study and the cloister, as Hester Prynne's womanly fancy failed not to recall, was slightly deformed, with the left shoulder a trifle higher than the right. Next rose before her, in memory's picture-gallery, the intricate and narrow thoroughfares, the tall, gray houses, the huge cathedrals, and the public edifices, ancient in date and quaint in architecture, of a Continental city; where a new life had awaited her, still in connection with the misshapen scholar; a new life, but feeding itself on time-worn materials, like a tuft of green moss on a crumbling wall. Lastly, in lieu of these shifting scenes, came back the rude market-place of the Puritan settlement, with all the townspeople assembled and levelling their stern regards at Hester Prynne, — yes, at herself, — who stood on the scaffold of the pillory, an infant on her arm, and the letter A, in scarlet, fantastically embroidered with gold thread, upon her bosom!

Could it be true? She clutched the child so fiercely to her breast, that it sent forth a cry; she turned her eyes downward at the scarlet letter, and even touched it with her finger, to assure herself that the infant and the shame were real. Yes! — these were her realities, — all else had vanished!

III. The Recognition

From this intense consciousness of being the object of severe and universal observation, the wearer of the scarlet letter was at length relieved by discerning, on the outskirts of the crowd, a figure which irresistibly took possession of her thoughts. An Indian, in his native garb, was standing there; but the red men were not so infrequent visitors of the English settlements, that one of them would have attracted any notice from Hester Prynne, at such a time; much less would he have excluded all other objects and ideas from her mind. By the Indian's side, and evidently sustaining a companionship with him, stood a white man, clad in a strange disarray of civilized and savage costume.

He was small in stature, with a furrowed visage, which, as yet, could hardly be termed aged. There was a remarkable intelligence in his features, as of a person who had so cultivated his mental part that it could not fail to mould the physical to itself, and become manifest by unmistakable tokens. Although, by a seemingly careless arrangement of his heterogeneous garb, he had endeavoured to conceal or abate the peculiarity, it was sufficiently evident to Hester Prynne, that one of this man's shoulders rose higher than the other. Again, at the first instant of perceiving that thin visage, and the slight deformity of the figure, she pressed her infant to her bosom, with so convulsive a force that the poor babe uttered another cry of pain. But the mother did not seem to hear it.

At his arrival in the market-place, and some time before she saw him, the stranger had bent his eyes on Hester Prynne. It was carelessly, at first, like a man chiefly accustomed to look inward, and to whom external matters are of little value and import, unless they bear relation to something within his mind. Very soon, however, his look became keen and penetrative. A writhing horror twisted itself across his features, like a snake gliding swiftly over them, and making one little pause, with all its wreathed intervolutions in open sight. His face darkened with some powerful emotion, which, nevertheless, he so instantaneously controlled by an effort of his will, that, save at a single moment, its expression might have passed for calmness. After a brief space, the convulsion grew almost imperceptible, and finally subsided into the depths of his nature. When he found the eyes of Hester Prynne fastened on his own, and saw that she appeared to recognize him, he slowly and calmly raised his finger, made a gesture with it in the air, and laid it on his lips.

Then, touching the shoulder of a townsman who stood next to him, he addressed him in a formal and courteous manner.

"I pray you, good Sir," said he, "who is this woman? — and wherefore is she here set up to public shame?"

"You must needs be a stranger in this region, friend," answered the townsman, looking curiously at the questioner and his savage companion; "else you would surely have heard of Mistress Hester Prynne, and her evil doings. She hath raised a great scandal, I promise you, in godly Master Dimmesdale's church."

"You say truly," replied the other. "I am a stranger, and have been a wanderer, sorely against my will. I have met with grievous mishaps by sea and land, and have been long held in bonds among the heathen-folk, to the southward; and am now brought hither by this Indian, to be redeemed out of my captivity. Will it please you, therefore, to tell me of Hester Prynne's, — have I her name rightly? — of this woman's offences, and what has brought her to yonder scaffold?"

"Truly, friend, and methinks it must gladden your heart, after your troubles and sojourn in the wilderness," said the townsman, "to find yourself, at length, in a land where iniquity is searched out, and punished in the sight of rulers and people; as here in our godly New England. Yonder woman, Sir, you must know, was the wife of a certain learned man, English by birth, but who had long dwelt in Amsterdam, whence, some good time agone, he was minded to cross over and cast in his lot with us of the Massachusetts. To this purpose, he sent his wife before him, remaining himself to look after some necessary affairs. Marry, good Sir, in some two years, or less, that the woman has been a dweller here in Boston, no tidings have come of this learned gentleman, Master Prynne; and his young wife, look you, being left to her own misguidance ——— "

"Ah! — aha! — I conceive you," said the stranger, with a bitter smile. "So learned a man as you speak of should have learned this too in his books. And who, by your favor, Sir, may be the father of yonder babe — it is some three or four months old, I should judge — which Mistress Prynne is holding in her arms?"

"Of a truth, friend, that matter remaineth a riddle; and the Daniel who shall expound it is yet a-wanting," answered the townsman. "Madam Hester absolutely refuseth to speak, and the magistrates have laid their heads together in vain. Peradventure the guilty one stands looking on at this sad spectacle, unknown of man, and forgetting that God sees him."

"The learned man," observed the stranger, with another smile, "should come himself to look into the mystery."

"It behooves him well, if he be still in life," responded the townsman. "Now, good Sir, our Massachusetts magistracy, bethinking themselves that this woman is youthful and fair, and doubtless was strongly tempted to her fall; — and that, moreover, as is most likely, her husband may be at the bottom of the sea; — they have not been bold to put in force the extremity of our righteous law against her. The penalty thereof is death. But, in their great mercy and tenderness of heart, they have doomed Mistress Prynne to stand only a space of three hours on the platform of the pillory, and then and thereafter, for the remainder of her natural life, to wear a mark of shame upon her bosom."

"A wise sentence!" remarked the stranger, gravely bowing his head. "Thus she will be a living sermon against sin, until the ignominious letter be engraved upon her tombstone. It irks me, nevertheless, that the partner of her iniquity should not, at least, stand on the scaffold by her side. But he will be known! — he will be known! — he will be known!"

He bowed courteously to the communicative townsman, and, whispering a few words to his Indian attendant, they both made their way through the crowd.

While this passed, Hester Prynne had been standing on her pedestal, still with a fixed gaze towards the stranger; so fixed a gaze, that, at moments of intense absorption, all other objects in the visible world seemed to vanish, leaving only him and her. Such an interview, perhaps, would have been more terrible than even to meet him as she now did, with the hot, midday sun burning down upon her face, and lighting up its shame; with the scarlet token of infamy on her breast; with the sin-born infant in her arms; with a whole people, drawn forth as to a festival, staring at the features that should have been seen only in the quiet gleam of the fireside, in the happy shadow of a home, or beneath a matronly veil, at church. Dreadful as it was, she was conscious of a shelter in the presence of these thousand witnesses. It was better to stand thus, with so many betwixt him and her, than to greet him, face to face, they two alone. She fled for refuge, as it were, to the public exposure, and dreaded the moment when its protection should be withdrawn from her. Involved in these thoughts, she scarcely heard a voice behind her, until it had repeated her name more than once, in a loud and solemn tone, audible to the whole multitude.

"Hearken unto me, Hester Prynne!" said the voice.

It has already been noticed, that directly over the platform on which Hester Prynne stood was a kind of balcony, or open gallery, appended to the meeting-house. It was the place whence proclamations were wont to be made, amidst an assemblage of the magistracy, with all the ceremonial that attended such public observances in those days. Here, to witness the scene which we are describing, sat Governor Bellingham himself, with four sergeants about his chair, bearing halberds, as a guard of honor. He wore a dark feather in his hat, a border of embroidery on his cloak, and a black velvet tunic beneath; a gentleman advanced in years, and with a hard experience written in his wrinkles. He was not ill fitted to be the head and representative of a community, which owed its origin and progress, and its present state of development, not to the impulses of youth, but to the stern and tempered energies of manhood, and the sombre sagacity of age; accomplishing so much, precisely because it imagined and hoped so little. The other eminent characters, by whom the chief ruler was surrounded, were distinguished by a dignity of mien, belonging to a period when the forms of authority were felt to possess the sacredness of divine institutions. They were, doubtless, good men, just, and sage. But, out of the whole human family, it would not have been easy to select the same number of wise and virtuous persons, who should be less capable of sitting in judgment on an erring woman's heart, and disentangling its mesh of good and evil, than the sages of rigid aspect towards whom Hester Prynne now turned her face. She seemed conscious, indeed, that whatever sympathy she might expect lay in the larger and warmer heart of the multitude; for, as she lifted her eyes towards the balcony, the unhappy woman grew pale and trembled.

The voice which had called her attention was that of the reverend and famous John Wilson, the eldest clergyman of Boston, a great scholar, like most of his contemporaries in the profession, and withal a man of kind and genial spirit. This last attribute, however, had been less carefully developed than his intellectual gifts, and was, in truth, rather a matter of shame than self-congratulation with him. There he stood, with a border of grizzled locks beneath his skull-cap; while his gray eyes, accustomed to the shaded light of his study, were winking, like those of Hester's infant, in the unadulterated sunshine. He looked like the darkly engraved portraits which we see prefixed to old volumes of sermons; and had no more right than one of those portraits would have, to step forth, as he now did, and meddle with a question of human guilt, passion, and anguish.

"Hester Prynne," said the clergyman, "I have striven with my young brother here, under whose preaching of the word you have been privileged to sit," — here Mr. Wilson laid his hand on the shoulder of a pale young man beside him, — "I have sought, I say, to persuade this godly youth, that he should deal with you, here in the face of Heaven, and before these wise and upright rulers, and in hearing of all the people, as touching the vileness and blackness of your sin. Knowing your natural temper better than I, he could the better judge what arguments to use, whether of tenderness or terror, such as might prevail over your hardness and obstinacy; insomuch that you should no longer hide the name of him who tempted you to this grievous fall. But he opposes to me, (with a young man's oversoftness, albeit wise beyond his years,) that it were wronging the very nature of woman to force her to lay open her heart's secrets in such broad daylight, and in presence of so great a multitude. Truly, as I sought to convince him, the shame lay in the commission of the sin, and not in the showing of it forth. What say you to it, once again, brother Dimmesdale? Must it be thou or I that shall deal with this poor sinner's soul?"

There was a murmur among the dignified and reverend occupants of the balcony; and Governor Bellingham gave expression to its purport, speaking in an authoritative voice, although tempered with respect towards the youthful clergyman whom he addressed.

"Good Master Dimmesdale," said he, "the responsibility of this woman's soul lies greatly with you. It behooves you, therefore, to exhort her to repentance, and to confession, as a proof and consequence thereof."

The directness of this appeal drew the eyes of the whole crowd upon the Reverend Mr. Dimmesdale; a young clergyman, who had come from one of the great English universities, bringing all the learning of the age into our wild forestland. His eloquence and religious fervor had already given the earnest of high eminence in his profession. He was a person of very striking aspect, with a white, lofty, and impending brow, large, brown, melancholy eyes, and a mouth which, unless when he forcibly compressed it, was apt to be tremulous, expressing both nervous sensibility and a vast power of self-restraint. Notwithstanding his high native gifts and scholar-like attainments, there was an air about this young minister, — an apprehensive, a startled, a half-frightened look, — as of a being who felt himself quite astray and at a loss in the pathway of human existence, and could only be at ease in some seclusion of his own. Therefore, so far as his duties would permit, he trode in the shadowy by-paths, and thus kept himself simple and childlike; coming forth, when occasion was, with a freshness, and fragrance, and dewy purity of thought, which, as many people said, affected them like the speech of an angel.

Such was the young man whom the Reverend Mr. Wilson and the

Governor had introduced so openly to the public notice, bidding him speak, in the hearing of all men, to that mystery of a woman's soul, so sacred even in its pollution. The trying nature of his position drove the blood from his cheek, and made his lips tremulous.

"Speak to the woman, my brother," said Mr. Wilson. "It is of moment to her soul, and therefore, as the worshipful Governor says, momentous to thine own, in whose charge hers is. Exhort her to confess the truth!"

The Reverend Mr. Dimmesdale bent his head, in silent prayer, as it seemed, and then came forward.

"Hester Prynne," said he, leaning over the balcony, and looking down stedfastly into her eyes, "thou hearest what this good man says, and seest the accountability under which I labor. If thou feelest it to be for thy soul's peace, and that thy earthly punishment will thereby be made more effectual to salvation, I charge thee to speak out the name of thy fellow-sinner and fellow-sufferer! Be not silent from any mistaken pity and tenderness for him; for, believe me, Hester, though he were to step down from a high place, and stand there beside thee, on thy pedestal of shame, yet better were it so, than to hide a guilty heart through life. What can thy silence do for him, except it tempt him — yea, compel him, as it were — to add hypocrisy to sin? Heaven hath granted thee an open ignominy, that thereby thou mayest work out an open triumph over the evil within thee, and the sorrow without. Take heed how thou deniest to him — who, perchance, hath not the courage to grasp it for himself — the bitter, but wholesome, cup that is now presented to thy lips!"

The young pastor's voice was tremulously sweet, rich, deep, and broken. The feeling that it so evidently manifested, rather than the direct purport of the words, caused it to vibrate within all hearts, and brought the listeners into one accord of sympathy. Even the poor baby, at Hester's bosom, was affected by the same influence; for it directed its hitherto vacant gaze towards Mr. Dimmesdale, and held up its little arms, with a half pleased, half plaintive murmur. So powerful seemed the minister's appeal, that the people could not believe but that Hester Prynne would speak out the guilty name; or else that the guilty one himself, in whatever high or lowly place he stood, would be drawn forth by an inward and inevitable necessity, and compelled to ascend the scaffold.

Hester shook her head.

"Woman, transgress not beyond the limits of Heaven's mercy!"

cried the Reverend Mr. Wilson, more harshly than before. "That little babe hath been gifted with a voice, to second and confirm the counsel which thou hast heard. Speak out the name! That, and thy repentance, may avail to take the scarlet letter off thy breast."

"Never!" replied Hester Prynne, looking, not at Mr. Wilson, but into the deep and troubled eyes of the younger clergyman. "It is too deeply branded. Ye cannot take it off. And would that I might endure his agony, as well as mine!"

"Speak, woman!" said another voice, coldly and sternly, proceeding from the crowd about the scaffold. "Speak; and give your child a father!"

"I will not speak!" answered Hester, turning pale as death, but responding to this voice, which she too surely recognized. "And my child must seek a heavenly Father; she shall never know an earthly one!"

"She will not speak!" murmured Mr. Dimmesdale, who, leaning over the balcony, with his hand upon his heart, had awaited the result of his appeal. He now drew back, with a long respiration. "Wondrous strength and generosity of a woman's heart! She will not speak!"

Discerning the impracticable state of the poor culprit's mind, the elder clergyman, who had carefully prepared himself for the occasion, addressed to the multitude a discourse on sin, in all its branches, but with continual reference to the ignominious letter. So forcibly did he dwell upon this symbol, for the hour or more during which his periods were rolling over the people's heads, that it assumed new terrors in their imagination, and seemed to derive its scarlet hue from the flames of the infernal pit. Hester Prynne, meanwhile, kept her place upon the pedestal of shame, with glazed eyes, and an air of weary indifference. She had borne, that morning, all that nature could endure; and as her temperament was not of the order that escapes from too intense suffering by a swoon, her spirit could only shelter itself beneath a stony crust of insensibility, while the faculties of animal life remained entire. In this state, the voice of the preacher thundered remorselessly, but unavailingly, upon her ears. The infant, during the latter portion of her ordeal, pierced the air with its wailings and screams; she strove to hush it, mechanically, but seemed scarcely to sympathize with its trouble. With the same hard demeanour, she was led back to prison, and vanished from the public gaze within its iron-clamped portal. It was whispered, by those who peered after her, that the scarlet letter threw a lurid gleam along the dark passage-way of the interior.

IV. The Interview

After her return to the prison, Hester Prynne was found to be in a state of nervous excitement that demanded constant watchfulness, lest she should perpetrate violence on herself, or do some half-frenzied mischief to the poor babe. As night approached, it proving impossible to quell her insubordination by rebuke or threats of punishment, Master Brackett, the jailer, thought fit to introduce a physician. He described him as a man of skill in all Christian modes of physical science, and likewise familiar with whatever the savage people could teach, in respect to medicinal herbs and roots that grew in the forest. To say the truth, there was much need of professional assistance, not merely for Hester herself, but still more urgently for the child; who, drawing its sustenance from the maternal bosom, seemed to have drank in with it all the turmoil, the anguish, and despair, which pervaded the mother's system. It now writhed in convulsions of pain, and was a forcible type, in its little frame, of the moral agony which Hester Prynne had borne throughout the day.

Closely following the jailer into the dismal apartment, appeared that individual, of singular aspect, whose presence in the crowd had been of such deep interest to the wearer of the scarlet letter. He was lodged in the prison, not as suspected of any offence, but as the most convenient and suitable mode of disposing of him, until the magistrates should have conferred with the Indian sagamores respecting his ransom. His name was announced as Roger Chillingworth. The jailer, after ushering him into the room, remained a moment, marvelling at the comparative quiet that followed his entrance; for Hester Prynne had immediately become as still as death, although the child continued to moan.

"Prithee, friend, leave me alone with my patient," said the practitioner. "Trust me, good jailer, you shall briefly have peace in your house; and, I promise you, Mistress Prynne shall hereafter be more amenable to just authority than you may have found her heretofore."

"Nay, if your worship can accomplish that," answered Master Brackett, "I shall own you for a man of skill indeed! Verily, the woman hath been like a possessed one; and there lacks little, that I should take in hand to drive Satan out of her with stripes."

The stranger had entered the room with the characteristic quietude of the profession to which he announced himself as belonging. Nor did his demeanour change, when the withdrawal of the prison-keeper left him face to face with the woman, whose absorbed notice of him, in the crowd, had intimated so close a relation between himself and her. His first care was given to the child; whose cries, indeed, as she lay writhing on the trundle-bed, made it of peremptory necessity to postpone all other business to the task of soothing her. He examined the infant carefully, and then proceeded to unclasp a leathern case, which he took from beneath his dress. It appeared to contain certain medical preparations, one of which he mingled with a cup of water.

"My old studies in alchemy," observed he, "and my sojourn, for above a year past, among a people well versed in the kindly properties of simples, have made a better physician of me than many that claim the medical degree. Here, woman! The child is yours, — she is none of mine, — neither will she recognize my voice or aspect as a father's. Administer this draught, therefore, with thine own hand."

Hester repelled the offered medicine, at the same time gazing with strongly marked apprehension into his face.

"Wouldst thou avenge thyself on the innocent babe?" whispered she.

"Foolish woman!" responded the physician, half coldly, half soothingly. "What should ail me to harm this misbegotten and miserable babe? The medicine is potent for good; and were it my child, — yea, mine own, as well as thine! — I could do no better for it."

As she still hesitated, being, in fact, in no reasonable state of mind, he took the infant in his arms, and himself administered the draught. It soon proved its efficacy, and redeemed the leech's pledge. The moans of the little patient subsided; its convulsive tossings gradually ceased; and in a few moments, as is the custom of young children after relief from pain, it sank into a profound and dewy slumber. The physician, as he had a fair right to be termed, next bestowed his attention on the mother. With calm and intent scrutiny, he felt her pulse, looked into her eyes, — a gaze that made her heart shrink and shudder, because so familiar, and yet so strange and cold, — and, finally, satisfied with his investigation, proceeded to mingle another draught.

"I know not Lethe or Nepenthe," remarked he; "but I have learned many new secrets in the wilderness, and here is one of them, — a recipe that an Indian taught me, in requital of some lessons of my own, that were as old as Paracelsus. Drink it! It may be less soothing than a sinless conscience. That I cannot give thee. But it will calm the swell and heaving of thy passion, like oil thrown on the waves of a tempestuous sea."

He presented the cup to Hester, who received it with a slow, earnest look into his face; not precisely a look of fear, yet full of doubt and questioning, as to what his purposes might be. She looked also at her slumbering child.

"I have thought of death," said she, — "have wished for it, — would even have prayed for it, were it fit that such as I should pray for any thing. Yet, if death be in this cup, I bid thee think again, ere thou beholdest me quaff it. See! It is even now at my lips."

"Drink, then," replied he, still with the same cold composure. "Dost thou know me so little, Hester Prynne? Are my purposes wont to be so shallow? Even if I imagine a scheme of vengeance, what could I do better for my object than to let thee live, — than to give thee medicines against all harm and peril of life, — so that this burning shame may still blaze upon thy bosom?" — As he spoke, he laid his long forefinger on the scarlet letter, which forthwith seemed to scorch into Hester's breast, as if it had been red-hot. He noticed her involuntary gesture, and smiled. — "Live, therefore, and bear about thy doom with thee, in the eyes of men and women, — in the eyes of him whom thou didst call thy husband, — in the eyes of yonder child! And, that thou mayest live, take off this draught."

Without further expostulation or delay, Hester Prynne drained the cup, and, at the motion of the man of skill, seated herself on the bed where the child was sleeping; while he drew the only chair which the room afforded, and took his own seat beside her. She could not but tremble at these preparations; for she felt that — having now done all that humanity, or principle, or, if so it were, a refined cruelty, impelled him to do, for the relief of physical suffering — he was next to treat with her as the man whom she had most deeply and irreparably injured.

"Hester," said he, "I ask not wherefore, nor how, thou hast fallen into the pit, or say rather, thou hast ascended to the pedestal of infamy, on which I found thee. The reason is not far to seek. It was my folly, and thy weakness. I, — a man of thought, — the book-worm of great libraries, — a man already in decay, having given my best years to feed the hungry dream of knowledge, — what had I to do with youth and beauty like thine own! Misshapen from my birth-hour, how could I delude myself with the idea that intellectual gifts might veil physical deformity in a young girl's fantasy! Men call me wise. If sages were ever wise in their own behoof, I might have foreseen all this. I might have known that, as I came out of the vast and dismal forest, and entered this settlement of Christian men, the very first object to meet my eyes would be thyself, Hester Prynne, standing up, a statue of ignominy, before the people. Nay, from the moment when we came down the old church-steps together, a married pair, I might have beheld the bale-fire of that scarlet letter blazing at the end of our path!"

"Thou knowest," said Hester, — for, depressed as she was, she could not endure this last quiet stab at the token of her shame, — "thou knowest that I was frank with thee. I felt no love, nor feigned any."

"True!" replied he. "It was my folly! I have said it. But, up to that epoch of my life, I had lived in vain. The world had been so cheerless! My heart was a habitation large enough for many guests, but lonely and chill, and without a household fire. I longed to kindle one! It seemed not so wild a dream, — old as I was, and sombre as I was, and misshapen as I was, — that the simple bliss, which is scattered far and wide, for all mankind to gather up, might yet be mine. And so, Hester, I drew thee into my heart, into its innermost chamber, and sought to warm thee by the warmth which thy presence made there!"

"I have greatly wronged thee," murmured Hester.

"We have wronged each other," answered he. "Mine was the first wrong, when I betrayed thy budding youth into a false and unnatural relation with my decay. Therefore, as a man who has not thought and philosophized in vain, I seek no vengeance, plot no evil against thee. Between thee and me, the scale hangs fairly balanced. But, Hester, the man lives who has wronged us both! Who is he?"

"Ask me not!" replied Hester Prynne, looking firmly into his face. "That thou shalt never know!"

"Never, sayest thou?" rejoined he, with a smile of dark and self-relying intelligence. "Never know him! Believe me, Hester, there are few things, — whether in the outward world, or, to a certain depth, in the invisible sphere of thought, — few things hidden from the man, who devotes himself earnestly and unreservedly to the solution of a mystery. Thou mayest cover up thy secret from the prying multitude. Thou mayest conceal it, too, from the ministers and magistrates, even as thou didst this day, when they sought to wrench the name out of thy heart, and give thee a partner on thy pedestal. But, as for me, I come to the inquest with other senses than they possess. I shall seek this man, as I have sought truth in books; as I have sought gold in alchemy. There is a sympathy that will make me conscious of him. I shall see him tremble. I shall feel myself shudder, suddenly and unawares. Sooner or later, he must needs be mine!"

The eyes of the wrinkled scholar glowed so intensely upon her, that

Hester Prynne clasped her hands over her heart, dreading lest he should read the secret there at once.

"Thou wilt not reveal his name? Not the less he is mine," resumed he, with a look of confidence, as if destiny were at one with him. "He bears no letter of infamy wrought into his garment, as thou dost; but I shall read it on his heart. Yet fear not for him! Think not that I shall interfere with Heaven's own method of retribution, or, to my own loss, betray him to the gripe of human law. Neither do thou imagine that I shall contrive aught against his life; no, nor against his fame, if, as I judge, he be a man of fair repute. Let him live! Let him hide himself in outward honor, if he may! Not the less he shall be mine!"

"Thy acts are like mercy," said Hester, bewildered and appalled. "But thy words interpret thee as a terror!"

"One thing, thou that wast my wife, I would enjoin upon thee," continued the scholar. "Thou hast kept the secret of thy paramour. Keep, likewise, mine! There are none in this land that know me. Breathe not, to any human soul, that thou didst ever call me husband! Here, on this wild outskirt of the earth, I shall pitch my tent; for, elsewhere a wanderer, and isolated from human interests, I find here a woman, a man, a child, amongst whom and myself there exist the closest ligaments. No matter whether of love or hate; no matter whether of right or wrong! Thou and thine, Hester Prynne, belong to me. My home is where thou art, and where he is. But betray me not!"

"Wherefore dost thou desire it?" inquired Hester, shrinking, she hardly knew why, from this secret bond. "Why not announce thyself openly, and cast me off at once?"

"It may be," he replied, "because I will not encounter the dishonor that besmirches the husband of a faithless woman. It may be for other reasons. Enough, it is my purpose to live and die unknown. Let, therefore, thy husband be to the world as one already dead, and of whom no tidings shall ever come. Recognize me not, by word, by sign, by look! Breathe not the secret, above all, to the man thou wottest of. Shouldst thou fail me in this, beware! His fame, his position, his life, will be in my hands. Beware!"

"I will keep thy secret, as I have his," said Hester.

"Swear it!" rejoined he.

And she took the oath.

"And now, Mistress Prynne," said old Roger Chillingworth, as he was hereafter to be named, "I leave thee alone; alone with thy infant, and the scarlet letter! How is it, Hester? Doth thy sentence bind thee to wear the token in thy sleep? Art thou not afraid of nightmares and hideous dreams?"

"Why dost thou smile so at me?" inquired Hester, troubled at the expression of his eyes. "Art thou like the Black Man that haunts the forest round about us? Hast thou enticed me into a bond that will prove the ruin of my soul?"

"Not thy soul," he answered, with another smile. "No, not thine!"

V. Hester at Her Needle

Hester Prynne's term of confinement was now at an end. Her prison-door was thrown open, and she came forth into the sunshine, which, falling on all alike, seemed, to her sick and morbid heart, as if meant for no other purpose than to reveal the scarlet letter on her breast. Perhaps there was a more real torture in her first unattended footsteps from the threshold of the prison, than even in the procession and spectacle that have been described, where she was made the common infamy, at which all mankind was summoned to point its finger. Then, she was supported by an unnatural tension of the nerves, and by all the combative energy of her character, which enabled her to convert the scene into a kind of lurid triumph. It was, moreover, a separate and insulated event, to occur but once in her lifetime, and to meet which, therefore, reckless of economy, she might call up the vital strength that would have sufficed for many quiet years. The very law that condemned her — a giant of stern features, but with vigor to support, as well as to annihilate, in his iron arm — had held her up, through the terrible ordeal of her ignominy. But now, with this unattended walk from her prison-door, began the daily custom, and she must either sustain and carry it forward by the ordinary resources of her nature, or sink beneath it. She could no longer borrow from the future, to help her through the present grief. To-morrow would bring its own trial with it; so would the next day, and so would the next; each its own trial, and yet the very same that was now so unutterably grievous to be borne. The days of the far-off future would toil onward, still with the same burden for her to take up, and bear along with her, but never to fling down; for the accumulating days, and added years, would pile up their misery upon the heap of shame. Throughout them all, giving up her individuality, she would become the general symbol at which the preacher and moralist might point, and in which they might vivify and embody their images of woman's frailty and sinful passion. Thus the young and pure would be taught to look at her, with the scarlet letter flaming on her breast, — at her, the child of honorable parents, — at her, the mother of a babe, that would hereafter be a woman, — at her, who had once been innocent, — as the figure, the body, the reality of sin. And over her grave, the infamy that she must carry thither would be her only monument.

It may seem marvellous, that, with the world before her, — kept by no restrictive clause of her condemnation within the limits of the Puritan settlement, so remote and so obscure, — free to return to her birthplace, or to any other European land, and there hide her character and identity under a new exterior, as completely as if emerging into another state of being, — and having also the passes of the dark, inscrutable forest open to her, where the wildness of her nature might assimilate itself with a people whose customs and life were alien from the law that had condemned her, — it may seem marvellous, that this woman should still call that place her home, where, and where only, she must needs be the type of shame. But there is a fatality, a feeling so irresistible and inevitable that it has the force of doom, which almost invariably compels human beings to linger around and haunt, ghost-like, the spot where some great and marked event has given the color to their lifetime; and still the more irresistibly, the darker the tinge that saddens it. Her sin, her ignominy, were the roots which she had struck into the soil. It was as if a new birth, with stronger assimilations than the first, had converted the forest-land, still so uncongenial to every other pilgrim and wanderer, into Hester Prynne's wild and dreary, but life-long home. All other scenes of earth — even that village of rural England, where happy infancy and stainless maidenhood seemed yet to be in her mother's keeping, like garments put off long ago — were foreign to her, in comparison. The chain that bound her here was of iron links, and galling to her inmost soul, but never could be broken.

It might be, too, — doubtless it was so, although she hid the secret from herself, and grew pale whenever it struggled out of her heart, like a serpent from its hole, — it might be that another feeling kept her within the scene and pathway that had been so fatal. There dwelt, there trode the feet of one with whom she deemed herself connected in a union, that, unrecognized on earth, would bring them together before the bar of final judgment, and make that their marriage-altar, for a joint futurity of endless retribution. Over and over again, the tempter of souls had thrust this idea upon Hester's contemplation, and laughed at the passionate and desperate joy with which she seized, and then strove to cast it from her. She barely looked the idea in the face, and hastened to bar it in its dungeon. What she compelled herself to believe, — what, finally, she reasoned upon, as her motive for continuing a resident of New England, — was half a truth, and half a self-delusion. Here, she said to herself, had been the scene of her guilt, and here should be the scene of her earthly punishment; and so, perchance, the torture of her daily shame would at length purge her soul, and work out another purity than that which she had lost; more saint-like, because the result of martyrdom.

Hester Prynne, therefore, did not flee. On the outskirts of the town, within the verge of the peninsula, but not in close vicinity to any other habitation, there was a small thatched cottage. It had been built by an earlier settler, and abandoned, because the soil about it was too sterile for cultivation, while its comparative remoteness put it out of the sphere of that social activity which already marked the habits of the emigrants. It stood on the shore, looking across a basin of the sea at the forest-covered hills, towards the west. A clump of scrubby trees, such as alone grew on the peninsula, did not so much conceal the cottage from view, as seem to denote that here was some object which would fain have been, or at least ought to be, concealed. In this little, lonesome dwelling, with some slender means that she possessed, and by the license of the magistrates, who still kept an inquisitorial watch over her, Hester established herself, with her infant child. A mystic shadow of suspicion immediately attached itself to the spot. Children, too young to comprehend wherefore this woman should be shut out from the sphere of human charities, would creep nigh enough to behold her plying her needle at the cottage-window, or standing in the door-way, or laboring in her little garden, or coming forth along the pathway that led townward; and, discerning the scarlet letter on her breast, would scamper off, with a strange, contagious fear.

Lonely as was Hester's situation, and without a friend on earth who dared to show himself, she, however, incurred no risk of want. She possessed an art that sufficed, even in a land that afforded comparatively little scope for its exercise, to supply food for her thriving infant and herself. It was the art — then, as now, almost the only one within a woman's grasp — of needle-work. She bore on her breast, in the curiously embroidered letter, a specimen of her delicate and imaginative skill, of which the dames of a court might gladly have availed themselves, to add the richer and more spiritual adornment of human ingenuity to their fabrics of silk and gold. Here, indeed, in the sable simplicity that generally characterized the Puritanic modes of dress, there might be an infrequent call for the finer productions of her handiwork. Yet the taste of the age, demanding whatever was elaborate in compositions of this kind, did not fail to extend its influence over our stern progenitors, who had cast behind them so many fashions which it might seem harder to dispense with. Public ceremonies, such as ordinations, the installation of magistrates, and all that could give majesty to the forms in which a new government manifested itself to the people, were, as a matter of policy, marked by a stately and well-conducted ceremonial, and a sombre, but yet a studied magnificence. Deep ruffs, painfully wrought bands, and gorgeously embroidered gloves, were all deemed necessary to the official state of men assuming the reins of power; and were readily allowed to individuals dignified by rank or wealth, even while sumptuary laws forbade these and similar extravagances to the plebeian order. In the array of funerals, too, — whether for the apparel of the dead body, or to typify, by manifold emblematic devices of sable cloth and snowy lawn, the sorrow of the survivors, — there was a frequent and characteristic demand for such labor as Hester Prynne could supply. Baby-linen — for babies then wore robes of state — afforded still another possibility of toil and emolument.

By degrees, nor very slowly, her handiwork became what would now be termed the fashion. Whether from commiseration for a woman of so miserable a destiny; or from the morbid curiosity that gives a fictitious value even to common or worthless things; or by whatever other intangible circumstance was then, as now, sufficient to bestow, on some persons, what others might seek in vain; or because Hester really filled a gap which must otherwise have remained vacant; it is certain that she had ready and fairly requited employment for as many hours as she saw fit to occupy with her needle. Vanity, it may be, chose to mortify itself, by putting on, for ceremonials of pomp and state, the garments that had been wrought by her sinful hands. Her needle-work was seen on the ruff of the Governor; military men wore it on their scarfs, and the minister on his band; it decked the baby's little cap; it was shut up, to be mildewed and moulder away, in the coffins of the dead. But it is not recorded that, in a single instance, her skill was called in aid to embroider the white veil which was to cover the pure blushes of a bride. The exception indicated the ever relentless vigor with which society frowned upon her sin.

Hester sought not to acquire any thing beyond a subsistence, of the plainest and most ascetic description, for herself, and a simple abundance for her child. Her own dress was of the coarsest materials and the most sombre hue; with only that one ornament, — the scarlet letter, — which it was her doom to wear. The child's attire, on the other hand, was distinguished by a fanciful, or, we might rather say, a fantastic ingenuity, which served, indeed, to heighten the airy charm that early began to develop itself in the little girl, but which appeared to have also a deeper meaning. We may speak further of it hereafter. Except for that small expenditure in the decoration of her infant, Hester bestowed all her superfluous means in charity, on wretches less miserable than herself, and who not unfrequently insulted the hand that fed them. Much of the time, which she might readily have applied to the better efforts of her art, she employed in making coarse garments for the poor. It is probable that there was an idea of penance in this mode of occupation, and that she offered up a real sacrifice of enjoyment, in devoting so many hours to such rude handiwork. She had in her nature a rich, voluptuous, Oriental characteristic, — a taste for the gorgeously beautiful, which, save in the exquisite productions of her needle, found nothing else, in all the possibilities of her life, to exercise itself upon. Women derive a pleasure, incomprehensible to the other sex, from the delicate toil of the needle. To Hester Prynne it might have been a mode of expressing, and therefore soothing, the passion of her life. Like all other joys, she rejected it as sin. This morbid meddling of conscience with an immaterial matter betokened, it is to be feared, no genuine and stedfast penitence, but something doubtful, something that might be deeply wrong, beneath.

In this manner, Hester Prynne came to have a part to perform in the world. With her native energy of character, and rare capacity, it could not entirely cast her off, although it had set a mark upon her, more intolerable to a woman's heart than that which branded the brow of Cain. In all her intercourse with society, however, there was nothing that made her feel as if she belonged to it. Every gesture, every word, and even the silence of those with whom she came in contact, implied, and often expressed, that she was banished, and as much alone as if she inhabited another sphere, or communicated with the common nature by other organs and senses than the rest of human kind. She stood apart from mortal interests, yet close beside them, like a ghost that revisits the familiar fireside, and can no longer make itself seen or felt; no more smile with the household joy, nor mourn with the kindred sorrow; or, should it succeed in manifesting its forbidden sympathy, awakening only terror and horrible repugnance. These emotions, in fact, and its bitterest scorn besides, seemed to be the sole portion that she retained in the universal heart. It was not an age of delicacy; and her position, although she understood it well, and was in little danger of forgetting it, was often brought before her vivid self-perception, like a new anguish, by the rudest touch upon the tenderest spot. The poor, as we have already said, whom she sought out to be the objects of her bounty, often reviled the hand that was stretched forth to succor them. Dames of elevated rank, likewise, whose doors she entered in the way of her occupation, were accustomed to distil drops of bitterness into her heart; sometimes through that alchemy of quiet malice, by which women can concoct a subtile poison from ordinary trifles; and sometimes, also, by a coarser expression, that fell upon the sufferer's defenceless breast like a rough blow upon an ulcerated wound. Hester had schooled herself long and well; she never responded to these attacks, save by a flush of crimson that rose irrepressibly over her pale cheek, and again subsided into the depths of her bosom. She was patient, — a martyr, indeed, — but she forbore to pray for her enemies; lest, in spite of her forgiving aspirations, the words of the blessing should stubbornly twist themselves into a curse.

Continually, and in a thousand other ways, did she feel the innumerable throbs of anguish that had been so cunningly contrived for her by the undying, the ever-active sentence of the Puritan tribunal. Clergymen paused in the street to address words of exhortation, that brought a crowd, with its mingled grin and frown, around the poor, sinful woman. If she entered a church, trusting to share the Sabbath smile of the Universal Father, it was often her mishap to find herself the text of the discourse. She grew to have a dread of children; for they had imbibed from their parents a vague idea of something horrible in this dreary woman, gliding silently through the town, with never any companion but one only child. Therefore, first allowing her to pass, they pursued her at a distance with shrill cries, and the utterance of a word that had no distinct purport to their own minds, but was none the less terrible to her, as proceeding from lips that babbled it unconsciously. It seemed to argue so wide a diffusion of her shame, that all nature knew of it; it could have caused her no deeper pang, had the leaves of the trees whispered the dark story among themselves, — had the summer breeze murmured about it, — had the wintry blast shrieked it aloud! Another peculiar torture was felt in the gaze of a new eye. When strangers looked curiously at the scarlet letter, — and none ever failed to do so, — they branded it afresh into Hester's soul; so that, oftentimes, she could scarcely refrain, yet always did refrain, from covering the symbol with her hand. But then, again, an accustomed eye had likewise its own anguish to inflict. Its cool stare of familiarity was intolerable. From first to last, in short, Hester Prynne had always this dreadful agony in feeling a human eye upon the token; the spot never grew callous; it seemed, on the contrary, to grow more sensitive with daily torture.

But sometimes, once in many days, or perchance in many months, she felt an eye — a human eye — upon the ignominious brand, that seemed to give a momentary relief, as if half of her agony were shared. The next instant, back it all rushed again, with still a deeper throb of pain; for, in that brief interval, she had sinned anew. Had Hester sinned alone?

Her imagination was somewhat affected, and, had she been of a softer moral and intellectual fibre, would have been still more so, by the strange and solitary anguish of her life. Walking to and fro, with those lonely footsteps, in the little world with which she was outwardly connected, it now and then appeared to Hester, — if altogether fancy, it was nevertheless too potent to be resisted, — she felt or fancied, then, that the scarlet letter had endowed her with a new sense. She shuddered to believe, yet could not help believing, that it gave her a sympathetic knowledge of the hidden sin in other hearts. She was terror-stricken by the revelations that were thus made. What were they? Could they be other than the insidious whispers of the bad angel, who would fain have persuaded the struggling woman, as yet only half his victim, that the outward guise of purity was but a lie, and that, if truth were everywhere to be shown, a scarlet letter would blaze forth on many a bosom besides Hester Prynne's? Or, must she receive those intimations — so obscure, yet so distinct — as truth? In all her miserable experience, there was nothing else so awful and so loathsome as this sense. It perplexed, as well as shocked her, by the irreverent inopportuneness of the occasions that brought it into vivid action. Sometimes, the red infamy upon her breast would give a sympathetic throb, as she passed near a venerable minister or magistrate, the model of piety and justice, to whom that age of antique reverence looked up, as to a mortal man in fellowship with angels. "What evil thing is at hand?" would Hester say to herself. Lifting her reluctant eyes, there would be nothing human within the scope of view, save the form of this earthly saint! Again, a mystic sisterhood would contumaciously assert itself, as she met the sanctified frown of some matron, who, according to the rumor of all tongues, had kept cold snow within her bosom throughout life. That unsunned snow in the matron's bosom, and the burning shame on Hester Prynne's, — what had the two in common? Or, once more, the electric thrill would give her warning, — "Behold, Hester, here is a companion!" — and, looking up, she would detect the eyes of a young maiden glancing at the scarlet letter, shyly and aside, and quickly averted, with a faint, chill crimson in her cheeks; as if her purity were somewhat sullied by that momentary glance. O Fiend, whose talisman was that fatal symbol, wouldst thou leave nothing, whether in youth or age, for this poor sinner to revere? — Such loss of faith is ever one of the saddest results of sin. Be it accepted as a proof that all was not corrupt in this poor victim of her own frailty, and man's hard law, that Hester Prynne yet struggled to believe that no fellow-mortal was guilty like herself.

The vulgar, who, in those dreary old times, were always contributing a grotesque horror to what interested their imaginations, had a story about the scarlet letter which we might readily work up into a terrific legend. They averred, that the symbol was not mere scarlet cloth, tinged in an earthly dye-pot, but was red-hot with infernal fire, and could be seen glowing all alight, whenever Hester Prynne walked abroad in the night-time. And we must needs say, it seared Hester's bosom so deeply, that perhaps there was more truth in the rumor than our modern incredulity may be inclined to admit.

VI. Pearl

We have as yet hardly spoken of the infant; that little creature, whose innocent life had sprung, by the inscrutable decree of Providence, a lovely and immortal flower, out of the rank luxuriance of a guilty passion. How strange it seemed to the sad woman, as she watched the growth, and the beauty that became every day more brilliant, and the intelligence that threw its quivering sunshine over the tiny features of this child! Her Pearl! — For so had Hester called her; not as a name expressive of her aspect, which had nothing of the calm, white, unimpassioned lustre that would be indicated by the comparison. But she named the infant "Pearl," as being of great price, — purchased with all she had, — her mother's only treasure! How strange, indeed! Man had marked this woman's sin by a scarlet letter, which had such potent and disastrous efficacy that no human sympathy could reach her, save it were sinful like herself. God, as a direct consequence of the sin which man thus punished, had given her a lovely child, whose place was on that same dishonored bosom, to connect her parent for ever with the race and descent of mortals, and to be finally a blessed soul in heaven! Yet these thoughts affected Hester Prynne less with hope than apprehension. She knew that her deed had been evil; she could have no faith, therefore, that its result would be for good. Day after day, she looked fearfully into the child's expanding nature; ever dreading to detect some dark and wild peculiarity, that should correspond with the guiltiness to which she owed her being.

Certainly, there was no physical defect. By its perfect shape, its vigor, and its natural dexterity in the use of all its untried limbs, the infant was worthy to have been brought forth in Eden; worthy to have been left there, to be the plaything of the angels, after the world's first parents were driven out. The child had a native grace which does not invariably coexist with faultless beauty; its attire, however simple, always impressed the beholder as if it were the very garb that precisely became it best. But little Pearl was not clad in rustic weeds. Her mother, with a morbid purpose that may be better understood hereafter, had bought the richest tissues that could be procured, and allowed her imaginative faculty its full play in the arrangement and decoration of the dresses which the child wore, before the public eye. So magnificent was the small figure, when thus arrayed, and such was the splendor of Pearl's own proper beauty, shining through the gorgeous robes which might have extinguished a paler loveliness, that there was an absolute circle of radiance around her, on the darksome cottage-floor. And yet a russet gown, torn and soiled with the child's rude play, made a picture of her just as perfect. Pearl's aspect was imbued with a spell of infinite variety; in this one child there were many children, comprehending the full scope between the wild-flower prettiness of a peasant-baby, and the pomp, in little, of an infant princess. Throughout all, however, there was a trait of passion, a certain depth of hue, which she never lost; and if, in any of her changes, she had grown fainter or paler, she would have ceased to be herself; — it would have been no longer Pearl!

This outward mutability indicated, and did not more than fairly express, the various properties of her inner life. Her nature appeared to possess depth, too, as well as variety; but — or else Hester's fears deceived her — it lacked reference and adaptation to the world into which she was born. The child could not be made amenable to rules. In giving her existence, a great law had been broken; and the result was a being, whose elements were perhaps beautiful and brilliant, but all in disorder; or with an order peculiar to themselves, amidst which the point of variety and arrangement was difficult or impossible to be discovered. Hester could only account for the child's character — and even then, most vaguely and imperfectly — by recalling what she herself had been, during that momentous period while Pearl was imbibing her soul from the spiritual world, and her bodily frame from its material of earth. The mother's impassioned state had been the medium through which were transmitted to the unborn infant the rays of its moral life;

and, however white and clear originally, they had taken the deep stains of crimson and gold, the fiery lustre, the black shadow, and the untempered light, of the intervening substance. Above all, the warfare of Hester's spirit, at that epoch, was perpetuated in Pearl. She could recognize her wild, desperate, defiant mood, the flightiness of her temper, and even some of the very cloud-shapes of gloom and despondency that had brooded in her heart. They were now illuminated by the morning radiance of a young child's disposition, but, later in the day of earthly existence, might be prolific of the storm and whirlwind.

The discipline of the family, in those days, was of a far more rigid kind than now. The frown, the harsh rebuke, the frequent application of the rod, enjoined by Scriptural authority, were used, not merely in the way of punishment for actual offences, but as a wholesome regimen for the growth and promotion of all childish virtues. Hester Prynne, nevertheless, the lonely mother of this one child, ran little risk of erring on the side of undue severity. Mindful, however, of her own errors and misfortunes, she early sought to impose a tender, but strict, control over the infant immortality that was committed to her charge. But the task was beyond her skill. After testing both smiles and frowns, and proving that neither mode of treatment possessed any calculable influence, Hester was ultimately compelled to stand aside, and permit the child to be swayed by her own impulses. Physical compulsion or restraint was effectual, of course, while it lasted. As to any other kind of discipline, whether addressed to her mind or heart, little Pearl might or might not be within its reach, in accordance with the caprice that ruled the moment. Her mother, while Pearl was yet an infant, grew acquainted with a certain peculiar look, that warned her when it would be labor thrown away to insist, persuade, or plead. It was a look so intelligent, yet inexplicable, so perverse, sometimes so malicious, but generally accompanied by a wild flow of spirits, that Hester could not help questioning, at such moments, whether Pearl was a human child. She seemed rather an airy sprite, which, after playing its fantastic sports for a little while upon the cottage-floor, would flit away with a mocking smile. Whenever that look appeared in her wild, bright, deeply black eyes, it invested her with a strange remoteness and intangibility; it was as if she were hovering in the air and might vanish, like a glimmering light that comes we know not whence, and goes we know not whither. Beholding it, Hester was constrained to rush towards the child, — to pursue the little elf in the flight which she invariably began, — to snatch her to her bosom, with a close pressure and earnest kisses, — not so much from overflowing love, as to assure herself that Pearl was flesh and blood, and not utterly delusive. But Pearl's laugh, when she was caught, though full of merriment and music, made her mother more doubtful than before.

Heart-smitten at this bewildering and baffling spell, that so often came between herself and her sole treasure, whom she had bought so dear, and who was all her world, Hester sometimes burst into passionate tears. Then, perhaps, — for there was no foreseeing how it might affect her, — Pearl would frown, and clench her little fist, and harden her small features into a stern, unsympathizing look of discontent. Not seldom, she would laugh anew, and louder than before, like a thing incapable and unintelligent of human sorrow. Or — but this more rarely happened — she would be convulsed with a rage of grief, and sob out her love for her mother, in broken words, and seem intent on proving that she had a heart, by breaking it. Yet Hester was hardly safe in confiding herself to that gusty tenderness; it passed, as suddenly as it came. Brooding over all these matters, the mother felt like one who has evoked a spirit, but, by some irregularity in the process of conjuration, has failed to win the master-word that should control this new and incomprehensible intelligence. Her only real comfort was when the child lay in the placidity of sleep. Then she was sure of her, and tasted hours of quiet, sad, delicious happiness; until — perhaps with that perverse expression glimmering from beneath her opening lids — little Pearl awoke!

How soon — with what strange rapidity, indeed! — did Pearl arrive at an age that was capable of social intercourse, beyond the mother's ever-ready smile and nonsense-words! And then what a happiness would it have been, could Hester Prynne have heard her clear, bird-like voice mingling with the uproar of other childish voices, and have distinguished and unravelled her own darling's tones, amid all the entangled outcry of a group of sportive children! But this could never be. Pearl was a born outcast of the infantile world. An imp of evil, emblem and product of sin, she had no right among christened infants. Nothing was more remarkable than the instinct, as it seemed, with which the child comprehended her loneliness; the destiny that had drawn an inviolable circle round about her; the whole peculiarity, in short, of her position in respect to other children. Never, since her release from prison, had Hester met the public gaze without her. In all her walks about the town, Pearl, too, was there; first as the babe in arms, and afterwards as the little girl, small companion of her mother, holding a forefinger with her whole grasp, and tripping along at the rate of three or four footsteps to one of Hester's. She saw the children of the settlement, on the grassy margin of the street, or at the domestic thresholds, disporting themselves in such grim fashion as the Puritanic nurture would permit; playing at going to church, perchance; or at scourging Quakers; or taking scalps in a sham-fight with the Indians; or scaring one another with freaks of imitative witchcraft. Pearl saw, and gazed intently, but never sought to make acquaintance. If spoken to, she would not speak again. If the children gathered about her, as they sometimes did, Pearl would grow positively terrible in her puny wrath, snatching up stones to fling at them, with shrill, incoherent exclamations that made her mother tremble, because they had so much the sound of a witch's anathemas in some unknown tongue.

The truth was, that the little Puritans, being of the most intolerant brood that ever lived, had got a vague idea of something outlandish, unearthly, or at variance with ordinary fashions, in the mother and child; and therefore scorned them in their hearts, and not unfrequently reviled them with their tongues. Pearl felt the sentiment, and requited it with the bitterest hatred that can be supposed to rankle in a childish bosom. These outbreaks of a fierce temper had a kind of value, and even comfort, for her mother; because there was at least an intelligible earnestness in the mood, instead of the fitful caprice that so often thwarted her in the child's manifestations. It appalled her, nevertheless, to discern here, again, a shadowy reflection of the evil that had existed in herself. All this enmity and passion had Pearl inherited, by inalienable right, out of Hester's heart. Mother and daughter stood together in the same circle of seclusion from human society; and in the nature of the child seemed to be perpetuated those unquiet elements that had distracted Hester Prynne before Pearl's birth, but had since begun to be soothed away by the softening influences of maternity.

At home, within and around her mother's cottage, Pearl wanted not a wide and various circle of acquaintance. The spell of life went forth from her ever creative spirit, and communicated itself to a thousand objects, as a torch kindles a flame wherever it may be applied. The unlikeliest materials, a stick, a bunch of rags, a flower, were the puppets of Pearl's witchcraft, and, without undergoing any outward change, became spiritually adapted to whatever drama occupied the stage of her inner world. Her one baby-voice served a multitude of imaginary personages, old and young, to talk withal. The pine-trees, aged, black, and solemn, and flinging groans and other melancholy utterances on the breeze, needed little transformation to figure as Puritan elders; the ugliest weeds of the garden were their children, whom Pearl smote down and uprooted, most unmercifully. It was wonderful, the vast variety of forms into which she threw her intellect, with no continuity, indeed, but darting up and dancing, always in a state of preternatural activity, — soon sinking down, as if exhausted by so rapid and feverish a tide of life, — and succeeded by other shapes of a similar wild energy. It was like nothing so much as the phantasmagoric play of the northern lights. In the mere exercise of the fancy, however, and the sportiveness of a growing mind, there might be little more than was observable in other children of bright faculties; except as Pearl, in the dearth of human playmates, was thrown more upon the visionary throng which she created. The singularity lay in the hostile feelings with which the child regarded all these offspring of her own heart and mind. She never created a friend, but seemed always to be sowing broadcast the dragon's teeth, whence sprung a harvest of armed enemies, against whom she rushed to battle. It was inexpressibly sad — then what depth of sorrow to a mother, who felt in her own heart the cause! — to observe, in one so young, this constant recognition of an adverse world, and so fierce a training of the energies that were to make good her cause, in the contest that must ensue.

Gazing at Pearl, Hester Prynne often dropped her work upon her knees, and cried out, with an agony which she would fain have hidden, but which made utterance for itself, betwixt speech and a groan, — "O Father in Heaven, — if Thou art still my Father, — what is this being which I have brought into the world!" And Pearl, overhearing the ejaculation, or aware, through some more subtile channel, of those throbs of anguish, would turn her vivid and beautiful little face upon her mother, smile with sprite-like intelligence, and resume her play.

One peculiarity of the child's deportment remains yet to be told. The very first thing which she had noticed, in her life was — what? — not the mother's smile, responding to it, as other babies do, by that faint, embryo smile of the little mouth, remembered so doubtfully afterwards, and with such fond discussion whether it were indeed a smile. By no means! But that first object of which Pearl seemed to become aware was — shall we say it? — the scarlet letter on Hester's bosom! One day, as her mother stooped over the cradle, the infant's eyes had been caught by the glimmering of the gold embroidery about the letter; and, putting up her little hand, she grasped at it, smiling, not doubtfully, but with a decided gleam that gave her face the look of a much older child. Then, gasping for breath, did Hester Prynne clutch the fatal token, instinctively endeavouring to tear it away; so infinite was the torture inflicted by the intelligent touch of Pearl's baby-hand. Again, as if her mother's agonized gesture were meant only to make sport for her, did little Pearl look into her eyes, and smile! From that epoch, except when the child was asleep, Hester had never felt a moment's safety; not a moment's calm enjoyment of her. Weeks, it is true, would sometimes elapse, during which Pearl's gaze might never once be fixed upon the scarlet letter; but then, again, it would come at unawares, like the stroke of sudden death, and always with that peculiar smile, and odd expression of the eyes.

Once, this freakish, elfish cast came into the child's eyes, while Hester was looking at her own image in them, as mothers are fond of doing; and, suddenly, — for women in solitude, and with troubled hearts, are pestered with unaccountable delusions, — she fancied that she beheld, not her own miniature portrait, but another face in the small black mirror of Pearl's eye. It was a face, fiend-like, full of smiling malice, yet bearing the semblance of features that she had known full well, though seldom with a smile, and never with malice, in them. It was as if an evil spirit possessed the child, and had just then peeped forth in mockery. Many a time afterwards had Hester been tortured, though less vividly, by the same illusion.

In the afternoon of a certain summer's day, after Pearl grew big enough to run about, she amused herself with gathering handfuls of wild-flowers, and flinging them, one by one, at her mother's bosom; dancing up and down, like a little elf, whenever she hit the scarlet letter. Hester's first motion had been to cover her bosom with her clasped hands. But, whether from pride or resignation, or a feeling that her penance might best be wrought out by this unutterable pain, she resisted the impulse, and sat erect, pale as death, looking sadly into little Pearl's wild eyes. Still came the battery of flowers, almost invariably hitting the mark, and covering the mother's breast with hurts for which she could find no balm in this world, nor knew how to seek it in another. At last, her shot being all expended, the child stood still and gazed at Hester, with that little, laughing image of a fiend peeping out — or, whether it peeped or no, her mother so imagined it — from the unsearchable abyss of her black eyes.

"Child, what art thou?" cried the mother.

"O, I am your little Pearl!" answered the child.

But, while she said it, Pearl laughed and began to dance up and down, with the humorsome gesticulation of a little imp, whose next freak might be to fly up the chimney.

"Art thou my child, in very truth?" asked Hester.

Nor did she put the question altogether idly, but, for the moment, with a portion of genuine earnestness; for, such was Pearl's wonderful intelligence, that her mother half doubted whether she were not acquainted with the secret spell of her existence, and might not now reveal herself.

"Yes; I am little Pearl!" repeated the child, continuing her antics.

"Thou art not my child! Thou art no Pearl of mine!" said the mother, half playfully; for it was often the case that a sportive impulse came over her, in the midst of her deepest suffering. "Tell me, then, what thou art, and who sent thee hither?"

"Tell me, mother!" said the child, seriously, coming up to Hester, and pressing herself close to her knees. "Do thou tell me!"

"Thy Heavenly Father sent thee!" answered Hester Prynne.

But she said it with a hesitation that did not escape the acuteness of the child. Whether moved only by her ordinary freakishness, or because an evil spirit prompted her, she put up her small forefinger, and touched the scarlet letter.

"He did not send me!" cried she, positively. "I have no Heavenly Father!"

"Hush, Pearl, hush! Thou must not talk so!" answered the mother, suppressing a groan. "He sent us all into this world. He sent even me, thy mother. Then, much more, thee! Or, if not, thou strange and elfish child, whence didst thou come?"

"Tell me! Tell me!" repeated Pearl, no longer seriously, but laughing, and capering about the floor. "It is thou that must tell me!"

But Hester could not resolve the query, being herself in a dismal labyrinth of doubt. She remembered — betwixt a smile and a shudder — the talk of the neighbouring townspeople; who, seeking vainly elsewhere for the child's paternity, and observing some of her odd attributes, had given out that poor little Pearl was a demon offspring; such as, ever since old Catholic times, had occasionally been seen on earth, through the agency of their mothers' sin, and to promote some foul and wicked purpose. Luther, according to the scandal of his monkish enemies, was a brat of that hellish breed; nor was Pearl the only child to whom this inauspicious origin was assigned, among the New England Puritans.

VII. The Governor's Hall

Hester Prynne went, one day, to the mansion of Governor Bellingham, with a pair of gloves, which she had fringed and embroidered to his order, and which were to be worn on some great occasion of state; for, though the chances of a popular election had caused this former ruler to descend a step or two from the highest rank, he still held an honorable and influential place among the colonial magistracy.

Another and far more important reason than the delivery of a pair of embroidered gloves impelled Hester, at this time, to seek an interview with a personage of so much power and activity in the affairs of the settlement. It had reached her ears, that there was a design on the part of some of the leading inhabitants, cherishing the more rigid order of principles in religion and government, to deprive her of her child. On the supposition that Pearl, as already hinted, was of demon origin, these good people not unreasonably argued that a Christian interest in the mother's soul required them to remove such a stumbling-block from her path. If the child, on the other hand, were really capable of moral and religious growth, and possessed the elements of ultimate salvation, then, surely, it would enjoy all the fairer prospect of these advantages by being transferred to wiser and better guardianship than Hester Prynne's. Among those who promoted the design, Governor Bellingham was said to be one of the most busy. It may appear singular, and, indeed, not a little ludicrous, that an affair of this kind, which, in later days, would have been referred to no higher jurisdiction than that of the selectmen of the town, should then have been a question publicly discussed, and on which statesmen of eminence took sides. At that epoch of pristine simplicity, however, matters of even slighter public interest, and of far less intrinsic weight than the welfare of Hester and her child, were strangely mixed up with the deliberations of legislators and acts of state. The period was hardly, if at all, earlier than that of our story, when a dispute concerning the right of property in a pig, not only caused a fierce and bitter contest in the legislative body of the colony, but resulted in an important modification of the framework itself of the legislature.

Full of concern, therefore, — but so conscious of her own right, that it seemed scarcely an unequal match between the public, on the one side, and a lonely woman, backed by the sympathies of nature, on the other, — Hester Prynne set forth from her solitary cottage. Little Pearl, of course, was her companion. She was now of an age to run lightly along by her mother's side, and, constantly in motion from morn till sunset, could have accomplished a much longer journey than that before her. Often, nevertheless, more from caprice than necessity, she demanded to be taken up in arms, but was soon as imperious to be set down again, and frisked onward before Hester on the grassy pathway, with many a harmless trip and tumble. We have spoken of Pearl's rich and luxuriant beauty; a beauty that shone with deep and vivid tints; a bright complexion, eyes possessing intensity both of depth and glow, and hair already of a deep, glossy brown, and which, in after years, would be nearly akin to black. There was fire in her and throughout her; she seemed the unpremeditated offshoot of a passionate moment. Her mother, in contriving the child's garb, had allowed the gorgeous tendencies of her imagination their full play; arraying her in a crimson velvet tunic, of a peculiar cut, abundantly embroidered with fantasies and flourishes of gold thread. So much strength of coloring, which must have given a wan and pallid aspect to cheeks of a fainter bloom, was admirably adapted to Pearl's beauty, and made her the very brightest little jet of flame that ever danced upon the earth.

But it was a remarkable attribute of this garb, and, indeed, of the child's whole appearance, that it irresistibly and inevitably reminded the beholder of the token which Hester Prynne was doomed to wear upon her bosom. It was the scarlet letter in another form; the scarlet letter endowed with life! The mother herself — as if the red ignominy were so deeply scorched into her brain, that all her conceptions assumed its form — had carefully wrought out the similitude; lavishing many hours of morbid ingenuity, to create an analogy between the object of her affection, and the emblem of her guilt and torture. But, in truth, Pearl was the one, as well as the other; and only in consequence of that identity had Hester contrived so perfectly to represent the scarlet letter in her appearance.

As the two wayfarers came within the precincts of the town, the children of the Puritans looked up from their play, — or what passed for play with those sombre little urchins, — and spake gravely one to another: —

"Behold, verily, there is the woman of the scarlet letter; and, of a truth, moreover, there is the likeness of the scarlet letter running along by her side! Come, therefore, and let us fling mud at them!"

But Pearl, who was a dauntless child, after frowning, stamping her foot, and shaking her little hand with a variety of threatening gestures, suddenly made a rush at the knot of her enemies, and put them all to flight. She resembled, in her fierce pursuit of them, an infant pestilence, — the scarlet fever, or some such half-fledged angel of judgment, — whose mission was to punish the sins of the rising generation. She screamed and shouted, too, with a terrific volume of sound, which doubtless caused the hearts of the fugitives to quake within them. The victory accomplished, Pearl returned quietly to her mother, and looked up smiling into her face.

Without further adventure, they reached the dwelling of Governor Bellingham. This was a large wooden house, built in a fashion of which there are specimens still extant in the streets of our elder towns; now moss-grown, crumbling to decay, and melancholy at heart with the many sorrowful or joyful occurrences, remembered or forgotten, that have happened, and passed away, within their dusky chambers. Then, however, there was the freshness of the passing year on its exterior, and the cheerfulness, gleaming forth from the sunny windows, of a human habitation into which death had never entered. It had indeed a very cheery aspect; the walls being overspread with a kind of stucco, in which fragments of broken glass were plentifully intermixed; so that, when the sunshine fell aslant-wise over the front of the edifice, it glittered and sparkled as if diamonds had been flung against it by the double handful. The brilliancy might have befitted Aladdin's palace, rather than the mansion of a grave old Puritan ruler. It was further decorated with strange and seemingly cabalistic figures and diagrams, suitable to the quaint taste of the age, which had been drawn in the stucco when newly laid on, and had now grown hard and durable, for the admiration of after times.

Pearl, looking at this bright wonder of a house, began to caper and dance, and imperatively required that the whole breadth of sunshine should be stripped off its front, and given her to play with.

"No, my little Pearl!" said her mother. "Thou must gather thine own sunshine. I have none to give thee!"

They approached the door; which was of an arched form, and flanked on each side by a narrow tower or projection of the edifice, in both of which were lattice-windows, with wooden shutters to close over them at need. Lifting the iron hammer that hung at the portal, Hester Prynne gave a summons, which was answered by one of the Governor's bond-servants; a free-born Englishman, but now a seven years' slave. During that term he was to be the property of his master, and as much a commodity of bargain and sale as an ox, or a joint-stool. The serf wore the blue coat, which was the customary garb of serving-men at that period, and long before, in the old hereditary halls of England.

"Is the worshipful Governor Bellingham within?" inquired Hester.

"Yea, forsooth," replied the bond-servant, staring with wide-open eyes at the scarlet letter, which, being a new-comer in the country, he had never before seen. "Yea, his honorable worship is within. But he hath a godly minister or two with him, and likewise a leech. Ye may not see his worship now."

"Nevertheless, I will enter," answered Hester Prynne; and the bond-servant, perhaps judging from the decision of her air and the glittering symbol in her bosom, that she was a great lady in the land, offered no opposition.

So the mother and little Pearl were admitted into the hall of entrance. With many variations, suggested by the nature of his building-materials, diversity of climate, and a different mode of social life, Governor Bellingham had planned his new habitation after the residences of gentlemen of fair estate in his native land. Here, then, was a wide and reasonably lofty hall, extending through the whole depth of the house, and forming a medium of general communication, more or less directly, with all the other apartments. At one extremity, this spacious room was lighted by the windows of the two towers, which formed a small recess on either side of the portal. At the other end, though partly muffled by a curtain, it was more powerfully illuminated by one of those embowed hall-windows which we read of in old books, and which was provided with a deep and cushioned seat. Here, on the cushion, lay a folio tome, probably of the Chronicles of England, or other such substantial literature; even as, in our own days, we scatter gilded volumes on the centre-table, to be turned over by the casual guest. The furniture of the hall consisted of some ponderous chairs, the backs of which were elaborately carved with wreaths of oaken flowers; and likewise a table in the same taste; the whole being of the Elizabethan age, or perhaps earlier, and heirlooms, transferred hither from the Governor's paternal home. On the table — in token that the sentiment of old English hospitality had not been left behind — stood a large pewter tankard, at the bottom of which, had Hester or Pearl peeped into it, they might have seen the frothy remnant of a recent draught of ale.

On the wall hung a row of portraits, representing the forefathers of the Bellingham lineage, some with armour on their breasts, and others with stately ruffs and robes of peace. All were characterized by the sternness and severity which old portraits so invariably put on; as if they were the ghosts, rather than the pictures, of departed worthies, and were gazing with harsh and intolerant criticism at the pursuits and enjoyments of living men.

At about the centre of the oaken panels, that lined the hall, was suspended a suit of mail, not, like the pictures, an ancestral relic, but of the most modern date; for it had been manufactured by a skilful armorer in London, the same year in which Governor Bellingham came over to New England. There was a steel head-piece, a cuirass, a gorget, and greaves, with a pair of gauntlets and a sword hanging beneath; all, and especially the helmet and breastplate, so highly burnished as to glow with white radiance, and scatter an illumination everywhere about upon the floor. This bright panoply was not meant for mere idle show, but had been worn by the Governor on many a solemn muster and training field, and had glittered, moreover, at the head of a regiment in the Pequod war. For, though bred a lawyer, and accustomed to speak of Bacon, Coke, Noye, and Finch, as his professional associates, the exigencies of this new country had transformed Governor Bellingham into a soldier, as well as a statesman and ruler.

Little Pearl — who was as greatly pleased with the gleaming armour as she had been with the glittering frontispiece of the house — spent some time looking into the polished mirror of the breastplate.

"Mother," cried she, "I see you here. Look! Look!"

Hester looked, by way of humoring the child; and she saw that, owing to the peculiar effect of this convex mirror, the scarlet letter was represented in exaggerated and gigantic proportions, so as to be greatly the most prominent feature of her appearance. In truth, she seemed absolutely hidden behind it. Pearl pointed upward, also, at a similar picture in the headpiece; smiling at her mother, with the elfish intelligence that was so familiar an expression on her small physiognomy. That look of naughty merriment was likewise reflected in the mirror, with so much breadth and intensity of effect, that it made Hester Prynne feel as if it could not be the image of her own child, but of an imp who was seeking to mould itself into Pearl's shape.

"Come along, Pearl!" said she, drawing her away. "Come and look into this fair garden. It may be, we shall see flowers there; more beautiful ones than we find in the woods."

Pearl, accordingly, ran to the bow-window, at the farther end of the hall, and looked along the vista of a garden-walk, carpeted with closely shaven grass, and bordered with some rude and immature attempt at shrubbery. But the proprietor appeared already to have relinquished, as hopeless, the effort to perpetuate on this side of the Atlantic, in a hard soil and amid the close struggle for subsistence, the native English taste for ornamental gardening. Cabbages grew in plain sight; and a pumpkin vine, rooted at some distance, had run across the intervening space, and deposited one of its gigantic products directly beneath the hall-window; as if to warn the Governor that this great lump of vegetable gold was as rich an ornament as New England earth would offer him. There were a few rose-bushes, however, and a number of apple-trees, probably the descendants of those planted by the

Reverend Mr. Blackstone, the first settler of the peninsula; that half mythological personage who rides through our early annals, seated on the back of a bull.

Pearl, seeing the rose-bushes, began to cry for a red rose, and would not be pacified.

"Hush, child, hush!" said her mother earnestly. "Do not cry, dear little Pearl! I hear voices in the garden. The Governor is coming, and gentlemen along with him!"

In fact, adown the vista of the garden-avenue, a number of persons were seen approaching towards the house. Pearl, in utter scorn of her mother's attempt to quiet her, gave an eldritch scream, and then became silent; not from any notion of obedience, but because the quick and mobile curiosity of her disposition was excited by the appearance of these new personages.

VIII. The Elf-Child and the Minister

Governor Bellingham, in a loose gown and easy cap, — such as elderly gentlemen loved to indue themselves with, in their domestic privacy, — walked foremost, and appeared to be showing off his estate, and expatiating on his projected improvements. The wide circumference of an elaborate ruff, beneath his gray beard, in the antiquated fashion of King James's reign, caused his head to look not a little like that of John the Baptist in a charger. The impression made by his aspect, so rigid and severe, and frost-bitten with more than autumnal age, was hardly in keeping with the appliances of worldly enjoyment wherewith he had evidently done his utmost to surround himself. But it is an error to suppose that our grave forefathers — though accustomed to speak and think of human existence as a state merely of trial and warfare, and though unfeignedly prepared to sacrifice goods and life at the behest of duty — made it a matter of conscience to reject such means of comfort, or even luxury, as lay fairly within their grasp. This creed was never taught, for instance, by the venerable pastor, John Wilson, whose beard, white as a snow-drift, was seen over Governor Bellingham's shoulder; while its wearer suggested that pears and peaches might yet be naturalized in the New England climate, and that purple grapes might possibly be compelled to flourish, against the sunny garden-wall. The old clergyman, nurtured at the rich bosom of the English Church, had a long established and legitimate taste for all good and comfortable things; and however stern he might show himself in the pulpit, or in his public reproof of such transgressions as that of Hester Prynne, still, the genial benevolence of his private life had won him warmer affection than was accorded to any of his professional contemporaries.

Behind the Governor and Mr. Wilson came two other guests; one, the Reverend Arthur Dimmesdale, whom the reader may remember, as having taken a brief and reluctant part in the scene of Hester Prynne's disgrace; and, in close companionship with him, old Roger Chillingworth, a person of great skill in physic, who, for two or three years past, had been settled in the town. It was understood that this learned man was the physician as well as friend of the young minister, whose health had severely suffered, of late, by his too unreserved self-sacrifice to the labors and duties of the pastoral relation.

The Governor, in advance of his visitors, ascended one or two steps, and, throwing open the leaves of the great hall window, found himself close to little Pearl. The shadow of the curtain fell on Hester Prynne, and partially concealed her.

"What have we here?" said Governor Bellingham, looking with surprise at the scarlet little figure before him. "I profess, I have never seen the like, since my days of vanity, in old King James's time, when I was wont to esteem it a high favor to be admitted to a court mask! There used to be a swarm of these small apparitions, in holiday-time; and we called them children of the Lord of Misrule. But how gat such a guest into my hall?"

"Ay, indeed!" cried good old Mr. Wilson. "What little bird of scarlet plumage may this be? Methinks I have seen just such figures, when the sun has been shining through a richly painted window, and tracing out the golden and crimson images across the floor. But that was in the old land. Prithee, young one, who art thou, and what has ailed thy mother to bedizen thee in this strange fashion? Art thou a Christian child, — ha? Dost know thy catechism? Or art thou one of those naughty elfs or fairies, whom we thought to have left behind us, with other relics of Papistry, in merry old England?"

"I am mother's child," answered the scarlet vision, "and my name is Pearl!"

"Pearl? — Ruby, rather! — or Coral! — or Red Rose, at the very least, judging from thy hue!" responded the old minister, putting forth his hand in a vain attempt to pat little Pearl on the cheek. "But where is this mother of thine? Ah! I see," he added; and, turning to Governor Bellingham, whispered, — "This is the selfsame child of whom we have held speech together; and behold here the unhappy woman, Hester Prynne, her mother!"

"Sayest thou so?" cried the Governor. "Nay, we might have judged that such a child's mother must needs be a scarlet woman, and a worthy type of her of Babylon! But she comes at a good time; and we will look into this matter forthwith."

Governor Bellingham stepped through the window into the hall, followed by his three guests.

"Hester Prynne," said he, fixing his naturally stern regard on the wearer of the scarlet letter, "there hath been much question concerning thee, of late. The point hath been weightily discussed, whether we, that are of authority and influence, do well discharge our consciences by trusting an immortal soul, such as there is in yonder child, to the guidance of one who hath stumbled and fallen, amid the pitfalls of this world. Speak thou, the child's own mother! Were it not, thinkest thou, for thy little one's temporal and eternal welfare, that she be taken out of thy charge, and clad soberly, and disciplined strictly, and instructed in the truths of heaven and earth? What canst thou do for the child, in this kind?"

"I can teach my little Pearl what I have learned from this!" answered Hester Prynne, laying her finger on the red token.

"Woman, it is thy badge of shame!" replied the stern magistrate. "It is because of the stain which that letter indicates, that we would transfer thy child to other hands."

"Nevertheless," said the mother calmly, though growing more pale, "this badge hath taught me, — it daily teaches me, — it is teaching me at this moment, — lessons whereof my child may be the wiser and better, albeit they can profit nothing to myself."

"We will judge warily," said Bellingham, "and look well what we are about to do. Good Master Wilson, I pray you, examine this Pearl, — since that is her name, — and see whether she hath had such Christian nurture as befits a child of her age."

The old minister seated himself in an arm-chair, and made an effort to draw Pearl betwixt his knees. But the child, unaccustomed to the touch or familiarity of any but her mother, escaped through the open window and stood on the upper step, looking like a wild, tropical bird, of rich plumage, ready to take flight into the upper air. Mr. Wilson, not a little astonished at this outbreak, — for he was a grandfatherly sort of personage, and usually a vast favorite with children, — essayed, however, to proceed with the examination.

"Pearl," said he, with great solemnity, "thou must take heed to instruction, that so, in due season, thou mayest wear in thy bosom the pearl of great price. Canst thou tell me, my child, who made thee?"

Now Pearl knew well enough who made her; for Hester Prynne,

the daughter of a pious home, very soon after her talk with the child about her Heavenly Father, had begun to inform her of those truths which the human spirit, at whatever stage of immaturity, imbibes with such eager interest. Pearl, therefore, so large were the attainments of her three years' lifetime, could have borne a fair examination in the New England Primer, or the first column of the Westminster Catechism, although unacquainted with the outward form of either of those celebrated works. But that perversity, which all children have more or less of, and of which little Pearl had a tenfold portion, now, at the most inopportune moment, took thorough possession of her, and closed her lips, or impelled her to speak words amiss. After putting her finger in her mouth, with many ungracious refusals to answer good Mr. Wilson's question, the child finally announced that she had not been made at all, but had been plucked by her mother off the bush of wild roses, that grew by the prison-door.

This fantasy was probably suggested by the near proximity of the Governor's red roses, as Pearl stood outside of the window; together with her recollection of the prison rose-bush, which she had passed in coming hither.

Old Roger Chillingworth, with a smile on his face, whispered something in the young clergyman's ear. Hester Prynne looked at the man of skill, and even then, with her fate hanging in the balance, was startled to perceive what a change had come over his features, — how much uglier they were, — how his dark complexion seemed to have grown duskier, and his figure more misshapen, — since the days when she had familiarly known him. She met his eyes for an instant, but was immediately constrained to give all her attention to the scene now going forward.

"This is awful!" cried the Governor, slowly recovering from the astonishment into which Pearl's response had thrown him. "Here is a child of three years old, and she cannot tell who made her! Without question, she is equally in the dark as to her soul, its present depravity, and future destiny! Methinks, gentlemen, we need inquire no further."

Hester caught hold of Pearl, and drew her forcibly into her arms, confronting the old Puritan magistrate with almost a fierce expression. Alone in the world, cast off by it, and with this sole treasure to keep her heart alive, she felt that she possessed indefeasible rights against the world, and was ready to defend them to the death.

"God gave me the child!" cried she. "He gave her, in requital of all things else, which ye had taken from me. She is my happiness! — she is my torture, none the less! Pearl keeps me here in life! Pearl punishes me too! See ye not, she is the scarlet letter, only capable of being loved, and so endowed with a million-fold the power of retribution for my sin? Ye shall not take her! I will die first!"

"My poor woman," said the not unkind old minister, "the child shall be well cared for! — far better than thou canst do it."

"God gave her into my keeping," repeated Hester Prynne, raising her voice almost to a shriek. "I will not give her up!" — And here, by a sudden impulse, she turned to the young clergyman, Mr. Dimmesdale, at whom, up to this moment, she had seemed hardly so much as once to direct her eyes. — "Speak thou for me!" cried she. "Thou wast my pastor, and hadst charge of my soul, and knowest me better than these men can. I will not lose the child! Speak for me! Thou knowest, — for thou hast sympathies which these men lack! — thou knowest what is in my heart, and what are a mother's rights, and how much the stronger they are, when that mother has but her child and the scarlet letter! Look thou to it! I will not lose the child! Look to it!"

At this wild and singular appeal, which indicated that Hester Prynne's situation had provoked her to little less than madness, the young minister at once came forward, pale, and holding his hand over his heart, as was his custom whenever his peculiarly nervous temperament was thrown into agitation. He looked now more careworn and emaciated than as we described him at the scene of Hester's public ignominy; and whether it were his failing health, or whatever the cause might be, his large dark eyes had a world of pain in their troubled and melancholy depth.

"There is truth in what she says," began the minister, with a voice sweet, tremulous, but powerful, insomuch that the hall reëchoed, and the hollow armour rang with it, — "truth in what Hester says, and in the feeling which inspires her! God gave her the child, and gave her, too, an instinctive knowledge of its nature and requirements, — both seemingly so peculiar, — which no other mortal being can possess. And, moreover, is there not a quality of awful sacredness in the relation between this mother and this child?"

"Ay! — how is that, good Master Dimmesdale?" interrupted the Governor. "Make that plain, I pray you!"

"It must be even so," resumed the minister. "For, if we deem it otherwise, do we not thereby say that the Heavenly Father, the Creator of all flesh, hath lightly recognized a deed of sin, and made of no account the distinction between unhallowed lust and holy love? This child of its father's guilt and its mother's shame hath come from the hand of God, to work in many ways upon her heart, who pleads so earnestly, and with such bitterness of spirit, the right to keep her. It was meant for a blessing; for the one blessing of her life! It was meant, doubtless, as the mother herself hath told us, for a retribution too; a torture, to be felt at many an unthought of moment; a pang, a sting, an ever-recurring agony, in the midst of a troubled joy! Hath she not expressed this thought in the garb of the poor child, so forcibly reminding us of that red symbol which sears her bosom?"

"Well said, again!" cried good Mr. Wilson. "I feared the woman had no better thought than to make a mountebank of her child!"

"O, not so! — not so!" continued Mr. Dimmesdale. "She recognizes, believe me, the solemn miracle which God hath wrought, in the existence of that child. And may she feel, too, — what, methinks, is the very truth, — that this boon was meant, above all things else, to keep the mother's soul alive, and to preserve her from blacker depths of sin into which Satan might else have sought to plunge her! Therefore it is good for this poor, sinful woman that she hath an infant immortality, a being capable of eternal joy or sorrow, confided to her care, — to be trained up by her to righteousness, — to remind her, at every moment, of her fall, — but yet to teach her, as it were by the Creator's sacred pledge, that, if she bring the child to heaven, the child also will bring its parent thither! Herein is the sinful mother happier than the sinful father. For Hester Prynne's sake, then, and no less for the poor child's sake, let us leave them as Providence hath seen fit to place them!"

"You speak, my friend, with a strange earnestness," said old Roger Chillingworth, smiling at him.

"And there is weighty import in what my young brother hath spoken," added the Reverend Mr. Wilson. "What say you, worshipful Master Bellingham? Hath he not pleaded well for the poor woman?"

"Indeed hath he," answered the magistrate, "and hath adduced such arguments, that we will even leave the matter as it now stands; so long, at least, as there shall be no further scandal in the woman. Care must be had, nevertheless, to put the child to due and stated examination in the catechism at thy hands or Master Dimmesdale's. Moreover, at a proper season, the tithing-men must take heed that she go both to school and to meeting."

The young minister, on ceasing to speak, had withdrawn a few steps from the group, and stood with his face partially concealed in the heavy folds of the window-curtain; while the shadow of his figure, which the sunlight cast upon the floor, was tremulous with the vehemence of his appeal. Pearl, that wild and flighty little elf, stole softly towards him, and, taking his hand in the grasp of both her own, laid her cheek against it; a caress so tender, and withal so unobtrusive, that her mother, who was looking on, asked herself, — "Is that my Pearl?" Yet she knew that there was love in the child's heart, although it mostly revealed itself in passion, and hardly twice in her lifetime had been softened by such gentleness as now. The minister, — for, save the long-sought regards of woman, nothing is sweeter than these marks of childish preference, accorded spontaneously by a spiritual instinct, and therefore seeming to imply in us something truly worthy to be loved, — the minister looked round, laid his hand on the child's head, hesitated an instant, and then kissed her brow. Little Pearl's unwonted mood of sentiment lasted no longer; she laughed, and went capering down the hall, so airily, that old Mr. Wilson raised a question whether even her tiptoes touched the floor.

"The little baggage hath witchcraft in her, I profess," said he to Mr. Dimmesdale. "She needs no old woman's broomstick to fly withal!"

"A strange child!" remarked old Roger Chillingworth. "It is easy to see the mother's part in her. Would it be beyond a philosopher's research, think ye, gentlemen, to analyze that child's nature, and, from its make and mould, to give a shrewd guess at the father?"

"Nay; it would be sinful, in such a question, to follow the clew of profane philosophy," said Mr. Wilson. "Better to fast and pray upon it; and still better, it may be, to leave the mystery as we find it, unless Providence reveal it of its own accord. Thereby, every good Christian man hath a title to show a father's kindness towards the poor, deserted babe."

The affair being so satisfactorily concluded, Hester Prynne, with Pearl, departed from the house. As they descended the steps, it is averred that the lattice of a chamber-window was thrown open, and forth into the sunny day was thrust the face of Mistress Hibbins, Governor Bellingham's bitter-tempered sister, and the same who, a few years later, was executed as a witch.

"Hist, hist!" said she, while her ill-omened physiognomy seemed to cast a shadow over the cheerful newness of the house. "Wilt thou go with us to-night? There will be a merry company in the forest; and I wellnigh promised the Black Man that comely Hester Prynne should make one."

"Make my excuse to him, so please you!" answered Hester, with a triumphant smile. "I must tarry at home, and keep watch over my little Pearl. Had they taken her from me, I would willingly have gone with thee into the forest, and signed my name in the Black Man's book too, and that with mine own blood!"

"We shall have thee there anon!" said the witch-lady, frowning, as she drew back her head.

But here — if we suppose this interview betwixt Mistress Hibbins and Hester Prynne to be authentic, and not a parable — was already an illustration of the young minister's argument against sundering the relation of a fallen mother to the offspring of her frailty. Even thus early had the child saved her from Satan's snare.

IX. The Leech

Under the appellation of Roger Chillingworth, the reader will remember, was hidden another name, which its former wearer had resolved should never more be spoken. It has been related, how, in the crowd that witnessed Hester Prynne's ignominious exposure, stood a man, elderly, travel-worn, who, just emerging from the perilous wilderness, beheld the woman, in whom he hoped to find embodied the warmth and cheerfulness of home, set up as a type of sin before the people. Her matronly fame was trodden under all men's feet. Infamy was babbling around her in the public market-place. For her kindred, should the tidings ever reach them, and for the companions of her unspotted life, there remained nothing but the contagion of her dishonor; which would not fail to be distributed in strict accordance and proportion with the intimacy and sacredness of their previous relationship. Then why — since the choice was with himself — should the individual, whose connection with the fallen woman had been the most intimate and sacred of them all, come forward to vindicate his claim to an inheritance so little desirable? He resolved not to be pilloried beside her on her pedestal of shame. Unknown to all but Hester Prynne, and possessing the lock and key of her silence, he chose to withdraw his name from the roll of mankind, and, as regarded his former ties and interests, to vanish out of life as completely as if he indeed lay at the bottom of the ocean, whither rumor had long ago consigned him. This purpose once effected, new interests would immediately spring up, and likewise a new purpose; dark, it is true, if not guilty, but of force enough to engage the full strength of his faculties.

In pursuance of this resolve, he took up his residence in the Puritan town, as Roger Chillingworth, without other introduction than the learning and intelligence of which he possessed more than a common measure. As his studies, at a previous period of his life, had made him extensively acquainted with the medical science of the day, it was as a physician that he presented himself, and as such was cordially received.

Skilful men, of the medical and chirurgical profession, were of rare occurrence in the colony. They seldom, it would appear, partook of the religious zeal that brought other emigrants across the Atlantic. In their researches into the human frame, it may be that the higher and more subtile faculties of such men were materialized, and that they lost the spiritual view of existence amid the intricacies of that wondrous mechanism, which seemed to involve art enough to comprise all of life within itself. At all events, the health of the good town of Boston, so far as medicine had aught to do with it, had hitherto lain in the guardianship of an aged deacon and apothecary, whose piety and godly deportment were stronger testimonials in his favor, than any that he could have produced in the shape of a diploma. The only surgeon was one who combined the occasional exercise of that noble art with the daily and habitual flourish of a razor. To such a professional body Roger Chillingworth was a brilliant acquisition. He soon manifested his familiarity with the ponderous and imposing machinery of antique physic; in which every remedy contained a multitude of far-fetched and heterogeneous ingredients, as elaborately compounded as if the proposed result had been the Elixir of Life. In his Indian captivity, moreover, he had gained much knowledge of the properties of native herbs and roots; nor did he conceal from his patients, that these simple medicines, Nature's boon to the untutored savage, had quite as large a share of his own confidence as the European pharmacopœia, which so many learned doctors had spent centuries in elaborating.

This learned stranger was exemplary, as regarded at least the outward forms of a religious life, and, early after his arrival, had chosen for his spiritual guide the Reverend Mr. Dimmesdale. The young divine, whose scholar-like renown still lived in Oxford, was considered by his more fervent admirers as little less than a heaven-ordained apostle, destined, should he live and labor for the ordinary term of life, to do as great deeds for the now feeble New England Church, as the early Fathers had achieved for the infancy of the Christian faith. About this period, however, the health of Mr. Dimmesdale had evidently begun to fail. By those best acquainted with his habits, the paleness of the young minister's cheek was accounted for by his too earnest devotion to study, his scrupulous fulfilment of parochial duty, and, more than all, by the fasts and vigils of which he made a frequent practice, in order to keep the grossness of this earthly state from clogging and obscuring his spiritual lamp. Some declared, that, if Mr. Dimmesdale were really going to die, it was cause enough, that the world was not worthy to be any longer trodden by his feet. He himself, on the other hand, with characteristic humility, avowed his belief, that, if Providence should see fit to remove him, it would be because of his own unworthiness to perform its humblest mission here on earth. With all this difference of opinion as to the cause of his decline, there could be no question of the fact. His form grew emaciated; his voice, though still rich and sweet, had a certain melancholy prophecy of decay in it; he was often observed, on any slight alarm or other sudden accident, to put his hand over his heart, with first a flush and then a paleness, indicative of pain.

Such was the young clergyman's condition, and so imminent the prospect that his dawning light would be extinguished, all untimely, when Roger Chillingworth made his advent to the town. His first entry on the scene, few people could tell whence, dropping down, as it were, out of the sky, or starting from the nether earth, had an aspect of mystery, which was easily heightened to the miraculous. He was now known to be a man of skill; it was observed that he gathered herbs, and the blossoms of wild-flowers, and dug up roots and plucked off twigs from the forest-trees, like one acquainted with hidden virtues in what was valueless to common eyes. He was heard to speak of Sir Kenelm Digby, and other famous men, — whose scientific attainments were esteemed hardly less than supernatural, — as having been his correspondents or associates. Why, with such rank in the learned world, had he come hither? What could he, whose sphere was in great cities, be seeking in the wilderness? In answer to this query, a rumor gained ground, — and, however absurd, was entertained by some very sensible people, — that Heaven had wrought an absolute miracle, by transporting an eminent Doctor of Physic, from a German university, bodily through the air, and setting him down at the door of Mr. Dimmesdale's study! Individuals of wiser faith, indeed, who knew that Heaven promotes its purposes without aiming at the stage-effect of what is called miraculous interposition, were inclined to see a providential hand in Roger Chillingworth's so opportune arrival.

This idea was countenanced by the strong interest which the physician ever manifested in the young clergyman; he attached himself to him as a parishioner, and sought to win a friendly regard and confidence from his naturally reserved sensibility. He expressed great alarm at his pastor's state of health, but was anxious to attempt the cure, and, if early undertaken, seemed not despondent of a favorable result. The elders, the deacons, the motherly dames, and the young and fair maidens, of Mr. Dimmesdale's flock, were alike importunate that he should make trial of the physician's frankly offered skill. Mr. Dimmesdale gently repelled their entreaties.

"I need no medicine," said he.

But how could the young minister say so, when, with every successive Sabbath, his cheek was paler and thinner, and his voice more tremulous than before, — when it had now become a constant habit, rather than a casual gesture, to press his hand over his heart? Was he weary of his labors? Did he wish to die? These questions were solemnly propounded to Mr. Dimmesdale by the elder ministers of Boston and the deacons of his church, who, to use their own phrase, "dealt with him" on the sin of rejecting the aid which Providence so manifestly held out. He listened in silence, and finally promised to confer with the physician.

"Were it God's will," said the Reverend Mr. Dimmesdale, when, in fulfilment of this pledge, he requested old Roger Chillingworth's professional advice, "I could be well content, that my labors, and my sorrows, and my sins, and my pains, should shortly end with me, and what is earthly of them be buried in my grave, and the spiritual go with me to my eternal state, rather than that you should put your skill to the proof in my behalf."

"Ah," replied Roger Chillingworth, with that quietness which, whether imposed or natural, marked all his deportment, "it is thus that a young clergyman is apt to speak. Youthful men, not having taken a deep root, give up their hold of life so easily! And saintly men, who walk with God on earth, would fain be away, to walk with him on the golden pavements of the New Jerusalem."

"Nay," rejoined the young minister, putting his hand to his heart, with a flush of pain flitting over his brow, "were I worthier to walk there, I could be better content to toil here."

"Good men ever interpret themselves too meanly," said the physician.

In this manner, the mysterious old Roger Chillingworth became the medical adviser of the Reverend Mr. Dimmesdale. As not only the disease interested the physician, but he was strongly moved to look into the character and qualities of the patient, these two men, so different in age, came gradually to spend much time together. For the sake of the minister's health, and to enable the leech to gather plants with healing balm in them, they took long walks on the sea-shore, or in the forest; mingling various talk with the plash and murmur of the waves, and the solemn wind-anthem among the tree-tops. Often, likewise, one was the guest of the other, in his place of study and retirement. There was a fascination for the minister in the company of the man of science, in whom he recognized an intellectual cultivation of no moderate depth or scope; together with a range and freedom of ideas, that he would have vainly looked for among the members of his own profession. In truth, he was startled, if not shocked, to find this attribute in the physician. Mr. Dimmesdale was a true priest, a true religionist, with the reverential sentiment largely developed, and an order of mind that impelled itself powerfully along the track of a creed, and wore its passage continually deeper with the lapse of time. In no state of society would he have been what is called a man of liberal views; it would always be essential to his peace to feel the pressure of a faith about him, supporting, while it confined him within its iron framework. Not the less, however, though with a tremulous enjoyment, did he feel the occasional relief of looking at the universe through the medium of another kind of intellect than those with which he habitually held converse. It was as if a window were thrown open, admitting a freer atmosphere into the close and stifled study, where his life was wasting itself away, amid lamp-light, or obstructed day-beams, and the musty fragrance, be it sensual or moral, that exhales from books. But the air was too fresh and chill to be long breathed, with comfort. So the minister, and the physician with him, withdrew again within the limits of what their church defined as orthodox.

Thus Roger Chillingworth scrutinized his patient carefully, both as he saw him in his ordinary life, keeping an accustomed pathway in the range of thoughts familiar to him, and as he appeared when thrown amidst other moral scenery, the novelty of which might call out something new to the surface of his character. He deemed it essential, it would seem, to know the man, before attempting to do him good. Wherever there is a heart and an intellect, the diseases of the physical frame are tinged with the peculiarities of these. In Arthur Dimmesdale, thought and imagination were so active, and sensibility so intense, that the bodily infirmity would be likely to have its groundwork there. So Roger Chillingworth — the man of skill, the kind and friendly physician — strove to go deep into his patient's bosom, delving among his principles, prying into his recollections, and probing every thing with a cautious touch, like a treasure-seeker in a dark cavern. Few secrets can escape an investigator, who has opportunity and license to undertake such a quest, and skill to follow it up. A man burdened with a secret should especially avoid the intimacy of his physician. If the latter possess native sagacity, and a nameless something more, — let us call it intuition; if he show no intrusive egotism, nor disagreeably prominent characteristics of his own; if he have the power, which must be born with him, to bring his mind into such affinity with his patient's, that this last shall unawares have spoken what he imagines himself only to have thought; if such revelations be received without tumult, and acknowledged not so often by an uttered sympathy, as by silence, an inarticulate breath, and here and there a word, to indicate that all is understood; if, to these qualifications of a confidant be joined the advantages afforded by his recognized character as a physician; — then, at some inevitable moment, will the soul of the sufferer be dissolved, and flow forth in a dark, but transparent stream, bringing all its mysteries into the daylight.

Roger Chillingworth possessed all, or most, of the attributes above enumerated. Nevertheless, time went on; a kind of intimacy, as we have said, grew up between these two cultivated minds, which had as wide a field as the whole sphere of human thought and study, to meet upon; they discussed every topic of ethics and religion, of public affairs, and private character; they talked much, on both sides, of matters that seemed personal to themselves; and yet no secret, such as the physician fancied must exist there, ever stole out of the minister's consciousness into his companion's ear. The latter had his suspicions, indeed, that even the nature of Mr Dimmesdale's bodily disease had never fairly been revealed to him. It was a strange reserve!

After a time, at a hint from Roger Chillingworth, the friends of Mr. Dimmesdale effected an arrangement by which the two were lodged in the same house; so that every ebb and flow of the minister's life-tide might pass under the eye of his anxious and attached physician. There was much joy throughout the town, when this greatly desirable object was attained. It was held to be the best possible measure for the young clergyman's welfare; unless, indeed, as often urged by such as felt authorized to do so, he had selected some one of the many blooming damsels, spiritually devoted to him, to become his devoted wife. This latter step, however, there was no present prospect that Arthur Dimmesdale would be prevailed upon to take; he rejected all suggestions of the kind, as if priestly celibacy were one of his articles of church-discipline. Doomed by his own choice, therefore, as Mr. Dimmesdale so evidently was, to eat his unsavory morsel always at another's board, and endure the life-long chill which must be his lot who seeks to warm himself only at another's fireside, it truly seemed that this sagacious, experienced, benevolent, old physician, with his concord of paternal and reverential love for the young pastor, was the very man, of all mankind, to be constantly within reach of his voice.

The new abode of the two friends was with a pious widow, of good social rank, who dwelt in a house covering pretty nearly the site on which the venerable structure of King's Chapel has since been built. It had the grave-yard, originally Isaac Johnson's home-field, on one side, and so was well adapted to call up serious reflections, suited to their respective employments, in both minister and man of physic. The motherly care of the good widow assigned to Mr. Dimmesdale a front apartment, with a sunny exposure, and heavy window-curtains to create a noontide shadow, when desirable. The walls were hung round with tapestry, said to be from the Gobelin looms, and, at all events, representing the Scriptural story of David and Bathsheba, and Nathan the Prophet, in colors still unfaded, but which made the fair woman of the scene almost as grimly picturesque as the woe-denouncing seer. Here, the pale clergyman piled up his library, rich with parchment-bound folios of the Fathers, and the lore of Rabbis, and monkish erudition, of which the Protestant divines, even while they vilified and decried that class of writers, were yet constrained often to avail themselves. On the other side of the house, old Roger Chillingworth arranged his study and laboratory; not such as a modern man of science would reckon even tolerably complete, but provided with a distilling apparatus, and the means of compounding drugs and chemicals, which the practised alchemist knew well how to turn to purpose. With such commodiousness of situation, these two learned persons sat themselves down, each in his own domain, yet familiarly passing from one apartment to the other, and bestowing a mutual and not incurious inspection into one another's business.

And the Reverend Arthur Dimmesdale's best discerning friends, as we have intimated, very reasonably imagined that the hand of Providence had done all this, for the purpose — besought in so many public, and domestic, and secret prayers — of restoring the young minister to health. But — it must now be said — another portion of the community had latterly begun to take its own view of the relation betwixt Mr. Dimmesdale and the mysterious old physician. When an uninstructed multitude attempts to see with its eyes, it is exceedingly apt to be deceived. When, however, it forms its judgment, as it usually does, on the intuitions of its great and warm heart, the conclusions thus attained are often so profound and so unerring, as to possess the character of truths supernaturally revealed. The people, in the case of which we speak, could justify its prejudice against Roger Chillingworth by no fact or argument worthy of serious refutation. There was an aged handicraftsman, it is true, who had been a citizen of London at the period of

Sir Thomas Overbury's murder, now some thirty years agone; he testified to having seen the physician, under some other name, which the narrator of the story had now forgotten, in company with Doctor Forman, the famous old conjurer, who was implicated in the affair of Overbury. Two or three individuals hinted, that the man of skill, during his Indian captivity, had enlarged his medical attainments by joining in the incantations of the savage priests; who were universally acknowledged to be powerful enchanters, often performing seemingly miraculous cures by their skill in the black art. A large number — and many of these were persons of such sober sense and practical observation, that their opinions would have been valuable, in other matters — affirmed that Roger Chillingworth's aspect had undergone a remarkable change while he had dwelt in town, and especially since his abode with Mr. Dimmesdale. At first, his expression had been calm, meditative, scholar-like. Now, there was something ugly and evil in his face, which they had not previously noticed, and which grew still the more obvious to sight, the oftener they looked upon him. According to the vulgar idea, the fire in his laboratory had been brought from the lower regions, and was fed with infernal fuel; and so, as might be expected, his visage was getting sooty with the smoke.

To sum up the matter, it grew to be a widely diffused opinion, that the Reverend Arthur Dimmesdale, like many other personages of especial sanctity, in all ages of the Christian world, was haunted either by Satan himself, or Satan's emissary, in the guise of old Roger Chillingworth. This diabolical agent had the Divine permission, for a season, to burrow into the clergyman's intimacy, and plot against his soul. No sensible man, it was confessed, could doubt on which side the victory would turn. The people looked, with an unshaken hope, to see the minister come forth out of the conflict, transfigured with the glory which he would unquestionably win. Meanwhile, nevertheless, it was sad to think of the perchance mortal agony through which he must struggle towards his triumph.

Alas, to judge from the gloom and terror in the depths of the poor minister's eyes, the battle was a sore one, and the victory any thing but secure!

X. The Leech and His Patient

Old Roger Chillingworth, throughout life, had been calm in temperament, kindly, though not of warm affections, but ever, and in all his relations with the world, a pure and upright man. He had begun an investigation, as he imagined, with the severe and equal integrity of a judge, desirous only of truth, even as if the question involved no more than the air-drawn lines and figures of a geometrical problem, instead of human passions, and wrongs inflicted on himself. But, as he proceeded, a terrible fascination, a kind of fierce, though still calm, necessity seized the old man within its gripe, and never set him free again, until he had done all its bidding. He now dug into the poor clergyman's heart, like a miner searching for gold; or, rather, like a sexton delving into a grave, possibly in quest of a jewel that had been buried on the dead man's bosom, but likely to find nothing save mortality and corruption. Alas for his own soul, if these were what he sought!

Sometimes, a light glimmered out of the physician's eyes, burning blue and ominous, like the reflection of a furnace, or, let us say, like one of those gleams of ghastly fire that darted from Bunyan's awful doorway in the hill-side, and quivered on the pilgrim's face. The soil where this dark miner was working had perchance shown indications that encouraged him.

"This man," said he, at one such moment, to himself, "pure as they deem him, — all spiritual as he seems, — hath inherited a strong animal nature from his father or his mother. Let us dig a little farther in the direction of this vein!"

Then, after long search into the minister's dim interior, and turning over many precious materials, in the shape of high aspirations for the welfare of his race, warm love of souls, pure sentiments, natural piety, strengthened by thought and study, and illuminated by revelation, — all of which invaluable gold was perhaps no better than rubbish to the seeker, — he would turn back, discouraged, and begin his quest towards another point. He groped along as stealthily, with as cautious a tread, and as wary an outlook, as a thief entering a chamber where a man lies only half asleep, — or, it may be, broad awake, — with purpose to steal the very treasure which this man guards as the apple of his eye. In spite of his premeditated carefulness, the floor would now and then creak; his garments would rustle; the shadow of his presence, in a forbidden proximity, would be thrown across his victim. In other words, Mr. Dimmesdale, whose sensibility of nerve often produced the effect of spiritual intuition, would become vaguely aware that something inimical to his peace had thrust itself into relation with him. But old Roger Chillingworth, too, had perceptions that were almost intuitive; and when the minister threw his startled eyes towards him, there the physician sat; his kind, watchful, sympathizing, but never intrusive friend.

Yet Mr. Dimmesdale would perhaps have seen this individual's character more perfectly, if a certain morbidness, to which sick hearts are liable, had not rendered him suspicious of all mankind. Trusting no man as his friend, he could not recognize his enemy when the latter actually appeared. He therefore still kept up a familiar intercourse with him, daily receiving the old physician in his study; or visiting the laboratory, and, for recreation's sake, watching the processes by which weeds were converted into drugs of potency.

One day, leaning his forehead on his hand, and his elbow on the sill of the open window, that looked towards the grave-yard, he talked with Roger Chillingworth, while the old man was examining a bundle of unsightly plants.

"Where," asked he, with a look askance at them, — for it was the clergyman's peculiarity that he seldom, now-a-days, looked straight-forth at any object, whether human or inanimate, — "where, my kind doctor, did you gather those herbs, with such a dark, flabby leaf?"

"Even in the grave-yard, here at hand," answered the physician, continuing his employment. "They are new to me. I found them growing on a grave, which bore no tombstone, nor other memorial of the dead man, save these ugly weeds that have taken upon themselves to keep him in remembrance. They grew out of his heart, and typify, it may be, some hideous secret that was buried with him, and which he had done better to confess during his lifetime."

"Perchance," said Mr. Dimmesdale, "he earnestly desired it, but could not."

"And wherefore?" rejoined the physician. "Wherefore not; since all the powers of nature call so earnestly for the confession of sin, that these black weeds have sprung up out of a buried heart, to make manifest an unspoken crime?"

"That, good Sir, is but a fantasy of yours," replied the minister. "There can be, if I forebode aright, no power, short of the Divine mercy, to disclose, whether by uttered words, or by type or emblem, the secrets that may be buried with a human heart. The heart, making itself guilty of such secrets, must perforce hold them, until the day when all hidden things shall be revealed. Nor have I so read or interpreted Holy Writ, as to understand that the disclosure of human thoughts and deeds, then to be made, is intended as a part of the retribution. That, surely, were a shallow view of it. No; these revelations, unless I greatly err, are meant merely to promote the intellectual satisfaction of all intelligent beings, who will stand waiting, on that day, to see the dark problem of this life made plain. A knowledge of men's hearts will be needful to the completest solution of that problem. And I conceive, moreover, that the hearts holding such miserable secrets as you speak of will yield them up, at that last day, not with reluctance, but with a joy unutterable."

"Then why not reveal them here?" asked Roger Chillingworth, glancing quietly aside at the minister. "Why should not the guilty ones sooner avail themselves of this unutterable solace?"

"They mostly do," said the clergyman, griping hard at his breast, as if afflicted with an importunate throb of pain. "Many, many a poor soul hath given its confidence to me, not only on the death-bed, but while strong in life, and fair in reputation. And ever, after such an outpouring, O, what a relief have I witnessed in those sinful brethren! even as in one who at last draws free air, after long stifling with his own polluted breath. How can it be otherwise? Why should a wretched man, guilty, we will say, of murder, prefer to keep the dead corpse buried in his own heart, rather than fling it forth at once, and let the universe take care of it!"

"Yet some men bury their secrets thus," observed the calm physician.

"True; there are such men," answered Mr. Dimmesdale. "But, not to suggest more obvious reasons, it may be that they are kept silent by the very constitution of their nature. Or, — can we not suppose it? — guilty as they may be, retaining, nevertheless, a zeal for God's glory and man's welfare, they shrink from displaying themselves black and filthy in the view of men; because, thenceforward, no good can be achieved by them; no evil of the past be redeemed by better service. So, to their own unutterable torment, they go about among their fellow-creatures, looking pure as new-fallen snow; while their hearts are all speckled and spotted with iniquity of which they cannot rid themselves."

"These men deceive themselves," said Roger Chillingworth, with somewhat more emphasis than usual, and making a slight gesture with his forefinger. "They fear to take up the shame that rightfully belongs to them. Their love for man, their zeal for God's service, — these holy impulses may or may not coexist in their hearts with the evil inmates to which their guilt has unbarred the door, and which must needs propagate a hellish breed within them. But, if they seek to glorify God, let them not lift heavenward their unclean hands! If they would serve their fellow-men, let them do it by making manifest the power and reality of conscience, in constraining them to penitential self-abasement! Wouldst thou have me to believe, O wise and pious friend, that a false show can be better — can be more for God's glory, or man's welfare — than God's own truth? Trust me, such men deceive themselves!"

"It may be so," said the young clergyman indifferently, as waiving a discussion that he considered irrelevant or unseasonable. He had a ready faculty, indeed, of escaping from any topic that agitated his too sensitive and nervous temperament. — "But, now, I would ask of my well-skilled physician, whether, in good sooth, he deems me to have profited by his kindly care of this weak frame of mine?"

Before Roger Chillingworth could answer, they heard the clear, wild laughter of a young child's voice, proceeding from the adjacent burial-ground. Looking instinctively from the open window, — for it was summer-time, — the minister beheld Hester Prynne and little Pearl passing along the footpath that traversed the inclosure. Pearl looked as beautiful as the day, but was in one of those moods of perverse merriment which, whenever they occurred, seemed to remove her entirely out of the sphere of sympathy or human contact. She now skipped irreverently from one grave to another; until, coming to the broad, flat, armorial tombstone of a departed worthy, — perhaps of Isaac Johnson himself, — she began to dance upon it. In reply to her mother's command and entreaty that she would behave more decorously, little Pearl paused to gather the prickly burrs from a tall burdock, which grew beside the tomb. Taking a handful of these, she arranged them along the lines of the scarlet letter that decorated the maternal bosom, to which the burrs, as their nature was, tenaciously adhered. Hester did not pluck them off.

Roger Chillingworth had by this time approached the window, and smiled grimly down.

"There is no law, nor reverence for authority, no regard for human ordinances or opinions, right or wrong, mixed up with that child's composition," remarked he, as much to himself as to his companion. "I saw her, the other day, bespatter the Governor himself with water, at the cattle-trough in Spring Lane. What, in Heaven's name, is she? Is the imp altogether evil? Hath she affections? Hath she any discoverable principle of being?"

"None, — save the freedom of a broken law," answered Mr. Dimmesdale, in a quiet way, as if he had been discussing the point within himself. "Whether capable of good, I know not."

The child probably overheard their voices; for, looking up to the window, with a bright, but naughty smile of mirth and intelligence, she threw one of the prickly burrs at the Reverend Mr. Dimmesdale. The sensitive clergyman shrunk, with nervous dread, from the light missile. Detecting his emotion, Pearl clapped her little hands in the most extravagant ecstasy. Hester Prynne, likewise, had involuntarily looked up; and all these four persons, old and young, regarded one another in silence, till the child laughed aloud, and shouted, — "Come away, mother! Come away, or yonder old Black Man will catch you! He hath got hold of the minister already. Come away, mother, or he will catch you! But he cannot catch little Pearl!"

So she drew her mother away, skipping, dancing, and frisking fantastically among the hillocks of the dead people, like a creature that had nothing in common with a bygone and buried generation, nor owned herself akin to it. It was as if she had been made afresh, out of new elements, and must perforce be permitted to live her own life, and be a law unto herself, without her eccentricities being reckoned to her for a crime.

"There goes a woman," resumed Roger Chillingworth, after a pause, "who, be her demerits what they may, hath none of that mystery of hidden sinfulness which you deem so grievous to be borne. Is Hester Prynne the less miserable, think you, for that scarlet letter on her breast?"

"I do verily believe it," answered the clergyman. "Nevertheless, I cannot answer for her. There was a look of pain in her face, which I would gladly have been spared the sight of. But still, methinks, it must needs be better for the sufferer to be free to show his pain, as this poor woman Hester is, than to cover it all up in his heart."

There was another pause; and the physician began anew to examine and arrange the plants which he had gathered.

"You inquired of me, a little time agone," said he, at length, "my judgment as touching your health."

"I did," answered the clergyman, "and would gladly learn it. Speak frankly, I pray you, be it for life or death."

"Freely, then, and plainly," said the physician, still busy with his plants, but keeping a wary eye on Mr. Dimmesdale, "the disorder is a strange one; not so much in itself, nor as outwardly manifested, — in so far, at least, as the symptoms have been laid open to my observation. Looking daily at you, my good Sir, and watching the tokens of your aspect, now for months gone by, I should deem you a man sore sick, it may be, yet not so sick but that an instructed and watchful physician might well hope to cure you. But — I know not what to say — the disease is what I seem to know, yet know it not."

"You speak in riddles, learned Sir," said the pale minister, glancing aside out of the window.

"Then, to speak more plainly," continued the physician, "and I crave pardon, Sir, — should it seem to require pardon, — for this needful plainness of my speech. Let me ask, — as your friend, — as one having charge, under Providence, of your life and physical well-being, — hath all the operation of this disorder been fairly laid open and recounted to me?"

"How can you question it?" asked the minister. "Surely, it were child's play to call in a physician, and then hide the sore!"

"You would tell me, then, that I know all?" said Roger Chillingworth, deliberately, and fixing an eye, bright with intense and concentrated intelligence, on the minister's face. "Be it so! But, again! He to whom only the outward and physical evil is laid open knoweth, oftentimes, but half the evil which he is called upon to cure. A bodily disease, which we look upon as whole and entire within itself, may, after all, be but a symptom of some ailment in the spiritual part. Your pardon, once again, good Sir, if my speech give the shadow of offence. You, Sir, of all men whom I have known, are he whose body is the closest conjoined, and imbued, and identified, so to speak, with the spirit whereof it is the instrument."

"Then I need ask no further," said the clergyman, somewhat hastily rising from his chair. "You deal not, I take it, in medicine for the soul!"

"Thus, a sickness," continued Roger Chillingworth, going on, in an unaltered tone, without heeding the interruption, — but standing up, and confronting the emaciated and white-cheeked minister with his low, dark, and misshapen figure, — "a sickness, a sore place, if we may so call it, in your spirit, hath immediately its appropriate manifestation in your bodily frame. Would you, therefore, that your physician heal the bodily evil? How may this be, unless you first lay open to him the wound or trouble in your soul?"

"No! — not to thee! — not to an earthly physician!" cried Mr. Dimmesdale, passionately, and turning his eyes, full and bright, and with a kind of fierceness, on old Roger Chillingworth. "Not to thee! But, if it be the soul's disease, then do I commit myself to the one Physician of the soul! He, if it stand with his good pleasure, can cure; or he can kill! Let him do with me as, in his justice and wisdom, he shall see good. But who art thou, that meddlest in this matter? — that dares thrust himself between the sufferer and his God?"

With a frantic gesture, he rushed out of the room.

"It is as well to have made this step," said Roger Chillingworth to himself, looking after the minister with a grave smile. "There is nothing lost. We shall be friends again anon. But see, now, how passion takes hold upon this man, and hurrieth him out of himself! As with one passion, so with another! He hath done a wild thing ere now, this pious Master Dimmesdale, in the hot passion of his heart!"

It proved not difficult to reëstablish the intimacy of the two companions, on the same footing and in the same degree as heretofore. The young clergyman, after a few hours of privacy, was sensible that the disorder of his nerves had hurried him into an unseemly outbreak of temper, which there had been nothing in the physician's words to excuse or palliate. He marvelled, indeed, at the violence with which he had thrust back the kind old man, when merely proffering the advice which it was his duty to bestow, and which the minister himself had expressly sought. With these remorseful feelings, he lost no time in making the amplest apologies, and besought his friend still to continue the care, which, if not successful in restoring him to health, had, in all probability, been the means of prolonging his feeble existence to that hour. Roger Chillingworth readily assented, and went on with his medical supervision of the minister; doing his best for him, in all good faith, but always quitting the patient's apartment, at the close of a professional interview, with a mysterious and puzzled smile upon his lips. This expression was invisible in Mr. Dimmesdale's presence, but grew strongly evident as the physician crossed the threshold.

"A rare case!" he muttered. "I must needs look deeper into it. A strange sympathy betwixt soul and body! Were it only for the art's sake, I must search this matter to the bottom!"

It came to pass, not long after the scene above recorded, that the Reverend Mr. Dimmesdale, at noonday, and entirely unawares, fell into a deep, deep slumber, sitting in his chair, with a large black-letter volume open before him on the table. It must have been a work of vast ability in the somniferous school of literature. The profound depth of the minister's repose was the more remarkable; inasmuch as he was one of those persons whose sleep, ordinarily, is as light, as fitful, and as easily scared away, as a small bird hopping on a twig. To such an unwonted remoteness, however, had his spirit now withdrawn into itself, that he stirred not in his chair, when old Roger Chillingworth, without any extraordinary precaution, came into the room. The physician advanced directly in front of his patient, laid his hand upon his bosom, and thrust aside the vestment, that, hitherto, had always covered it even from the professional eye.

Then, indeed, Mr. Dimmesdale shuddered, and slightly stirred.

After a brief pause, the physician turned away.

But with what a wild look of wonder, joy, and horror! With what a ghastly rapture, as it were, too mighty to be expressed only by the eye and features, and therefore bursting forth through the whole ugliness of his figure, and making itself even riotously manifest by the extravagant gestures with which he threw up his arms towards the ceiling, and stamped his foot upon the floor! Had a man seen old Roger Chillingworth, at that moment of his ecstasy, he would have had no need to ask how Satan comports himself, when a precious human soul is lost to heaven, and won into his kingdom.

But what distinguished the physician's ecstasy from Satan's was the trait of wonder in it!

XI. The Interior of a Heart

After the incident last described, the intercourse between the clergyman and the physician, though externally the same, was really of another character than it had previously been. The intellect of Roger Chillingworth had now a sufficiently plain path before it. It was not, indeed, precisely that which he had laid out for himself to tread. Calm, gentle, passionless, as he appeared, there was yet, we fear, a quiet depth of malice, hitherto latent, but active now, in this unfortunate old man, which led him to imagine a more intimate revenge than any mortal had ever wreaked upon an enemy. To make himself the one trusted friend, to whom should be confided all the fear, the remorse, the agony, the ineffectual repentance, the backward rush of sinful thoughts, expelled in vain! All that guilty sorrow, hidden from the world, whose great heart would have pitied and forgiven, to be revealed to him, the Pitiless, to him, the Unforgiving! All that dark treasure to be lavished on the very man, to whom nothing else could so adequately pay the debt of vengeance!

The clergyman's shy and sensitive reserve had balked this scheme. Roger Chillingworth, however, was inclined to be hardly, if at all, less satisfied with the aspect of affairs, which Providence — using the avenger and his victim for its own purposes, and, perchance, pardoning, where it seemed most to punish — had substituted for his black devices. A revelation, he could almost say, had been granted to him. It mattered little, for his object, whether celestial, or from what other region. By its aid, in all the subsequent relations betwixt him and Mr. Dimmesdale, not merely the external presence, but the very inmost soul of the latter seemed to be brought out before his eyes, so that he could see and comprehend its every movement. He became, thenceforth, not a spectator only, but a chief actor, in the poor minister's interior world. He could play upon him as he chose. Would he arouse him with a throb of agony? The victim was for ever on the rack; it needed only to know the spring that controlled the engine; — and the physician knew it well!

Would he startle him with sudden fear? As at the waving of a magician's wand, uprose a grisly phantom, — uprose a thousand phantoms, — in many shapes, of death, or more awful shame, all flocking roundabout the clergyman, and pointing with their fingers at his breast!

All this was accomplished with a subtlety so perfect, that the minister, though he had constantly a dim perception of some evil influence watching over him, could never gain a knowledge of its actual nature. True, he looked doubtfully, fearfully, — even, at times, with horror and the bitterness of hatred, — at the deformed figure of the old physician. His gestures, his gait, his grizzled beard, his slightest and most indifferent acts, the very fashion of his garments, were odious in the clergyman's sight; a token, implicitly to be relied on, of a deeper antipathy in the breast of the latter than he was willing to acknowledge to himself. For, as it was impossible to assign a reason for such distrust and abhorrence, so Mr. Dimmesdale, conscious that the poison of one morbid spot was infecting his heart's entire substance, attributed all his presentiments to no other cause. He took himself to task for his bad sympathies in reference to Roger Chillingworth, disregarded the lesson that he should have drawn from them, and did his best to root them out. Unable to accomplish this, he nevertheless, as a matter of principle, continued his habits of social familiarity with the old man, and thus gave him constant opportunities for perfecting the purpose to which — poor, forlorn creature that he was, and more wretched than his victim — the avenger had devoted himself.

While thus suffering under bodily disease, and gnawed and tortured by some black trouble of the soul, and given over to the machinations of his deadliest enemy, the Reverend Mr. Dimmesdale had achieved a brilliant popularity in his sacred office. He won it, indeed, in great part, by his sorrows. His intellectual gifts, his moral perceptions, his power of experiencing and communicating emotion, were kept in a state of preternatural activity by the prick and anguish of his daily life. His fame, though still on its upward slope, already overshadowed the soberer reputations of his fellow-clergymen, eminent as several of them were. There were scholars among them, who had spent more years in acquiring abstruse lore, connected with the divine profession, than Mr. Dimmesdale had lived; and who might well, therefore, be more profoundly versed in such solid and valuable attainments than their youthful brother. There were men, too, of a sturdier texture of mind than his, and endowed with a far greater share of shrewd, hard, iron or granite understanding; which, duly mingled with a fair proportion of doctrinal ingredient, constitutes a highly respectable, efficacious, and unamiable variety of the clerical species. There were others, again, true saintly fathers, whose faculties had been elaborated by weary toil among their books, and by patient thought, and etherealized, moreover, by spiritual communications with the better world, into which their purity of life had almost introduced these holy personages, with their garments of mortality still clinging to them. All that they lacked was the gift that descended upon the chosen disciples, at Pentecost, in tongues of flame; symbolizing, it would seem, not the power of speech in foreign and unknown languages, but that of addressing the whole human brotherhood in the heart's native language. These fathers, otherwise so apostolic, lacked Heaven's last and rarest attestation of their office, the Tongue of Flame. They would have vainly sought — had they ever dreamed of seeking — to express the highest truths through the humblest medium of familiar words and images. Their voices came down, afar and indistinctly, from the upper heights where they habitually dwelt.

Not improbably, it was to this latter class of men that Mr. Dimmesdale, by many of his traits of character, naturally belonged. To their high mountain-peaks of faith and sanctity he would have climbed, had not the tendency been thwarted by the burden, whatever it might be, of crime or anguish, beneath which it was his doom to totter. It kept him down, on a level with the lowest; him, the man of ethereal attributes, whose voice the angels might else have listened to and answered! But this very burden it was, that gave him sympathies so intimate with the sinful brotherhood of mankind; so that his heart vibrated in unison with theirs, and received their pain into itself, and sent its own throb of pain through a thousand other hearts, in gushes of sad, persuasive eloquence. Oftenest persuasive, but sometimes terrible! The people knew not the power that moved them thus. They deemed the young clergyman a miracle of holiness. They fancied him the mouth-piece of Heaven's messages of wisdom, and rebuke, and love. In their eyes, the very ground on which he trod was sanctified. The virgins of his church grew pale around him, victims of a passion so imbued with religious sentiment that they imagined it to be all religion, and brought it openly, in their white bosoms, as their most acceptable sacrifice before the altar. The aged members of his flock, beholding Mr. Dimmesdale's frame so feeble, while they were themselves so rugged in their infirmity, believed that he would go heavenward before them, and enjoined it upon their children, that their old bones should be buried close to their young pastor's holy grave. And, all this time, perchance, when poor Mr. Dimmesdale was thinking of his grave, he questioned with himself whether the grass would ever grow on it, because an accursed thing must there be buried!

It is inconceivable, the agony with which this public veneration tortured him! It was his genuine impulse to adore the truth, and to reckon all things shadow-like, and utterly devoid of weight or value, that had not its divine essence as the life within their life. Then, what was he? — a substance? — or the dimmest of all shadows? He longed to speak out, from his own pulpit, at the full height of his voice, and tell the people what he was. "I, whom you behold in these black garments of the priesthood, — I, who ascend the sacred desk, and turn my pale face heavenward, taking upon myself to hold communion, in your behalf, with the Most High Omniscience, — I, in whose daily life you discern the sanctity of Enoch, — I, whose footsteps, as you suppose, leave a gleam along my earthly track, whereby the pilgrims that shall come after me may be guided to the regions of the blest, — I, who have laid the hand of baptism upon your children, — I, who have breathed the parting prayer over your dying friends, to whom the Amen sounded faintly from a world which they had quitted, — I, your pastor, whom you so reverence and trust, am utterly a pollution and a lie!"

More than once, Mr. Dimmesdale had gone into the pulpit, with a purpose never to come down its steps, until he should have spoken words like the above. More than once, he had cleared his throat, and drawn in the long, deep, and tremulous breath, which, when sent forth again, would come burdened with the black secret of his soul. More than once — nay, more than a hundred times — he had actually spoken! Spoken! But how? He had told his hearers that he was altogether vile, a viler companion of the vilest, the worst of sinners, an abomination, a thing of unimaginable iniquity; and that the only wonder was, that they did not see his wretched body shrivelled up before their eyes, by the burning wrath of the Almighty! Could there be plainer speech than this? Would not the people start up in their seats, by a simultaneous impulse, and tear him down out of the pulpit which he defiled? Not so, indeed! They heard it all, and did but reverence him the more. They little guessed what deadly purport lurked in those self-condemning words. "The godly youth!" said they among themselves. "The saint on earth! Alas, if he discern such sinfulness in his own white soul, what horrid spectacle would he behold in thine or mine!" The minister well knew — subtle, but remorseful hypocrite that he was! — the light in which his vague confession would be viewed. He had striven to put a cheat upon himself by making the avowal of a guilty conscience, but had gained only one other sin, and a self-acknowledged shame, without the momentary relief of being self-deceived. He had spoken the very truth, and transformed it into the veriest falsehood. And yet, by the constitution of his nature, he loved the truth, and loathed the lie, as few men ever did. Therefore, above all things else, he loathed his miserable self!

His inward trouble drove him to practices, more in accordance with the old, corrupted faith of Rome, than with the better light of the church in which he had been born and bred. In Mr. Dimmesdale's secret closet, under lock and key, there was a bloody scourge. Oftentimes, this Protestant and Puritan divine had plied it on his own shoulders; laughing bitterly at himself the while, and smiting so much the more pitilessly, because of that bitter laugh. It was his custom, too, as it has been that of many other pious Puritans, to fast, — not, however, like them, in order to purify the body and render it the fitter medium of celestial illumination, — but rigorously, and until his knees trembled beneath him, as an act of penance. He kept vigils, likewise, night after night, sometimes in utter darkness; sometimes with a glimmering lamp; and sometimes, viewing his own face in a looking-glass, by the most powerful light which he could throw upon it. He thus typified the constant introspection wherewith he tortured, but could not purify, himself. In these lengthened vigils, his brain often reeled, and visions seemed to flit before him; perhaps seen doubtfully, and by a faint light of their own, in the remote dimness of the chamber, or more vividly, and close beside him, within the looking-glass. Now it was a herd of diabolic shapes, that grinned and mocked at the pale minister, and beckoned him away with them; now a group of shining angels, who flew upward heavily, as sorrow-laden, but grew more ethereal as they rose. Now came the dead friends of his youth, and his white-bearded father, with a saint-like frown, and his mother, turning her face away as she passed by. Ghost of a mother, — thinnest fantasy of a mother, — methinks she might yet have thrown a pitying glance towards her son! And now, through the chamber which these spectral thoughts had made so ghastly, glided Hester Prynne, leading along little Pearl, in her scarlet garb, and pointing her forefinger, first, at the scarlet letter on her bosom, and then at the clergyman's own breast.

None of these visions ever quite deluded him. At any moment, by an effort of his will, he could discern substances through their misty lack of substance, and convince himself that they were not solid in their nature, like yonder table of carved oak, or that big, square, leathern-bound and brazen-clasped volume of divinity. But, for all that, they were, in one sense, the truest and most substantial things which the poor minister now dealt with. It is the unspeakable misery of a life so false as his, that it steals the pith and substance out of whatever realities there are around us, and which were meant by Heaven to be the spirit's joy and nutriment. To the untrue man, the whole universe is false, — it is impalpable, — it shrinks to nothing within his grasp. And he himself, in so far as he shows himself in a false light, becomes a shadow, or, indeed, ceases to exist. The only truth, that continued to give Mr. Dimmesdale a real existence on this earth, was the anguish in his inmost soul, and the undissembled expression of it in his aspect. Had he once found power to smile, and wear a face of gayety, there would have been no such man!

On one of those ugly nights, which we have faintly hinted at, but forborne to picture forth, the minister started from his chair. A new thought had struck him. There might be a moment's peace in it. Attiring himself with as much care as if it had been for public worship, and precisely in the same manner, he stole softly down the staircase, undid the door, and issued forth.

XII. The Minister's Vigil

Walking in the shadow of a dream, as it were, and perhaps actually under the influence of a species of somnambulism, Mr. Dimmesdale reached the spot, where, now so long since, Hester Prynne had lived through her first hour of public ignominy. The same platform or scaffold, black and weather-stained with the storm or sunshine of seven long years, and foot-worn, too, with the tread of many culprits who had since ascended it, remained standing beneath the balcony of the meeting-house. The minister went up the steps.

It was an obscure night of early May. An unvaried pall of cloud muffled the whole expanse of sky from zenith to horizon. If the same multitude which had stood as eyewitnesses while Hester Prynne sustained her punishment could now have been summoned forth, they would have discerned no face above the platform, nor hardly the outline of a human shape, in the dark gray of the midnight. But the town was all asleep. There was no peril of discovery. The minister might stand there, if it so pleased him, until morning should redden in the east, without other risk than that the dank and chill night-air would creep into his frame, and stiffen his joints with rheumatism, and clog his throat with catarrh and cough; thereby defrauding the expectant audience of to-morrow's prayer and sermon. No eye could see him, save that ever-wakeful one which had seen him in his closet, wielding the bloody scourge. Why, then, had he come hither? Was it but the mockery of penitence? A mockery, indeed, but in which his soul trifled with itself! A mockery at which angels blushed and wept, while fiends rejoiced, with jeering laughter! He had been driven hither by the impulse of that Remorse which dogged him everywhere, and whose own sister and closely linked companion was that Cowardice which invariably drew him back, with her tremulous gripe, just when the other impulse had hurried him to the verge of a disclosure. Poor, miserable man! what right had infirmity like his to burden itself with crime? Crime is for the iron-nerved, who have their choice either to endure it, or, if it press too hard, to exert their fierce and savage strength for a good purpose, and fling it off at once! This feeble and most sensitive of spirits could do neither, yet continually did one thing or another, which intertwined, in the same inextricable knot, the agony of heaven-defying guilt and vain repentance.

And thus, while standing on the scaffold, in this vain show of expiation, Mr. Dimmesdale was overcome with a great horror of mind, as if the universe were gazing at a scarlet token on his naked breast, right over his heart. On that spot, in very truth, there was, and there had long been, the gnawing and poisonous tooth of bodily pain. Without any effort of his will, or power to restrain himself, he shrieked aloud; an outcry that went pealing through the night, and was beaten back from one house to another, and reverberated from the hills in the background; as if a company of devils, detecting so much misery and terror in it, had made a plaything of the sound, and were bandying it to and fro.

"It is done!" muttered the minister, covering his face with his hands. "The whole town will awake, and hurry forth, and find me here!"

But it was not so. The shriek had perhaps sounded with a far greater power, to his own startled ears, than it actually possessed. The town did not awake; or, if it did, the drowsy slumberers mistook the cry either for something frightful in a dream, or for the noise of witches; whose voices, at that period, were often heard to pass over the settlements or lonely cottages, as they rode with Satan through the air. The clergyman, therefore, hearing no symptoms of disturbance, uncovered his eyes and looked about him. At one of the chamber-windows of Governor Bellingham's mansion, which stood at some distance, on the line of another street, he beheld the appearance of the old magistrate himself, with a lamp in his hand, a white night-cap on his head, and a long white gown enveloping his figure. He looked like a ghost, evoked unseasonably from the grave. The cry had evidently startled him. At another window of the same house, moreover, appeared old Mistress Hibbins, the Governor's sister, also with a lamp, which, even thus far off, revealed the expression of her sour and discontented face. She thrust forth her head from the lattice, and looked anxiously upward. Beyond the shadow of a doubt, this venerable witch-lady had heard Mr. Dimmesdale's outcry, and interpreted it, with its multitudinous echoes and reverberations, as the clamor of the fiends and night-hags, with whom she was well known to make excursions into the forest.

Detecting the gleam of Governor Bellingham's lamp, the old lady quickly extinguished her own, and vanished. Possibly, she went up among the clouds. The minister saw nothing further of her motions. The magistrate, after a wary observation of the darkness — into which, nevertheless, he could see but little farther than he might into a mill-stone — retired from the window.

The minister grew comparatively calm. His eyes, however, were soon greeted by a little, glimmering light, which, at first a long way off, was approaching up the street. It threw a gleam of recognition on here a post, and there a garden-fence, and here a latticed window-pane, and there a pump, with its full trough of water, and here, again, an arched door of oak, with an iron knocker, and a rough log for the door-step. The Reverend Mr. Dimmesdale noted all these minute particulars, even while firmly convinced that the doom of his existence was stealing onward, in the footsteps which he now heard; and that the gleam of the lantern would fall upon him, in a few moments more, and reveal his long-hidden secret. As the light drew nearer, he beheld, within its illuminated circle, his brother clergyman, — or, to speak more accurately, his professional father, as well as highly valued friend, — the Reverend Mr. Wilson; who, as Mr. Dimmesdale now conjectured, had been praying at the bedside of some dying man. And so he had. The good old minister came freshly from the death-chamber of Governor Winthrop, who had passed from earth to heaven within that very hour. And now, surrounded, like the saint-like personages of olden times, with a radiant halo, that glorified him amid this gloomy night of sin, — as if the departed Governor had left him an inheritance of his glory, or as if he had caught upon himself the distant shine of the celestial city, while looking thitherward to see the triumphant pilgrim pass within its gates, — now, in short, good Father Wilson was moving homeward, aiding his footsteps with a lighted lantern! The glimmer of this luminary suggested the above conceits to Mr. Dimmesdale, who smiled, — nay, almost laughed at them, — and then wondered if he were going mad.

As the Reverend Mr. Wilson passed beside the scaffold, closely muffling his Geneva cloak about him with one arm, and holding the lantern before his breast with the other, the minister could hardly restrain himself from speaking.

"A good evening to you, venerable Father Wilson! Come up hither, I pray you, and pass a pleasant hour with me!"

Good heavens! Had Mr. Dimmesdale actually spoken? For one instant, he believed that these words had passed his lips. But they were uttered only within his imagination. The venerable Father Wilson continued to step slowly onward, looking carefully at the muddy pathway before his feet, and never once turning his head towards the guilty platform. When the light of the glimmering lantern had faded quite away, the minister discovered, by the faintness which came over him, that the last few moments had been a crisis of terrible anxiety; although his mind had made an involuntary effort to relieve itself by a kind of lurid playfulness.

Shortly afterwards, the like grisly sense of the humorous again stole in among the solemn phantoms of his thought. He felt his limbs growing stiff with the unaccustomed chilliness of the night, and doubted whether he should be able to descend the steps of the scaffold. Morning would break, and find him there. The neighbourhood would begin to rouse itself. The earliest riser, coming forth in the dim twilight, would perceive a vaguely defined figure aloft on the place of shame; and, half crazed betwixt alarm and curiosity, would go, knocking from door to door, summoning all the people to behold the ghost — as he needs must think it — of some defunct transgressor. A dusky tumult would flap its wings from one house to another. Then — the morning light still waxing stronger — old patriarchs would rise up in great haste, each in his flannel gown, and matronly dames, without pausing to put off their night-gear. The whole tribe of decorous personages, who had never heretofore been seen with a single hair of their heads awry, would start into public view, with the disorder of a nightmare in their aspects. Old Governor Bellingham would come grimly forth, with his King James's ruff fastened askew; and Mistress Hibbins, with some twigs of the forest clinging to her skirts, and looking sourer than ever, as having hardly got a wink of sleep after her night ride; and good Father Wilson, too, after spending half the night at a death-bed, and liking ill to be disturbed, thus early, out of his dreams about the glorified saints. Hither, likewise, would come the elders and deacons of Mr. Dimmesdale's church, and the young virgins who so idolized their minister, and had made a shrine for him in their white bosoms; which, now, by the by, in their hurry and confusion, they would scantly have given themselves time to cover with their kerchiefs. All people, in a word, would come stumbling over their thresholds, and turning up their amazed and horror-stricken visages around the scaffold. Whom would they discern there, with the red eastern light upon his brow? Whom, but the Reverend Arthur Dimmesdale, half frozen to death, overwhelmed with shame, and standing where Hester Prynne had stood!

Carried away by the grotesque horror of this picture, the minister, unawares, and to his own infinite alarm, burst into a great peal of laughter. It was immediately responded to by a light, airy, childish laugh, in which, with a thrill of the heart, — but he knew not whether of exquisite pain, or pleasure as acute, — he recognized the tones of little Pearl.

"Pearl! Little Pearl!" cried he, after a moment's pause; then, suppressing his voice, — "Hester! Hester Prynne! Are you there?"

"Yes, it is Hester Prynne!" she replied, in a tone of surprise; and the minister heard her footsteps approaching from the sidewalk, along which she had been passing. — "It is I, and my little Pearl."

"Whence come you, Hester?" asked the minister. "What sent you hither?"

"I have been watching at a death-bed," answered Hester Prynne; — "at Governor Winthrop's death-bed, and have taken his measure for a robe, and am now going homeward to my dwelling."

"Come up hither, Hester, thou and little Pearl," said the Reverend Mr. Dimmesdale. "Ye have both been here before, but I was not with you. Come up hither once again, and we will stand all three together!"

She silently ascended the steps, and stood on the platform, holding little Pearl by the hand. The minister felt for the child's other hand, and took it. The moment that he did so, there came what seemed a tumultuous rush of new life, other life than his own, pouring like a torrent into his heart, and hurrying through all his veins, as if the mother and the child were communicating their vital warmth to his half-torpid system. The three formed an electric chain.

"Minister!" whispered little Pearl.

"What wouldst thou say, child?" asked Mr. Dimmesdale.

"Wilt thou stand here with mother and me, to-morrow noontide?" inquired Pearl.

"Nay; not so, my little Pearl!" answered the minister; for, with the new energy of the moment, all the dread of public exposure, that had so long been the anguish of his life, had returned upon him; and he was already trembling at the conjunction in which — with a strange joy, nevertheless — he now found himself. "Not so, my child. I shall, indeed, stand with thy mother and thee one other day, but not to-morrow!"

Pearl laughed, and attempted to pull away her hand. But the minister held it fast.

"A moment longer, my child!" said he.

"But wilt thou promise," asked Pearl, "to take my hand, and mother's hand, to-morrow noontide?"

"Not then, Pearl," said the minister, "but another time!"

"And what other time?" persisted the child.

"At the great judgment day!" whispered the minister, — and, strangely enough, the sense that he was a professional teacher of the truth impelled him to answer the child so. "Then, and there, before the judgment-seat, thy mother, and thou, and I, must stand together! But the daylight of this world shall not see our meeting!"

Pearl laughed again.

But, before Mr. Dimmesdale had done speaking, a light gleamed far and wide over all the muffled sky. It was doubtless caused by one of those meteors, which the night-watcher may so often observe burning out to waste, in the vacant regions of the atmosphere. So powerful was its radiance, that it thoroughly illuminated the dense medium of cloud betwixt the sky and earth. The great vault brightened, like the dome of an immense lamp. It showed the familiar scene of the street, with the distinctness of mid-day, but also with the awfulness that is always imparted to familiar objects by an unaccustomed light. The wooden houses, with their jutting stories and quaint gable-peaks; the doorsteps and thresholds, with the early grass springing up about them; the garden-plots, black with freshly turned earth; the wheel-track, little worn, and, even in the market-place, margined with green on either side; — all were visible, but with a singularity of aspect that seemed to give another moral interpretation to the things of this world than they had ever borne before. And there stood the minister, with his hand over his heart; and Hester Prynne, with the embroidered letter glimmering on her bosom; and little Pearl, herself a symbol, and the connecting link between those two. They stood in the noon of that strange and solemn splendor, as if it were the light that is to reveal all secrets, and the daybreak that shall unite all who belong to one another.

There was witchcraft in little Pearl's eyes; and her face, as she glanced upward at the minister, wore that naughty smile which made its expression frequently so elfish. She withdrew her hand from Mr. Dimmesdale's, and pointed across the street. But he clasped both his hands over his breast, and cast his eyes towards the zenith.

Nothing was more common, in those days, than to interpret all meteoric appearances, and other natural phenomena, that occurred with less regularity than the rise and set of sun and moon, as so many revelations from a supernatural source. Thus, a blazing spear, a sword of flame, a bow, or a sheaf of arrows, seen in the midnight sky, prefigured Indian warfare. Pestilence was known to have been foreboded by a shower of crimson light. We doubt whether any marked event, for good or evil, ever befell New England, from its settlement down to Revolutionary times, of which the inhabitants had not been previously warned by some spectacle of this nature. Not seldom, it had been seen by multitudes. Oftener, however, its credibility rested on the faith of some lonely eyewitness, who beheld the wonder through the colored, magnifying, and distorting medium of his imagination, and shaped it more distinctly in his after-thought. It was, indeed, a majestic idea, that the destiny of nations should be revealed, in these awful hieroglyphics, on the cope of heaven. A scroll so wide might not be deemed too expansive for Providence to write a people's doom upon. The belief was a favorite one with our fore-fathers, as betokening that their infant commonwealth was under a celestial guardianship of peculiar intimacy and strictness. But what shall we say, when an individual discovers a revelation, addressed to himself alone, on the same vast sheet of record! In such a case, it could only be the symptom of a highly disordered mental state, when a man, rendered morbidly self-contemplative by long, intense, and secret pain, had extended his egotism over the whole expanse of nature, until the firmament itself should appear no more than a fitting page for his soul's history and fate.

We impute it, therefore, solely to the disease in his own eye and heart, that the minister, looking upward to the zenith, beheld there the appearance of an immense letter, — the letter A, — marked out in lines of dull red light. Not but the meteor may have shown itself at that point, burning duskily through a veil of cloud; but with no such shape as his guilty imagination gave it; or, at least, with so little definiteness, that another's guilt might have seen another symbol in it.

There was a singular circumstance that characterized Mr. Dimmesdale's psychological state, at this moment. All the time that he gazed upward to the zenith, he was, nevertheless, perfectly aware that little Pearl was pointing her finger towards old Roger Chillingworth, who stood at no great distance from the scaffold. The minister appeared to see him, with the same glance that discerned the miraculous letter. To his features, as to all other objects, the meteoric light imparted a new expression; or it might well be that the physician was not careful then, as at all other times, to hide the malevolence with which he looked upon his victim. Certainly, if the meteor kindled up the sky, and disclosed the earth, with an awfulness that admonished Hester Prynne and the clergyman of the day of judgment, then might Roger Chillingworth have passed with them for the arch-fiend, standing there, with a smile and scowl, to claim his own. So vivid was the expression, or so intense the minister's perception of it, that it seemed still to remain painted on the darkness, after the meteor had vanished, with an effect as if the street and all things else were at once annihilated.

"Who is that man, Hester?" gasped Mr. Dimmesdale, overcome with terror. "I shiver at him! Dost thou know the man? I hate him, Hester!"

She remembered her oath, and was silent.

"I tell thee, my soul shivers at him," muttered the minister again. "Who is he? Who is he? Canst thou do nothing for me? I have a nameless horror of the man."

"Minister," said little Pearl, "I can tell thee who he is!"

"Quickly, then, child!" said the minister, bending his ear close to her lips. "Quickly! — and as low as thou canst whisper."

Pearl mumbled something into his ear, that sounded, indeed, like human language, but was only such gibberish as children may be heard amusing themselves with, by the hour together. At all events, if it involved any secret information in regard to old Roger Chillingworth, it was in a tongue unknown to the erudite clergyman, and did but increase the bewilderment of his mind. The elfish child then laughed aloud.

"Dost thou mock me now?" said the minister.

"Thou wast not bold! — thou wast not true!" answered the child. "Thou wouldst not promise to take my hand, and mother's hand, tomorrow noontide!"

"Worthy Sir," said the physician, who had now advanced to the foot of the platform. "Pious Master Dimmesdale! can this be you? Well, well, indeed! We men of study, whose heads are in our books, have need to be straitly looked after! We dream in our waking moments, and walk in our sleep. Come, good Sir, and my dear friend, I pray you, let me lead you home!"

"How knewest thou that I was here?" asked the minister, fearfully.

"Verily, and in good faith," answered Roger Chillingworth, "I knew nothing of the matter. I had spent the better part of the night at the bedside of the worshipful Governor Winthrop, doing what my poor skill might to give him ease. He going home to a better world, I, likewise, was on my way homeward, when this strange light shone out.

Come with me, I beseech you, Reverend Sir; else you will be poorly able to do Sabbath duty to-morrow. Aha! see now, how they trouble the brain, — these books! — these books! You should study less, good Sir, and take a little pastime; or these night-whimseys will grow upon you!"

"I will go home with you," said Mr. Dimmesdale.

With a chill despondency, like one awaking, all nerveless, from an ugly dream, he yielded himself to the physician, and was led away.

The next day, however, being the Sabbath, he preached a discourse which was held to be the richest and most powerful, and the most replete with heavenly influences, that had ever proceeded from his lips. Souls, it is said, more souls than one, were brought to the truth by the efficacy of that sermon, and vowed within themselves to cherish a holy gratitude towards Mr. Dimmesdale throughout the long hereafter. But, as he came down the pulpit-steps, the gray-bearded sexton met him, holding up a black glove, which the minister recognized as his own.

"It was found," said the sexton, "this morning, on the scaffold, where evil-doers are set up to public shame. Satan dropped it there, I take it, intending a scurrilous jest against your reverence. But, indeed, he was blind and foolish, as he ever and always is. A pure hand needs no glove to cover it!"

"Thank you, my good friend," said the minister gravely, but startled at heart; for, so confused was his remembrance, that he had almost brought himself to look at the events of the past night as visionary. "Yes, it seems to be my glove indeed!"

"And, since Satan saw fit to steal it, your reverence must needs handle him without gloves, henceforward," remarked the old sexton, grimly smiling. "But did your reverence hear of the portent that was seen last night? A great red letter in the sky, — the letter A, — which we interpret to stand for Angel. For, as our good Governor Winthrop was made an angel this past night, it was doubtless held fit that there should be some notice thereof!"

"No," answered the minister. "I had not heard of it."

XIII. Another View of Hester

In her late singular interview with Mr. Dimmesdale, Hester Prynne was shocked at the condition to which she found the clergyman reduced. His nerve seemed absolutely destroyed. His moral force was abased into more than childish weakness. It grovelled helpless on the ground, even while his intellectual faculties retained their pristine strength, or had perhaps acquired a morbid energy, which disease only could have given them. With her knowledge of a train of circumstances hidden from all others, she could readily infer, that, besides the legitimate action of his own conscience, a terrible machinery had been brought to bear, and was still operating, on Mr. Dimmesdale's well-being and repose. Knowing what this poor, fallen man had once been, her whole soul was moved by the shuddering terror with which he had appealed to her, — the outcast woman, — for support against his instinctively discovered enemy. She decided, moreover, that he had a right to her utmost aid. Little accustomed, in her long seclusion from society, to measure her ideas of right and wrong by any standard external to herself, Hester saw — or seemed to see — that there lay a responsibility upon her, in reference to the clergyman, which she owed to no other, nor to the whole world besides. The links that united her to the rest of human kind — links of flowers, or silk, or gold, or whatever the material — had all been broken. Here was the iron link of mutual crime, which neither he nor she could break. Like all other ties, it brought along with it its obligations.

Hester Prynne did not now occupy precisely the same position in which we beheld her during the earlier periods of her ignominy. Years had come, and gone. Pearl was now seven years old. Her mother, with the scarlet letter on her breast, glittering in its fantastic embroidery, had long been a familiar object to the townspeople. As is apt to be the case when a person stands out in any prominence before the community, and, at the same time, interferes neither with public nor individual interests and convenience, a species of general regard had ultimately grown up in reference to Hester Prynne. It is to the credit of human nature, that, except where its selfishness is brought into play, it loves more readily than it hates. Hatred, by a gradual and quiet process, will even be transformed to love, unless the change be impeded by a continually new irritation of the original feeling of hostility. In this matter of Hester Prynne, there was neither irritation nor irksomeness. She never battled with the public, but submitted uncomplainingly to its worst usage; she made no claim upon it, in requital for what she suffered; she did not weigh upon its sympathies. Then, also, the blameless purity of her life, during all these years in which she had been set apart to infamy, was reckoned largely in her favor. With nothing now to lose, in the sight of mankind, and with no hope, and seemingly no wish, of gaining any thing, it could only be a genuine regard for virtue that had brought back the poor wanderer to its paths.

It was perceived, too, that, while Hester never put forward even the humblest title to share in the world's privileges, — farther than to breathe the common air, and earn daily bread for little Pearl and herself by the faithful labor of her hands, — she was quick to acknowledge her sisterhood with the race of man, whenever benefits were to be conferred. None so ready as she to give of her little substance to every demand of poverty; even though the bitter-hearted pauper threw back a gibe in requital of the food brought regularly to his door, or the garments wrought for him by the fingers that could have embroidered a monarch's robe. None so self-devoted as Hester, when pestilence stalked through the town. In all seasons of calamity, indeed, whether general or of individuals, the outcast of society at once found her place. She came, not as a guest, but as a rightful inmate, into the household that was darkened by trouble; as if its gloomy twilight were a medium in which she was entitled to hold intercourse with her fellow-creatures. There glimmered the embroidered letter, with comfort in its unearthly ray. Elsewhere the token of sin, it was the taper of the sick-chamber. It had even thrown its gleam, in the sufferer's hard extremity, across the verge of time. It had shown him where to set his foot, while the light of earth was fast becoming dim, and ere the light of futurity could reach him. In such emergencies, Hester's nature showed itself warm and rich; a well-spring of human tenderness, unfailing to every real demand, and inexhaustible by the largest. Her breast, with its badge of shame, was but the softer pillow for the head that needed one. She was self-ordained a Sister of Mercy; or, we may rather say, the world's heavy hand had so ordained her, when neither the world nor she looked forward to this result. The letter was the symbol of her calling. Such helpfulness was found in her, — so much power to do, and power to sympathize, — that many people refused to interpret the scarlet A by its original signification. They said that it meant Able; so strong was Hester Prynne, with a woman's strength.

It was only the darkened house that could contain her. When sunshine came again, she was not there. Her shadow had faded across the threshold. The helpful inmate had departed, without one backward glance to gather up the meed of gratitude, if any were in the hearts of those whom she had served so zealously. Meeting them in the street, she never raised her head to receive their greeting. If they were resolute to accost her, she laid her finger on the scarlet letter, and passed on. This might be pride, but was so like humility, that it produced all the softening influence of the latter quality on the public mind. The public is despotic in its temper; it is capable of denying common justice, when too strenuously demanded as a right; but quite as frequently it awards more than justice, when the appeal is made, as despots love to have it made, entirely to its generosity. Interpreting Hester Prynne's deportment as an appeal of this nature, society was inclined to show its former victim a more benign countenance than she cared to be favored with, or, perchance, than she deserved.

The rulers, and the wise and learned men of the community, were longer in acknowledging the influence of Hester's good qualities than the people. The prejudices which they shared in common with the latter were fortified in themselves by an iron framework of reasoning, that made it a far tougher labor to expel them. Day by day, nevertheless, their sour and rigid wrinkles were relaxing into something which, in the due course of years, might grow to be an expression of almost benevolence. Thus it was with the men of rank, on whom their eminent position imposed the guardianship of the public morals. Individuals in private life, meanwhile, had quite forgiven Hester Prynne for her frailty; nay, more, they had begun to look upon the scarlet letter as the token, not of that one sin, for which she had borne so long and dreary a penance, but of her many good deeds since. "Do you see that woman with the embroidered badge?" they would say to strangers. "It is our Hester, — the town's own Hester, — who is so kind to the poor, so helpful to the sick, so comfortable to the afflicted!" Then, it is true, the propensity of human nature to tell the very worst of itself, when embodied in the person of another, would constrain them to whisper the black scandal of bygone years. It was none the less a fact, however, that, in the eyes of the very men who spoke thus, the scarlet letter had the effect of the cross on a nun's bosom. It imparted to the wearer a kind of sacredness, which enabled her to walk securely amid all peril. Had she fallen among thieves, it would have kept her safe. It was reported, and believed by many, that an Indian had drawn his arrow against the badge, and that the missile struck it, but fell harmless to the ground.

The effect of the symbol — or rather, of the position in respect to society that was indicated by it — on the mind of Hester Prynne herself, was powerful and peculiar. All the light and graceful foliage of her character had been withered up by this red-hot brand, and had long ago fallen away, leaving a bare and harsh outline, which might have been repulsive, had she possessed friends or companions to be repelled by it. Even the attractiveness of her person had undergone a similar change. It might be partly owing to the studied austerity of her dress, and partly to the lack of demonstration in her manners. It was a sad transformation, too, that her rich and luxuriant hair had either been cut off, or was so completely hidden by a cap, that not a shining lock of it ever once gushed into the sunshine. It was due in part to all these causes, but still more to something else, that there seemed to be no longer any thing in Hester's face for Love to dwell upon; nothing in Hester's form, though majestic and statue-like, that Passion would ever dream of clasping in its embrace; nothing in Hester's bosom, to make it ever again the pillow of Affection. Some attribute had departed from her, the permanence of which had been essential to keep her a woman. Such is frequently the fate, and such the stern development, of the feminine character and person, when the woman has encountered, and lived through, an experience of peculiar severity. If she be all tenderness, she will die. If she survive, the tenderness will either be crushed out of her, or — and the outward semblance is the same — crushed so deeply into her heart that it can never show itself more. The latter is perhaps the truest theory. She who has once been woman, and ceased to be so, might at any moment become a woman again, if there were only the magic touch to effect the transfiguration. We shall see whether Hester Prynne were ever afterwards so touched, and so transfigured.

Much of the marble coldness of Hester's impression was to be attributed to the circumstance that her life had turned, in a great measure, from passion and feeling, to thought. Standing alone in the world, — alone, as to any dependence on society, and with little Pearl to be guided and protected, — alone, and hopeless of retrieving her position, even had she not scorned to consider it desirable, — she cast away the fragments of a broken chain. The world's law was no law for her mind. It was an age in which the human intellect, newly emancipated, had taken a more active and a wider range than for many centuries before. Men of the sword had overthrown nobles and kings. Men bolder than these had overthrown and rearranged — not actually, but within the sphere of theory, which was their most real abode — the whole system of ancient prejudice, wherewith was linked much of ancient principle. Hester Prynne imbibed this spirit. She assumed a freedom of speculation, then common enough on the other side of the Atlantic, but which our forefathers, had they known of it, would have held to be a deadlier crime than that stigmatized by the scarlet letter. In her lonesome cottage, by the sea-shore, thoughts visited her, such as dared to enter no other dwelling in New England; shadowy guests, that would have been as perilous as demons to their entertainer, could they have been seen so much as knocking at her door.

It is remarkable, that persons who speculate the most boldly often conform with the most perfect quietude to the external regulations of society. The thought suffices them, without investing itself in the flesh and blood of action. So it seemed to be with Hester. Yet, had little Pearl never come to her from the spiritual world, it might have been far otherwise. Then, she might have come down to us in history, hand in hand with Ann Hutchinson, as the foundress of a religious sect. She might, in one of her phases, have been a prophetess. She might, and not improbably would, have suffered death from the stern tribunals of the period, for attempting to undermine the foundations of the Puritan establishment. But, in the education of her child, the mother's enthusiasm of thought had something to wreak itself upon. Providence, in the person of this little girl, had assigned to Hester's charge the germ and blossom of womanhood, to be cherished and developed amid a host of difficulties. Every thing was against her. The world was hostile. The child's own nature had something wrong in it, which continually betokened that she had been born amiss, — the effluence of her mother's lawless passion, — and often impelled Hester to ask, in bitterness of heart, whether it were for ill or good that the poor little creature had been born at all.

Indeed, the same dark question often rose into her mind, with reference to the whole race of womanhood. Was existence worth accepting, even to the happiest among them? As concerned her own individual existence, she had long ago decided in the negative, and dismissed the point as settled. A tendency to speculation, though it may keep woman quiet, as it does man, yet makes her sad. She discerns, it may be, such a hopeless task before her. As a first step, the whole system of society is to be torn down, and built up anew. Then, the very nature of the opposite sex, or its long hereditary habit, which has become like nature, is to be essentially modified, before woman can be allowed to assume what seems a fair and suitable position. Finally, all other difficulties being obviated, woman cannot take advantage of these preliminary reforms, until she herself shall have undergone a still mightier change; in which, perhaps, the ethereal essence, wherein she has her truest life, will be found to have evaporated. A woman never overcomes these problems by any exercise of thought. They are not to be solved, or only in one way. If her heart chance to come uppermost, they vanish. Thus, Hester Prynne, whose heart had lost its regular and healthy throb, wandered without a clew in the dark labyrinth of mind; now turned aside by an insurmountable precipice; now starting back from a deep chasm. There was wild and ghastly scenery all around her, and a home and comfort nowhere. At times, a fearful doubt strove to possess her soul, whether it were not better to send Pearl at once to heaven, and go herself to such futurity as Eternal Justice should provide.

The scarlet letter had not done its office.

Now, however, her interview with the Reverend Mr. Dimmesdale, on the night of his vigil, had given her a new theme of reflection, and held up to her an object that appeared worthy of any exertion and sacrifice for its attainment. She had witnessed the intense misery beneath which the minister struggled, or, to speak more accurately, had ceased to struggle. She saw that he stood on the verge of lunacy, if he had not already stepped across it. It was impossible to doubt, that, whatever painful efficacy there might be in the secret sting of remorse, a deadlier venom had been infused into it by the hand that proffered relief. A secret enemy had been continually by his side, under the semblance of a friend and helper, and had availed himself of the opportunities thus afforded for tampering with the delicate springs of Mr. Dimmesdale's nature. Hester could not but ask herself, whether there had not originally been a defect of truth, courage, and loyalty, on her own part, in allowing the minister to be thrown into a position where so much evil was to be foreboded, and nothing auspicious to be hoped. Her only justification lay in the fact, that she had been able to discern no method of rescuing him from a blacker ruin than had overwhelmed herself, except by acquiescing in Roger Chillingworth's scheme of disguise. Under that impulse, she had made her choice, and had chosen, as it now appeared, the more wretched alternative of the two. She determined to redeem her error, so far as it might yet be possible. Strengthened by years of hard and solemn trial, she felt herself no longer so inadequate to cope with Roger Chillingworth as on that night, abased by sin, and half maddened by the ignominy that was still new, when they had talked together in the prison-chamber. She had climbed her way, since then, to a higher point. The old man, on the other hand, had brought himself nearer to her level, or perhaps below it, by the revenge which he had stooped for.

In fine, Hester Prynne resolved to meet her former husband, and do what might be in her power for the rescue of the victim on whom he had so evidently set his gripe. The occasion was not long to seek. One afternoon, walking with Pearl in a retired part of the peninsula, she beheld the old physician, with a basket on one arm, and a staff in the other hand, stooping along the ground, in quest of roots and herbs to concoct his medicines withal.

XIV. Hester and the Physician

Hester bade little Pearl run down to the margin of the water, and play with the shells and tangled sea-weed, until she should have talked awhile with yonder gatherer of herbs. So the child flew away like a bird, and, making bare her small white feet, went pattering along the moist margin of the sea. Here and there, she came to a full stop, and peeped curiously into a pool, left by the retiring tide as a mirror for Pearl to see her face in. Forth peeped at her, out of the pool, with dark, glistening curls around her head, and an elf-smile in her eyes, the image of a little maid, whom Pearl, having no other playmate, invited to take her hand and run a race with her. But the visionary little maid, on her part, beckoned likewise, as if to say, — "This is a better place! Come thou into the pool!" And Pearl, stepping in, mid-leg deep, beheld her own white feet at the bottom; while, out of a still lower depth, came the gleam of a kind of fragmentary smile, floating to and fro in the agitated water.

Meanwhile, her mother had accosted the physician.

"I would speak a word with you," said she, — "a word that concerns us much."

"Aha! And is it Mistress Hester that has a word for old Roger Chillingworth?" answered he, raising himself from his stooping posture. "With all my heart! Why, Mistress, I hear good tidings of you on all hands! No longer ago than yester-eve, a magistrate, a wise and godly man, was discoursing of your affairs, Mistress Hester, and whispered me that there had been question concerning you in the council. It was debated whether or no, with safety to the common weal, yonder scarlet letter might be taken off your bosom. On my life, Hester, I made my entreaty to the worshipful magistrate that it might be done forthwith!"

"It lies not in the pleasure of the magistrates to take off this badge," calmly replied Hester. "Were I worthy to be quit of it, it would fall away of its own nature, or be transformed into something that should speak a different purport."

"Nay, then, wear it, if it suit you better," rejoined he. "A woman must needs follow her own fancy, touching the adornment of her person. The letter is gayly embroidered, and shows right bravely on your bosom!"

All this while, Hester had been looking steadily at the old man, and was shocked, as well as wonder-smitten, to discern what a change had been wrought upon him within the past seven years. It was not so much that he had grown older; for though the traces of advancing life were visible, he bore his age well, and seemed to retain a wiry vigor and alertness. But the former aspect of an intellectual and studious man, calm and quiet, which was what she best remembered in him, had altogether vanished, and been succeeded by an eager, searching, almost fierce, yet carefully guarded look. It seemed to be his wish and purpose to mask this expression with a smile; but the latter played him false, and flickered over his visage so derisively, that the spectator could see his blackness all the better for it. Ever and anon, too, there came a glare of red light out of his eyes; as if the old man's soul were on fire, and kept on smouldering duskily within his breast, until, by some casual puff of passion, it was blown into a momentary flame. This he repressed as speedily as possible, and strove to look as if nothing of the kind had happened.

In a word, old Roger Chillingworth was a striking evidence of man's faculty of transforming himself into a devil, if he will only, for a reasonable space of time, undertake a devil's office. This unhappy person had effected such a transformation by devoting himself, for seven years, to the constant analysis of a heart full of torture, and deriving his enjoyment thence, and adding fuel to those fiery tortures which he analyzed and gloated over.

The scarlet letter burned on Hester Prynne's bosom. Here was another ruin, the responsibility of which came partly home to her.

"What see you in my face," asked the physician, "that you look at it so earnestly?"

"Something that would make me weep, if there were any tears bitter enough for it," answered she. "But let it pass! It is of yonder miserable man that I would speak."

"And what of him?" cried Roger Chillingworth eagerly, as if he loved the topic, and were glad of an opportunity to discuss it with the only person of whom he could make a confidant. "Not to hide the truth, Mistress Hester, my thoughts happen just now to be busy with the gentleman. So speak freely; and I will make an answer."

"When we last spake together," said Hester, "now seven years ago, it was your pleasure to extort a promise of secrecy, as touching the former relation betwixt yourself and me. As the life and good fame of yonder man were in your hands, there seemed no choice to me, save to be silent, in accordance with your behest. Yet it was not without heavy misgivings that I thus bound myself; for, having cast off all duty towards other human beings, there remained a duty towards him; and something whispered me that I was betraying it, in pledging myself to keep your counsel. Since that day, no man is so near to him as you. You tread behind his every footstep. You are beside him, sleeping and waking. You search his thoughts. You burrow and rankle in his heart! Your clutch is on his life, and you cause him to die daily a living death; and still he knows you not. In permitting this, I have surely acted a false part by the only man to whom the power was left me to be true!"

"What choice had you?" asked Roger Chillingworth. "My finger, pointed at this man, would have hurled him from his pulpit into a dungeon, — thence, peradventure, to the gallows!"

"It had been better so!" said Hester Prynne.

"What evil have I done the man?" asked Roger Chillingworth again. "I tell thee, Hester Prynne, the richest fee that ever physician earned from monarch could not have bought such care as I have wasted on this miserable priest! But for my aid, his life would have burned away in torments, within the first two years after the perpetration of his crime and thine. For, Hester, his spirit lacked the strength that could have borne up, as thine has, beneath a burden like thy scarlet letter. O, I could reveal a goodly secret! But enough! What art can do, I have exhausted on him. That he now breathes, and creeps about on earth, is owing all to me!"

"Better he had died at once!" said Hester Prynne.

"Yea, woman, thou sayest truly!" cried old Roger Chillingworth, letting the lurid fire of his heart blaze out before her eyes. "Better had he died at once! Never did mortal suffer what this man has suffered. And all, all, in the sight of his worst enemy! He has been conscious of me. He has felt an influence dwelling always upon him like a curse. He knew, by some spiritual sense, — for the Creator never made another being so sensitive as this, — he knew that no friendly hand was pulling at his heart-strings, and that an eye was looking curiously into him, which sought only evil, and found it. But he knew not that the eye and hand were mine! With the superstition common to his brotherhood, he fancied himself given over to a fiend, to be tortured with frightful dreams, and desperate thoughts, the sting of remorse, and despair of pardon; as a foretaste of what awaits him beyond the grave. But it was the constant shadow of my presence! — the closest propinquity of the man whom he had most vilely wronged! — and who had grown to exist only by this perpetual poison of the direst revenge! Yea, indeed! — he did not err! — there was a fiend at his elbow! A mortal man, with once a human heart, has become a fiend for his especial torment!"

The unfortunate physician, while uttering these words, lifted his hands with a look of horror, as if he had beheld some frightful shape, which he could not recognize, usurping the place of his own image in a glass. It was one of those moments — which sometimes occur only at the interval of years — when a man's moral aspect is faithfully revealed to his mind's eye. Not improbably, he had never before viewed himself as he did now.

"Hast thou not tortured him enough?" said Hester, noticing the old man's look. "Has he not paid thee all?"

"No! — no! — He has but increased the debt!" answered the physician; and, as he proceeded, his manner lost its fiercer characteristics, and subsided into the gloom. "Dost thou remember me, Hester, as I was nine years agone? Even then, I was in the autumn of my days, nor was it the early autumn. But all my life had been made up of earnest, studious, thoughtful, quiet years, bestowed faithfully for the increase of mine own knowledge, and faithfully, too, though this latter object was but casual to the other, — faithfully for the advancement of human welfare. No life had been more peaceful and innocent than mine; few lives so rich with benefits conferred. Dost thou remember me? Was I not, though you might deem me cold, nevertheless a man thoughtful for others, craving little for himself, — kind, true, just, and of constant, if not warm affections? Was I not all this?"

"All this, and more," said Hester.

"And what am I now?" demanded he, looking into her face, and permitting the whole evil within him to be written on his features. "I have already told thee what I am! A fiend! Who made me so?"

"It was myself!" cried Hester, shuddering. "It was I, not less than he. Why hast thou not avenged thyself on me?"

"I have left thee to the scarlet letter," replied Roger Chillingworth. "If that have not avenged me, I can do no more!"

He laid his finger on it, with a smile.

"It has avenged thee!" answered Hester Prynne.

"I judged no less," said the physician. "And now, what wouldst thou with me touching this man?"

"I must reveal the secret," answered Hester, firmly. "He must discern thee in thy true character. What may be the result, I know not. But this long debt of confidence, due from me to him, whose bane and ruin I have been, shall at length be paid. So far as concerns the overthrow or preservation of his fair fame and his earthly state, and perchance his life, he is in thy hands. Nor do I, — whom the scarlet letter has disciplined to truth, though it be the truth of red-hot iron, entering into the soul, — nor do I perceive such advantage in his living any longer a life of ghastly emptiness, that I shall stoop to implore thy mercy. Do with him as thou wilt! There is no good for him, — no good for me, — no good for thee! There is no good for little Pearl! There is no path to guide us out of this dismal maze!"

"Woman, I could wellnigh pity thee!" said Roger Chillingworth, unable to restrain a thrill of admiration too; for there was a quality almost majestic in the despair which she expressed. "Thou hadst great elements. Peradventure, hadst thou met earlier with a better love than mine, this evil had not been. I pity thee, for the good that has been wasted in thy nature!"

"And I thee," answered Hester Prynne, "for the hatred that has transformed a wise and just man to a fiend! Wilt thou yet purge it out of thee, and be once more human? If not for his sake, then doubly for thine own! Forgive, and leave his further retribution to the Power that claims it! I said, but now, that there could be no good event for him, or thee, or me, who are here wandering together in this gloomy maze of evil, and stumbling, at every step, over the guilt wherewith we have strewn our path. It is not so! There might be good for thee, and thee alone, since thou hast been deeply wronged, and hast it at thy will to pardon. Wilt thou give up that only privilege? Wilt thou reject that priceless benefit?"

"Peace, Hester, peace!" replied the old man, with gloomy sternness. "It is not granted me to pardon. I have no such power as thou tellest me of. My old faith, long forgotten, comes back to me, and explains all that we do, and all we suffer. By thy first step awry, thou didst plant the germ of evil; but, since that moment, it has all been a dark necessity. Ye that have wronged me are not sinful, save in a kind of typical illusion; neither am I fiend-like, who have snatched a fiend's office from his hands. It is our fate. Let the black flower blossom as it may! Now go thy ways, and deal as thou wilt with yonder man."

He waved his hand, and betook himself again to his employment of gathering herbs.

XV. Hester and Pearl

So Roger Chillingworth — a deformed old figure, with a face that haunted men's memories longer than they liked — took leave of Hester Prynne, and went stooping away along the earth. He gathered here and there an herb, or grubbed up a root, and put it into the basket on his arm. His gray beard almost touched the ground, as he crept onward. Hester gazed after him a little while, looking with a half-fantastic curiosity to see whether the tender grass of early spring would not be blighted beneath him, and show the wavering track of his footsteps, sere and brown, across its cheerful verdure. She wondered what sort of herbs they were, which the old man was so sedulous to gather. Would not the earth, quickened to an evil purpose by the sympathy of his eye, greet him with poisonous shrubs, of species hitherto unknown, that would start up under his fingers? Or might it suffice him, that every wholesome growth should be converted into something deleterious and malignant at his touch? Did the sun, which shone so brightly everywhere else, really fall upon him? Or was there, as it rather seemed, a circle of ominous shadow moving along with his deformity, whichever way he turned himself? And whither was he now going? Would he not suddenly sink into the earth, leaving a barren and blasted spot, where, in due course of time, would be seen deadly nightshade, dogwood, henbane, and whatever else of vegetable wickedness the climate could produce, all flourishing with hideous luxuriance? Or would he spread bat's wings and flee away, looking so much the uglier, the higher he rose towards heaven?

"Be it sin or no," said Hester Prynne bitterly, as she still gazed after him, "I hate the man!"

She upbraided herself for the sentiment, but could not overcome or lessen it. Attempting to do so, she thought of those long-past days, in a distant land, when he used to emerge at eventide from the seclusion of his study, and sit down in the fire-light of their home, and in the light of her nuptial smile. He needed to bask himself in that smile, he said, in order that the chill of so many lonely hours among his books might be taken off the scholar's heart. Such scenes had once appeared not otherwise than happy, but now, as viewed through the dismal medium of her subsequent life, they classed themselves among her ugliest remembrances. She marvelled how such scenes could have been! She marvelled how she could ever have been wrought upon to marry him! She deemed it her crime most to be repented of, that she had ever endured, and reciprocated, the lukewarm grasp of his hand, and had suffered the smile of her lips and eyes to mingle and melt into his own. And it seemed a fouler offence committed by Roger Chillingworth, than any which had since been done him, that, in the time when her heart knew no better, he had persuaded her to fancy herself happy by his side.

"Yes, I hate him!" repeated Hester, more bitterly than before. "He betrayed me! He has done me worse wrong than I did him!"

Let men tremble to win the hand of woman, unless they win along with it the utmost passion of her heart! Else it may be their miserable fortune, as it was Roger Chillingworth's, when some mightier touch than their own may have awakened all her sensibilities, to be reproached even for the calm content, the marble image of happiness, which they will have imposed upon her as the warm reality. But Hester ought long ago to have done with this injustice. What did it betoken? Had seven long years, under the torture of the scarlet letter, inflicted so much of misery, and wrought out no repentance?

The emotions of that brief space, while she stood gazing after the crooked figure of old Roger Chillingworth, threw a dark light on Hester's state of mind, revealing much that she might not otherwise have acknowledged to herself.

He being gone, she summoned back her child.

"Pearl! Little Pearl! Where are you?"

Pearl, whose activity of spirit never flagged, had been at no loss for amusement while her mother talked with the old gatherer of herbs. At first, as already told, she had flirted fancifully with her own image in a pool of water, beckoning the phantom forth, and — as it declined to venture — seeking a passage for herself into its sphere of impalpable earth and unattainable sky. Soon finding, however, that either she or the image was unreal, she turned elsewhere for better pastime. She made little boats out of birch-bark, and freighted them with snail-shells, and sent out more ventures on the mighty deep than any merchant in New England; but the larger part of them foundered near the shore. She seized a live horse-shoe by the tail, and made prize of several five-fingers, and laid out a jelly-fish to melt in the warm sun. Then she took up the white foam, that streaked the line of the advancing tide, and threw it upon the breeze, scampering after it with winged footsteps, to catch the great snow-flakes ere they fell. Perceiving a flock of beach-birds, that fed and fluttered along the shore, the naughty child picked up her apron full of pebbles, and, creeping from rock to rock after these small sea-fowl, displayed remarkable dexterity in pelting them. One little gray bird, with a white breast, Pearl was almost sure, had been hit by a pebble, and fluttered away with a broken wing. But then the elf-child sighed, and gave up her sport; because it grieved her to have done harm to a little being that was as wild as the sea-breeze, or as wild as Pearl herself.

Her final employment was to gather sea-weed, of various kinds, and make herself a scarf, or mantle, and a head-dress, and thus assume the aspect of a little mermaid. She inherited her mother's gift for devising drapery and costume. As the last touch to her mermaid's garb, Pearl took some eel-grass, and imitated, as best she could, on her own bosom, the decoration with which she was so familiar on her mother's. A letter, — the letter A, — but freshly green, instead of scarlet! The child bent her chin upon her breast, and contemplated this device with strange interest; even as if the only thing for which she had been sent into the world was to make out its hidden import.

"I wonder if mother will ask me what it means!" thought Pearl.

Just then, she heard her mother's voice, and, flitting along as lightly as one of the little sea-birds, appeared before Hester Prynne, dancing, laughing, and pointing her finger to the ornament upon her bosom.

"My little Pearl," said Hester, after a moment's silence, "the green letter, and on thy childish bosom, has no purport. But dost thou know, my child, what this letter means which thy mother is doomed to wear?"

"Yes, mother," said the child. "It is the great letter A. Thou hast taught it me in the horn-book."

Hester looked steadily into her little face; but, though there was that singular expression which she had so often remarked in her black eyes, she could not satisfy herself whether Pearl really attached any meaning to the symbol. She felt a morbid desire to ascertain the point.

"Dost thou know, child, wherefore thy mother wears this letter?"

"Truly do I!" answered Pearl, looking brightly into her mother's face. "It is for the same reason that the minister keeps his hand over his heart!"

"And what reason is that?" asked Hester, half smiling at the absurd incongruity of the child's observation; but, on second thoughts, turning pale. "What has the letter to do with any heart, save mine?"

"Nay, mother, I have told all I know," said Pearl, more seriously than she was wont to speak. "Ask yonder old man whom thou hast been talking with! It may be he can tell. But in good earnest now, mother dear, what does this scarlet letter mean? — and why dost thou wear it on thy bosom? — and why does the minister keep his hand over his heart?"

She took her mother's hand in both her own, and gazed into her eyes with an earnestness that was seldom seen in her wild and capricious character. The thought occurred to Hester, that the child might really be seeking to approach her with childlike confidence, and doing what she could, and as intelligently as she knew how, to establish a meeting-point of sympathy. It showed Pearl in an unwonted aspect. Heretofore, the mother, while loving her child with the intensity of a sole affection, had schooled herself to hope for little other return than the waywardness of an April breeze; which spends its time in airy sport, and has its gusts of inexplicable passion, and is petulant in its best of moods, and chills oftener than caresses you, when you take it to your bosom; in requital of which misdemeanours, it will sometimes, of its own vague purpose, kiss your cheek with a kind of doubtful tenderness, and play gently with your hair, and then begone about its other idle business, leaving a dreamy pleasure at your heart. And this, moreover, was a mother's estimate of the child's disposition. Any other observer might have seen few but unamiable traits, and have given them a far darker coloring. But now the idea came strongly into Hester's mind, that Pearl, with her remarkable precocity and acuteness, might already have approached the age when she could be made a friend, and intrusted with as much of her mother's sorrows as could be imparted, without irreverence either to the parent or the child. In the little chaos of Pearl's character, there might be seen emerging — and could have been, from the very first — the stedfast principles of an unflinching courage, — an uncontrollable will, — a sturdy pride, which might be disciplined into self-respect, — and a bitter scorn of many things, which, when examined, might be found to have the taint of falsehood in them. She possessed affections, too, though hitherto acrid and disagreeable, as are the richest flavors of unripe fruit. With all these sterling attributes, thought Hester, the evil which she inherited from her mother must be great indeed, if a noble woman do not grow out of this elfish child.

Pearl's inevitable tendency to hover about the enigma of the scarlet letter seemed an innate quality of her being. From the earliest epoch of her conscious life, she had entered upon this as her appointed mission. Hester had often fancied that Providence had a design of justice and retribution, in endowing the child with this marked propensity; but never, until now, had she bethought herself to ask, whether, linked with that design, there might not likewise be a purpose of mercy and beneficence. If little Pearl were entertained with faith and trust, as a spirit-messenger no less than an earthly child, might it not be her errand to soothe away the sorrow that lay cold in her mother's heart, and converted it into a tomb? — and to help her to overcome the passion, once so wild, and even yet neither dead nor asleep, but only imprisoned within the same tomb-like heart?

Such were some of the thoughts that now stirred in Hester's mind, with as much vivacity of impression as if they had actually been whispered into her ear. And there was little Pearl, all this while, holding her mother's hand in both her own, and turning her face upward, while she put these searching questions, once, and again, and still a third time.

"What does the letter mean, mother? — and why dost thou wear it? — and why does the minister keep his hand over his heart?"

"What shall I say?" thought Hester to herself. — "No! If this be the price of the child's sympathy, I cannot pay it!"

Then she spoke aloud.

"Silly Pearl," said she, "what questions are these? There are many things in this world that a child must not ask about. What know I of the minister's heart? And as for the scarlet letter, I wear it for the sake of its gold thread!"

In all the seven bygone years, Hester Prynne had never before been false to the symbol on her bosom. It may be that it was the talisman of a stern and severe, but yet a guardian spirit, who now forsook her; as recognizing that, in spite of his strict watch over her heart, some new evil had crept into it, or some old one had never been expelled. As for little Pearl, the earnestness soon passed out of her face.

But the child did not see fit to let the matter drop. Two or three times, as her mother and she went homeward, and as often at supper-time, and while Hester was putting her to bed, and once after she seemed to be fairly asleep, Pearl looked up, with mischief gleaming in her black eyes.

"Mother," said she, "what does the scarlet letter mean?"

And the next morning, the first indication the child gave of being awake was by popping up her head from the pillow, and making that other inquiry, which she had so unaccountably connected with her investigations about the scarlet letter: —

"Mother! — Mother! — Why does the minister keep his hand over his heart?"

"Hold thy tongue, naughty child!" answered her mother, with an asperity that she had never permitted to herself before. "Do not tease me; else I shall shut thee into the dark closet!"

XVI. A Forest Walk

Hester Prynne remained constant in her resolve to make known to Mr. Dimmesdale, at whatever risk of present pain or ulterior consequences, the true character of the man who had crept into his intimacy. For several days, however, she vainly sought an opportunity of addressing him in some of the meditative walks which she knew him to be in the habit of taking, along the shores of the peninsula, or on the wooded hills of the neighbouring country. There would have been no scandal, indeed, nor peril to the holy whiteness of the clergyman's good fame, had she visited him in his own study; where many a penitent, ere now, had confessed sins of perhaps as deep a dye as the one betokened by the scarlet letter. But, partly that she dreaded the secret or undisguised interference of old Roger Chillingworth, and partly that her conscious heart imputed suspicion where none could have been felt, and partly that both the minister and she would need the whole wide world to breathe in, while they talked together, — for all these reasons, Hester never thought of meeting him in any narrower privacy than beneath the open sky.

At last, while attending in a sick-chamber, whither the Reverend Mr. Dimmesdale had been summoned to make a prayer, she learnt that he had gone, the day before, to visit the Apostle Eliot, among his Indian converts. He would probably return, by a certain hour, in the afternoon of the morrow. Betimes, therefore, the next day, Hester took little Pearl, — who was necessarily the companion of all her mother's expeditions, however inconvenient her presence, — and set forth.

The road, after the two wayfarers had crossed from the peninsula to the mainland, was no other than a footpath. It straggled onward into the mystery of the primeval forest. This hemmed it in so narrowly, and stood so black and dense on either side, and disclosed such imperfect glimpses of the sky above, that, to Hester's mind, it imaged not amiss the moral wilderness in which she had so long been wandering. The day was chill and sombre. Overhead was a gray expanse of cloud, slightly stirred, however, by a breeze; so that a gleam of flickering sunshine might now and then be seen at its solitary play along the path. This flitting cheerfulness was always at the farther extremity of some long vista through the forest. The sportive sunlight — feebly sportive, at best, in the predominant pensiveness of the day and scene — withdrew itself as they came nigh, and left the spots where it had danced the drearier, because they had hoped to find them bright.

"Mother," said little Pearl, "the sunshine does not love you. It runs away and hides itself, because it is afraid of something on your bosom. Now, see! There it is, playing, a good way off. Stand you here, and let me run and catch it. I am but a child. It will not flee from me; for I wear nothing on my bosom yet!"

"Nor ever will, my child, I hope," said Hester.

"And why not, mother?" asked Pearl, stopping short, just at the beginning of her race. "Will not it come of its own accord, when I am a woman grown?"

"Run away, child," answered her mother, "and catch the sunshine! It will soon be gone."

Pearl set forth, at a great pace, and, as Hester smiled to perceive, did actually catch the sunshine, and stood laughing in the midst of it, all brightened by its splendor, and scintillating with the vivacity excited by rapid motion. The light lingered about the lonely child, as if glad of such a playmate, until her mother had drawn almost nigh enough to step into the magic circle too.

"It will go now!" said Pearl, shaking her head.

"See!" answered Hester, smiling. "Now I can stretch out my hand, and grasp some of it."

As she attempted to do so, the sunshine vanished; or, to judge from the bright expression that was dancing on Pearl's features, her mother could have fancied that the child had absorbed it into herself, and would give it forth again, with a gleam about her path, as they should plunge into some gloomier shade. There was no other attribute that so much impressed her with a sense of new and untransmitted vigor in Pearl's nature, as this never-failing vivacity of spirits; she had not the disease of sadness, which almost all children, in these latter days, inherit, with the scrofula, from the troubles of their ancestors. Perhaps this too was a disease, and but the reflex of the wild energy with which Hester had fought against her sorrows, before Pearl's birth. It was certainly a doubtful charm, imparting a hard, metallic lustre to the child's character. She wanted — what some people want throughout life — a grief that should deeply touch her, and thus humanize and make her capable of sympathy. But there was time enough yet for little Pearl!

"Come, my child!" said Hester, looking about her, from the spot where Pearl had stood still in the sunshine. "We will sit down a little way within the wood, and rest ourselves."

"I am not aweary, mother," replied the little girl. "But you may sit down, if you will tell me a story meanwhile."

"A story, child!" said Hester. "And about what?"

"O, a story about the Black Man!" answered Pearl, taking hold of her mother's gown, and looking up, half earnestly, half mischievously, into her face. "How he haunts this forest, and carries a book with him, — a big, heavy book, with iron clasps; and how this ugly Black Man offers his book and an iron pen to every body that meets him here among the trees; and they are to write their names with their own blood. And then he sets his mark on their bosoms! Didst thou ever meet the Black Man, mother?"

"And who told you this story, Pearl?" asked her mother, recognizing a common superstition of the period.

"It was the old dame in the chimney-corner, at the house where you watched last night," said the child. "But she fancied me asleep while she was talking of it. She said that a thousand and a thousand people had met him here, and had written in his book, and have his mark on them. And that ugly-tempered lady, old Mistress Hibbins, was one. And, mother, the old dame said that this scarlet letter was the Black Man's mark on thee, and that it glows like a red flame when thou meetest him at midnight, here in the dark wood. Is it true, mother? And dost thou go to meet him in the night-time?"

"Didst thou ever awake, and find thy mother gone?" asked Hester.

"Not that I remember," said the child. "If thou fearest to leave me in our cottage, thou mightest take me along with thee. I would very gladly go! But, mother, tell me now! Is there such a Black Man? And didst thou ever meet him? And is this his mark?"

"Wilt thou let me be at peace, if I once tell thee?" asked her mother.

"Yes, if thou tellest me all," answered Pearl.

"Once in my life I met the Black Man!" said her mother. "This scarlet letter is his mark!"

Thus conversing, they entered sufficiently deep into the wood to secure themselves from the observation of any casual passenger along the forest-track. Here they sat down on a luxuriant heap of moss; which, at some epoch of the preceding century, had been a gigantic pine, with its roots and trunk in the darksome shade, and its head aloft in the upper atmosphere. It was a little dell where they had seated themselves, with a leaf-strewn bank rising gently on either side, and a brook flowing through the midst, over a bed of fallen and drowned leaves. The trees impending over it had flung down great branches, from time to time, which choked up the current, and compelled it to form eddies and black depths at some points; while, in its swifter and livelier passages, there appeared a channel-way of pebbles, and brown, sparkling sand. Letting the eyes follow along the course of the stream, they could catch the reflected light from its water, at some short distance within the forest, but soon lost all traces of it amid the bewilderment of tree-trunks and underbrush, and here and there a huge rock, covered over with gray lichens. All these giant trees and boulders of granite seemed intent on making a mystery of the course of this small brook; fearing, perhaps, that, with its never-ceasing loquacity, it should whisper tales out of the heart of the old forest whence it flowed, or mirror its revelations on the smooth surface of a pool. Continually, indeed, as it stole onward, the streamlet kept up a babble, kind, quiet, soothing, but melancholy, like the voice of a young child that was spending its infancy without playfulness, and knew not how to be merry among sad acquaintance and events of sombre hue.

"O brook! O foolish and tiresome little brook!" cried Pearl, after listening awhile to its talk. "Why art thou so sad? Pluck up a spirit, and do not be all the time sighing and murmuring!"

But the brook, in the course of its little lifetime among the forest-trees, had gone through so solemn an experience that it could not help talking about it, and seemed to have nothing else to say. Pearl resembled the brook, inasmuch as the current of her life gushed from a well-spring as mysterious, and had flowed through scenes shadowed as heavily with gloom. But, unlike the little stream, she danced and sparkled, and prattled airily along her course.

"What does this sad little brook say, mother?" inquired she.

"If thou hadst a sorrow of thine own, the brook might tell thee of it," answered her mother, "even as it is telling me of mine! But now, Pearl, I hear a footstep along the path, and the noise of one putting aside the branches. I would have thee betake thyself to play, and leave me to speak with him that comes yonder."

"Is it the Black Man?" asked Pearl.

"Wilt thou go and play, child?" repeated her mother. "But do not stray far into the wood. And take heed that thou come at my first call."

"Yes, mother," answered Pearl. "But, if it be the Black Man, wilt thou not let me stay a moment, and look at him, with his big book under his arm?"

"Go, silly child!" said her mother, impatiently. "It is no Black Man! Thou canst see him now through the trees. It is the minister!"

"And so it is!" said the child. "And, mother, he has his hand over his heart! Is it because, when the minister wrote his name in the book, the Black Man set his mark in that place? But why does he not wear it outside his bosom, as thou dost, mother?"

"Go now, child, and thou shalt tease me as thou wilt another time!" cried Hester Prynne. "But do not stray far. Keep where thou canst hear the babble of the brook."

The child went singing away, following up the current of the brook, and striving to mingle a more lightsome cadence with its melancholy voice. But the little stream would not be comforted, and still kept telling its unintelligible secret of some very mournful mystery that had happened — or making a prophetic lamentation about something that was yet to happen — within the verge of the dismal forest. So Pearl, who had enough of shadow in her own little life, chose to break off all acquaintance with this repining brook. She set herself, therefore, to gathering violets and wood-anemones, and some scarlet columbines that she found growing in the crevices of a high rock.

When her elf-child had departed, Hester Prynne made a step or two towards the track that led through the forest, but still remained under the deep shadow of the trees. She beheld the minister advancing along the path, entirely alone, and leaning on a staff which he had cut by the way-side. He looked haggard and feeble, and betrayed a nerveless despondency in his air, which had never so remarkably characterized him in his walks about the settlement, nor in any other situation where he deemed himself liable to notice. Here it was wofully visible, in this intense seclusion of the forest, which of itself would have been a heavy trial to the spirits. There was a listlessness in his gait; as if he saw no reason for taking one step farther, nor felt any desire to do so, but would have been glad, could he be glad of any thing, to fling himself down at the root of the nearest tree, and lie there passive for evermore. The leaves might bestrew him, and the soil gradually accumulate and form a little hillock over his frame, no matter whether there were life in it or no. Death was too definite an object to be wished for, or avoided.

To Hester's eye, the Reverend Mr. Dimmesdale exhibited no symptom of positive and vivacious suffering, except that, as little Pearl had remarked, he kept his hand over his heart.

XVII. The Pastor and His Parishioner

Slowly as the minister walked, he had almost gone by, before Hester Prynne could gather voice enough to attract his observation. At length, she succeeded.

"Arthur Dimmesdale!" she said, faintly at first; then louder, but hoarsely. "Arthur Dimmesdale!"

"Who speaks?" answered the minister.

Gathering himself quickly up, he stood more erect, like a man taken by surprise in a mood to which he was reluctant to have witnesses. Throwing his eyes anxiously in the direction of the voice, he indistinctly beheld a form under the trees, clad in garments so sombre, and so little relieved from the gray twilight into which the clouded sky and the heavy foliage had darkened the noontide, that he knew not whether it were a woman or a shadow. It may be, that his pathway through life was haunted thus, by a spectre that had stolen out from among his thoughts.

He made a step nigher, and discovered the scarlet letter.

"Hester! Hester Prynne!" said he. "Is it thou? Art thou in life?"

"Even so!" she answered. "In such life as has been mine these seven years past! And thou, Arthur Dimmesdale, dost thou yet live?"

It was no wonder that they thus questioned one another's actual and bodily existence, and even doubted of their own. So strangely did they meet, in the dim wood, that it was like the first encounter, in the world beyond the grave, of two spirits who had been intimately connected in their former life, but now stood coldly shuddering, in mutual dread; as not yet familiar with their state, nor wonted to the companionship of disembodied beings. Each a ghost, and awe-stricken at the other ghost! They were awe-stricken likewise at themselves; because the crisis flung back to them their consciousness, and revealed to each heart its history and experience, as life never does, except at such breathless epochs. The soul beheld its features in the mirror of the passing moment. It was with fear, and tremulously, and, as it were, by a slow, reluctant necessity, that Arthur Dimmesdale put forth his hand, chill as death, and touched the chill hand of Hester Prynne. The grasp, cold as it was, took away what was dreariest in the interview. They now felt themselves, at least, inhabitants of the same sphere.

Without a word more spoken, — neither he nor she assuming the guidance, but with an unexpressed consent, — they glided back into the shadow of the woods, whence Hester had emerged, and sat down on the heap of moss where she and Pearl had before been sitting. When they found voice to speak, it was, at first, only to utter remarks and inquiries such as any two acquaintance might have made, about the gloomy sky, the threatening storm, and, next, the health of each. Thus they went onward, not boldly, but step by step, into the themes that were brooding deepest in their hearts. So long estranged by fate and circumstances, they needed something slight and casual to run before, and throw open the doors of intercourse, so that their real thoughts might be led across the threshold.

After a while, the minister fixed his eyes on Hester Prynne's.

"Hester," said he, "hast thou found peace?"

She smiled drearily, looking down upon her bosom.

"Hast thou?" she asked.

"None! — nothing but despair!" he answered. "What else could I look for, being what I am, and leading such a life as mine? Were I an atheist, — a man devoid of conscience, — a wretch with coarse and brutal instincts, — I might have found peace, long ere now. Nay, I never should have lost it! But, as matters stand with my soul, whatever of good capacity there originally was in me, all of God's gifts that were the choicest have become the ministers of spiritual torment. Hester, I am most miserable!"

"The people reverence thee," said Hester. "And surely thou workest good among them! Doth this bring thee no comfort?"

"More misery, Hester! — only the more misery!" answered the

clergyman, with a bitter smile. "As concerns the good which I may appear to do, I have no faith in it. It must needs be a delusion. What can a ruined soul, like mine, effect towards the redemption of other souls? — or a polluted soul, towards their purification? And as for the people's reverence, would that it were turned to scorn and hatred! Canst thou deem it, Hester, a consolation, that I must stand up in my pulpit, and meet so many eyes turned upward to my face, as if the light of heaven were beaming from it! — must see my flock hungry for the truth, and listening to my words as if a tongue of Pentecost were speaking! — and then look inward, and discern the black reality of what they idolize? I have laughed, in bitterness and agony of heart, at the contrast between what I seem and what I am! And Satan laughs at it!"

"You wrong yourself in this," said Hester, gently. "You have deeply and sorely repented. Your sin is left behind you, in the days long past. Your present life is not less holy, in very truth, than it seems in people's eyes. Is there no reality in the penitence thus sealed and witnessed by good works? And wherefore should it not bring you peace?"

"No, Hester, no!" replied the clergyman. "There is no substance in it! It is cold and dead, and can do nothing for me! Of penance I have had enough! Of penitence there has been none! Else, I should long ago have thrown off these garments of mock holiness, and have shown myself to mankind as they will see me at the judgment-seat. Happy are you, Hester, that wear the scarlet letter openly upon your bosom! Mine burns in secret! Thou little knowest what a relief it is, after the torment of a seven years' cheat, to look into an eye that recognizes me for what I am! Had I one friend, — or were it my worst enemy! — to whom, when sickened with the praises of all other men, I could daily betake myself, and be known as the vilest of all sinners, methinks my soul might keep itself alive thereby. Even thus much of truth would save me! But, now, it is all falsehood! — all emptiness! — all death!"

Hester Prynne looked into his face, but hesitated to speak. Yet, uttering his long-restrained emotions so vehemently as he did, his words here offered her the very point of circumstances in which to interpose what she came to say. She conquered her fears, and spoke.

"Such a friend as thou hast even now wished for," said she, "with whom to weep over thy sin, thou hast in me, the partner of it!" — Again she hesitated, but brought out the words with an effort. — "Thou hast long had such an enemy, and dwellest with him under the same roof!"

The minister started to his feet, gasping for breath, and clutching at his heart as if he would have torn it out of his bosom.

"Ha! What sayest thou?" cried he. "An enemy! And under mine own roof! What mean you?"

Hester Prynne was now fully sensible of the deep injury for which she was responsible to this unhappy man, in permitting him to lie for so many years, or, indeed, for a single moment, at the mercy of one, whose purposes could not be other than malevolent. The very contiguity of his enemy, beneath whatever mask the latter might conceal himself, was enough to disturb the magnetic sphere of a being so sensitive as Arthur Dimmesdale. There had been a period when Hester was less alive to this consideration; or, perhaps, in the misanthropy of her own trouble, she left the minister to bear what she might picture to herself as a more tolerable doom. But of late, since the night of his vigil, all her sympathies towards him had been both softened and invigorated. She now read his heart more accurately. She doubted not, that the continual presence of Roger Chillingworth, — the secret poison of his malignity, infecting all the air about him, — and his authorized interference, as a physician, with the minister's physical and spiritual infirmities, — that these bad opportunities had been turned to a cruel purpose. By means of them, the sufferer's conscience had been kept in an irritated state, the tendency of which was, not to cure by wholesome pain, but to disorganize and corrupt his spiritual being. Its result, on earth, could hardly fail to be insanity, and hereafter, that eternal alienation from the Good and True, of which madness is perhaps the earthly type.

Such was the ruin to which she had brought the man, once, — nay, why should we not speak it? — still so passionately loved! Hester felt that the sacrifice of the clergyman's good name, and death itself, as she had already told Roger Chillingworth, would have been infinitely preferable to the alternative which she had taken upon herself to choose. And now, rather than have had this grievous wrong to confess, she would gladly have lain down on the forest-leaves, and died there, at Arthur Dimmesdale's feet.

"O Arthur," cried she, "forgive me! In all things else, I have striven to be true! Truth was the one virtue which I might have held fast, and did hold fast through all extremity; save when thy good, — thy life, — thy fame, — were put in question! Then I consented to a deception. But a lie is never good, even though death threaten on the other side! Dost thou not see what I would say? That old man! — the physician! — he whom they call Roger Chillingworth! — he was my husband!"

The minister looked at her, for an instant, with all that violence of passion, which — intermixed, in more shapes than one, with his higher, purer, softer qualities — was, in fact, the portion of him which the

Devil claimed, and through which he sought to win the rest. Never was there a blacker or a fiercer frown, than Hester now encountered. For the brief space that it lasted, it was a dark transfiguration. But his character had been so much enfeebled by suffering, that even its lower energies were incapable of more than a temporary struggle. He sank down on the ground, and buried his face in his hands.

"I might have known it!" murmured he. "I did know it! Was not the secret told me in the natural recoil of my heart, at the first sight of him, and as often as I have seen him since? Why did I not understand? O Hester Prynne, thou little, little knowest all the horror of this thing! And the shame! — the indelicacy! — the horrible ugliness of this exposure of a sick and guilty heart to the very eye that would gloat over it! Woman, woman, thou art accountable for this! I cannot forgive thee!"

"Thou shalt forgive me!" cried Hester, flinging herself on the fallen leaves beside him. "Let God punish! Thou shalt forgive!"

With sudden and desperate tenderness, she threw her arms around him, and pressed his head against her bosom; little caring though his cheek rested on the scarlet letter. He would have released himself, but strove in vain to do so. Hester would not set him free, lest he should look her sternly in the face. All the world had frowned on her, — for seven long years had it frowned upon this lonely woman, — and still she bore it all, nor ever once turned away her firm, sad eyes. Heaven, likewise, had frowned upon her, and she had not died. But the frown of this pale, weak, sinful, and sorrow-stricken man was what Hester could not bear, and live!

"Wilt thou yet forgive me?" she repeated, over and over again. "Wilt thou not frown? Wilt thou forgive?"

"I do forgive you, Hester," replied the minister, at length, with a deep utterance out of an abyss of sadness, but no anger. "I freely forgive you now. May God forgive us both! We are not, Hester, the worst sinners in the world. There is one worse than even the polluted priest! That old man's revenge has been blacker than my sin. He has violated, in cold blood, the sanctity of a human heart. Thou and I, Hester, never did so!"

"Never, never!" whispered she. "What we did had a consecration of its own. We felt it so! We said so to each other! Hast thou forgotten it?"

"Hush, Hester!" said Arthur Dimmesdale, rising from the ground. "No; I have not forgotten!"

They sat down again, side by side, and hand clasped in hand, on the mossy trunk of the fallen tree. Life had never brought them a gloomier hour; it was the point whither their pathway had so long been tending, and darkening ever, as it stole along; — and yet it inclosed a charm that made them linger upon it, and claim another, and another, and, after all, another moment. The forest was obscure around them, and creaked with a blast that was passing through it. The boughs were tossing heavily above their heads; while one solemn old tree groaned dolefully to another, as if telling the sad story of the pair that sat beneath, or constrained to forebode evil to come.

And yet they lingered. How dreary looked the forest-track that led backward to the settlement, where Hester Prynne must take up again the burden of her ignominy, and the minister the hollow mockery of his good name! So they lingered an instant longer. No golden light had ever been so precious as the gloom of this dark forest. Here, seen only by his eyes, the scarlet letter need not burn into the bosom of the fallen woman! Here, seen only by her eyes, Arthur Dimmesdale, false to God and man, might be, for one moment, true!

He started at a thought that suddenly occurred to him.

"Hester," cried he, "here is a new horror! Roger Chillingworth knows your purpose to reveal his true character. Will he continue, then, to keep our secret? What will now be the course of his revenge?"

"There is a strange secrecy in his nature," replied Hester, thoughtfully; "and it has grown upon him by the hidden practices of his revenge. I deem it not likely that he will betray the secret. He will doubtless seek other means of satiating his dark passion."

"And I! — how am I to live longer, breathing the same air with this deadly enemy?" exclaimed Arthur Dimmesdale, shrinking within himself, and pressing his hand nervously against his heart, — a gesture that had grown involuntary with him. "Think for me, Hester! Thou art strong. Resolve for me!"

"Thou must dwell no longer with this man," said Hester, slowly and firmly. "Thy heart must be no longer under his evil eye!"

"It were far worse than death!" replied the minister. "But how to avoid it? What choice remains to me? Shall I lie down again on these withered leaves, where I cast myself when thou didst tell me what he was? Must I sink down there, and die at once?"

"Alas, what a ruin has befallen thee!" said Hester, with the tears gushing into her eyes. "Wilt thou die for very weakness? There is no other cause!"

"The judgment of God is on me," answered the conscience-stricken priest. "It is too mighty for me to struggle with!"

"Heaven would show mercy," rejoined Hester, "hadst thou but the strength to take advantage of it."

"Be thou strong for me!" answered he. "Advise me what to do."

"Is the world then so narrow?" exclaimed Hester Prynne, fixing her deep eyes on the minister's, and instinctively exercising a magnetic power over a spirit so shattered and subdued, that it could hardly hold itself erect. "Doth the universe lie within the compass of yonder town, which only a little time ago was but a leaf-strewn desert, as lonely as this around us? Whither leads yonder forest-track? Backward to the settlement, thou sayest! Yes; but onward, too! Deeper it goes, and deeper, into the wilderness, less plainly to be seen at every step; until, some few miles hence, the yellow leaves will show no vestige of the white man's tread. There thou art free! So brief a journey would bring thee from a world where thou hast been most wretched, to one where thou mayest still be happy! Is there not shade enough in all this boundless forest to hide thy heart from the gaze of Roger Chillingworth?"

"Yes, Hester; but only under the fallen leaves!" replied the minister, with a sad smile.

"Then there is the broad pathway of the sea!" continued Hester. "It brought thee hither. If thou so choose, it will bear thee back again. In our native land, whether in some remote rural village or in vast London, — or, surely, in Germany, in France, in pleasant Italy, — thou wouldst be beyond his power and knowledge! And what hast thou to do with all these iron men, and their opinions? They have kept thy better part in bondage too long already!"

"It cannot be!" answered the minister, listening as if he were called upon to realize a dream. "I am powerless to go. Wretched and sinful as I am, I have had no other thought than to drag on my earthly existence in the sphere where Providence hath placed me. Lost as my own soul is, I would still do what I may for other human souls! I dare not quit my post, though an unfaithful sentinel, whose sure reward is death and dishonor, when his dreary watch shall come to an end!"

"Thou art crushed under this seven years' weight of misery," replied Hester, fervently resolved to buoy him up with her own energy. "But thou shalt leave it all behind thee! It shall not cumber thy steps, as thou treadest along the forest-path; neither shalt thou freight the ship with it, if thou prefer to cross the sea. Leave this wreck and ruin here where it hath happened! Meddle no more with it! Begin all anew! Hast thou exhausted possibility in the failure of this one trial? Not so! The future is yet full of trial and success. There is happiness to be enjoyed! There is good to be done! Exchange this false life of thine for a true one. Be, if thy spirit summon thee to such a mission, the teacher and apostle of the red men. Or, — as is more thy nature, — be a scholar and a sage among the wisest and the most renowned of the cultivated world.

Preach! Write! Act! Do any thing, save to lie down and die! Give up this name of Arthur Dimmesdale, and make thyself another, and a high one, such as thou canst wear without fear or shame. Why shouldst thou tarry so much as one other day in the torments that have so gnawed into thy life! — that have made thee feeble to will and to do! — that will leave thee powerless even to repent! Up, and away!"

"O Hester!" cried Arthur Dimmesdale, in whose eyes a fitful light, kindled by her enthusiasm, flashed up and died away, "thou tellest of running a race to a man whose knees are tottering beneath him! I must die here. There is not the strength or courage left me to venture into the wide, strange, difficult world, alone!"

It was the last expression of the despondency of a broken spirit. He lacked energy to grasp the better fortune that seemed within his reach.

He repeated the word.

"Alone, Hester!"

"Thou shalt not go alone!" answered she, in a deep whisper.

Then, all was spoken!

XVIII. A Flood of Sunshine

Arthur Dimmesdale gazed into Hester's face with a look in which hope and joy shone out, indeed, but with fear betwixt them, and a kind of horror at her boldness, who had spoken what he vaguely hinted at, but dared not speak.

But Hester Prynne, with a mind of native courage and activity, and for so long a period not merely estranged, but outlawed, from society, had habituated herself to such latitude of speculation as was altogether foreign to the clergyman. She had wandered, without rule or guidance, in a moral wilderness; as vast, as intricate and shadowy, as the untamed forest, amid the gloom of which they were now holding a colloquy that was to decide their fate. Her intellect and heart had their home, as it were, in desert places, where she roamed as freely as the wild Indian in his woods. For years past she had looked from this estranged point of view at human institutions, and whatever priests or legislators had established; criticizing all with hardly more reverence than the Indian would feel for the clerical band, the judicial robe, the pillory, the gallows, the fireside, or the church. The tendency of her fate and fortunes had been to set her free. The scarlet letter was her passport into regions where other women dared not tread. Shame, Despair, Solitude! These had been her teachers, — stern and wild ones, — and they had made her strong, but taught her much amiss.

The minister, on the other hand, had never gone through an experience calculated to lead him beyond the scope of generally received laws; although, in a single instance, he had so fearfully transgressed one of the most sacred of them. But this had been a sin of passion, not of principle, nor even purpose. Since that wretched epoch, he had watched, with morbid zeal and minuteness, not his acts, — for those it was easy to arrange, — but each breath of emotion, and his every thought. At the head of the social system, as the clergymen of that day stood, he was only the more trammelled by its regulations, its principles, and even its prejudices. As a priest, the framework of his order inevitably hemmed him in. As a man who had once sinned, but who kept his conscience all alive and painfully sensitive by the fretting of an unhealed wound, he might have been supposed safer within the line of virtue, than if he had never sinned at all.

Thus, we seem to see that, as regarded Hester Prynne, the whole seven years of outlaw and ignominy had been little other than a preparation for this very hour. But Arthur Dimmesdale! Were such a man once more to fall, what plea could be urged in extenuation of his crime? None; unless it avail him somewhat, that he was broken down by long and exquisite suffering; that his mind was darkened and confused by the very remorse which harrowed it; that, between fleeing as an avowed criminal, and remaining as a hypocrite, conscience might find it hard to strike the balance; that it was human to avoid the peril of death and infamy, and the inscrutable machinations of an enemy; that, finally, to this poor pilgrim, on his dreary and desert path, faint, sick, miserable, there appeared a glimpse of human affection and sympathy, a new life, and a true one, in exchange for the heavy doom which he was now expiating. And be the stern and sad truth spoken, that the breach which guilt has once made into the human soul is never, in this mortal state, repaired. It may be watched and guarded; so that the enemy shall not force his way again into the citadel, and might even, in his subsequent assaults, select some other avenue, in preference to that where he had formerly succeeded. But there is still the ruined wall, and, near it, the stealthy tread of the foe that would win over again his unforgotten triumph.

The struggle, if there were one, need not be described. Let it suffice, that the clergyman resolved to flee, and not alone.

"If, in all these past seven years," thought he, "I could recall one instant of peace or hope, I would yet endure, for the sake of that earnest of Heaven's mercy. But now, — since I am irrevocably doomed, —

wherefore should I not snatch the solace allowed to the condemned culprit before his execution? Or, if this be the path to a better life, as Hester would persuade me, I surely give up no fairer prospect by pursuing it! Neither can I any longer live without her companionship; so powerful is she to sustain, — so tender to soothe! O Thou to whom I dare not lift mine eyes, wilt Thou yet pardon me!"

"Thou wilt go!" said Hester calmly, as he met her glance.

The decision once made, a glow of strange enjoyment threw its flickering brightness over the trouble of his breast. It was the exhilarating effect — upon a prisoner just escaped from the dungeon of his own heart — of breathing the wild, free atmosphere of an unredeemed, unchristianized, lawless region. His spirit rose, as it were, with a bound, and attained a nearer prospect of the sky, than throughout all the misery which had kept him grovelling on the earth. Of a deeply religious temperament, there was inevitably a tinge of the devotional in his mood.

"Do I feel joy again?" cried he, wondering at himself. "Methought the germ of it was dead in me! O Hester, thou art my better angel! I seem to have flung myself — sick, sin-stained, and sorrow-blackened — down upon these forest-leaves, and to have risen up all made anew, and with new powers to glorify Him that hath been merciful! This is already the better life! Why did we not find it sooner?"

"Let us not look back," answered Hester Prynne. "The past is gone! Wherefore should we linger upon it now? See! With this symbol, I undo it all, and make it as it had never been!"

So speaking, she undid the clasp that fastened the scarlet letter, and, taking it from her bosom, threw it to a distance among the withered leaves. The mystic token alighted on the hither verge of the stream. With a hand's breadth farther flight it would have fallen into the water, and have given the little brook another woe to carry onward, besides the unintelligible tale which it still kept murmuring about. But there lay the embroidered letter, glittering like a lost jewel, which some ill-fated wanderer might pick up, and thenceforth be haunted by strange phantoms of guilt, sinkings of the heart, and unaccountable misfortune.

The stigma gone, Hester heaved a long, deep sigh, in which the burden of shame and anguish departed from her spirit. O exquisite relief! She had not known the weight, until she felt the freedom! By another impulse, she took off the formal cap that confined her hair; and down it fell upon her shoulders, dark and rich, with at once a shadow and a light in its abundance, and imparting the charm of softness to her features. There played around her mouth, and beamed out of her eyes, a radiant and tender smile, that seemed gushing from the very heart of womanhood. A crimson flush was glowing on her cheek, that had been long so pale. Her sex, her youth, and the whole richness of her beauty, came back from what men call the irrevocable past, and clustered themselves, with her maiden hope, and a happiness before unknown, within the magic circle of this hour. And, as if the gloom of the earth and sky had been but the effluence of these two mortal hearts, it vanished with their sorrow. All at once, as with a sudden smile of heaven, forth burst the sunshine, pouring a very flood into the obscure forest, gladdening each green leaf, transmuting the yellow fallen ones to gold, and gleaming adown the gray trunks of the solemn trees. The objects that had made a shadow hitherto, embodied the brightness now. The course of the little brook might be traced by its merry gleam afar into the wood's heart of mystery, which had become a mystery of joy.

Such was the sympathy of Nature — that wild, heathen Nature of the forest, never subjugated by human law, nor illumined by higher truth — with the bliss of these two spirits! Love, whether newly born, or aroused from a deathlike slumber, must always create a sunshine, filling the heart so full of radiance, that it overflows upon the outward world. Had the forest still kept its gloom, it would have been bright in Hester's eyes, and bright in Arthur Dimmesdale's!

Hester looked at him with the thrill of another joy.

"Thou must know Pearl!" said she. "Our little Pearl! Thou hast seen her, — yes, I know it! — but thou wilt see her now with other eyes. She is a strange child! I hardly comprehend her! But thou wilt love her dearly, as I do, and wilt advise me how to deal with her."

"Dost thou think the child will be glad to know me?" asked the minister, somewhat uneasily. "I have long shrunk from children, because they often show a distrust, — a backwardness to be familiar with me. I have even been afraid of little Pearl!"

"Ah, that was sad!" answered the mother. "But she will love thee dearly, and thou her. She is not far off. I will call her! Pearl! Pearl!"

"I see the child," observed the minister. "Yonder she is, standing in a streak of sunshine, a good way off, on the other side of the brook. So thou thinkest the child will love me?"

Hester smiled, and again called to Pearl, who was visible, at some distance, as the minister had described her, like a bright-apparelled vision, in a sunbeam, which fell down upon her through an arch of boughs. The ray quivered to and fro, making her figure dim or distinct, — now like a real child, now like a child's spirit, — as the splendor went and came again. She heard her mother's voice, and approached slowly through the forest.

Pearl had not found the hour pass wearisomely, while her mother sat talking with the clergyman. The great black forest — stern as it showed itself to those who brought the guilt and troubles of the world into its bosom — became the playmate of the lonely infant, as well as it knew how. Sombre as it was, it put on the kindest of its moods to welcome her. It offered her the partridge-berries, the growth of the preceding autumn, but ripening only in the spring, and now red as drops of blood upon the withered leaves. These Pearl gathered, and was pleased with their wild flavor. The small denizens of the wilderness hardly took pains to move out of her path. A partridge, indeed, with a brood of ten behind her, ran forward threateningly, but soon repented of her fierceness, and clucked to her young ones not to be afraid. A pigeon, alone on a low branch, allowed Pearl to come beneath, and uttered a sound as much of greeting as alarm. A squirrel, from the lofty depths of his domestic tree, chattered either in anger or merriment, — for a squirrel is such a choleric and humorous little personage that it is hard to distinguish between his moods, — so he chattered at the child, and flung down a nut upon her head. It was a last year's nut, and already gnawed by his sharp tooth. A fox, startled from his sleep by her light footstep on the leaves, looked inquisitively at Pearl, as doubting whether it were better to steal off, or renew his nap on the same spot. A wolf, it is said, — but here the tale has surely lapsed into the improbable, — came up, and smelt of Pearl's robe, and offered his savage head to be patted by her hand. The truth seems to be, however, that the mother-forest, and these wild things which it nourished, all recognized a kindred wildness in the human child.

And she was gentler here than in the grassy-margined streets of the settlement, or in her mother's cottage. The flowers appeared to know it; and one and another whispered, as she passed, "Adorn thyself with me, thou beautiful child, adorn thyself with me!" — and, to please them, Pearl gathered the violets, and anemones, and columbines, and some twigs of the freshest green, which the old trees held down before her eyes. With these she decorated her hair, and her young waist, and became a nymph-child, or an infant dryad, or whatever else was in closest sympathy with the antique wood. In such guise had Pearl adorned herself, when she heard her mother's voice, and came slowly back.

Slowly; for she saw the clergyman!

XIX. The Child at the Brook-Side

"Thou wilt love her dearly," repeated Hester Prynne, as she and the minister sat watching little Pearl. "Dost thou not think her beautiful? And see with what natural skill she has made those simple flowers adorn her! Had she gathered pearls, and diamonds, and rubies, in the wood, they could not have become her better. She is a splendid child! But I know whose brow she has!"

"Dost thou know, Hester," said Arthur Dimmesdale, with an unquiet smile, "that this dear child, tripping about always at thy side, hath caused me many an alarm? Methought — O Hester, what a thought is that, and how terrible to dread it! — that my own features were partly repeated in her face, and so strikingly that the world might see them! But she is mostly thine!"

"No, no! Not mostly!" answered the mother with a tender smile. "A little longer, and thou needest not to be afraid to trace whose child she is. But how strangely beautiful she looks, with those wild flowers in her hair! It is as if one of the fairies, whom we left in our dear old England, had decked her out to meet us."

It was with a feeling which neither of them had ever before experienced, that they sat and watched Pearl's slow advance. In her was visible the tie that united them. She had been offered to the world, these seven years past, as the living hieroglyphic, in which was revealed the secret they so darkly sought to hide, — all written in this symbol, — all plainly manifest, — had there been a prophet or magician skilled to read the character of flame! And Pearl was the oneness of their being. Be the foregone evil what it might, how could they doubt that their earthly lives and future destinies were conjoined, when they beheld at once the material union, and the spiritual idea, in whom they met, and were to dwell immortally together? Thoughts like these — and perhaps other thoughts, which they did not acknowledge or define — threw an awe about the child, as she came onward.

"Let her see nothing strange — no passion nor eagerness — in thy way of accosting her," whispered Hester. "Our Pearl is a fitful and fantastic little elf, sometimes. Especially, she is seldom tolerant of emotion, when she does not fully comprehend the why and wherefore. But the child hath strong affections! She loves me, and will love thee!"

"Thou canst not think," said the minister, glancing aside at Hester Prynne, "how my heart dreads this interview, and yearns for it! But, in truth, as I already told thee, children are not readily won to be familiar with me. They will not climb my knee, nor prattle in my ear, nor answer to my smile; but stand apart, and eye me strangely. Even little babes, when I take them in my arms, weep bitterly. Yet Pearl, twice in her little lifetime, hath been kind to me! The first time, — thou knowest it well! The last was when thou ledst her with thee to the house of yonder stern old Governor."

"And thou didst plead so bravely in her behalf and mine!" answered the mother. "I remember it; and so shall little Pearl. Fear nothing! She may be strange and shy at first, but will soon learn to love thee!"

By this time Pearl had reached the margin of the brook, and stood on the farther side, gazing silently at Hester and the clergyman, who still sat together on the mossy tree-trunk, waiting to receive her. Just where she had paused the brook chanced to form a pool, so smooth and quiet that it reflected a perfect image of her little figure, with all the brilliant picturesqueness of her beauty, in its adornment of flowers and wreathed foliage, but more refined and spiritualized than the reality. This image, so nearly identical with the living Pearl, seemed to communicate somewhat of its own shadowy and intangible quality to the child herself. It was strange, the way in which Pearl stood, looking so stedfastly at them through the dim medium of the forest-gloom; herself, meanwhile, all glorified with a ray of sunshine, that was attracted thitherward as by a certain sympathy. In the brook beneath stood another child, — another and the same, — with likewise its ray of golden light. Hester felt herself, in some indistinct and tantalizing manner, estranged from Pearl; as if the child, in her lonely ramble through the forest, had strayed out of the sphere in which she and her mother dwelt together, and was now vainly seeking to return to it.

There was both truth and error in the impression; the child and mother were estranged, but through Hester's fault, not Pearl's. Since the latter rambled from her side, another inmate had been admitted within the circle of the mother's feelings, and so modified the aspect of them all, that Pearl, the returning wanderer, could not find her wonted place, and hardly knew where she was.

"I have a strange fancy," observed the sensitive minister, "that this brook is the boundary between two worlds, and that thou canst never meet thy Pearl again. Or is she an elfish spirit, who, as the legends of our childhood taught us, is forbidden to cross a running stream? Pray hasten her; for this delay has already imparted a tremor to my nerves."

"Come, dearest child!" said Hester encouragingly, and stretching out both her arms. "How slow thou art! When hast thou been so sluggish before now? Here is a friend of mine, who must be thy friend also. Thou wilt have twice as much love, henceforward, as thy mother alone could give thee! Leap across the brook and come to us. Thou canst leap like a young deer!"

Pearl, without responding in any manner to these honey-sweet expressions, remained on the other side of the brook. Now she fixed her bright, wild eyes on her mother, now on the minister, and now included them both in the same glance; as if to detect and explain to herself the relation which they bore to one another. For some unaccountable reason, as Arthur Dimmesdale felt the child's eyes upon himself, his hand — with that gesture so habitual as to have become involuntary — stole over his heart. At length, assuming a singular air of authority, Pearl stretched out her hand, with the small forefinger extended, and pointing evidently towards her mother's breast. And beneath, in the mirror of the brook, there was the flower-girdled and sunny image of little Pearl, pointing her small forefinger too.

"Thou strange child, why dost thou not come to me?" exclaimed Hester.

Pearl still pointed with her forefinger; and a frown gathered on her brow; the more impressive from the childish, the almost baby-like aspect of the features that conveyed it. As her mother still kept beckoning to her, and arraying her face in a holiday suit of unaccustomed smiles, the child stamped her foot with a yet more imperious look and gesture. In the brook, again, was the fantastic beauty of the image, with its reflected frown, its pointed finger, and imperious gesture, giving emphasis to the aspect of little Pearl.

"Hasten, Pearl; or I shall be angry with thee!" cried Hester Prynne, who, however inured to such behaviour on the elf-child's part at other seasons, was naturally anxious for a more seemly deportment now. "Leap across the brook, naughty child, and run hither! Else I must come to thee!"

But Pearl, not a whit startled at her mother's threats, any more than mollified by her entreaties, now suddenly burst into a fit of passion, gesticulating violently, and throwing her small figure into the most extravagant contortions. She accompanied this wild outbreak with piercing shrieks, which the woods reverberated on all sides; so that, alone as she was in her childish and unreasonable wrath, it seemed as if a hidden multitude were lending her their sympathy and encouragement. Seen in the brook, once more, was the shadowy wrath of Pearl's image, crowned and girdled with flowers, but stamping its foot, wildly gesticulating, and, in the midst of all, still pointing its small forefinger at Hester's bosom!

"I see what ails the child," whispered Hester to the clergyman, and turning pale in spite of a strong effort to conceal her trouble and annoyance. "Children will not abide any, the slightest, change in the accustomed aspect of things that are daily before their eyes. Pearl misses something which she has always seen me wear!"

"I pray you," answered the minister, "if thou hast any means of pacifying the child, do it forthwith! Save it were the cankered wrath of an old witch, like Mistress Hibbins," added he, attempting to smile, "I know nothing that I would not sooner encounter than this passion in a child. In Pearl's young beauty, as in the wrinkled witch, it has a preternatural effect. Pacify her, if thou lovest me!"

Hester turned again towards Pearl, with a crimson blush upon her cheek, a conscious glance aside at the clergyman, and then a heavy sigh; while, even before she had time to speak, the blush yielded to a deadly pallor.

"Pearl," said she, sadly, "look down at thy feet! There! — before thee! — on the hither side of the brook!"

The child turned her eyes to the point indicated; and there lay the scarlet letter, so close upon the margin of the stream, that the gold embroidery was reflected in it.

"Bring it hither!" said Hester.

"Come thou and take it up!" answered Pearl.

"Was ever such a child!" observed Hester aside to the minister. "O, I have much to tell thee about her. But, in very truth, she is right as regards this hateful token. I must bear its torture yet a little longer, — only a few days longer, — until we shall have left this region, and look back hither as to a land which we have dreamed of. The forest cannot hide it! The mid-ocean shall take it from my hand, and swallow it up for ever!"

With these words, she advanced to the margin of the brook, took up the scarlet letter, and fastened it again into her bosom. Hopefully, but a moment ago, as Hester had spoken of drowning it in the deep sea, there was a sense of inevitable doom upon her, as she thus received back this deadly symbol from the hand of fate. She had flung it into infinite space! — she had drawn an hour's free breath! — and here again was the scarlet misery, glittering on the old spot! So it ever is, whether thus typified or no, that an evil deed invests itself with the character of doom. Hester next gathered up the heavy tresses of her hair, and confined them beneath her cap. As if there were a withering spell in the sad letter, her beauty, the warmth and richness of her womanhood, departed, like fading sunshine; and a gray shadow seemed to fall across her.

When the dreary change was wrought, she extended her hand to Pearl.

"Dost thou know thy mother now, child?" asked she, reproachfully, but with a subdued tone. "Wilt thou come across the brook, and own thy mother, now that she has her shame upon her, — now that she is sad?"

"Yes; now I will!" answered the child, bounding across the brook, and clasping Hester in her arms. "Now thou art my mother indeed! And I am thy little Pearl!"

In a mood of tenderness that was not usual with her, she drew down her mother's head, and kissed her brow and both her cheeks. But then — by a kind of necessity that always impelled this child to alloy whatever comfort she might chance to give with a throb of anguish — Pearl put up her mouth, and kissed the scarlet letter too!

"That was not kind!" said Hester. "When thou hast shown me a little love, thou mockest me!"

"Why doth the minister sit yonder?" asked Pearl.

"He waits to welcome thee," replied her mother. "Come thou, and entreat his blessing! He loves thee, my little Pearl, and loves thy mother too. Wilt thou not love him? Come! he longs to greet thee!"

"Doth he love us?" said Pearl, looking up with acute intelligence into her mother's face. "Will he go back with us, hand in hand, we three together, into the town?"

"Not now, dear child," answered Hester. "But in days to come he will walk hand in hand with us. We will have a home and fireside of our own; and thou shalt sit upon his knee; and he will teach thee many things, and love thee dearly. Thou wilt love him; wilt thou not?"

"And will he always keep his hand over his heart?" inquired Pearl.

"Foolish child, what a question is that!" exclaimed her mother. "Come and ask his blessing!"

But, whether influenced by the jealousy that seems instinctive with every petted child towards a dangerous rival, or from whatever caprice of her freakish nature, Pearl would show no favor to the clergyman. It was only by an exertion of force that her mother brought her up to him, hanging back, and manifesting her reluctance by odd grimaces; of which, ever since her babyhood, she had possessed a singular variety, and could transform her mobile physiognomy into a series of different aspects, with a new mischief in them, each and all. The minister —

painfully embarrassed, but hoping that a kiss might prove a talisman to admit him into the child's kindlier regards — bent forward, and impressed one on her brow. Hereupon, Pearl broke away from her mother, and, running to the brook, stooped over it, and bathed her forehead, until the unwelcome kiss was quite washed off, and diffused through a long lapse of the gliding water. She then remained apart, silently watching Hester and the clergyman; while they talked together, and made such arrangements as were suggested by their new position, and the purposes soon to be fulfilled.

And now this fateful interview had come to a close. The dell was to be left a solitude among its dark, old trees, which, with their multitudinous tongues, would whisper long of what had passed there, and no mortal be the wiser. And the melancholy brook would add this other tale to the mystery with which its little heart was already overburdened, and whereof it still kept up a murmuring babble, with not a whit more cheerfulness of tone than for ages heretofore.

XX. The Minister in a Maze

As the minister departed, in advance of Hester Prynne and little Pearl, he threw a backward glance; half expecting that he should discover only some faintly traced features or outline of the mother and the child, slowly fading into the twilight of the woods. So great a vicissitude in his life could not at once be received as real. But there was Hester, clad in her gray robe, still standing beside the tree-trunk, which some blast had overthrown a long antiquity ago, and which time had ever since been covering with moss, so that these two fated ones, with earth's heaviest burden on them, might there sit down together, and find a single hour's rest and solace. And there was Pearl, too, lightly dancing from the margin of the brook, — now that the intrusive third person was gone, — and taking her old place by her mother's side. So the minister had not fallen asleep, and dreamed!

In order to free his mind from this indistinctness and duplicity of impression, which vexed it with a strange disquietude, he recalled and more thoroughly defined the plans which Hester and himself had sketched for their departure. It had been determined between them, that the Old World, with its crowds and cities, offered them a more eligible shelter and concealment than the wilds of New England, or all America, with its alternatives of an Indian wigwam, or the few settlements of Europeans, scattered thinly along the seaboard. Not to speak of the clergyman's health, so inadequate to sustain the hardships of a forest life, his native gifts, his culture, and his entire development would secure him a home only in the midst of civilization and refinement; the higher the state, the more delicately adapted to it the man. In furtherance of this choice, it so happened that a ship lay in the harbour; one of those questionable cruisers, frequent at that day, which, without being absolutely outlaws of the deep, yet roamed over its surface with a remarkable irresponsibility of character. This vessel had recently arrived from the Spanish Main, and, within three days' time, would sail for Bristol. Hester Prynne — whose vocation, as a self-enlisted Sister of Charity, had brought her acquainted with the captain and crew — could take upon herself to secure the passage of two individuals and a child, with all the secrecy which circumstances rendered more than desirable.

The minister had inquired of Hester, with no little interest, the precise time at which the vessel might be expected to depart. It would probably be on the fourth day from the present. "That is most fortunate!" he had then said to himself. Now, why the Reverend Mr. Dimmesdale considered it so very fortunate, we hesitate to reveal. Nevertheless, — to hold nothing back from the reader, — it was because, on the third day from the present, he was to preach the Election Sermon; and, as such an occasion formed an honorable epoch in the life of a New England clergyman, he could not have chanced upon a more suitable mode and time of terminating his professional career. "At least, they shall say of me," thought this exemplary man, "that I leave no public duty unperformed, nor ill performed!" Sad, indeed, that an introspection so profound and acute as this poor minister's should be so miserably deceived! We have had, and may still have, worse things to tell of him; but none, we apprehend, so pitiably weak; no evidence, at once so slight and irrefragable, of a subtle disease, that had long since begun to eat into the real substance of his character. No man, for any considerable period, can wear one face to himself, and another to the multitude, without finally getting bewildered as to which may be the true.

The excitement of Mr. Dimmesdale's feelings, as he returned from his interview with Hester, lent him unaccustomed physical energy, and hurried him townward at a rapid pace. The pathway among the woods seemed wilder, more uncouth with its rude natural obstacles, and less trodden by the foot of man, than he remembered it on his outward journey. But he leaped across the plashy places, thrust himself through the clinging underbrush, climbed the ascent, plunged into the hollow, and overcame, in short, all the difficulties of the track, with an unwearia-ble activity that astonished him. He could not but recall how feebly, and with what frequent pauses for breath, he had toiled over the same ground only two days before. As he drew near the town, he took an impression of change from the series of familiar objects that presented themselves. It seemed not yesterday, not one, nor two, but many days, or even years ago, since he had quitted them. There, indeed, was each former trace of the street, as he remembered it, and all the peculiarities of the houses, with the due multitude of gable-peaks, and a weathercock at every point where his memory suggested one. Not the less, however, came this importunately obtrusive sense of change. The same was true as regarded the acquaintances whom he met, and all the well-known shapes of human life, about the little town. They looked neither older nor younger, now; the beards of the aged were no whiter, nor could the creeping babe of yesterday walk on his feet to-day; it was impossible to describe in what respect they differed from the individuals on whom he had so recently bestowed a parting glance; and yet the minister's deepest sense seemed to inform him of their mutability. A similar impression struck him most remarkably, as he passed under the walls of his own church. The edifice had so very strange, and yet so familiar, an aspect, that Mr. Dimmesdale's mind vibrated between two ideas; either that he had seen it only in a dream hitherto, or that he was merely dreaming about it now.

This phenomenon, in the various shapes which it assumed, indicated no external change, but so sudden and important a change in the spectator of the familiar scene, that the intervening space of a single day had operated on his consciousness like the lapse of years. The minister's own will, and Hester's will, and the fate that grew between them, had wrought this transformation. It was the same town as heretofore; but the same minister returned not from the forest. He might have said to the friends who greeted him, — "I am not the man for whom you take me! I left him yonder in the forest, withdrawn into a secret dell, by a mossy tree-trunk, and near a melancholy brook! Go, seek your minister, and see if his emaciated figure, his thin cheek, his white, heavy, pain-wrinkled brow, be not flung down there like a cast-off garment!" His friends, no doubt, would still have insisted with him, — "Thou art thyself the man!" — but the error would have been their own, not his.

Before Mr. Dimmesdale reached home, his inner man gave him other evidences of a revolution in the sphere of thought and feeling. In truth, nothing short of a total change of dynasty and moral code, in that interior kingdom, was adequate to account for the impulses now communicated to the unfortunate and startled minister. At every step he was incited to do some strange, wild, wicked thing or other, with a sense that it would be at once involuntary and intentional; in spite of himself, yet growing out of a profounder self than that which opposed the impulse. For instance, he met one of his own deacons. The good old man addressed him with the paternal affection and patriarchal privilege, which his venerable age, his upright and holy character, and his station in the Church, entitled him to use; and, conjoined with this, the deep, almost worshipping respect, which the minister's professional and private claims alike demanded. Never was there a more beautiful example of how the majesty of age and wisdom may comport with the obeisance and respect enjoined upon it, as from a lower social rank and inferior order of endowment, towards a higher. Now, during a conversation of some two or three moments between the Reverend Mr. Dimmesdale and this excellent and hoary-bearded deacon, it was only by the most careful self-control that the former could refrain from uttering certain blasphemous suggestions that rose into his mind, respecting the communion-supper. He absolutely trembled and turned pale as ashes, lest his tongue should wag itself, in utterance of these horrible matters, and plead his own consent for so doing, without his having fairly given it. And, even with this terror in his heart, he could hardly avoid laughing to imagine how the sanctified old patriarchal deacon would have been petrified by his minister's impiety!

Again, another incident of the same nature. Hurrying along the street, the Reverend Mr. Dimmesdale encountered the eldest female member of his church; a most pious and exemplary old dame; poor, widowed, lonely, and with a heart as full of reminiscences about her dead husband and children, and her dead friends of long ago, as a burial-ground is full of storied grave-stones. Yet all this, which would else have been such heavy sorrow, was made almost a solemn joy to her devout old soul by religious consolations and the truths of Scripture, wherewith she had fed herself continually for more than thirty years. And, since Mr. Dimmesdale had taken her in charge, the good grandam's chief earthly comfort — which, unless it had been likewise a heavenly comfort, could have been none at all — was to meet her pastor, whether casually, or of set purpose, and be refreshed with a word of warm, fragrant, heaven-breathing Gospel truth from his beloved lips into her dulled, but rapturously attentive ear. But, on this occasion, up to the moment of putting his lips to the old woman's ear, Mr. Dimmesdale, as the great enemy of souls would have it, could recall no text of Scripture, nor aught else, except a brief, pithy, and, as it then appeared to him, unanswerable argument against the immortality of the human soul. The instilment thereof into her mind would probably have caused this aged sister to drop down dead, at once, as by the effect of an intensely poisonous infusion. What he really did whisper, the minister could never afterwards recollect. There was, perhaps, a fortunate disorder in his utterance, which failed to impart any distinct idea to the good widow's comprehension, or which Providence interpreted after a method of its own. Assuredly, as the minister looked back, he beheld an expression of divine gratitude and ecstasy that seemed like the shine of the celestial city on her face, so wrinkled and ashy pale.

Again, a third instance. After parting from the old church-member, he met the youngest sister of them all. It was a maiden newly won — and won by the Reverend Mr. Dimmesdale's own sermon, on the Sabbath after his vigil — to barter the transitory pleasures of the world for the heavenly hope, that was to assume brighter substance as life grew dark around her, and which would gild the utter gloom with final glory. She was fair and pure as a lily that had bloomed in Paradise. The minister knew well that he was himself enshrined within the stainless sanctity of her heart, which hung its snowy curtains about his image, imparting to religion the warmth of love, and to love a religious purity. Satan, that afternoon, had surely led the poor young girl away from her mother's side, and thrown her into the pathway of this sorely tempted, or — shall we not rather say? — this lost and desperate man. As she drew nigh, the arch-fiend whispered him to condense into small compass and drop into her tender bosom a germ of evil that would be sure to blossom darkly soon, and bear black fruit betimes. Such was his sense of power over this virgin soul, trusting him as she did, that the minister felt potent to blight all the field of innocence with but one wicked look, and develop all its opposite with but a word. So — with a mightier struggle than he had yet sustained — he held his Geneva cloak before his face, and hurried onward, making no sign of recognition, and leaving the young sister to digest his rudeness as she might. She ransacked her conscience, — which was full of harmless little matters, like her pocket or her work-bag, — and took herself to task, poor thing, for a thousand imaginary faults; and went about her household duties with swollen eyelids the next morning.

Before the minister had time to celebrate his victory over this last temptation, he was conscious of another impulse, more ludicrous, and almost as horrible. It was, — we blush to tell it, — it was to stop short in the road, and teach some very wicked words to a knot of little Puritan children who were playing there, and had but just begun to talk.

Denying himself this freak, as unworthy of his cloth, he met a drunken seaman, one of the ship's crew from the Spanish Main. And, here, since he had so valiantly forborne all other wickedness, poor Mr. Dimmesdale longed, at least, to shake hands with the tarry blackguard, and recreate himself with a few improper jests, such as dissolute sailors so abound with, and a volley of good, round, solid, satisfactory, and heaven-defying oaths! It was not so much a better principle, as partly his natural good taste, and still more his buckramed habit of clerical decorum, that carried him safely through the latter crisis.

"What is it that haunts and tempts me thus?" cried the minister to himself, at length, pausing in the street, and striking his hand against his forehead. "Am I mad? or am I given over utterly to the fiend? Did I make a contract with him in the forest, and sign it with my blood? And does he now summon me to its fulfilment, by suggesting the performance of every wickedness which his most foul imagination can conceive?"

At the moment when the Reverend Mr. Dimmesdale thus communed with himself, and struck his forehead with his hand, old Mistress Hibbins, the reputed witch-lady, is said to have been passing by. She made a very grand appearance; having on a high head-dress, a rich gown of velvet, and a ruff done up with the famous yellow starch, of which Ann Turner, her especial friend, had taught her the secret, before this last good lady had been hanged for Sir Thomas Overbury's murder. Whether the witch had read the minister's thoughts, or no, she came to a full stop, looked shrewdly into his face, smiled craftily, and — though little given to converse with clergymen — began a conversation.

"So, reverend Sir, you have made a visit into the forest," observed the witch-lady, nodding her high head-dress at him. "The next time, I pray you to allow me only a fair warning, and I shall be proud to bear you company. Without taking overmuch upon myself, my good word will go far towards gaining any strange gentleman a fair reception from yonder potentate you wot of!"

"I profess, madam," answered the clergyman, with a grave obeisance, such as the lady's rank demanded, and his own good-breeding made imperative, — "I profess, on my conscience and character, that I am utterly bewildered as touching the purport of your words! I went not into the forest to seek a potentate; neither do I, at any future time, design a visit thither, with a view to gaining the favor of such personage. My one sufficient object was to greet that pious friend of mine, the Apostle Eliot, and rejoice with him over the many precious souls he hath won from heathendom!"

"Ha, ha, ha!" cackled the old witch-lady, still nodding her high head-dress at the minister. "Well, well, we must needs talk thus in the daytime! You carry it off like an old hand! But at midnight, and in the forest, we shall have other talk together!"

She passed on with her aged stateliness, but often turning back her head and smiling at him, like one willing to recognize a secret intimacy of connection.

"Have I then sold myself," thought the minister, "to the fiend whom, if men say true, this yellow-starched and velveted old hag has chosen for her prince and master!"

The wretched minister! He had made a bargain very like it! Tempted by a dream of happiness, he had yielded himself with deliberate choice, as he had never done before, to what he knew was deadly sin. And the infectious poison of that sin had been thus rapidly diffused throughout his moral system. It had stupefied all blessed impulses, and awakened into vivid life the whole brotherhood of bad ones. Scorn, bitterness, unprovoked malignity, gratuitous desire of ill, ridicule of whatever was good and holy, all awoke, to tempt, even while they frightened him. And his encounter with old Mistress Hibbins, if it were a real incident, did but show his sympathy and fellowship with wicked mortals and the world of perverted spirits.

He had by this time reached his dwelling, on the edge of the burial-ground, and, hastening up the stairs, took refuge in his study. The minister was glad to have reached this shelter, without first betraying himself to the world by any of those strange and wicked eccentricities to which he had been continually impelled while passing through the streets. He entered the accustomed room, and looked around him on its books, its windows, its fireplace, and the tapestried comfort of the walls, with the same perception of strangeness that had haunted him throughout his walk from the forest-dell into the town, and thitherward. Here he had studied and written; here, gone through fast and vigil, and come forth half alive; here, striven to pray; here, borne a hundred thousand agonies! There was the Bible, in its rich old Hebrew, with Moses and the Prophets speaking to him, and God's voice through all! There, on the table, with the inky pen beside it, was an unfinished sermon, with a sentence broken in the midst, where his thoughts had ceased to gush out upon the page two days before. He knew that it was himself, the thin and white-cheeked minister, who had done and suffered these things, and written thus far into the Election Sermon! But he seemed to stand apart, and eye this former self with scornful, pitying, but half-envious curiosity. That self was gone! Another man had returned out of the forest; a wiser one; with a knowledge of hidden mysteries which the simplicity of the former never could have reached. A bitter kind of knowledge that!

While occupied with these reflections, a knock came at the door of the study, and the minister said, "Come in!" — not wholly devoid of an idea that he might behold an evil spirit. And so he did! It was old Roger Chillingworth that entered. The minister stood, white and speechless, with one hand on the Hebrew Scriptures, and the other spread upon his breast.

"Welcome home, reverend Sir!" said the physician. "And how found you that godly man, the Apostle Eliot? But methinks, dear Sir, you look pale; as if the travel through the wilderness had been too sore for you. Will not my aid be requisite to put you in heart and strength to preach your Election Sermon?"

"Nay, I think not so," rejoined the Reverend Mr. Dimmesdale. "My journey, and the sight of the holy Apostle yonder, and the free air which I have breathed, have done me good, after so long confinement in my study. I think to need no more of your drugs, my kind physician, good though they be, and administered by a friendly hand."

All this time, Roger Chillingworth was looking at the minister with the grave and intent regard of a physician towards his patient. But, in spite of this outward show, the latter was almost convinced of the old man's knowledge, or, at least, his confident suspicion, with respect to his own interview with Hester Prynne. The physician knew, then, that, in the minister's regard, he was no longer a trusted friend, but his bitterest enemy. So much being known, it would appear natural that a part of it should be expressed. It is singular, however, how long a time often passes before words embody things; and with what security two persons, who choose to avoid a certain subject, may approach its very verge, and retire without disturbing it. Thus, the minister felt no apprehension that Roger Chillingworth would touch, in express words, upon the real position which they sustained towards one another. Yet did the physician, in his dark way, creep frightfully near the secret.

"Were it not better," said he, "that you use my poor skill to-night? Verily, dear Sir, we must take pains to make you strong and vigorous for this occasion of the Election discourse. The people look for great things from you; apprehending that another year may come about, and find their pastor gone."

"Yea, to another world," replied the minister, with pious resignation. "Heaven grant it be a better one; for, in good sooth, I hardly think to tarry with my flock through the flitting seasons of another year! But, touching your medicine, kind Sir, in my present frame of body I need it not."

"I joy to hear it," answered the physician. "It may be that my remedies, so long administered in vain, begin now to take due effect. Happy man were I, and well deserving of New England's gratitude, could I achieve this cure!"

"I thank you from my heart, most watchful friend," said the Reverend Mr. Dimmesdale, with a solemn smile. "I thank you, and can but requite your good deeds with my prayers."

"A good man's prayers are golden recompense!" rejoined old Roger Chillingworth, as he took his leave. "Yea, they are the current gold coin of the New Jerusalem, with the King's own mint-mark on them!"

Left alone, the minister summoned a servant of the house, and requested food, which, being set before him, he ate with ravenous appetite. Then, flinging the already written pages of the Election Sermon into the fire, he forthwith began another, which he wrote with such an impulsive flow of thought and emotion, that he fancied himself inspired; and only wondered that Heaven should see fit to transmit the grand and solemn music of its oracles through so foul an organ-pipe as he. However, leaving that mystery to solve itself, or go unsolved for ever, he drove his task onward, with earnest haste and ecstasy. Thus the night fled away, as if it were a winged steed, and he careering on it; morning came, and peeped blushing through the curtains; and at last sunrise threw a golden beam into the study, and laid it right across the minister's bedazzled eyes. There he was, with the pen still between his fingers, and a vast, immeasurable tract of written space behind him!

XXI. The New England Holiday

Betimes in the morning of the day on which the new Governor was to receive his office at the hands of the people, Hester Prynne and little Pearl came into the market-place. It was already thronged with the craftsmen and other plebeian inhabitants of the town, in considerable numbers; among whom, likewise, were many rough figures, whose attire of deer-skins marked them as belonging to some of the forest settlements, which surrounded the little metropolis of the colony.

On this public holiday, as on all other occasions, for seven years past, Hester was clad in a garment of coarse gray cloth. Not more by its hue than by some indescribable peculiarity in its fashion, it had the effect of making her fade personally out of sight and outline; while, again, the scarlet letter brought her back from this twilight indistinctness, and revealed her under the moral aspect of its own illumination. Her face, so long familiar to the townspeople, showed the marble quietude which they were accustomed to behold there. It was like a mask; or rather, like the frozen calmness of a dead woman's features; owing this dreary resemblance to the fact that Hester was actually dead, in respect to any claim of sympathy, and had departed out of the world with which she still seemed to mingle.

It might be, on this one day, that there was an expression unseen before, nor, indeed, vivid enough to be detected now; unless some preternaturally gifted observer should have first read the heart, and have afterwards sought a corresponding development in the countenance and mien. Such a spiritual seer might have conceived, that, after sustaining the gaze of the multitude through seven miserable years as a necessity, a penance, and something which it was a stern religion to endure, she now, for one last time more, encountered it freely and voluntarily, in order to convert what had so long been agony into a kind of triumph. "Look your last on the scarlet letter and its wearer!" — the people's victim and life-long bond-slave, as they fancied her, might say to them. "Yet a little while, and she will be beyond your reach! A few hours longer, and the deep, mysterious ocean will quench and hide for ever the symbol which ye have caused to burn upon her bosom!" Nor were it an inconsistency too improbable to be assigned to human nature, should we suppose a feeling of regret in Hester's mind, at the moment when she was about to win her freedom from the pain which had been thus deeply incorporated with her being. Might there not be an irresistible desire to quaff a last, long, breathless draught of the cup of wormwood and aloes, with which nearly all her years of womanhood had been perpetually flavored? The wine of life, henceforth to be presented to her lips, must be indeed rich, delicious, and exhilarating, in its chased and golden beaker; or else leave an inevitable and weary languor, after the lees of bitterness wherewith she had been drugged, as with a cordial of intensest potency.

Pearl was decked out with airy gayety. It would have been impossible to guess that this bright and sunny apparition owed its existence to the shape of gloomy gray; or that a fancy, at once so gorgeous and so delicate as must have been requisite to contrive the child's apparel, was the same that had achieved a task perhaps more difficult, in imparting so distinct a peculiarity to Hester's simple robe. The dress, so proper was it to little Pearl, seemed an effluence, or inevitable development and outward manifestation of her character, no more to be separated from her than the many-hued brilliancy from a butterfly's wing, or the painted glory from the leaf of a bright flower. As with these, so with the child; her garb was all of one idea with her nature. On this eventful day, moreover, there was a certain singular inquietude and excitement in her mood, resembling nothing so much as the shimmer of a diamond, that sparkles and flashes with the varied throbbings of the breast on which it is displayed. Children have always a sympathy in the agitations of those connected with them; always, especially, a sense of any trouble or impending revolution, of whatever kind, in domestic circumstances; and therefore Pearl, who was the gem on her mother's unquiet bosom, betrayed, by the very dance of her spirits, the emotions which none could detect in the marble passiveness of Hester's brow.

This effervescence made her flit with a bird-like movement, rather than walk by her mother's side. She broke continually into shouts of a wild, inarticulate, and sometimes piercing music. When they reached the market-place, she became still more restless, on perceiving the stir and bustle that enlivened the spot; for it was usually more like the broad and lonesome green before a village meeting-house, than the centre of a town's business.

"Why, what is this, mother?" cried she. "Wherefore have all the people left their work to-day? Is it a play-day for the whole world? See, there is the blacksmith! He has washed his sooty face, and put on his Sabbath-day clothes, and looks as if he would gladly be merry, if any kind body would only teach him how! And there is Master Brackett, the old jailer, nodding and smiling at me. Why does he do so, mother?"

"He remembers thee a little babe, my child," answered Hester.

"He should not nod and smile at me, for all that, — the black, grim, ugly-eyed old man!" said Pearl. "He may nod at thee if he will; for thou art clad in gray, and wearest the scarlet letter. But, see, mother, how many faces of strange people, and Indians among them, and sailors! What have they all come to do here in the market-place?"

"They wait to see the procession pass," said Hester. "For the Governor and the magistrates are to go by, and the ministers, and all the great people and good people, with the music, and the soldiers marching before them."

"And will the minister be there?" asked Pearl. "And will he hold out both his hands to me, as when thou ledst me to him from the brook-side?"

"He will be there, child," answered her mother. "But he will not greet thee to-day; nor must thou greet him."

"What a strange, sad man is he!" said the child, as if speaking partly to herself. "In the dark night-time, he calls us to him, and holds thy hand and mine, as when we stood with him on the scaffold yonder! And in the deep forest, where only the old trees can hear, and the strip of sky see it, he talks with thee, sitting on a heap of moss! And he kisses my forehead, too, so that the little brook would hardly wash it off! But here in the sunny day, and among all the people, he knows us not; nor must we know him! A strange, sad man is he, with his hand always over his heart!"

"Be quiet, Pearl! Thou understandest not these things," said her mother. "Think not now of the minister, but look about thee, and see how cheery is every body's face to-day. The children have come from their schools, and the grown people from their workshops and their fields, on purpose to be happy. For, to-day, a new man is beginning to rule over them; and so — as has been the custom of mankind ever since a nation was first gathered — they make merry and rejoice; as if a good and golden year were at length to pass over the poor old world!"

It was as Hester said, in regard to the unwonted jollity that brightened the faces of the people. Into this festal season of the year — as it already was, and continued to be during the greater part of two centuries — the Puritans compressed whatever mirth and public joy they deemed allowable to human infirmity; thereby so far dispelling the customary cloud, that, for the space of a single holiday, they appeared scarcely more grave than most other communities at a period of general affliction.

But we perhaps exaggerate the gray or sable tinge, which undoubtedly characterized the mood and manners of the age. The persons now in the market-place of Boston had not been born to an inheritance of Puritanic gloom. They were native Englishmen, whose fathers had lived in the sunny richness of the Elizabethan epoch; a time when the life of England, viewed as one great mass, would appear to have been as stately, magnificent, and joyous, as the world has ever witnessed. Had they followed their hereditary taste, the New England settlers would have illustrated all events of public importance by bonfires, banquets, pageantries, and processions. Nor would it have been impracticable, in the observance of majestic ceremonies, to combine mirthful recreation with solemnity, and give, as it were, a grotesque and brilliant embroidery to the great robe of state, which a nation, at such festivals, puts on. There was some shadow of an attempt of this kind in the mode of celebrating the day on which the political year of the colony commenced. The dim reflection of a remembered splendor, a colorless and manifold diluted repetition of what they had beheld in proud old London, — we will not say at a royal coronation, but at a Lord Mayor's show, — might be traced in the customs which our forefathers instituted, with reference to the annual installation of magistrates. The fathers and founders of the commonwealth — the statesman, the priest, and the soldier — deemed it a duty then to assume the outward state and majesty, which, in accordance with antique style, was looked upon as the proper garb of public or social eminence. All came forth, to move in procession before the people's eye, and thus impart a needed dignity to the simple framework of a government so newly constructed.

Then, too, the people were countenanced, if not encouraged, in relaxing the severe and close application to their various modes of rugged industry, which, at all other times, seemed of the same piece and material with their religion. Here, it is true, were none of the appliances which popular merriment would so readily have found in the England of Elizabeth's time, or that of James; — no rude shows of a theatrical kind; no minstrel with his harp and legendary ballad, nor gleeman, with an ape dancing to his music; no juggler, with his tricks of mimic witchcraft; no Merry Andrew, to stir up the multitude with jests, perhaps hundreds of years old, but still effective, by their appeals to the very broadest sources of mirthful sympathy. All such professors of the several branches of jocularity would have been sternly repressed, not only by the rigid discipline of law, but by the general sentiment which gives law its vitality. Not the less, however, the great, honest face of the people smiled, grimly, perhaps, but widely too. Nor were sports wanting, such as the colonists had witnessed, and shared in, long ago, at the country fairs and on the village-greens of England; and which it was thought well to keep alive on this new soil, for the sake of the courage and manliness that were essential in them. Wrestling-matches, in the differing fashions of Cornwall and Devonshire, were seen here and there about the market-place; in one corner, there was a friendly bout at quarterstaff; and — what attracted most interest of all — on the platform of the pillory, already so noted in our pages, two masters of defence were commencing an exhibition with the buckler and broadsword. But, much to the disappointment of the crowd, this latter business was broken off by the interposition of the town beadle, who had no idea of permitting the majesty of the law to be violated by such an abuse of one of its consecrated places.

It may not be too much to affirm, on the whole, (the people being then in the first stages of joyless deportment, and the offspring of sires who had known how to be merry, in their day,) that they would compare favorably, in point of holiday keeping, with their descendants, even at so long an interval as ourselves. Their immediate posterity, the generation next to the early emigrants, wore the blackest shade of Puritanism, and so darkened the national visage with it, that all the subsequent years have not sufficed to clear it up. We have yet to learn again the forgotten art of gayety.

The picture of human life in the market-place, though its general tint was the sad gray, brown, or black of the English emigrants, was yet enlivened by some diversity of hue. A party of Indians — in their savage finery of curiously embroidered deer-skin robes, wampum-belts, red and yellow ochre, and feathers, and armed with the bow and arrow and stone-headed spear — stood apart, with countenances of inflexible gravity, beyond what even the Puritan aspect could attain. Nor, wild as were these painted barbarians, were they the wildest feature of the scene. This distinction could more justly be claimed by some mariners, — a part of the crew of the vessel from the Spanish Main, — who had come ashore to see the humors of Election Day. They were rough-looking desperadoes, with sun-blackened faces, and an immensity of beard; their wide, short trousers were confined about the waist by belts, often clasped with a rough plate of gold, and sustaining always a long knife, and, in some instances, a sword. From beneath their broad-brimmed hats of palm-leaf, gleamed eyes which, even in good nature and merriment, had a kind of animal ferocity. They transgressed, without fear or scruple, the rules of behaviour that were binding on all others; smoking tobacco under the beadle's very nose, although each whiff would have cost a townsman a shilling; and quaffing, at their pleasure, draughts of wine or aqua-vitae from pocket-flasks, which they freely tendered to the gaping crowd around them. It remarkably characterized the incomplete morality of the age, rigid as we call it, that a license was allowed the seafaring class, not merely for their freaks on shore, but for far more desperate deeds on their proper element. The sailor of that day would go near to be arraigned as a pirate in our own. There could be little doubt, for instance, that this very ship's crew, though no unfavorable specimens of the nautical brotherhood, had been guilty, as we should phrase it, of depredations on the Spanish commerce, such as would have perilled all their necks in a modern court of justice.

But the sea, in those old times, heaved, swelled, and foamed very much at its own will, or subject only to the tempestuous wind, with hardly any attempts at regulation by human law. The buccaneer on the wave might relinquish his calling, and become at once, if he chose, a man of probity and piety on land; nor, even in the full career of his reckless life, was he regarded as a personage with whom it was disreputable to traffic, or casually associate. Thus, the Puritan elders, in their black cloaks, starched bands, and steeple-crowned hats, smiled not unbenignantly at the clamor and rude deportment of these jolly seafaring men; and it excited neither surprise nor animadversion when so reputable a citizen as old Roger Chillingworth, the physician, was seen to enter the market-place, in close and familiar talk with the commander of the questionable vessel.

The latter was by far the most showy and gallant figure, so far as apparel went, anywhere to be seen among the multitude. He wore a profusion of ribbons on his garment, and gold lace on his hat, which was also encircled by a gold chain, and surmounted with a feather. There was a sword at his side, and a sword-cut on his forehead, which, by the arrangement of his hair, he seemed anxious rather to display than hide. A landsman could hardly have worn this garb and shown his face, and worn and shown them both with such a galliard air, without undergoing stern question before a magistrate, and probably incurring fine or imprisonment, or perhaps an exhibition in the stocks. As regarded the shipmaster, however, all was looked upon as pertaining to the character, as to a fish his glistening scales.

After parting from the physician, the commander of the Bristol ship strolled idly through the market-place; until, happening to approach the spot where Hester Prynne was standing, he appeared to recognize, and did not hesitate to address her. As was usually the case wherever Hester stood, a small, vacant area — a sort of magic circle — had formed itself about her, into which, though the people were elbowing one another at a little distance, none ventured, or felt disposed to intrude. It was a forcible type of the moral solitude in which the scarlet letter enveloped its fated wearer; partly by her own reserve, and partly by the instinctive, though no longer so unkindly, withdrawal of her fellow-creatures. Now, if never before, it answered a good purpose, by enabling Hester and the seaman to speak together without risk of being overheard; and so changed was Hester Prynne's repute before the public, that the matron in town most eminent for rigid morality could not have held such intercourse with less result of scandal than herself.

"So, mistress," said the mariner, "I must bid the steward make ready one more berth than you bargained for! No fear of scurvy or ship-fever, this voyage! What with the ship's surgeon and this other doctor, our only danger will be from drug or pill; more by token, as there is a lot of apothecary's stuff aboard, which I traded for with a Spanish vessel."

"What mean you?" inquired Hester, startled more than she permitted to appear. "Have you another passenger?"

"Why, know you not," cried the shipmaster, "that this physician here — Chillingworth, he calls himself — is minded to try my cabin-fare with you? Ay, ay, you must have known it; for he tells me he is of your party, and a close friend to the gentleman you spoke of, — he that is in peril from these sour old Puritan rulers!"

"They know each other well, indeed," replied Hester, with a mien of calmness, though in the utmost consternation. "They have long dwelt together."

Nothing further passed between the mariner and Hester Prynne. But, at that instant, she beheld old Roger Chillingworth himself, standing in the remotest corner of the market-place, and smiling on her; a smile which — across the wide and bustling square, and through all the talk and laughter, and various thoughts, moods, and interests of the crowd — conveyed secret and fearful meaning.

XXII. The Procession

Before Hester Prynne could call together her thoughts, and consider what was practicable to be done in this new and startling aspect of affairs, the sound of military music was heard approaching along a contiguous street. It denoted the advance of the procession of magistrates and citizens, on its way towards the meeting-house; where, in compliance with a custom thus early established, and ever since observed, the Reverend Mr. Dimmesdale was to deliver an Election Sermon.

Soon the head of the procession showed itself, with a slow and stately march, turning a corner, and making its way across the market-place. First came the music. It comprised a variety of instruments, perhaps imperfectly adapted to one another, and played with no great skill, but yet attaining the great object for which the harmony of drum and clarion addresses itself to the multitude, — that of imparting a higher and more heroic air to the scene of life that passes before the eye. Little Pearl at first clapped her hands, but then lost, for an instant, the restless agitation that had kept her in a continual effervescence throughout the morning; she gazed silently, and seemed to be borne upward, like a floating sea-bird, on the long heaves and swells of sound. But she was brought back to her former mood by the shimmer of the sunshine on the weapons and bright armour of the military company, which followed after the music, and formed the honorary escort of the procession. This body of soldiery — which still sustains a corporate existence, and marches down from past ages with an ancient and honorable fame — was composed of no mercenary materials. Its ranks were filled with gentlemen, who felt the stirrings of martial impulse, and sought to establish a kind of College of Arms, where, as in an association of Knights Templars, they might learn the science, and, so far as peaceful exercise would teach them, the practices of war. The high estimation then placed upon the military character might be seen in the lofty port of each individual member of the company. Some of them, indeed, by their services in the Low Countries and on other fields of European warfare, had fairly won their title to assume the name and pomp of soldiership. The entire array, moreover, clad in burnished steel, and with plumage nodding over their bright morions, had a brilliancy of effect which no modern display can aspire to equal.

And yet the men of civil eminence, who came immediately behind the military escort, were better worth a thoughtful observer's eye. Even in outward demeanour they showed a stamp of majesty that made the warrior's haughty stride look vulgar, if not absurd. It was an age when what we call talent had far less consideration than now, but the massive materials which produce stability and dignity of character a great deal more. The people possessed, by hereditary right, the quality of reverence; which, in their descendants, if it survive at all, exists in smaller proportion, and with a vastly diminished force in the selection and estimate of public men. The change may be for good or ill, and is partly, perhaps, for both. In that old day, the English settler on these rude shores, — having left king, nobles, and all degrees of awful rank behind, while still the faculty and necessity of reverence were strong in him, — bestowed it on the white hair and venerable brow of age; on long-tried integrity; on solid wisdom and sad-colored experience; on endowments of that grave and weighty order, which gives the idea of permanence, and comes under the general definition of respectability. These primitive statesmen, therefore, — Bradstreet, Endicott, Dudley, Bellingham, and their compeers, — who were elevated to power by the early choice of the people, seem to have been not often brilliant, but distinguished by a ponderous sobriety, rather than activity of intellect. They had fortitude and self-reliance, and, in time of difficulty or peril, stood up for the welfare of the state like a line of cliffs against a tempestuous tide. The traits of character here indicated were well represented in the square cast of countenance and large physical development of the new colonial magistrates. So far as a demeanour of natural authority was concerned, the mother country need not have been ashamed to see these foremost men of an actual democracy adopted into the House of Peers, or made the Privy Council of the sovereign.

Next in order to the magistrates came the young and eminently distinguished divine, from whose lips the religious discourse of the anniversary was expected. His was the profession, at that era, in which intellectual ability displayed itself far more than in political life; for — leaving a higher motive out of the question — it offered inducements powerful enough, in the almost worshipping respect of the community, to win the most aspiring ambition into its service. Even political power — as in the case of Increase Mather — was within the grasp of a successful priest.

It was the observation of those who beheld him now, that never, since Mr. Dimmesdale first set his foot on the New England shore, had he exhibited such energy as was seen in the gait and air with which he kept his pace in the procession. There was no feebleness of step, as at other times; his frame was not bent; nor did his hand rest ominously upon his heart. Yet, if the clergyman were rightly viewed, his strength seemed not of the body. It might be spiritual, and imparted to him by angelic ministrations. It might be the exhilaration of that potent cordial, which is distilled only in the furnace-glow of earnest and long-continued thought. Or, perchance, his sensitive temperament was invigorated by the loud and piercing music, that swelled heavenward, and uplifted him on its ascending wave. Nevertheless, so abstracted was his look, it might be questioned whether Mr. Dimmesdale even heard the music. There was his body, moving onward, and with an unaccustomed force. But where was his mind? Far and deep in its own region, busying itself, with preternatural activity, to marshal a procession of stately thoughts that were soon to issue thence; and so he saw nothing, heard nothing, knew nothing, of what was around him; but the spiritual element took up the feeble frame, and carried it along, unconscious of the burden, and converting it to spirit like itself. Men of uncommon intellect, who have grown morbid, possess this occasional power of mighty effort, into which they throw the life of many days, and then are lifeless for as many more.

Hester Prynne, gazing stedfastly at the clergyman, felt a dreary influence come over her, but wherefore or whence she knew not; unless that he seemed so remote from her own sphere, and utterly beyond her reach. One glance of recognition, she had imagined, must needs pass between them. She thought of the dim forest, with its little dell of solitude, and love, and anguish, and the mossy tree-trunk, where, sitting hand in hand, they had mingled their sad and passionate talk with the melancholy murmur of the brook. How deeply had they known each other then! And was this the man? She hardly knew him now! He, moving proudly past, enveloped, as it were, in the rich music, with the procession of majestic and venerable fathers; he, so unattainable in his worldly position, and still more so in that far vista of his unsympathizing thoughts, through which she now beheld him! Her spirit sank with the idea that all must have been a delusion, and that, vividly as she had dreamed it, there could be no real bond betwixt the clergyman and herself. And thus much of woman was there in Hester, that she could scarcely forgive him, — least of all now, when the heavy footstep of their approaching Fate might be heard, nearer, nearer, nearer! — for being able so completely to withdraw himself from their mutual world; while she groped darkly, and stretched forth her cold hands, and found him not.

Pearl either saw and responded to her mother's feelings, or herself felt the remoteness and intangibility that had fallen around the minister. While the procession passed, the child was uneasy, fluttering up and down, like a bird on the point of taking flight. When the whole had gone by, she looked up into Hester's face.

"Mother," said she, "was that the same minister who kissed me by the brook?"

"Hold thy peace, dear little Pearl!" whispered her mother. "We must not always talk in the market-place of what happens to us in the forest."

"I could not be sure that it was he; so strange he looked," continued the child. "Else I would have run to him, and bid him kiss me now, before all the people; even as he did yonder among the dark old trees. What would the minister have said, mother? Would he have clapped his hand over his heart, and scowled on me, and bid me begone?"

"What should he say, Pearl," answered Hester, "save that it was no time to kiss, and that kisses are not to be given in the market-place? Well for thee, foolish child, that thou didst not speak to him!"

Another shade of the same sentiment, in reference to Mr. Dimmesdale, was expressed by a person whose eccentricities — or insanity, as we should term it — led her to do what few of the townspeople would have ventured on; to begin a conversation with the wearer of the scarlet letter, in public. It was Mistress Hibbins, who, arrayed in great magnificence, with a triple ruff, a broidered stomacher, a gown of rich velvet, and a gold-headed cane, had come forth to see the procession. As this ancient lady had the renown (which subsequently cost her no less a price than her life) of being a principal actor in all the works of necromancy that were continually going forward, the crowd gave way before her, and seemed to fear the touch of her garment, as if it carried the plague among its gorgeous folds. Seen in conjunction with Hester Prynne, — kindly as so many now felt towards the latter, — the dread inspired by Mistress Hibbins was doubled, and caused a general movement from that part of the market-place in which the two women stood.

"Now, what mortal imagination could conceive it!" whispered the old lady confidentially to Hester. "Yonder divine man! That saint on earth, as the people uphold him to be, and as — I must needs say — he really looks! Who, now, that saw him pass in the procession, would think how little while it is since he went forth out of his study, — chewing a Hebrew text of Scripture in his mouth, I warrant, — to take an airing in the forest! Aha! we know what that means, Hester Prynne! But, truly, forsooth, I find it hard to believe him the same man. Many a church-member saw I, walking behind the music, that has danced in the same measure with me, when Somebody was fiddler, and, it might be, an Indian powwow or a Lapland wizard changing hands with us! That is but a trifle, when a woman knows the world. But this minister! Couldst thou surely tell, Hester, whether he was the same man that encountered thee on the forest-path!"

"Madam, I know not of what you speak," answered Hester Prynne, feeling Mistress Hibbins to be of infirm mind; yet strangely startled and awe-stricken by the confidence with which she affirmed a personal connection between so many persons (herself among them) and the Evil One. "It is not for me to talk lightly of a learned and pious minister of the Word, like the Reverend Mr. Dimmesdale!"

"Fie, woman, fie!" cried the old lady, shaking her finger at Hester. "Dost thou think I have been to the forest so many times, and have yet no skill to judge who else has been there? Yea; though no leaf of the wild garlands, which they wore while they danced, be left in their hair! I know thee, Hester; for I behold the token. We may all see it in the sunshine; and it glows like a red flame in the dark. Thou wearest it openly; so there need be no question about that. But this minister! Let me tell thee in thine ear! When the Black Man sees one of his own servants, signed and sealed, so shy of owning to the bond as is the Reverend Mr. Dimmesdale, he hath a way of ordering matters so that the mark shall be disclosed in open daylight to the eyes of all the world!

What is it that the minister seeks to hide, with his hand always over his heart? Ha, Hester Prynne!"

"What is it, good Mistress Hibbins?" eagerly asked little Pearl. "Hast thou seen it?"

"No matter, darling!" responded Mistress Hibbins, making Pearl a profound reverence. "Thou thyself wilt see it, one time or another. They say, child, thou art of the lineage of the Prince of the Air! Wilt thou ride with me, some fine night, to see thy father? Then thou shalt know wherefore the minister keeps his hand over his heart!"

Laughing so shrilly that all the market-place could hear her, the weird old gentlewoman took her departure.

By this time the preliminary prayer had been offered in the meeting-house, and the accents of the Reverend Mr. Dimmesdale were heard commencing his discourse. An irresistible feeling kept Hester near the spot. As the sacred edifice was too much thronged to admit another auditor, she took up her position close beside the scaffold of the pillory. It was in sufficient proximity to bring the whole sermon to her ears, in the shape of an indistinct, but varied, murmur and flow of the minister's very peculiar voice.

This vocal organ was in itself a rich endowment; insomuch that a listener, comprehending nothing of the language in which the preacher spoke, might still have been swayed to and fro by the mere tone and cadence. Like all other music, it breathed passion and pathos, and emotions high or tender, in a tongue native to the human heart, wherever educated. Muffled as the sound was by its passage through the church-walls, Hester Prynne listened with such intentness, and sympathized so intimately, that the sermon had throughout a meaning for her, entirely apart from its indistinguishable words. These, perhaps, if more distinctly heard, might have been only a grosser medium, and have clogged the spiritual sense. Now she caught the low undertone, as of the wind sinking down to repose itself; then ascended with it, as it rose through progressive gradations of sweetness and power, until its volume seemed to envelop her with an atmosphere of awe and solemn grandeur. And yet, majestic as the voice sometimes became, there was for ever in it an essential character of plaintiveness. A loud or low expression of anguish, — the whisper, or the shriek, as it might be conceived, of suffering humanity, that touched a sensibility in every bosom! At times this deep strain of pathos was all that could be heard, and scarcely heard, sighing amid a desolate silence. But even when the minister's voice grew high and commanding, — when it gushed irrepressibly upward, — when it assumed its utmost breadth and power, so overfilling the church as to burst its way through the solid walls, and diffuse itself in the open air, — still, if the auditor listened intently, and for the purpose, he could detect the same cry of pain. What was it? The complaint of a human heart, sorrow-laden, perchance guilty, telling its secret, whether of guilt or sorrow, to the great heart of mankind; beseeching its sympathy or forgiveness, — at every moment, — in each accent, — and never in vain! It was this profound and continual undertone that gave the clergyman his most appropriate power.

During all this time Hester stood, statue-like, at the foot of the scaffold. If the minister's voice had not kept her there, there would nevertheless have been an inevitable magnetism in that spot, whence she dated the first hour of her life of ignominy. There was a sense within her, — too ill-defined to be made a thought, but weighing heavily on her mind, — that her whole orb of life, both before and after, was connected with this spot, as with the one point that gave it unity.

Little Pearl, meanwhile, had quitted her mother's side, and was playing at her own will about the market-place. She made the sombre crowd cheerful by her erratic and glistening ray; even as a bird of bright plumage illuminates a whole tree of dusky foliage by darting to and fro, half seen and half concealed, amid the twilight of the clustering leaves. She had an undulating, but, oftentimes, a sharp and irregular movement. It indicated the restless vivacity of her spirit, which to-day was doubly indefatigable in its tiptoe dance, because it was played upon and vibrated with her mother's disquietude. Whenever Pearl saw any thing to excite her ever active and wandering curiosity, she flew thitherward, and, as we might say, seized upon that man or thing as her own property, so far as she desired it; but without yielding the minutest degree of control over her motions in requital. The Puritans looked on, and, if they smiled, were none the less inclined to pronounce the child a demon offspring, from the indescribable charm of beauty and eccentricity that shone through her little figure, and sparkled with its activity. She ran and looked the wild Indian in the face; and he grew conscious of a nature wilder than his own. Thence, with native audacity, but still with a reserve as characteristic, she flew into the midst of a group of mariners, the swarthy-cheeked wild men of the ocean, as the Indians were of the land; and they gazed wonderingly and admiringly at Pearl, as if a flake of the sea-foam had taken the shape of a little maid, and were gifted with a soul of the sea-fire, that flashes beneath the prow in the night-time.

One of these seafaring men — the shipmaster, indeed, who had spoken to Hester Prynne — was so smitten with Pearl's aspect, that he attempted to lay hands upon her, with purpose to snatch a kiss. Finding it as impossible to touch her as to catch a humming-bird in the air, he took from his hat the gold chain that was twisted about it, and threw it to the child. Pearl immediately twined it around her neck and waist, with such happy skill, that, once seen there, it became a part of her, and it was difficult to imagine her without it.

"Thy mother is yonder woman with the scarlet letter," said the seaman. "Wilt thou carry her a message from me?"

"If the message pleases me I will," answered Pearl.

"Then tell her," rejoined he, "that I spake again with the black-a-visaged, hump-shouldered old doctor, and he engages to bring his friend, the gentleman she wots of, aboard with him. So let thy mother take no thought, save for herself and thee. Wilt thou tell her this, thou witch-baby?"

"Mistress Hibbins says my father is the Prince of the Air!" cried Pearl, with her naughty smile. "If thou callest me that ill name, I shall tell him of thee; and he will chase thy ship with a tempest!"

Pursuing a zigzag course across the market-place, the child returned to her mother, and communicated what the mariner had said. Hester's strong, calm, stedfastly enduring spirit almost sank, at last, on beholding this dark and grim countenance of an inevitable doom, which — at the moment when a passage seemed to open for the minister and herself out of their labyrinth of misery — showed itself, with an unrelenting smile, right in the midst of their path.

With her mind harassed by the terrible perplexity in which the shipmaster's intelligence involved her, she was also subjected to another trial. There were many people present, from the country roundabout, who had often heard of the scarlet letter, and to whom it had been made terrific by a hundred false or exaggerated rumors, but who had never beheld it with their own bodily eyes. These, after exhausting other modes of amusement, now thronged about Hester Prynne with rude and boorish intrusiveness. Unscrupulous as it was, however, it could not bring them nearer than a circuit of several yards. At that distance they accordingly stood, fixed there by the centrifugal force of the repugnance which the mystic symbol inspired. The whole gang of sailors, likewise, observing the press of spectators, and learning the purport of the scarlet letter, came and thrust their sunburnt and desperado-looking faces into the ring. Even the Indians were affected by a sort of cold shadow of the white man's curiosity, and, gliding through the crowd, fastened their snake-like black eyes on Hester's bosom; conceiving, perhaps, that the wearer of this brilliantly embroidered badge must needs be a personage of high dignity among her people. Lastly, the inhabitants of the town (their own interest in this worn-out subject languidly reviving itself, by sympathy with what they saw others feel) lounged idly to the same quarter, and tormented Hester Prynne, perhaps more than all the rest, with their cool, well-acquainted gaze at her familiar shame. Hester saw and recognized the self-same faces of that group of matrons, who had awaited her forthcoming from the prison-door, seven years ago; all save one, the youngest and only compassionate among them, whose burial-robe she had since made. At the final hour, when she was so soon to fling aside the burning letter, it had strangely become the centre of more remark and excitement, and was thus made to sear her breast more painfully, than at any time since the first day she put it on.

While Hester stood in that magic circle of ignominy, where the cunning cruelty of her sentence seemed to have fixed her for ever, the admirable preacher was looking down from the sacred pulpit upon an audience, whose very inmost spirits had yielded to his control. The sainted minister in the church! The woman of the scarlet letter in the market-place! What imagination would have been irreverent enough to surmise that the same scorching stigma was on them both?

XXIII. The Revelation of the Scarlet Letter

The eloquent voice, on which the souls of the listening audience had been borne aloft, as on the swelling waves of the sea, at length came to a pause. There was a momentary silence, profound as what should follow the utterance of oracles. Then ensued a murmur and half-hushed tumult; as if the auditors, released from the high spell that had transported them into the region of another's mind, were returning into themselves, with all their awe and wonder still heavy on them. In a moment more, the crowd began to gush forth from the doors of the church. Now that there was an end, they needed other breath, more fit to support the gross and earthly life into which they relapsed, than that atmosphere which the preacher had converted into words of flame, and had burdened with the rich fragrance of his thought.

In the open air their rapture broke into speech. The street and the market-place absolutely babbled, from side to side, with applauses of the minister. His hearers could not rest until they had told one another of what each knew better than he could tell or hear. According to their united testimony, never had man spoken in so wise, so high, and so holy a spirit, as he that spake this day; nor had inspiration ever breathed through mortal lips more evidently than it did through his. Its influence could be seen, as it were, descending upon him, and possessing him, and continually lifting him out of the written discourse that lay before him, and filling him with ideas that must have been as marvellous to himself as to his audience. His subject, it appeared, had been the relation between the Deity and the communities of mankind, with a special reference to the New England which they were here planting in the wilderness. And, as he drew towards the close, a spirit as of prophecy had come upon him, constraining him to its purpose as mightily as the old prophets of Israel were constrained; only with this difference, that, whereas the Jewish seers had denounced judgments and ruin on their country, it was his mission to foretell a high and glorious destiny for the newly gathered people of the Lord. But, throughout it all, and through the whole discourse, there had been a certain deep, sad undertone of pathos, which could not be interpreted otherwise than as the natural regret of one soon to pass away. Yes; their minister whom they so loved — and who so loved them all, that he could not depart heavenward without a sigh — had the foreboding of untimely death upon him, and would soon leave them in their tears! This idea of his transitory stay on earth gave the last emphasis to the effect which the preacher had produced; it was as if an angel, in his passage to the skies, had shaken his bright wings over the people for an instant, — at once a shadow and a splendor, — and had shed down a shower of golden truths upon them.

Thus, there had come to the Reverend Mr. Dimmesdale — as to most men, in their various spheres, though seldom recognized until they see it far behind them — an epoch of life more brilliant and full of triumph than any previous one, or than any which could hereafter be. He stood, at this moment, on the very proudest eminence of superiority, to which the gifts of intellect, rich lore, prevailing eloquence, and a reputation of whitest sanctity, could exalt a clergyman in New England's earliest days, when the professional character was of itself a lofty pedestal. Such was the position which the minister occupied, as he bowed his head forward on the cushions of the pulpit, at the close of his Election Sermon. Meanwhile, Hester Prynne was standing beside the scaffold of the pillory, with the scarlet letter still burning on her breast!

Now was heard again the clangor of the music, and the measured tramp of the military escort, issuing from the church-door. The procession was to be marshalled thence to the town-hall, where a solemn banquet would complete the ceremonies of the day.

Once more, therefore, the train of venerable and majestic fathers was seen moving through a broad pathway of the people, who drew back reverently, on either side, as the Governor and magistrates, the old and wise men, the holy ministers, and all that were eminent and renowned, advanced into the midst of them. When they were fairly in the market-place, their presence was greeted by a shout. This — though doubtless it might acquire additional force and volume from the child-like loyalty which the age awarded to its rulers — was felt to be an irrepressible outburst of the enthusiasm kindled in the auditors by that high strain of eloquence which was yet reverberating in their ears. Each felt the impulse in himself, and, in the same breath, caught it from his neighbour. Within the church, it had hardly been kept down; beneath the sky, it pealed upward to the zenith. There were human beings enough, and enough of highly wrought and symphonious feeling, to produce that more impressive sound than the organ-tones of the blast, or the thunder, or the roar of the sea; even that mighty swell of many voices, blended into one great voice by the universal impulse which makes likewise one vast heart out of the many. Never, from the soil of New England, had gone up such a shout! Never, on New England soil, had stood the man so honored by his mortal brethren as the preacher!

How fared it with him then? Were there not the brilliant particles of a halo in the air about his head? So etherealized by spirit as he was, and so apotheosized by worshipping admirers, did his footsteps in the procession really tread upon the dust of earth?

As the ranks of military men and civil fathers moved onward, all eyes were turned towards the point where the minister was seen to approach among them. The shout died into a murmur, as one portion of the crowd after another obtained a glimpse of him. How feeble and pale he looked amid all his triumph! The energy — or say, rather, the inspiration which had held him up, until he should have delivered the sacred message that brought its own strength along with it from heaven — was withdrawn, now that it had so faithfully performed its office. The glow, which they had just before beheld burning on his cheek, was extinguished, like a flame that sinks down hopelessly among the late-decaying embers. It seemed hardly the face of a man alive, with such a deathlike hue; it was hardly a man with life in him, that tottered on his path so nervelessly, yet tottered, and did not fall!

One of his clerical brethren, — it was the venerable John Wilson, — observing the state in which Mr. Dimmesdale was left by the retiring wave of intellect and sensibility, stepped forward hastily to offer his support. The minister tremulously, but decidedly, repelled the old man's arm. He still walked onward, if that movement could be so described, which rather resembled the wavering effort of an infant, with its mother's arms in view, outstretched to tempt him forward. And now, almost imperceptible as were the latter steps of his progress, he had come opposite the well-remembered and weather-darkened scaffold, where, long since, with all that dreary lapse of time between, Hester Prynne had encountered the world's ignominious stare. There stood Hester, holding little Pearl by the hand! And there was the scarlet letter on her breast! The minister here made a pause; although the music still played the stately and rejoicing march to which the procession moved. It summoned him onward, — onward to the festival! — but here he made a pause.

Bellingham, for the last few moments, had kept an anxious eye upon him. He now left his own place in the procession, and advanced to give assistance; judging from Mr. Dimmesdale's aspect that he must otherwise inevitably fall. But there was something in the latter's expression that warned back the magistrate, although a man not readily obeying the vague intimations that pass from one spirit to another. The crowd, meanwhile, looked on with awe and wonder. This earthly faintness was, in their view, only another phase of the minister's celestial strength; nor would it have seemed a miracle too high to be wrought for one so holy, had he ascended before their eyes, waxing dimmer and brighter, and fading at last into the light of heaven!

He turned towards the scaffold, and stretched forth his arms.

"Hester," said he, "come hither! Come, my little Pearl!"

It was a ghastly look with which he regarded them; but there was something at once tender and strangely triumphant in it. The child, with the bird-like motion which was one of her characteristics, flew to him, and clasped her arms about his knees. Hester Prynne — slowly, as if impelled by inevitable fate, and against her strongest will — likewise drew near, but paused before she reached him. At this instant old Roger Chillingworth thrust himself through the crowd, — or, perhaps, so dark, disturbed, and evil was his look, he rose up out of some nether region, — to snatch back his victim from what he sought to do! Be that as it might, the old man rushed forward and caught the minister by the arm.

"Madman, hold! What is your purpose?" whispered he. "Wave back that woman! Cast off this child! All shall be well! Do not blacken your fame, and perish in dishonor! I can yet save you! Would you bring infamy on your sacred profession?"

"Ha, tempter! Methinks thou art too late!" answered the minister, encountering his eye, fearfully, but firmly. "Thy power is not what it was! With God's help, I shall escape thee now!"

He again extended his hand to the woman of the scarlet letter.

"Hester Prynne," cried he, with a piercing earnestness, "in the name of Him, so terrible and so merciful, who gives me grace, at this last moment, to do what — for my own heavy sin and miserable agony — I withheld myself from doing seven years ago, come hither now, and twine thy strength about me! Thy strength, Hester; but let it be guided by the will which God hath granted me! This wretched and wronged old man is opposing it with all his might! — with all his own might and the fiend's! Come, Hester, come! Support me up yonder scaffold!"

The crowd was in a tumult. The men of rank and dignity, who stood more immediately around the clergyman, were so taken by surprise, and so perplexed as to the purport of what they saw, — unable to receive the explanation which most readily presented itself, or to imagine any other, — that they remained silent and inactive spectators of the judgment which Providence seemed about to work. They beheld the minister, leaning on Hester's shoulder and supported by her arm around him, approach the scaffold, and ascend its steps; while still the little hand of the sin-born child was clasped in his. Old Roger Chillingworth followed, as one intimately connected with the drama of guilt and sorrow in which they had all been actors, and well entitled, therefore, to be present at its closing scene.

"Hadst thou sought the whole earth over," said he, looking darkly at the clergyman, "there was no one place so secret, — no high place nor lowly place, where thou couldst have escaped me, — save on this very scaffold!"

"Thanks be to Him who hath led me hither!" answered the minister.

Yet he trembled, and turned to Hester with an expression of doubt and anxiety in his eyes, not the less evidently betrayed, that there was a feeble smile upon his lips.

"Is not this better," murmured he, "than what we dreamed of in the forest?"

"I know not! I know not!" she hurriedly replied. "Better? Yea; so we may both die, and little Pearl die with us!"

"For thee and Pearl, be it as God shall order," said the minister; "and God is merciful! Let me now do the will which he hath made plain before my sight. For, Hester, I am a dying man. So let me make haste to take my shame upon me."

Partly supported by Hester Prynne, and holding one hand of little Pearl's, the Reverend Mr. Dimmesdale turned to the dignified and venerable rulers; to the holy ministers, who were his brethren; to the people, whose great heart was thoroughly appalled, yet overflowing with tearful sympathy, as knowing that some deep life-matter — which, if full of sin, was full of anguish and repentance likewise — was now to be laid open to them. The sun, but little past its meridian, shone down upon the clergyman, and gave a distinctness to his figure, as he stood out from all the earth to put in his plea of guilty at the bar of Eternal Justice.

"People of New England!" cried he, with a voice that rose over them, high, solemn, and majestic, — yet had always a tremor through it, and sometimes a shriek, struggling up out of a fathomless depth of remorse and woe, — "ye, that have loved me! — ye, that have deemed me holy! — behold me here, the one sinner of the world! At last! — at last! — I stand upon the spot where, seven years since, I should have stood; here, with this woman, whose arm, more than the little strength wherewith I have crept hitherward, sustains me, at this dreadful moment, from grovelling down upon my face! Lo, the scarlet letter which Hester wears! Ye have all shuddered at it! Wherever her walk hath been, — wherever, so miserably burdened, she may have hoped to find repose, — it hath cast a lurid gleam of awe and horrible repugnance roundabout her. But there stood one in the midst of you, at whose brand of sin and infamy ye have not shuddered!"

It seemed, at this point, as if the minister must leave the remainder of his secret undisclosed. But he fought back the bodily weakness, — and, still more, the faintness of heart, — that was striving for the mastery with him. He threw off all assistance, and stepped passionately forward a pace before the woman and the child.

"It was on him!" he continued, with a kind of fierceness; so determined was he to speak out the whole. "God's eye beheld it! The angels were for ever pointing at it! The Devil knew it well, and fretted it continually with the touch of his burning finger! But he hid it cunningly from men, and walked among you with the mien of a spirit, mournful, because so pure in a sinful world! — and sad, because he missed his heavenly kindred! Now, at the death-hour, he stands up before you! He bids you look again at Hester's scarlet letter! He tells you, that, with all its mysterious horror, it is but the shadow of what he bears on his own breast, and that even this, his own red stigma, is no more than the type of what has seared his inmost heart! Stand any here that question God's judgment on a sinner? Behold! Behold a dreadful witness of it!"

With a convulsive motion he tore away the ministerial band from before his breast. It was revealed! But it were irreverent to describe that revelation. For an instant the gaze of the horror-stricken multitude was concentred on the ghastly miracle; while the minister stood with a flush of triumph in his face, as one who, in the crisis of acutest pain, had won a victory. Then, down he sank upon the scaffold! Hester partly raised him, and supported his head against her bosom. Old Roger Chillingworth knelt down beside him, with a blank, dull countenance, out of which the life seemed to have departed.

"Thou hast escaped me!" he repeated more than once. "Thou hast escaped me!"

"May God forgive thee!" said the minister. "Thou, too, hast deeply sinned!"

He withdrew his dying eyes from the old man, and fixed them on the woman and the child.

"My little Pearl," said he feebly, — and there was a sweet and gentle smile over his face, as of a spirit sinking into deep repose; nay, now that the burden was removed, it seemed almost as if he would be sportive with the child, — "dear little Pearl, wilt thou kiss me now? Thou wouldst not yonder, in the forest! But now thou wilt?"

Pearl kissed his lips. A spell was broken. The great scene of grief, in which the wild infant bore a part, had developed all her sympathies; and as her tears fell upon her father's cheek, they were the pledge that she would grow up amid human joy and sorrow, nor for ever do battle with the world, but be a woman in it. Towards her mother, too, Pearl's errand as a messenger of anguish was all fulfilled.

"Hester," said the clergyman, "farewell!"

"Shall we not meet again?" whispered she, bending her face down close to his. "Shall we not spend our immortal life together? Surely, surely, we have ransomed one another, with all this woe! Thou lookest far into eternity, with those bright dying eyes! Then tell me what thou seest?"

"Hush, Hester, hush!" said he, with tremulous solemnity. "The law we broke! — the sin here so awfully revealed! — let these alone be in thy thoughts! I fear! I fear! It may be, that, when we forgot our God, — when we violated our reverence each for the other's soul, — it was thenceforth vain to hope that we could meet hereafter, in an everlasting and pure reunion. God knows; and He is merciful! He hath proved his mercy, most of all, in my afflictions. By giving me this burning torture to bear upon my breast! By sending yonder dark and terrible old man, to keep the torture always at red-heat! By bringing me hither, to die this death of triumphant ignominy before the people! Had either of these agonies been wanting, I had been lost for ever! Praised be his name! His will be done! Farewell!"

That final word came forth with the minister's expiring breath. The multitude, silent till then, broke out in a strange, deep voice of awe and wonder, which could not as yet find utterance, save in this murmur that rolled so heavily after the departed spirit.

XXIV. Conclusion

After many days, when time sufficed for the people to arrange their thoughts in reference to the foregoing scene, there was more than one account of what had been witnessed on the scaffold.

Most of the spectators testified to having seen, on the breast of the unhappy minister, a SCARLET LETTER — the very semblance of that worn by Hester Prynne — imprinted in the flesh. As regarded its origin, there were various explanations, all of which must necessarily have been conjectural. Some affirmed that the Reverend Mr. Dimmesdale, on the very day when Hester Prynne first wore her ignominious badge, had begun a course of penance, — which he afterwards, in so many futile methods, followed out, — by inflicting a hideous torture on himself. Others contended that the stigma had not been produced until a long time subsequent, when old Roger Chillingworth, being a potent necromancer, had caused it to appear, through the agency of magic and poisonous drugs. Others, again, — and those best able to appreciate the minister's peculiar sensibility, and the wonderful operation of his spirit upon the body, — whispered their belief, that the awful symbol was the effect of the ever active tooth of remorse, gnawing from the inmost heart outwardly, and at last manifesting Heaven's dreadful judgment by the visible presence of the letter. The reader may choose among these theories. We have thrown all the light we could acquire upon the portent, and would gladly, now that it has done its office, erase its deep print out of our own brain; where long meditation has fixed it in very undesirable distinctness.

It is singular, nevertheless, that certain persons, who were spectators of the whole scene, and professed never once to have removed their eyes from the Reverend Mr. Dimmesdale, denied that there was any mark whatever on his breast, more than on a new-born infant's. Neither, by their report, had his dying words acknowledged, nor even remotely implied, any, the slightest connection, on his part, with the guilt for which Hester Prynne had so long worn the scarlet letter. According to these highly respectable witnesses, the minister, conscious that he was dying, — conscious, also, that the reverence of the multitude placed him already among saints and angels, — had desired, by yielding up his breath in the arms of that fallen woman, to express to the world how utterly nugatory is the choicest of man's own righteousness. After exhausting life in his efforts for mankind's spiritual good, he had made the manner of his death a parable, in order to impress on his admirers the mighty and mournful lesson, that, in the view of Infinite Purity, we are sinners all alike. It was to teach them, that the holiest among us has but attained so far above his fellows as to discern more clearly the Mercy which looks down, and repudiate more utterly the phantom of human merit, which would look aspiringly upward. Without disputing a truth so momentous, we must be allowed to consider this version of Mr. Dimmesdale's story as only an instance of that stubborn fidelity with which a man's friends — and especially a clergyman's — will sometimes uphold his character; when proofs, clear as the mid-day sunshine on the scarlet letter, establish him a false and sin-stained creature of the dust.

The authority which we have chiefly followed — a manuscript of old date, drawn up from the verbal testimony of individuals, some of whom had known Hester Prynne, while others had heard the tale from contemporary witnesses — fully confirms the view taken in the foregoing pages. Among many morals which press upon us from the poor minister's miserable experience, we put only this into a sentence: — "Be true! Be true! Be true! Show freely to the world, if not your worst, yet some trait whereby the worst may be inferred!"

Nothing was more remarkable than the change which took place, almost immediately after Mr. Dimmesdale's death, in the appearance and demeanour of the old man known as Roger Chillingworth. All his strength and energy — all his vital and intellectual force — seemed at once to desert him; insomuch that he positively withered up, shrivelled away, and almost vanished from mortal sight, like an uprooted weed that lies wilting in the sun. This unhappy man had made the very principle of his life to consist in the pursuit and systematic exercise of revenge; and when, by its completest triumph and consummation, that evil principle was left with no further material to support it, — when, in short, there was no more devil's work on earth for him to do, it only remained for the unhumanized mortal to betake himself whither his Master would find him tasks enough, and pay him his wages duly. But, to all these shadowy beings, so long our near acquaintances, — as well

Roger Chillingworth as his companions, — we would fain be merciful. It is a curious subject of observation and inquiry, whether hatred and love be not the same thing at bottom. Each, in its utmost development, supposes a high degree of intimacy and heart-knowledge; each renders one individual dependent for the food of his affections and spiritual life upon another; each leaves the passionate lover, or the no less passionate hater, forlorn and desolate by the withdrawal of his object. Philosophically considered, therefore, the two passions seem essentially the same, except that one happens to be seen in a celestial radiance, and the other in a dusky and lurid glow. In the spiritual world, the old physician and the minister — mutual victims as they have been — may, unawares, have found their earthly stock of hatred and antipathy transmuted into golden love.

Leaving this discussion apart, we have a matter of business to communicate to the reader. At old Roger Chillingworth's decease (which took place within the year), and by his last will and testament, of which Governor Bellingham and the Reverend Mr. Wilson were executors, he bequeathed a very considerable amount of property, both here and in England, to little Pearl, the daughter of Hester Prynne.

So Pearl — the elf-child, — the demon offspring, as some people, up to that epoch, persisted in considering her — became the richest heiress of her day, in the New World. Not improbably, this circumstance wrought a very material change in the public estimation; and, had the mother and child remained here, little Pearl, at a marriageable period of life, might have mingled her wild blood with the lineage of the devoutest Puritan among them all. But, in no long time after the physician's death, the wearer of the scarlet letter disappeared, and Pearl along with her. For many years, though a vague report would now and then find its way across the sea, — like a shapeless piece of driftwood tost ashore, with the initials of a name upon it, — yet no tidings of them unquestionably authentic were received. The story of the scarlet letter grew into a legend. Its spell, however, was still potent, and kept the scaffold awful where the poor minister had died, and likewise the cottage by the sea-shore, where Hester Prynne had dwelt. Near this latter spot, one afternoon, some children were at play, when they beheld a tall woman, in a gray robe, approach the cottage-door. In all those years it had never once been opened; but either she unlocked it, or the decaying wood and iron yielded to her hand, or she glided shadow-like through these impediments, — and, at all events, went in.

On the threshold she paused, — turned partly round, — for, perchance, the idea of entering, all alone, and all so changed, the home of so intense a former life, was more dreary and desolate than even she could bear. But her hesitation was only for an instant, though long enough to display a scarlet letter on her breast.

And Hester Prynne had returned, and taken up her long-forsaken shame. But where was little Pearl? If still alive, she must now have been in the flush and bloom of early womanhood. None knew — nor ever learned, with the fulness of perfect certainty — whether the elf-child had gone thus untimely to a maiden grave; or whether her wild, rich nature had been softened and subdued, and made capable of a woman's gentle happiness. But, through the remainder of Hester's life, there were indications that the recluse of the scarlet letter was the object of love and interest with some inhabitant of another land. Letters came, with armorial seals upon them, though of bearings unknown to English heraldry. In the cottage there were articles of comfort and luxury, such as Hester never cared to use, but which only wealth could have purchased, and affection have imagined for her. There were trifles, too, little ornaments, beautiful tokens of a continual remembrance, that must have been wrought by delicate fingers, at the impulse of a fond heart. And, once, Hester was seen embroidering a baby-garment, with such a lavish richness of golden fancy as would have raised a public tumult, had any infant, thus apparelled, been shown to our sombre-hued community.

In fine, the gossips of that day believed, — and Mr. Surveyor Pue, who made investigations a century later, believed, — and one of his recent successors in office, moreover, faithfully believes, — that Pearl was not only alive, but married, and happy, and mindful of her mother; and that she would most joyfully have entertained that sad and lonely mother at her fireside.

But there was a more real life for Hester Prynne, here, in New England, than in that unknown region where Pearl had found a home. Here had been her sin; here, her sorrow; and here was yet to be her penitence. She had returned, therefore, and resumed, — of her own free will, for not the sternest magistrate of that iron period would have imposed it, — resumed the symbol of which we have related so dark a tale. Never afterwards did it quit her bosom. But, in the lapse of the toilsome, thoughtful, and self-devoted years that made up Hester's life, the scarlet letter ceased to be a stigma which attracted the world's scorn and bitterness, and became a type of something to be sorrowed over, and looked upon with awe, yet with reverence too. And, as Hester Prynne had no selfish ends, nor lived in any measure for her own profit and enjoyment, people brought all their sorrows and perplexities, and besought her counsel, as one who had herself gone through a mighty trouble. Women, more especially, — in the continually recurring trials of wounded, wasted, wronged, misplaced, or erring and sinful passion, — or with the dreary burden of a heart unyielded, because unvalued and unsought, — came to Hester's cottage, demanding why they were so wretched, and what the remedy! Hester comforted and counselled them, as best she might. She assured them, too, of her firm belief, that, at some brighter period, when the world should have grown ripe for it, in Heaven's own time, a new truth would be revealed, in order to establish the whole relation between man and woman on a surer ground of mutual happiness. Earlier in life, Hester had vainly imagined that she herself might be the destined prophetess, but had long since recognized the impossibility that any mission of divine and mysterious truth should be confided to a woman stained with sin, bowed down with shame, or even burdened with a life-long sorrow. The angel and apostle of the coming revelation must be a woman, indeed, but lofty, pure, and beautiful; and wise, moreover, not through dusky grief, but the ethereal medium of joy; and showing how sacred love should make us happy, by the truest test of a life successful to such an end!

So said Hester Prynne, and glanced her sad eyes downward at the scarlet letter. And, after many, many years, a new grave was delved, near an old and sunken one, in that burial-ground beside which King's Chapel has since been built. It was near that old and sunken grave, yet with a space between, as if the dust of the two sleepers had no right to mingle. Yet one tombstone served for both. All around, there were monuments carved with armorial bearings; and on this simple slab of slate — as the curious investigator may still discern, and perplex himself with the purport — there appeared the semblance of an engraved escutcheon. It bore a device, a herald's wording of which might serve for a motto and brief description of our now concluded legend; so sombre is it, and relieved only by one ever-glowing point of light gloomier than the shadow: —

"ON A FIELD, SABLE, THE LETTER A, GULES."

THE END.

PART TWO

The Scarlet Letter: A Case Study in Contemporary Criticism

Introduction: The Critical Background

In a letter dated 1850 and written to his friend and old Bowdoin classmate, Horatio Bridge, Hawthorne began to write the history of his most famous novel's critical reception. First, he sums up the response of his wife to the concluding chapter of *The Scarlet Letter:* "It broke her heart and sent her to bed with a grievous headache — which I look upon as a triumphant success! Judging from its effect on her and the publisher, I may calculate on what bowlers call a ten-strike. Yet I do not make any such calculation," Hawthorne goes on immediately to say. "My writings do not, nor ever will, appeal to the broadest class of sympathies." In fact, he proceeds by predicting that if anything the introduction to his novel, "The Custom-House," which has "an imaginative touch here and there — . . . may be more widely attractive than the main narrative." *The Scarlet Letter,* he admits, "lacks sunshine" (Crowley 151). (These comments and other reviews quoted from Hawthorne's contemporaries may be found in J. Donald Crowley's *Hawthorne: The Critical Heritage* [1971].)

Hawthorne's predictions proved prophetic, in the sense that many of the volume's first reviewers *were* pleased by the imaginative touches of "The Custom-House" and *did* find the novel that followed it depressing. George Ripley, writing in the *New York Tribune Supplement,* praised "The Custom-House" for its "unrivalled force of graphic delineation" and predicted it "will furnish an agreeable amusement to those who are so far from the scene of action as to feel no wound in their personal relations" (Crowley 155, 159). "We confess," Anne W. Abbott wrote in the *North American Review,* "that to our individual taste, this naughty [Custom-House] chapter is more piquant than anything in the book. . . . We like the preface better than the tale" (Crowley 164–65).

As for "the tale," it left no small number of book reviewers of Hawthorne's day with headaches, although not for the same reason the novel left Sophia Hawthorne with one. Contemporary reviewers saw *The Scarlet Letter* as evidence of national moral decay as well as of the decline of the novel. "Our interest" in Hester Prynne, Abbott claims, "only continues while we have hope for her soul"; once Hester's "humility catches a new tint, and we find it pride, . . . she disappoints us. . . . We were looking to behold a Christian." As for Arthur Dimmesdale, "we are told repeatedly, that the Christian element yet pervades his character and guides its efforts; but it seems strangely wanting" (165–66).

A self-described Christian, Abbott was not writing in a Christian forum; those reviewers who did were even more severe. According to Orestes Brownson, Hawthorne misused his God-given faculties by investing a subject (adultery) "not fit . . . for popular literature" with "all the fascinations of genius, and all the charms of a highly polished style." He created an adulteress who "suffers not from remorse, but from regret," together with an adulterer who "suffers . . . not from the fact of the crime itself but from the consciousness of not being what he seems to the world, from his having permitted the partner in his guilt . . . to be punished, without his having the manliness to avow his share in the guilt" (Crowley 176).

Even more disapproving was Arthur Cleveland Coxe in the *Church Review*. Believing that stories should be of "moral benefit," Coxe declares himself "astonished" that Hawthorne would choose adultery for his subject. Such incidents may have been common even in Puritan times, he admits, but "good taste might be pardoned for not giving them prominence in fiction." Summarizing the story as the "nauseous amour" of a Puritan pastor, and a woman whose mind is even more "debauched" than her body, Coxe goes on to ask whether "filth" is now requisite to romance and whether "the French era" has "actually begun in our literature."

To be sure, there were some reviewers who did not see *The Scarlet Letter* as either a danger to morals or a precursor to a "French" (that is, amoral or immoral) era in American literature. George Bailey Loring, for instance, writing in the *Massachusetts Quarterly Review,* went so far as to say that the novel was a "vehicle of religion and ethics" because it properly exposed the inhumanity of Puritanism, which repressed the sensuous element in human nature" (Crowley 169). But most of those who assessed the morality of *The Scarlet Letter* positively did so by claiming that the novel was actually a morally instructive, even Puritanical, work that warned against the pitfalls of sensuality in general and adulterous misdeeds in particular. E. A. Duyckinck took that tack in *The Literary World*. As for "the moral," he writes, "though severe, it is wholesome, and is a sounder bit of Puritan divinity than we have been of late accustomed to hear from the degenerate successors of Cotton Mather. . . . The spirit of his old Puritan ancestors, to whom he refers in the preface, lives in Nathaniel Hawthorne" (Crowley 156–57).

E. P. Whipple agreed, stating in *Graham's Magazine* that the "moral purpose of the book" is so "definite" that "the most abandoned libertine could not read the volume without being thrilled into something like virtuous resolution." In Whipple's view no novel could be more *un*-French: "to those who have theories of seduction and adultery modeled after the French school of novelists," he says,

> the volume may afford matter for very instructive and edifying contemplation; for, in truth, Hawthorne, in *The Scarlet Letter*, has utterly undermined the whole philosophy on which the French novel rests. . . . He has made his guilty parties end, not as his own fancy or his own benevolent sympathies might dictate, but as the spiritual laws, lying back of all persons, dictated to him. (Crowley 156, 157, 161–62)

In addition to finding sound moral teaching in the book, both Whipple and Duyckinck detected philosophy and artfulness. Duyckinck referred to the novel as "a drama in which thoughts are acts," while describing as "perfect" the "atmosphere of the piece." Whipple called *The Scarlet Letter* a "beautiful and touching romance" with "a profound philosophy underlying the story"; Hawthorne's regular readers, he predicted, "will hardly be prepared for a novel of so much tragic interest and tragic power, so deep in thought and so condensed in style." The only fault he finds in the book, "if fault it have, is the almost morbid intensity with which the characters are realized, and the consequent lack of sufficient geniality in the delineation" (Crowley 160–61).

This criticism of the novel's morbid intensity is perhaps stated most strongly in an essay by Henry F. Chorley and published in the *Athenaeum*. Calling the novel "most powerful" but "more than ordinarily painful," Chorley explains that the "misery of the woman" at the center of the story "is . . . present in every page," but that "her slow and painful purification through repentance is crowned by no perfect happiness." As for "Dimmesdale, the faithlesss priest," Chorley calls "appalling" the "gradual corrosion" of his heart. . . . His final confession and expiation are merely a relief, not a reconciliation." Like those other critics who fault the novel for its amoral or immoral teachings, Chorley suggests that "passions and tragedies like these" are not "the legitimate subjects for fiction" (Crowley 162–63).

Hawthorne, certainly, did not share the view that he had produced a work destructive to American morals. But he could not justly have resented the recurring claim that his book was perhaps too tragic, too passionately painful. Those who made the claim were, after all, unwittingly echoing his own private assessment that it is a dark and dismal work. Having admitted that his novel "lacks sunshine," Hawthorne had proceeded in his letter to Horatio Bridge by remaking the point with a directness unexceeded by Chorley or any other reviewer. "To tell you the truth," he had concluded, "it is . . . positively a h—ll-fired story, into which I found it almost impossible to throw any cheering light" (Crowley 151).

In the century following the appearance of these early reviews, *The Scarlet Letter* was of course often discussed. But because literary criticism had not yet developed into the intellectual discipline that it has become since the 1940s, Hawthorne's novel was not written about — certainly it was not carefully and systematically analyzed — with the frequency that it has been in the past fifty years.

Nonetheless, a few interesting studies were published between the last of the contemporary reviews and the advent of modern Hawthorne criticism. In 1879, a book was published simply entitled *Hawthorne,* written by the great American novelist Henry James. James, who praised the novel as "the finest piece of imaginative writing yet put forth in this country" and as "something" that could be "sent to Europe as exquisite in quality as anything that had been received" (James 110–11), nonetheless had much that was critical to say as well. Like his predecessors, and like Hawthorne himself, he found the story somewhat too painful, too somber: "It is densely dark," he writes, "with a single spot of vivid colour in it; and will probably long remain the most consistently gloomy of English novels of the first order" (109). Also like the first reviewers, he viewed the novel as a novel of ideas. But whereas E. A. Duyckinck had approved of the novel for being one in which "thoughts are acts," James objected to the fact that even "characters," when examined closely, turn out to be "representatives of a single state of mind" (114). He felt that the philosophical abstractness of the novel made it somewhat frigid; as for the "symbolism" contributing to that abstractness, "there is," James writes, "I think, too much." Especially excessive, in James's view, is Hawthorne's placement of the letter A in the sky toward the end of the novel. Here, James politely suggests, "We feel that he goes too far" (114, 117, 118).

On the question of the book's ethical content (or lack thereof), James sides squarely with that minority who had found the book highly moral in character. In fact, he refuses even to say that the book is *about* adultery, which, he points out, has been committed long before the story begins. "To Hawthorne's imagination," James argues, "the fact that these two persons had loved each other too well was of an interest comparatively vulgar; what appealed to him was the idea of their moral situation in the long years that were to follow" (112). Because the plot turns on that situation, it is, in James's view, "full of the moral presence of the race that invented Hester's penance":

> Puritanism, in a word is there, not only objectively, as Hawthorne tried to place it there, but subjectively as well. Not, I mean in his judgment of his characters, in any harshness of prejudice, or in the obtrusion of a moral lesson; but in the very quality of his own vision, in a certain coldness and exclusiveness of treatment. (112–14)

It is hard not to recall, while reading James's words, those written by Duyckinck some thirty years earlier: "The spirit of his old Puritan ancestors, to whom he refers in the preface, lives in Nathaniel Hawthorne." The difference between Duyckinck and James is that the former approved of what the latter found "cold," or a weakness in an otherwise great artistic sensibility.

In 1902, a little more than twenty years after James published *Hawthorne,* the scholar George Edward Woodberry brought out a book entitled *Nathaniel Hawthorne*. Woodberry, like James, emphasizes symbolism in *The Scarlet Letter*. But rather than saying that there is "too much" symbolism, Woodberry comments approvingly, particularly on the symbolism surrounding the scarlet A. The symbolic letter, Woodberry argues, like the recurring stage-setting, provides the tale with unity: "it multiplies itself, as the tale unfolds, . . . as if in mirrors set round about it, — in the slowly disclosed and fearful stigma on the minister's hidden heart," "in the growing elf-like figure of the child, who . . . embodies it," and even in the apparition that James found so excessive: the one that "lightens forth over the whole heavens" in the novel's climactic scene. Along with unity of plot, continues Woodberry, the symbol of the scarlet letter provides the novel with unity of meaning — the meaning it stands for. That meaning, in Woodberry's words, "is the brand of sin on life" (192–93).

In 1923, just over twenty years after Woodberry published his interpretation and just over forty after James had published his evaluation, *The Scarlet Letter* was once again being debated by an influential writer. This time, it was D. H. Lawrence, author of *Sons and Lovers* and *Lady Chatterley's Lover,* who was refocusing critical attention on the novel. Lawrence, who devoted the seventh chapter of his *Studies in Classic American Literature* (1923) to "Hawthorne and *The Scarlet Letter,*" in many ways brings to culmination the views of his critical predecessors, while at the same time writing a highly idiosyncratic and provocative account of Hawthorne's novel meant to justify his own agnostic and sensual world view.

Lawrence agreed with James that the story was not a romance, calling the book "a sort of parable, an earthly story with a hellish meaning" (121). Like James and a few of the early reviewers, he finds the book *too* dark, painful, and hellish; like them, he sees the spirit of the book as essentially moral and didactic and the author of the book as essentially Puritan in spirit. But he goes further, attacking the book as a deeply destructive myth that teaches hypocrisy and the sinfulness of the sensual and instinctive life. *The Scarlet Letter,* in Lawrence's view, is a particularly American reworking of the myth of the Fall of Man, with a particularly American message: one should either learn to deny the body and die, as Dimmesdale does, or one should deny the sensual through self-sacrifice, by becoming a sister of mercy, as does Hester. Finally, one should keep up appearances — as do both Hester and Dimmesdale.

In a sense, Lawrence weaves together two long-divergent strands of argument about *The Scarlet Letter.* Along with some of his precursors, he finds the novel to be Puritanical and moral, but he doesn't believe the novel great in *spite* of that fact. Like the pious reviewers for Christian journals, he regards the novel as "hellish[ly]" dangerous and destructive. But to Lawrence, its danger resides not in any approval of the life of the flesh, but rather in what he sees as the novel's "devilish" parable: "*Be good! Be good!* warbles Nathaniel. *Be good, and never sin! Be sure your sins will find you out*" (123).

Modern Hawthorne criticism has been considerably influenced by both nineteenth-century and early modern studies. Sometimes the mark of influence stands out prominently against new critical insights as the old scarlet letter stands out against the newer garments that Hester has fashioned for herself. For example, when Leslie Fiedler published *Love and Death in the American Novel* (1960), the influence of James and Lawrence was obvious. James had pointed out that *The Scarlet Letter* is not about adultery, but about the "moral situation" that ensues; Lawrence had found in the novel a revision of the story of the Fall. Fiedler calls it "a seduction story without a seduction," "a parable of the Fall with the Fall offstage and before the action proper begins" (224).

But in discussing Fiedler, we are getting ahead of our story of *The Scarlet Letter* and its interpretive history. In the 1940s, when academic criticism began to flourish as a discipline, it was the artistry of *The Scarlet Letter* — not its moral or mythical content — that critics such as F. O. Matthiessen, Leland Schubert, and Richard Harter Fogle tended to stress. These critics and others of their generation, the "New Critics," were far more prone to follow James by discussing the symbolism of *The Scarlet Letter* than to expand on Lawrence's perception of the novel as a destructive revision of the myth of the Fall as worked out by an American moralist with a Puritan bent.

The New Criticism, or formalism as it is now usually called, was a reaction against the tendency to read the literary work as a product of its author's personal experience and historical context. Formalists, such as William K. Wimsatt, warned against trying to determine or discern an author's purpose in writing a work (Wimsatt and Monroe C. Beardsley referred to this as the "Intentional Fallacy"); our time as readers is better spent, the formalists suggested, in describing the way the parts of a work relate to form a beautiful artistic unity. Formalists avoided talking about the effects that works of literature might have on readers (or on the national morality); they believed the critic's job to be that of identifying the form and meaning of a work, not of describing the responses of readers to it.

When F. O. Matthiessen discussed *The Scarlet Letter* in *American Renaissance: Art and Expression in the Age of Emerson and Whitman* (1941), he stressed the artfulness of the novel, developing an idea first advanced by Woodberry, namely, that *The Scarlet Letter* is intrinsically theatrical. Matthiessen argues that in this novel Hawthorne

> developed his most coherent plot. Its symmetrical design is built around the three scenes on the scaffold or the pillory. There Hester endures her public shaming in the opening chapter. There, midway through the book, the minister . . . ascends one midnight for

> self-torture, and is joined by Hester. . . . There also, at the end, . . . the exhausted and death-stricken Dimmesdale totters to confess his sin . . . and to die in Hester's arms. (275)

Matthiessen's stress on the "coherence" and "symmetrical[ity]" provided by the twice-repeated scaffold setting is typical of formalist criticism.

Three years after Matthiessen published this major formalist study, Leland Schubert built upon it in *Hawthorne, the Artist: Fine Art Devices in Fiction* (1944). Schubert, who begins by referring to *The Scarlet Letter* as "perfect," "thoroughly fused," "whole," "complete," and wonderfully "artificial," continues by exposing the "pattern, rhythm, balance, and the other elements of form" that "hold the book together" (136–37).

Following Matthiessen, he argues that the book is "built around the scaffold." In fact, he points out, if we consider "The Custom-House" and the "Conclusion" to stand apart from and to form "a kind of frame around" the work of art, then we see that the scaffold scene is repeated in precisely "the middle chapter (when we omit the concluding chapter)" and "the last (omitting the conclusion)." But "there is more to the pattern than this two-fold division," Schubert continues. "The setting of the first three and the last three chapters is the market-place. . . . The chapters between the first three and the middle one fall nicely into two groups of five and three chapters each," the group of five dealing "chiefly with Pearl and Hester," the group of three dealing "with Chillingworth and Dimmesdale." Another group of three chapters (dealing with Hester and Pearl) follows the middle scaffold chapter, and another group of five chapters follows that second group of three. "So it is," Schubert concludes, "that we find *The Scarlet Letter* falling into a structural pattern of seven parts (exclusive of the frame)" (138–39).

In addition to outlining the novel's plot, Schubert discusses the way the novel is structured by repeated images (of trembling, sunlight, and the scarlet letter itself), repeated words ("live," "forgive"), repeated ideas or suggestions (Dimmesdale may be Pearl's father), and repeated colors (red, black, gold). All of these repetitions contribute to the overall pattern of the work, giving it a "rhythmic motif" like that found in musical works (150, 153).

Schubert's notion that the structure of *The Scarlet Letter* is made up of "motifs" created by repetition was developed by a number of formalist critics. In *Hawthorne: A Critical Study,* Hyatt Waggoner shows how a given image, like that of flowers or weeds, "is established as a motif" and how, once established, it is able to function symbolically (127). Waggoner shows that Hawthorne begins by presenting a "pure sensory image" (the prison is described as dark), then "expands it into a mixed image, exploring its connotations" (Chillingworth's "face darkened with some powerful emotion"), repeating the process until the image, "enriched by the relations," is "drained" of its original status as a sensory descriptor and becomes part of "a work of symbolism" (119–29 passim). Thus, by the time "Governor Bellingham says that Pearl is 'in the dark' concerning her soul, the expression means far more to the reader than that she is not . . . properly instructed: it calls up the whole range of colors, and the moral and other values attached to them, which the reader has absorbed by this time" (127).

Richard Harter Fogle was another New Critic who followed Schubert's lead in analyzing motifs involving color, light, and darkness in *The Scarlet Letter;* indeed, his most influential critical study, published in 1952, was entitled *Hawthorne's Fiction: The Light and the Dark*. In addition to showing how the interconnected imagery of darkness, of the "waxing and waning of sunlight," and of "the . . . hell-fire which occurs throughout *The Scarlet Letter*" come to serve as indices of the emotional or spiritual states of characters, Fogle also discusses another kind of unity: that provided by the book's "sustained and rigorous dramatic irony" resulting from its repetition of scenes in which one character is aware of something known to some, but not all, of the characters present in the scene. For instance, when Dimmesdale tries to persuade Hester to confess publicly the name of her partner in adultery, "his words have a double meaning — one to the onlookers, another far different to Hester and the speaker himself" (*Hawthorne's Fiction* 111, 114–15).

Fogle argues that these dramatic ironies not only help advance the theme of tragic concealment, but also provide the basis for the novel's climax, in which Chillingworth arrives at "a moment of terrible self-knowledge." The old man's sudden realization that the ultimate result of his long-concealed purpose is the destruction not so much of Dimmesdale as of himself provides not only the book's final dramatic irony but also "an Aristotelian reversal, where a conscious and deep-laid purpose brings about totally unforeseen and opposite results" (*Hawthorne's Fiction* 112).

Fogle's use of Aristotle, of course, takes us beyond Hawthorne's text and causes us to see *The Scarlet Letter* in the light of a wider context, that of literary history. In a later book, *Hawthorne's Imagery,* Fogle expands on his thesis about Hawthorne's repeated symbolic use of light and dark, sunlight and shadow, as well as on the role of literary history in Hawthorne. He suggests that both the novel's heavenly light and its "distinctness of mid-day" need to be referred back to poems by Coleridge and Wordsworth — especially to Wordsworth's great "Ode: Intimations of Immortality," in which "celestial light" is distinguished from "the light of common day" (*Hawthorne's Imagery* 27–28, 34).

Darrel Abel was another critic writing during the 1950s who combined a formalist attention to artistic structure with an interest in literary antecedents. In writing about Arthur Dimmesdale, he adheres closely to the text, developing Matthiessen's argument about the structural importance of the three scaffold scenes by showing that these scenes prove that Dimmesdale, not Hester Prynne, is the novel's main character. In his study, *The Moral Picturesque* (articles published in book form in 1988), Abel outlines the scenes as follows: at the beginning of the book, Dimmesdale is not on the scaffold with Hester but knows he should be; in the middle, he ascends the scaffold alone, at night; at the end he does so in public, to confess his sin. The plot of the novel, in Abel's view, "exhibits the protracted struggle between influences seeking to prevent the minister from ascending this emblematic scaffold . . . and influences seeking to induce him to do so" (227). But when Abel turns his attention from this character whose "role is the structural and thematic center of the romance" (225) to other characters, he widens the angle of his vision to encompass not just the form of one novel, but also the backdrop of literary history. Through Hester, who "typifies romantic individualism" (180), Hawthorne supposedly showed that it is not enough to be a sincere self living in nature and believing that all true love has a consecration of its own. Through Pearl, according to Abel, Hawthorne argued even more specifically with a specific Romantic poet, Wordsworth, and showed that the Wordsworthian child of nature is not necessarily a pure and moral child, because humanity, not nature, is the source of morality. With the remaining main character in the story, Chillingworth, Hawthorne took on a group of belated *American* Romantics, according to Abel: the Transcendentalists of Hawthorne's own place and time. Through the "diabolized physician," Hawthorne allegedly showed the Transcendentalists' "optimism" about "human nature and its possibilities" to be questionable, if not unjustified (207).

The debate about whether Hester or Dimmesdale lies at the novel's center was, to some extent, finessed by Roy R. Male in his book *Hawthorne's Tragic Vision* (1957). Male argues that the first third of *The Scarlet Letter* describes Hester's "limited ascension," as she "recognizes her guilt" and "reaches the peak of her moral development"; that the second third of the novel is concerned with the shifting of the burden of guilt, represented by Chillingworth, from Hester to Dimmesdale; and that "the final third (Chapters XVII to XXIV) deals with Dimmesdale's ascension. . . . Where Hester's ascension was limited," Male explains, Dimmesdale's "is complete" (97–98). Male's reading turns the novel into something like a Christian tragedy: Christian in that it is about the burden of original sin (symbolized for Male by the act of adultery committed before the opening of the novel); tragic in that, "like *Oedipus Tyrannus* and *King Lear,* [it] is about ways of seeing" (recognition, discovery, insight, self-recognition) and, finally, about cathartic revelation (101 passim).

With the advantage of hindsight we can see that formalism was in flux by 1957, the year Male published his study depicting *The Scarlet Letter* as a kind of Christian tragedy and Richard Chase published his even more influential book, *The American Novel and Its Tradition.* Chase not only sought to define Hawthorne's novel in light of literary tradition (his chapter on *The Scarlet Letter* was entitled "Hawthorne and the Limits of Romance") but also politely attacked formalism, or "the New Criticism." "The New Criticism," Chase writes with prophetic antagonism, "has been interested primarily in poetry and when it has turned to the novel it has too often assumed that the techniques of criticism which are suitable to poetry are sufficient for the novel." Specifically, Chase identifies as inappropriate the New Critics' intense interest in novelistic "metaphor and symbol" (70).

That the novel in general and *The Scarlet Letter* in particular were becoming subject to new and hybrid critical approaches became even clearer in 1964. In that year Charles Feidelson, Jr., who in 1953 had published a typically formalist analysis of "Hawthorne the Symbolist," revisited *The Scarlet Letter,* this time paying relatively little attention to symbols and symmetry while showing a willingness to read the novel in light of conditions and situations that once might have seemed utterly extrinsic and therefore irrelevant. "The book is most profoundly historical," Feidelson argues; "it is not only *about* but also *written out of* a felt historical situation" (Pearce 32).

Drawing on biography, which only a little while ago had been out of bounds to formalists, and "The Custom-House," which had proved of little interest except insofar as it helped "frame" the novel proper, Feidelson argues that an isolated and lonely Hawthorne forged a link with the human community through his writing of *The Scarlet Letter.*

(Interestingly, in making the case, Feidelson may have committed what Wimsatt and Beardsley had called "the Intentional Fallacy.") Hawthorne may seem to have gone about his business in an odd or even paradoxical way, that is, by writing about a woman who was herself alienated from a community that was itself a community of exiles. But in fact Hester is able to accomplish in the novel exactly what Hawthorne needed to accomplish in life, for she comes to transform her enforced life apart from others into a positive individuality. "She converts disinheritance into freedom, isolation into individuality, excommunication into a personal presence that is actual and communicable," Feidelson wrote (Pearce 35).

Feidelson's reading of *The Scarlet Letter* could almost be called a psychoanalytic interpretation, because it views the novel as the product of an author's struggle with a complex personal problem. What this interpretation lacks, the explicit application of the psychoanalytic theories of a Sigmund Freud, was not long in coming. In *The Sins of the Fathers: Hawthorne's Psychological Themes* (1966), Frederick C. Crews was to reread the novel in light of Freudian terms and concepts, such as the *libido*, or sex drive, and the *ego*, or that part of the mind that typically censors, or sublimates, forbidden desires into more socially acceptable alternatives.

As a result of his Freudian applications, Crews came up with a reading of *The Scarlet Letter* quite different from all preceding ones, and very different, indeed, from formalist and quasiformalist accounts. Taking seriously Hawthorne's own description of the novel as a "h—ll-fired story, into which I found it almost impossible to throw any cheering light," Crews dismisses as particularly wrongheaded recent interpretations (by Male, specifically, but presumably by Fogle and Abel as well) representing *The Scarlet Letter* as culminating in self-recognition, revelation, and redemption. In Crews's view, the novel is a dark piece of psychological realism throughout. It explores libidinous desire, the ego's repression of such desire, and the variety of ways in which desire may be gratified after it has been disguised or sublimated.

Central to Crews's analysis is that passage in the novel in which Hawthorne speaks of the psyche or "soul" as "a ruined wall" continually "watched and guarded," lest the "enemy . . . force his way" through again or circumvent the "breach" via "some other avenue" (158). The enemy, according to Crews, would be a forbidden impulse (and the guilt that accompanies it); the guardian of the wall would, in Freudian terms, be the repressive or censoring ego. But the ego is a less than effective sentry; disguised or sublimated, the forbidden impulse may be readmitted and entertained via other avenues. In scourging himself, Crews suggests, Dimmesdale reindulges libidinous desire in a disguised and twisted form; similarly, in rewriting and delivering the impassioned Election Day sermon, the minister draws on and sublimates the same sexual energies that once drove him to break the law of his society. "Dimmesdale's penance," according to Crews, continually "fail[s] to purify him because it . . . has incorporated and embodied the very urge it has been punishing" (141).

Whereas the New Critics, or formalists, had viewed works of literature as self-contained, self-reflexive, self-referential objects of art, critics such as Crews were suddenly making a new kind of sense by referring texts to other texts: not just to literary works narrowly defined (Freud's psychoanalytic writings are not, strictly speaking, works of literary art) and not just to older, influential works, either. (Obviously, Hawthorne didn't learn psychology from Freud, who wrote roughly half a century later than he did.) What critics like Crews were suggesting was that great works of literature at once re-present and anticipate themes or ideas so fundamental to human nature and experience that they find expression in a variety of times, places, and forms. It is these universal themes, not internal artistic interconnections, that we should be looking for when we interpret literature.

Any number of postformalist studies of Hawthorne make these same suggestions, implicitly or explicitly. In one of the first, Harry Levin's *The Power of Blackness* (1958), "the continuity of human awareness" and "the universality of its means of expression" hold the most interest; works by Hawthorne, Poe, and Melville are seen (re)expressing timeless parables or fables that survive the centuries and "pass from one environment to another," each being "an irreducible unit of what [Carl] Jung," a contemporary of Freud's who proposed an alternative psychoanalytic theory, "would call the collective unconscious" (9–10).

The fable Levin discovers — in Hawthorne, but in Poe and Melville as well — concerns the struggle between good and evil. More specifically, however, it concerns what Melville called "the power of blackness," a blackness "from whose visitations, in some shape or other, no deeply thinking mind is always and wholly free." Citing D. H. Lawrence's description of "the Pilgrim Fathers" as " 'black, masterful men' who had crossed a 'black sea' in 'black revulsion' from Europe," Levin finds in the fable what Lawrence had found in it: something particularly American. And yet, he hastens to remind us, the "obsession" with the awful power of blackness "takes us back to the very beginning of things, the primal darkness, the void that God shaped by creating light and dividing night from day." The world's religions "all . . . seem to posit some dichotomy [between darkness and light], such as the Yin and Yang of the Orient" (26, 29). Whereas Hawthorne's images of black flowers and black weeds had interested formalist critics because such images provided unity within *The Scarlet Letter,* these same images captivate postformalists like Levin because they exemplify an ancient mythology of blackness and thus a unity within human consciousness.

Levin was not the first critic to read *The Scarlet Letter* in light of a persistent fable or mythology. As early as 1953, when formalism was still the dominant critical approach, William Bysshe Stein viewed Hawthorne's novel as a relatively recent version of the ancient Faust myth in his *Hawthorne's Faust: A Study of the Devil Archetype.* Faust, of course, was the scholar-magician who sold his soul to the devil in exchange for secret or forbidden knowledge. Stein first points out a parallel between Faust and Chillingworth, the scholar-alchemist who has learned his magic among the New England "Indians." Chillingworth, like Faust, pays a terrible price for the knowledge he seeks:

> After Hester refuses to reveal the identity of her lover, [Chillingworth] extorts a pledge of silence from her on the legal state of their relations. But something in his cruel smile causes her to regret her promise, and she inquires in fear: "Art thou like the Black Man that haunts the forest round about us? Hast thou enticed me into a bond that will prove the ruin of my soul?" His answer is sardonically elusive: "Not thy soul! No, not thine!" (109)

Having yielded to the temptation to exchange his own soul for knowledge, Chillingworth, like Faust, becomes a tempter himself. And Hester, by entering into a pact with her husband not to tell anyone that she is his wife, becomes a secondary Faust figure.

She is Faustian in her suffering: suffering that is in large part caused by the pact she has entered into with the evil Chillingworth. She is Faustian, too, in that she becomes an intellectual rebel in whose mind, the novel tells us, "the world's law was no law." Finally, she is Faustian because she, too, becomes a temptress. And Dimmesdale, whom she tempts in the forest to run away with her, exits the forest as the novel's third Faust: "Nothing short of a total change of dynasty and moral code," the novel tells us, "was adequate to account for [Dimmesdale's] impulses" to make blasphemous and seductive suggestions to pious members of his congregation. "Am I given over utterly to the fiend?" he wonders. "Did I make a contract with him in the forest and sign it with my blood?" (Stein 117–18).

Stein's study of "the devil archetype" in Hawthorne, we can now see, was one of the earliest examples of a kind of criticism that came to be known as archetypal or "myth criticism." Now usually associated with Northrop Frye, the new kind of criticism taught the importance of uncovering not only the larger cultural myths (of the Fall, of Faust, or of the Power of Blackness) that underlie individual literary works, but also the personal mythology of an individual writer, part of which is expressed in each work.

Hugo McPherson accomplished both of these ends in *Hawthorne as Myth-Maker* (1969), in which *The Scarlet Letter* is said to be "allied" to universal "patterns of fairytale, romance, and myth." The romance is also seen as part of a longer and continuous myth, or fairy tale, that Hawthorne told throughout his career, for "the total creation of [an] artist is not his written works," according to McPherson, "but a living, interior drama," "one facet or another" of which is "expresse[d]" by "each of his works" (3, 5). McPherson alludes to Frye at key points in his study: "if — as Northrop Frye has argued — a personal myth 'is in fact . . . the source of [an author's] argument,' " McPherson maintains, "then the critic must recognize that myth, or fail, beyond certain limits, to understand both the artist's statement and method" (5).

McPherson suggests that Hawthorne's overarching myth concerns the quest of a "mercurial hero" for love, social intercourse, and meaning, and that "each of his works expresses one facet or another of the total structure" (5). In the larger tale, or "total structure," the hero is beset by the Dark Lady, the Black Man, and numerous Iron Men before discovering the veiled secret and earning the frail princess. In *The Scarlet Letter,* Chillingworth is the Black Man; Puritan Boston is a community of iron men (and women); and the quest is "for the meaning of *A* or Pearl" (171). Hester is the Scarlet Lady, and

> the "seven long years" of [her] torture are like the seven generations, or Seven Gables, of the Pyncheon-Maule conflict [in *The House of the Seven Gables*], and the seven years of Hollingsworth's quest to establish an institution for criminal reform. In the same way, the embroidered or scarlet *A* is a "talisman" or token of "our common nature"; it is the talisman which later appears in *Blithedale* as Zenobia's exotic flower . . . and in *The Marble Faun* as the seven stones in the bracelet which Miriam presents as a wedding gift to Hilda. (190)

McPherson identifies himself with Frye and may himself be identified as part of a critical movement commonly referred to as "myth criticism." But McPherson also anticipates phenomenological criticism, or "criticism of consciousness," by his suggestion that a given novel is only a page or a chapter in that larger work that phenomenologists refer to as the "*oeuvre*." Defining "the mythological situations that give his work coherence as an *oeuvre*," McPherson writes, draws us "closer to the spirit of his art than interpretations which stress . . . New-critical analysis of image patterns" (13).

Psychoanalytic, archetypal, and phenomenological criticism afford three examples of contemporary critical theories whose practitioners are skeptical of New Critical or formalist analysis. Another, perhaps more interesting example is afforded by feminist criticism. Nina Baym begins a ground-breaking feminist study with the reminder that just "prior to" the advent of formalism or "the New Criticism," the novel "was widely agreed to be a glorification of Hester." Then, New Critics like Abel had come along, arguing that "Dimmesdale was the novelist's true protagonist" and that "Hawthorne portrayed Hester as woefully inadequate." But "to minimize Hester's significance . . . it is necessary to minimize or ignore the plot which points so unequivocally to her importance," Baym protests (49–50, 59). Thus, even "from a structural point of view, this position is untenable. Of the romance's twenty-four chapters, thirteen are 'about' Hester, three are 'about' Hester and Dimmesdale both, and eight are 'about' Dimmesdale" (51).

"I have asked myself over and over," Baym continues, "why it is that critics of the 1950s were almost unanimously concerned to deny Hester her place as protagonist of *The Scarlet Letter*." One answer Baym comes up with is that Hester is associated with "passion, freedom, and individualism," whereas the New Critics valued form and order. "Beyond this," Baym writes,

> I have come to the regretful conclusion that some of the unwillingness, perhaps much of it, to recognize Hester as the protagonist came from a more covert aspect of the New Critical social ideology, its strong sense of appropriate male/female roles and its consequent conviction that it would be improper for a woman character to be the protagonist in what might well be the greatest American book. (51–52)

As evidence that formalists were straining to "diminish the significance of Hester," Baym points to the fact that, in order to accomplish their end, they had to associate her with "romantic individualism," whereas "almost nothing that she does in *The Scarlet Letter* can be labeled as an example of romantic individualism" (53).

Although mainly feminist in her orientation, Baym draws on and anticipates insights developed by other contemporary critics. In arguing that different readers and communities of readers make sense of the same work differently, Baym shows some affinity with deconstructors, who would argue that interpretations are inevitably *metafictions,* that is, fictions about fictions. She also builds significantly on the insights of reader-oriented critics like Richard Brodhead and Kenneth Dauber, who have shown how the text of *The Scarlet Letter* invites or even forces us to choose between different, sometimes contradictory meanings. In suggesting that every critical methodology (including the supposedly objective New Criticism) is the product of a historical period and harbors its own covert social purpose or ideology, she anticipates the new historicism, which attempts to situate historically the act of interpretation as well as the text being interpreted.

In the five introductions that follow, the new historicism, reader-response criticism, and deconstruction, as well as feminist and psychoanalytic criticism, will be further described and explained. Introductions to the five critical approaches will conclude with a brief account of several recent examples of that approach. For instance, the introduction "What Is Reader-Response Criticism?" will end with a summary of the arguments of Brodhead and Dauber. Following each introduction and a selected bibliography is a contemporary essay of the kind of criticism described in that introduction.

The five representative essays — by Shari Benstock (feminist criticism), Sacvan Bercovitch (the new historicism), Joanne Feit Diehl (psychoanalytic criticism), David Leverenz (reader-response criticism), and Michael Ragussis (deconstruction) — demonstrate more than five contemporary approaches to literature. They also prove how changing and vital Hawthorne criticism is today, while affording us glimpses into the continuity of literary criticism. In each provocative new essay, we can see affinities with past approaches, not to mention with other contemporary approaches. For example, Joanne Diehl's psychoanalytic reading is also a feminist reading, as is David Leverenz's reader-response reading, which has psychoanalytic implications as well.

A great work of literature such as *The Scarlet Letter* elicits a host of different interpretive responses, no one of which stands alone or is entirely adequate to unpack its significance. Such texts beget community in that they continually attract new generations of readers, sending them in search not only of meaning but also of the meanings other readers — and generations of readers — have found in them.

WORKS CITED

Abel, Darrel. *The Moral Picturesque: Studies in Hawthorne's Fiction*. West Lafayette: Purdue UP, 1988. This is a collection of essays first printed in various journals in the 1950s.

Baym, Nina. "The Significance of Plot in Hawthorne's Romances." *Ruined Eden of the Present: Hawthorne, Melville, and Poe*. Ed. G. R. Thompson and Virgil L. Lokke. West Lafayette: Purdue UP, 1981. 49–70.

Chase, Richard. *The American Novel and Its Tradition*. Garden City: Doubleday, 1957.

Crews, Frederick C. *The Sins of the Fathers: Hawthorne's Psychological Themes*. New York: Oxford UP, 1966.

Crowley, J. Donald, ed. *Hawthorne: The Critical Heritage*. New York: Barnes, 1971. Contains all the early reviews quoted in the preceding essay.

Fiedler, Leslie. *Love and Death in the American Novel*. Rev. ed. New York: Stein and Day, 1966.

Fogle, Richard Harter. *Hawthorne's Fiction: The Light and the Dark*. Norman: U of Oklahoma P, 1952.

———. *Hawthorne's Imagery*. Norman: U of Oklahoma P, 1969.

James, Henry. *Hawthorne*. 1879. New York: AMS, 1968.

Lawrence, D. H. *Studies in Classic American Literature*. New York: Seltzer, 1923.

Levin, Harry. *The Power of Blackness*. New York: Knopf, 1958.

Male, Roy R. *Hawthorne's Tragic Vision*. New York: Norton, 1957.

Matthiessen, F. O. *American Renaissance: Art and Expression in the Age of Emerson and Whitman*. New York: Oxford UP, 1941.

McPherson, Hugo. *Hawthorne as Myth-Maker: A Study in Imagination*. Toronto: U of Toronto P, 1969.

Pearce, Roy Harvey. *Hawthorne Centenary Essays*. Columbus: Ohio State UP, 1964. Contains the essay on *The Scarlet Letter* by Charles Feidelson, Jr., cited in the preceding essay.

Schubert, Leland. *Hawthorne, the Artist: Fine Art Devices in Fiction*. Chapel Hill: U of North Carolina P, 1944.

Stein, William Bysshe. *Hawthorne's Faust: A Study of the Devil Archetype*. Gainesville: U of Florida P, 1953.

Waggoner, Hyatt H. *Hawthorne: A Critical Study*. Cambridge: Belknap-Harvard UP, 1955.

Woodberry, George, E. *Nathaniel Hawthorne*. Boston: Houghton, 1902. American Men of Letters series. Cambridge: Riverside Press.

Psychoanalytic Criticism and *The Scarlet Letter*

WHAT IS PSYCHOANALYTIC CRITICISM?

It seems natural to think about novels in terms of dreams. Like dreams, novels are fictions, inventions of the mind that, though based on reality, are by definition not literally true. Like a novel, a dream may have some truth to tell, but, like a novel, it may need to be interpreted before that truth can be grasped.

There are other reasons why it seems natural to make an analogy between dreams and novels. We can live vicariously through romantic fictions, much as we can through daydreams. Terrifying novels and nightmares affect us in much the same way, plunging us into an atmosphere that continues to cling, even after the last chapter has been read — or the alarm clock has sounded. Thus, it is not surprising to hear someone say that Mary Shelley's *Frankenstein* is like a nightmare. Nor is it surprising to read an analysis of *The Scarlet Letter* in which the critic compares reading the novel to having a long and complex dream: "Our experience in the world of this novel is akin to Hawthorne's own in the moonlit room," Richard Brodhead has written, referring to the passage in "The Custom-House" in which Hawthorne discusses the world of romance in terms of a familiar room made strange by moonlight. "Ordinary boundaries become fluid" in Hawthorne's world, which is characterized, in Brodhead's words, by a "haunted interconnectedness. . . . Its fluid interrelatedness of parts and its supersaturation with significant patterns give it the quality of overdetermination that Freud ascribes to dreams" (53).

Brodhead here goes a step further than the person who compares *Frankenstein* to a nightmare. We may even say he practices psychoanalytic criticism, for in comparing *The Scarlet Letter* to a dream he invokes the name of Sigmund Freud, the famous Austrian psychoanalyst who in 1900 published a seminal essay, *The Interpretation of Dreams*. He also suggests that Freud's observations — for instance, that dreams are supersaturated with significance and thus overdetermined — may be used to appreciate and better understand literary works. But is the reader who simply calls *Frankenstein* a nightmarish tale a Freudian as well? And is it even *valid* to apply concepts advanced in 1900 to novels like *Frankenstein* and *The Scarlet Letter,* both of which were written long before Freud was born?

To some extent the answer to the first question has to be yes. Freud is one of the reasons it seems "natural" to think of literary works in terms of dreams. We are all Freudians, really, whether or not we have read anything by Freud. At one time or another, most of us have referred to ego, libido, complexes, unconscious desires, and sexual repression. The premises of Freud's thought have changed the way the Western world thinks about itself. To a lesser extent, we are all psychoanalytic interpreters as well. Psychoanalytic criticism has influenced the teachers our teachers studied from, the works of scholarship and criticism they read, and the critical and creative writers we read as well.

But was Hawthorne a Freudian? Obviously, he didn't study from teachers conversant with psychoanalytic terminology; he lived in a world unchanged by Freud. Does it make sense, then, to apply Freudian ideas about the psyche to his books? Freud, after all, didn't *invent* dreams or unconscious desires or libidinous impulses or even the idea that we can learn from dreams.

What he did do, though, was to develop a language that described, a model that explained, a theory that encompassed, human psychology. Many of the elements of psychology he sought to explain are present in the literary works of various ages and cultures, from Sophocles' *Oedipus Rex* to Shakespeare's *Hamlet* to Hawthorne's *The Scarlet Letter*. When the great novel of the twenty-first century is written, many of these same psychological elements will probably inform its discourse as well. If, by understanding human psychology according to Freud, we can appreciate literature on a new level, then we should acquaint ourselves with his insights.

Freud's theories are either directly or indirectly concerned with the nature of the unconscious mind. Freud didn't invent the unconscious; others before him had suggested that even the supposedly "sane" human mind was only conscious and rational at times, and even then at possibly only one level. But Freud went further, suggesting that the powers motivating men and women are *mainly* and *normally* unconscious.

Freud, then, powerfully developed an old idea: that the human mind is essentially dual in nature. He called the predominantly passional, irrational, unknown, and unconscious part of the psyche the *id,* or "it." The *ego,* or "I," was his term for the predominantly rational, logical, orderly, conscious part. Another aspect of the psyche, which he called the *superego,* is really a projection of the ego. The superego almost seems to be outside of the self, making moral judgments, telling us to make sacrifices for good causes even though self-sacrifice may not be quite logical or rational. And, in a sense, the superego *is* "outside," since much of what it tells us to do or think we have learned from our parents, our schools, or our religious institutions.

What the ego and superego tell us *not* to do or think is repressed, forced into the unconscious mind. One of Freud's most important contributions to the study of the psyche, the theory of repression, goes something like this: much of what lies in the unconscious mind has been put there by consciousness, which acts as a censor, driving underground unconscious or conscious thoughts or instincts that it deems unacceptable. Censored materials often involve infantile sexual desires, Freud postulated. Repressed to an unconscious state, they emerge only in disguised forms: in dreams, in language (so-called Freudian slips), in creative activity that may produce art (including literature), and in neurotic behavior.

According to Freud, all of us have repressed wishes and fears; we all have dreams in which repressed materials emerge disguised, and thus we all could, in theory, have our dreams analyzed. One of the unconscious desires most commonly repressed is the childhood wish to displace the parent of our own sex and take his or her place in the affections of the parent of the opposite sex. This desire really involves a number of different but related wishes and fears. (A boy — and it should be remarked in passing that Freud here concerns himself mainly with the male — may fear that his father will castrate him, and he may wish that his mother would return to nursing him.) Freud referred to the whole complex of feelings by the word "oedipal," naming the complex after the Greek tragic hero Oedipus, who unwittingly killed his father and married his mother.

Why are oedipal wishes and fears repressed by the conscious side of the mind? And what happens to them after they have been censored? As Roy P. Basler puts it in *Sex, Symbolism, and Psychology in Literature* (1975), "from the beginning of recorded history such wishes have been restrained by the most powerful religious and social taboos, and as a result have come to be regarded as 'unnatural,'" even though "Freud found that such wishes are more or less characteristic of normal human development":

> In dreams, particularly, Freud found ample evidence that such wishes persisted. . . . Hence he conceived that natural urges, when identified as "wrong," may be repressed but not obliterated. . . . In the unconscious, these urges take on symbolic garb, regarded as nonsense by the waking mind that does not recognize their significance. (14)

Freud's belief in the significance of dreams, of course, was no more original than his belief that there is an unconscious side to the psyche. Again, it was the extent to which he developed a theory of how dreams work — and the extent to which that theory helped him, by analogy, to understand far more than just dreams — that made him unusual, important, and influential beyond the perimeters of medical schools and psychiatrists' offices.

The psychoanalytic approach to literature rests not only on the theories of Freud; it may even be said to have *begun* with Freud, who was interested in writers, especially those who relied heavily on symbols. Such writers regularly cloak or mystify ideas in figures that only make sense once interpreted, much as the unconscious mind of a neurotic disguises secret thoughts in dream stories or bizarre actions that need to be interpreted by an analyst. Freud's interest in literary artists led him to make some unfortunate generalizations about creativity; for example, in the twenty-third lecture in *Introductory Lectures on Psycho-Analysis* (1922), he defined the artist as "one urged on by instinctive needs that are too clamorous" (314). But it also led him to write creative literary criticism of his own, including an influential essay on "The Relation of a Poet to Daydreaming" (1908) and "The Uncanny" (1919), a provocative psychoanalytic reading of E. T. A. Hoffmann's supernatural tale, "The Sandman."

Freud's application of psychoanalytic theory to literature quickly caught on. In 1909, only a year after Freud had published "The Relation of a Poet to Daydreaming," the psychoanalyst Otto Rank published *The Myth of the Birth of the Hero*. In that work, Rank subscribes to the notion that the artist turns a powerful, secret wish into a literary fantasy, and he uses Freud's notion about the oedipal complex to explain why the popular stories of so many heroes in literature are so similar. A year after Rank had published his psychoanalytic account of heroic texts, Ernest Jones, Freud's student and eventual biographer, turned his attention to a tragic text: Shakespeare's *Hamlet*. In an essay first published in the *American Journal of Psychology,* Jones, like Rank, makes use of the oedipal concept; he suggests that Hamlet is a victim of strong feelings toward his mother, the queen.

Between 1909 and 1949 numerous other critics decided that psychological and psychoanalytic theory could assist in the understanding of literature. I. A. Richards, Kenneth Burke, and Edmund Wilson were among the most influential to become interested in the new approach. Not all of the early critics were committed to the approach, neither were all of them Freudians. Some followed Alfred Adler, who believed that writers write out of inferiority complexes, and others applied the ideas of Carl Gustav Jung, who had broken with Freud over Freud's emphasis on sex and who had developed a theory of the *collective* unconscious. According to Jungian theory, a great novel like *The Scarlet Letter* is not a disguised expression of Hawthorne's personal, repressed wishes; rather, it is a manifestation of desires once held by the whole human race but now repressed because of the advent of civilization.

It is important to point out that among those who relied on Freud's models were a number of critics who were poets and novelists as well. Conrad Aiken wrote a Freudian study of American literature, and poets such as Robert Graves and W. H. Auden applied Freudian insights when writing critical prose. William Faulkner, Henry James, James Joyce, D. H. Lawrence, Marcel Proust, and Dylan Thomas are only a few of the novelists who have either written criticism influenced by Freud or who have written novels that conceive of character, conflict, and creative writing itself in Freudian terms. The poet H. D. (Hilda Doolittle) was actually a patient of Freud's and provided an account of her analysis in her book *Tribute to Freud*. By giving Freudian theory credibility among students of literature that only they could bestow, such writers helped to endow psychoanalytic criticism with the largely Freudian orientation that, one could argue, it still exhibits today.

The willingness, even eagerness, of writers to use Freudian models in producing literature and criticism of their own consummated a relationship that, to Freud and other pioneering psychoanalytic theorists, had seemed fated from the beginning; after all, therapy involves the close analysis of language. René Wellek and Austin Warren included "psychological" criticism as one of the five "extrinsic" approaches to literature described in their influential book, *Theory of Literature* (1942). Psychological criticism, they suggest, typically attempts to do at least one of the following: provide a psychological study of an individual writer; explore the nature of the creative process; generalize about "types and laws present within works of literature"; or theorize about the psychological "effects of literature upon its readers" (81). Entire books on psychoanalytic criticism even began to appear, such as Frederick J. Hoffman's *Freudianism and the Literary Mind* (1945).

Probably because of Freud's characterization of the creative mind as "clamorous" if not ill, psychoanalytic criticism written before 1950 tended to psychoanalyze the individual author. Poems were read as fantasies that allowed authors to indulge repressed wishes, to protect themselves from deep-seated anxieties, or both. A perfect example of author analysis would be Marie Bonaparte's 1933 study of Edgar Allan Poe. Bonaparte found Poe to be so fixated on his mother that his repressed longing emerges in his stories in images such as the white spot on a black cat's breast, said to represent mother's milk.

A later generation of psychoanalytic critics often paused to analyze the characters in novels and plays before proceeding to the authors. But not for long, since characters, both evil and good, tended to be seen by these critics as the author's potential selves, or projections of various repressed aspects of his or her psyche. For instance, in *A Psychoanalytic Study of the Double in Literature* (1970), Robert Rogers begins with the view that human beings are double or multiple in nature. Using this assumption, along with the psychoanalytic concept of "dissociation" (best known by its result, the dual or multiple personality), Rogers concludes that writers reveal instinctual or repressed selves in their books, often without realizing that they have done so.

In the view of critics attempting to arrive at more psychological insights into an author than biographical materials can provide, a work of literature is a fantasy or a dream — or at least so analogous to daydream or dream that Freudian analysis can help explain the nature of the mind that produced it. The author's purpose in writing is to gratify secretly some forbidden wish, in particular an infantile wish or desire that has been repressed into the unconscious mind. To discover what the wish is, the psychoanalytic critic employs many of the terms and procedures developed by Freud to analyze dreams.

The literal surface of a work is sometimes spoken of as its "manifest content" and treated as a "manifest dream" or "dream story" would be treated by a Freudian analyst. Just as the analyst tries to figure out the "dream thought" behind the dream story, that is, the latent content hidden in the manifest dream, the psychoanalytic literary critic tries to expose the latent, underlying content of a work. Freud used the words "condensation" and "displacement" to explain two of the mental processes whereby the mind disguises its wishes and fears in dream stories. In condensation, several thoughts or persons may be condensed into a single manifestation or image in a dream story; in displacement, an anxiety, a wish, or a person may be displaced onto the image of another, with which or whom it is loosely connected through a string of associations that only an analyst can untangle. Psychoanalytic critics treat metaphors as if they were dream condensations; they treat metonyms — figures of speech based on extremely loose, arbitrary associations — as if they were dream displacements. Thus, figurative literary language in general is treated as something that evolves as the writer's conscious mind resists what the unconscious tells it to picture or describe. A symbol is, in Daniel Weiss's words, "a meaningful concealment of truth as the truth promises to emerge as some frightening or forbidden idea" (20).

In a 1970 article entitled "The 'Unconscious' of Literature," Norman Holland, a literary critic trained in psychoanalysis, succinctly sums up the attitudes held by critics who psychoanalyze authors, but without quite saying that it is the *author* that is being analyzed by the psychoanalytic critic. "When one looks at a poem psychoanalytically," he writes, "one considers it as though it were a dream or as though some ideal patient [were speaking] from the couch in iambic pentameter." One "looks for the general level or levels of fantasy associated with the language. By level I mean the familiar stages of childhood development — oral [when desires for nourishment and infantile sexual desires overlap], anal [when infants receive their primary pleasure from defecation], urethral [when urinary functions are the locus of sexual pleasure], phallic [when the penis or, in girls, some penis substitute is of primary interest], oedipal." Holland continues by analyzing not Robert Frost but Frost's poem, "Mending Wall," in terms of a specifically oral fantasy that is *not* particular to its author. "Mending Wall" is "about breaking down the wall which marks the separated or individuated self so as to return to a state of closeness to some Other" — including and perhaps essentially the nursing mother ("Unconscious" 136, 139).

While not denying the idea that the unconscious plays a role in creativity, psychoanalytic critics such as Holland began to focus more on the ways in which authors create works that appeal to *our* repressed wishes and fancies. Consequently, they shifted their focus away from the psyche of the author and toward the psychology of the reader and the text. Holland's theories, which have concerned themselves more with the reader than with the text, have helped to establish another school of critical theory: reader-response criticism. Elizabeth Wright explains Holland's brand of modern psychoanalytic criticism in this way:

> What draws us as readers to a text is the secret expression of what we desire to hear, much as we protest we do not. The disguise must be good enough to fool the censor into thinking that the text is respectable, but bad enough to allow the unconscious to glimpse the unrespectable. (117)

Whereas Holland came increasingly to focus on the reader rather than on the work being read, others who turned away from character and author diagnosis preferred to concentrate on texts; they remained skeptical that readers regularly fulfill wishes by reading. Following the theories of D. W. Winnicott, a psychoanalytic theorist who has argued that even young babies have relationships as well as raw wishes, these textually oriented psychoanalytic critics contend that the relationship between reader and text depends greatly on the text. To be sure, some works fulfill the reader's secret wishes, but others — maybe most — do not. The texts created by some authors effectively resist the reader's involvement.

In determining the nature of the text, such critics may regard the text in terms of a dream. But no longer do they assume that dreams are meaningful in the way that works of literature are. Rather, they assume something more complex. "If we move outward" from one "scene to others in the [same] novel," Meredith Skura writes, "as Freud moves from the dream to its associations, we find that the paths of movement are really quite similar" (181). Dreams are viewed more as a language than as symptoms of repression. In fact, the French structuralist psychoanalyst Jacques Lacan treats the unconscious *as* a language, as a form of discourse. Thus, we may study dreams psychoanalytically in order to learn about literature, even as we may study literature in order to learn more about the unconscious. In Lacan's seminar on Poe's "The Purloined Letter," a pattern of repetition like that used by psychoanalysts in their analyses is used to arrive at a reading of the story. According to Wright, "the new psychoanalytic structural approach to literature" employs "analogies from psychoanalysis . . . to explain the workings of the text as distinct from the workings of a particular author's, character's, or even reader's mind" (125).

Joanne Feit Diehl, whose essay begins on page 235, is far from being the first critic to use Freudian concepts in coming to terms with *The Scarlet Letter*. Joseph Levi published a ground-breaking study in *American Imago* in 1953, and slightly more than a decade later Frederick C. Crews published his classic Freudian reading of the novel in his book, *The Sins of the Fathers: Hawthorne's Psychological Themes* (1966). (A summary of Crews's argument may be found in the preceding "Introduction: The Critical Background.") Other psychoanalytic readings of the novel, most of them Freudian but some of them based on the theories of Lacan and others, have been published since 1966.

Whereas Crews had focused on Arthur Dimmesdale's libidinous (and forbidden) desire for Hester Prynne, and on how that desire, because it has been suppressed, must be fulfilled through other disguised means (scourging, writing, etc.), most of the more recent Freudian readings have developed Levi's somewhat older idea that the novel is grounded in the author's oedipal feelings. As Clay Daniel puts it in "*The Scarlet Letter:* Hawthorne, Freud, and the Transcendentalists" (1986), "Hawthorne's masterwork in part is the product of the author's attempt to resolve his Oedipal complex, which was reactivated immediately prior to his writing the story by the death of his mother" (23).

Most Freudians who have interpreted the novel since Daniel have similarly assumed that Hawthorne expresses his disguised oedipal desire through his portrayal of Dimmesdale's relationship with Hester. Hester, after all, *is* a mother, and the reason Dimmesdale can't have her is that she already has a husband. But not all Freudians have seen in the Dimmesdale-Hester relationship Hawthorne's longing for his lost mother being worked out. In an article published in *Literature and Psychology* (1974), Allan Lefcowitz has argued provocatively that it is Dimmesdale, not Chillingworth, who represents the father (he, after all, is the father of Hester's only child, conceived in a scene prior to the novel's opening), and that it is Chillingworth, not Dimmesdale, who represents the oedipal son. Like the boy who feels hostility toward the man who first claimed the mother's affections, Chillingworth hovers near Hester and goads the father of her child. To the objection that Chillingworth is old, ugly, and married to Hester, Lefcowitz would respond with the reminder that an author's self-projection into an oedipal fantasy would inevitably involve disguise.

In "Re-Reading *The Letter:* Hawthorne, the Fetish, and the (Family) Romance," Diehl follows the lead of predecessors such as Daniel and Lefcowitz in reading the novel as an expression of its author's oedipal feelings. (She follows Daniel in interpreting Dimmesdale, not

Chillingworth, as the author's self-projection.) Using Freud's discussion of the guilt felt by sons on the death of their fathers, she discusses Hawthorne's particular biographical situation of being left, as a young child, by a father he practically never saw, to be raised by a mother whose eventual death he found emotionally overwhelming. And, making use of the text of *The Scarlet Letter,* she discusses scenes in which Hester is figured as a distant, unattainable, even dead mother and in which Dimmesdale, through language, tries to reach and regain the woman he has lost.

But Diehl's argument is more complex than those of either Daniel or Lefcowitz. Her focus is neither just on the Dimmesdale-Hester relationship nor on Hawthorne's feelings toward his mother. Rather, Diehl concentrates on the scarlet letter itself, which she maintains is, in Freud's terms, a fetishistic object.

According to Freud, certain things replace and stand for other things that are desired but taboo (a foot fetish isn't really a desire for feet, for example). The A in *The Scarlet Letter,* Diehl maintains, "functions in several ways that parallel Freud's concept of the fetish, which by its very presence recalls the conflict between desire and repression." Along with other characters, Dimmesdale is fascinated by the letter, which seems to signify adultery as it suggests something else to the beholder's unconscious. Thus the A, like all fetishistic objects, conceals what it ultimately signifies and "represents what cannot be spoken, the inviolate truth of what is most desired and what must be repressed, predominantly the longing for the mother."

Diehl goes beyond her precursors by focusing on the letter and by showing how it functions fetishistically for characters other than Dimmesdale. She also breaks new ground by showing how *The Scarlet Letter* (like the scarlet letter) engages the psychology of the reader, thus implicating the reader in the novel's "family romance." One of the most difficult passages in Diehl's essay is also one that is worth pondering:

> For just as Dimmesdale depends on the Puritan community's misinterpretation of narrative events (the appearance of the lost glove on the scaffold and the revelation of the A shining in the night sky) to protect his guilt and not to expose it, so the narrative establishes a pattern of substitutive identifications that play equally on the community of its readers to *fail* to recognize the sublimated incestuous wishes covered by the text.

We too, in other words, are drawn to *The Letter* both because we don't know what it signifies and because, at some level, we do.

PSYCHOANALYTIC CRITICISM: A SELECTED BIBLIOGRAPHY

Some Short Introductions to Psychological and Psychoanalytic Criticism

Holland, Norman. "The 'Unconscious' of Literature." *Contemporary Criticism*. Ed. Norman Bradbury and David Palmer. Stratford-upon-Avon Series, vol. 12. New York: St. Martin's, 1970.

Natoli, Joseph, and Frederik L. Rusch, comps. *Psychocriticism: An Annotated Bibliography*. Westport: Greenwood, 1984.

Scott, Wilbur. *Five Approaches to Literary Criticism*. London: Collier-Macmillan, 1962. See the essays by Burke and Gorer, as well as Scott's introduction to the section "The Psychological Approach: Literature in the Light of Psychological Theory."

Wellek, René, and Austin Warren. *Theory of Literature*. New York: Harcourt, 1942. See the chapter "Literature and Psychology" in Part Three, "The Extrinsic Approach to the Study of Literature."

Wright, Elizabeth. "Modern Psychoanalytic Criticism." *Modern Literary Theory: A Comparative Introduction*. Ed. Ann Jefferson and David Robey. Totowa: Barnes, 1982. 113–33.

Freud and His Influence

Basler, Roy P. *Sex, Symbolism, and Psychology in Literature*. New York: Octagon, 1975. See especially pp. 13–19.

Freud, Sigmund. *Introductory Lectures on Psycho-Analysis*. Trans. Joan Riviere. London: Allen, 1922.

Hoffman, Frederick J. *Freudianism and the Literary Mind*. Baton Rouge: Louisiana State UP, 1945.

Kazin, Alfred. "Freud and His Consequences." *Contemporaries*. Boston: Little, 1962.

Meisel, Perry, ed. *Freud: Twentieth Century Views*. Englewood Cliffs: Prentice, 1981.

Porter, Laurence M. *The Interpretation of Dreams: Freud's Theories Revisited*. Twayne's Masterwork Studies Series. Boston: Hall, 1986.

Reppen, Joseph, and Maurice Charney. *The Psychoanalytic Study of Literature*. Hillsdale: Analytic, 1985.

Trilling, Lionel. "Art and Neurosis." *The Liberal Imagination*. New York: Scribner's, 1950.

Psychological or Psychoanalytic Studies of Literature

Bettelheim, Bruno. *The Uses of Enchantment: The Meaning and Importance of Fairy Tales*. New York: Knopf, 1977. Although this book is about fairy tales instead of literary works written for publication, it offers model Freudian readings of well-known stories.

Crews, Frederick C. *Out of My System: Psychoanalysis, Ideology, and Critical Method*. New York: Oxford UP, 1975.

———. *Relations of Literary Study*. New York: MLA, 1967. See the chapter "Literature and Psychology."

Hallman, Ralph. *Psychology of Literature: A Study of Alienation and Tragedy*. New York: Philosophical Library, 1961.

Hartman, Geoffrey. *Psychoanalysis and the Question of the Text*. Baltimore: Johns Hopkins UP, 1979. See especially the essays by Hartman, Johnson, Nelson, and Schwartz.

Hertz, Neil. *The End of the Line: Essays on Psychoanalysis and the Sublime*. New York: Columbia UP, 1985.

Holland, Norman N. *Dynamics of Literary Response*. New York: Oxford UP, 1968.

———. *Poems in Persons: An Introduction to The Psychoanalysis of Literature*. New York: Norton, 1973.

Kris, Ernest. *Psychoanalytic Explorations in Art*. New York: International Universities, 1952.

Lucas, F. L. *Literature and Psychology*. London: Cassell, 1951.

Natoli, Joseph, ed. *Psychological Perspectives on Literature: Freudian Dissidents and Non-Freudians: A Casebook*. Hamden: Archon Books-Shoe String, 1984.

Phillips, William, ed. *Art and Psychoanalysis*. New York: Columbia UP, 1977.

Rogers, Robert. *A Psychoanalytic Study of the Double in Literature*. Detroit: Wayne State UP, 1970.

Skura, Meredith. *The Literary Use of the Psychoanalytic Process*. New Haven: Yale UP, 1981.

Strelka, Joseph P. *Literary Criticism and Psychology*. University Park: Pennsylvania State UP, 1976. See especially the essays by Lerner and Peckham.

Weiss, Daniel. *The Critic Agonistes: Psychology, Myth, and the Art of Fiction*. Ed. Stephen Arkin and Eric Solomon. Seattle: U of Washington P, 1985.

Freudian Psychoanalytic Approaches to Hawthorne

Crews, Frederick C. *The Sins of the Fathers: Hawthorne's Psychological Themes*. New York: Oxford UP, 1966.

Daniel, Clay. "*The Scarlet Letter:* Hawthorne, Freud, and the Transcendentalists." *American Transcendental Quarterly* 61 (1986): 23–35.

Lefcowitz, Allan. "*Apologia* Pro Roger Prynne: A Psychological Study." *Literature and Psychology* 24 (1974): 34–43.

Levi, Joseph. "Hawthorne's *The Scarlet Letter:* (A Psychoanalytic Interpretation)." *American Imago* 10 (1953): 291–305.

Other Psychoanalytic Approaches to Hawthorne

Hilgers, Thomas L. "The Psychology of Conflict Resolution in *The Scarlet Letter:* A Non-Freudian Perspective." *American Transcendental Quarterly* 43 (1979): 211–23. Hilgers uses Leon Festinger's theory of cognitive dissonance to explain the actions of the novel's major characters.

Irwin, John T. *American Hieroglyphics: The Symbol of the Egyptian Hieroglyphics in the American Renaissance*. New Haven: Yale UP, 1980. Part Three, "Hawthorne and Melville," begins with a Lacanian reading of *The Scarlet Letter*.

Other Works Referred to in "What Is Psychoanalytic Criticism?"

Brodhead, Richard H. *Hawthorne, Melville, and the Novel*. Chicago: U of Chicago P, 1973.

A PSYCHOANALYTIC CRITIC AT WORK

JOANNE FEIT DIEHL

Re-Reading *The Letter:* Hawthorne, the Fetish, and the (Family) Romance

The text is a fetish object, and *this fetish desires me*. The text chooses me, by a whole disposition of invisible screens, selec-

> tive baffles: vocabulary, references, readability, etc.; and, lost in the midst of a text (not *behind* it, like a *deus ex machina*) there is always the other, the author.
>
> –ROLAND BARTHES, *The Pleasure of the Text*

> "Your father — where is your father? Your mother — is she living? have you been much with her? and has she been much with you?"
>
> –WALT WHITMAN

Almost halfway through *The Scarlet Letter,* in a nightmarish inversion of the moonlit-room description of the conditions necessary for the writing of romance, Arthur Dimmesdale ends a night of vigilant introspection by gazing into the mirror, viewing his face in a looking glass, by the most powerful light which he could throw upon it. "He thus typified," Hawthorne writes, "the constant introspection wherewith he tortured, but could not purify, himself. In these lengthened vigils, his brain often reeled, and visions seemed to flit before him; . . . Now came the dead friends of his youth, and his white-bearded father, with a saint-like frown, and his mother, turning her face away as she passed by. Ghost of a mother, — thinnest fantasy of a mother, — methinks she might yet have thrown a pitying glance towards her son!" (120). Other images come and go without comment; the rejecting mother alone receives a direct appeal, voiced not in the third person that speaks throughout the passage, but in the first. The dispassionate objectivity that hitherto separated the authorial voice from his description dissolves with the "methinks," which, in its very immediacy, breaks through the fabric of reserve and seems to speak straight from the heart.

This search for the redemptive mother's pitying glance echoes throughout *The Scarlet Letter,* for, although Hawthorne narratively conceptualizes the work of his romance as the enactment of a desire to reestablish relations with those patriarchal forebears who would so severely judge him, although competition with the father is everywhere on the surface of the text, *The Scarlet Letter* nevertheless harbors a subtext that links the motives for writing to a search for the lost mother, whom the novel envisions as having rejected her only son. Nina Baym has recently argued for the centrality of the maternal in *The Scarlet Letter;* however, my discussion differs from hers in that I am interested in examining what I understand to be a much more ambivalent relationship between the authorial self and the lost mother as it functions in the narrative. Furthermore, I would question her assertion that "the consciously articulated intentions of *The Scarlet Letter,* one might say, are to rescue its heroine from the oblivion of death and to rectify the injustices that were done to her in life" (Baym 21). In my estimation, the romance's "intentions" have less to do with rescuing the heroine/mother from death than they do with returning the son to his mother's presence and exposing a deep authorial conflict toward Hester as the lover/mother.

Consequently, rather than following any single line of interpretation based on character, my discussion will focus on the letter A and its matrix of energies, for it is within the sign's history that the conflicts engendered from repressed authorial desires are most compellingly and intricately articulated. It is, furthermore, in the figure of the letter A itself that the conflict between desire for the mother and the guilt associated with this desire finds its boldest articulation. Specifically, what I want to suggest is that the A functions in several ways that parallel Freud's concept of the fetish, which by its very presence recalls the conflict between desire and its necessary repression. The desire for the mother and the censoring power of custom conjoin in Hawthorne's "A," both in its geometric patterning and in its scarlet threads.

Before expanding on the ways that I understand the A to function as a fetishistic object, however, I want briefly to recall the specific biographical circumstances that would have led Hawthorne to this complex and deeply ambivalent sign. Writing on "Mourning and Melancholia," Freud asserts that the son's guilt at the death of the father is associated with his wish to vanquish him, to destroy the father in order to clear the way to sleep with the mother. The greater the intensity of the previously unresolved oedipal feelings, the more severe the guilt following a parent's death. In the case of the father's death, the son experiences the guilt of harboring a death wish for him that has now come true. In the case of the death of the mother, the guilt is complicated by resentment, by the feeling that she has deprived him both of a means of fulfilling his oedipal fantasy and of finding forgiveness for it; her death, then, becomes a kind of double deprivation. Incest, as fantasy and as taboo, lies at the center of his multiple guilt. How great a factor such guilt would have been in Hawthorne's own psychosexual development must be left to surmise; however, pertinent to an interpretation of *The Scarlet Letter* is an understanding of the narrative's treatment of issues related to early conflicts from Hawthorne's own history. Nathaniel's father, a sea captain, was mostly absent during the first three years of his son's life. That the absence of the father would have intensified the boy's feelings toward the mother there is little doubt. Moreover, the conversion of the father's absence into permanent separation through his death when Nathaniel was four years old — unmarked by any visible event at home — would have offered the young boy no sign to substantiate his father's disappearance in actuality, thus enhancing its importance to him on the level of fantasy.

In regard to the mother, Hawthorne's experience reveals an aspect of the Family Romance that is equally intense. Once again, the particular circumstances of the early life are crucial: one recalls Nathaniel's mother's rejection by her husband's family and the later difficulties the mother found in making an independent home for her children. Such early trauma may lie at the origins of the extraordinary burst of energy Hawthorne experienced following what his wife Sophia called his "brain fever," suffered immediately after his mother's death, an energy related to the reawakening of early repressed drives associated with ambivalent feelings toward his mother and as-yet-unresolved guilt over his father's failure to return.

In two descriptions that mark endings, one physical, the other literary, Hawthorne recounts his attempt and failure to achieve control over a flood of feeling. Here is Hawthorne on his last moments with his mother:

> At about five o'clock, I went to my mother's chamber, and was shocked to see such an alteration since my last visit, the day before yesterday. I love my mother; but there has been, ever since my boyhood, a sort of coldness of intercourse between us, such as is apt to come between persons of strong feelings, if they are not managed rightly. I did not expect to be much moved at the time — that is to say, to feel any overpowering emotion struggling, just then — though I knew that I should deeply remember and regret. . . . Mrs. Dike left the chamber, and then I found the tears slowly gathering in my eyes. I tried to keep them down; but it would not be — I kept filling up, till, for a few moments, I shook with sobs. For a long time, I knelt there, holding her hand; and surely it is the darkest hour I ever lived. (*American Notebooks* 428–29)

Hawthorne confesses to a similar struggle to attain control in only one other instance — when he read the closing pages of *The Scarlet Letter* to his wife: ". . . my emotions when I read the last scene . . . to my wife, just after writing it, — tried to read it, rather, for my voice swelled and heaved, as if I were tossed up and down on an ocean as it subsides after a storm" (*English Notebooks* 95). Once again Hawthorne is surprised by the power of the emotions that overwhelm him. And as in the earlier description, he employs rhythms of ebb and flow to characterize the conflict between attempts to stifle tears and their reemergence against his will. This struggle for control and the necessity to express his longing for his mother are the precipitating psychological occasions for the composition of Hawthorne's romance. For in its gestures of intermittent withdrawal and return, in its provisional endings, in its associative images of oceanic rhythms and vast tracts of land, *The Scarlet Letter* continually reenacts an unfulfilled or thwarted desire: the desire to traverse a distance that becomes more specifically an authorial search for a discourse that can carry Hawthorne back not simply into an amorphous time past, but, more precisely, into the lost mother's presence. Such yearnings are, however, everywhere restricted as enclosure dominates the characters' movements; jail, scaffold, governor's mansion, even the clandestine forest contribute to a claustrophobic intensity in which the human glance at times seems the only possible form of action.

On a narrative level, the antithetical significance of the A manifests itself as a tension between stricture and flight that determines the very texture of the romance. In a crucial conjunction between motive and image, for example, Hawthorne describes the moment when Dimmesdale, returning from the forest reunion with Hester where he has agreed to flee with her (the most extreme attempt to break away found in the book), sits down to write, or rather to rewrite, the Election Day sermon. Dimmesdale associates the power of inspired composition with a voyage over time and space as the text enacts the only journey of which Dimmesdale will prove capable, a distance traversed by language: "Thus the night fled away, as if it were a winged steed, and he careering on it; . . . There he was, with the pen still between his fingers, and a vast, immeasurable tract of written space behind him!" (175). The scene of writing has become the space over which Dimmesdale travels, a ground he traverses to attain his goal; and although Hawthorne does not dwell on the implications of his description, the reader surmises, given the power of language, that the "word" might just possibly transport its author (as narratively it will carry Dimmesdale) past life itself.

That such verbal power should be tied to violation of order is not surprising; that it should be accompanied by a fear of perversion, by an aura of unreality, suggests the extent to which "inspiration" incurs psychic risk. The knowledge Dimmesdale gains in the forest is the self-knowledge that results from his having chosen to flee Boston with Hester. What he learns about himself enforces a sense of doubleness that, although valuable in terms of self-consciousness, tortures his soul:

> The wretched minister! . . . Tempted by a dream of happiness, he had yielded himself with deliberate choice, as he had never done before, to what he knew was deadly sin. And the infectious poison of that sin had been thus rapidly diffused throughout his moral system. It had stupefied all blessed impulses, and awakened into vivid life the whole brotherhood of bad ones. Scorn, bitterness, unprovoked malignity, gratuitous desire of ill, ridicule of whatever was good and holy, all awoke, to tempt, even while they frightened him. (173)

Such pervasive self-alienation comes from an uncensored desire rising to the surface and articulating its demands. Despite the cloud of wickedness in which Dimmesdale perceives himself to be wandering, that release of unchecked desire serves on another level to free his imagination so that he can write the most powerful sermon of his career. His flight into the forest and subsequent self-knowledge allow access to previously unconscious powers associated with the repressed self.

When Dimmesdale delivers the sermon he composed in his newly released fires of thought, the narrative again associates the language of travel with the power of words. Articulated speech now assumes less importance than the power of the voice itself as the reader listens to the sermon as Hester Prynne does, the words obliterated by the distance between herself and the minister. Despite their socially determined positions, Dimmesdale in the church at the center of his congregation and Hester near the scaffold beyond the church walls, the minister's voice nonetheless speaks straight to *her* heart. Communication thus escapes the confines of articulated speech as Hester experiences the sermon's power without recourse to language; voice triumphs over word. "Muffled as the sound was by its passage through the church-walls," the cry of pain reaches out to Hester and "the complaint of a human heart, sorrow-laden, perchance guilty, telling its secret, whether of guilt or sorrow, to the great heart of mankind; beseeching its sympathy or forgiveness, — at every moment, — in each accent, — and never in vain!" (187–88).

Hawthorne follows this description of oracular power with a vision of Hester immobile, almost lifeless, listening attentively to the muffled strains of Dimmesdale's voice:

> During all this time Hester stood, statue-like, at the foot of the scaffold. If the minister's voice had not kept her there, there would nevertheless have been an inevitable magnetism in that spot, whence she dated the first hour of her life of ignominy. (188)

She is transfixed by history (*his story*), objectified by the passion of the past. The sinful minister reaches out to the mute woman through his voice; but by the close of the afternoon, he will have fallen into her arms in an ultimate appeal for disclosure and reunification.

Before observing this climactic moment, however, the reader should note how Hawthorne's language prepares his audience to imagine this public reunion between Dimmesdale and Hester not simply as the meeting of two formerly clandestine lovers, but as a reunion of mother and son as well. The dynamics of family interaction (specifically, between infant and mother) and the anxiety over language's capacity to carry the self into the presence of what it most desires dominate the descriptions that precede Dimmesdale and Hester's final meeting. Throughout the Election Day scene, Hawthorne employs images that associate Dimmesdale with the rejected, ever-apprehensive son who longs to journey back to the sexually tainted, yet longed-for mother. Within the description of communal activities of Election Day, Hawthorne sketches the drama of the toddler, reaching out to an immobile, statue-like woman who welcomes him only when he collapses, on the verge of death, in her arms. Stasis and movement acquire great poignancy, as the extreme efforts of a dying man evoke his earliest beginnings. Furthermore, Hawthorne partly builds his sustained narrative of filial return on his characterizations of Hester as an image of death. Her face, he writes, resembled "a mask; or rather . . . the frozen calmness of a dead woman's features; owing this dreary resemblance to the fact that Hester was actually dead, in respect to any claim of sympathy, and had departed out of the world with which she still seemed to mingle" (176).

This portrayal of Hester as death mask and statue reinforces the prohibition associated with the son's incestuous fantasy and through its very lifelessness serves to protect the perceiver from his own desires. The scarlet letter alone shines out from the grayness of maternal death, at once preserving the sign of desire and barring the possibility of its fulfillment. The simultaneity of the A's function as both signifier and denier of desire opens the letter to ever-recurrent *mis*interpretation, for just as Dimmesdale depends on the Puritan community's misinterpretation of narrative events (the appearance of the lost glove on the scaffold and the revelation of the A shining in the night sky) to protect his guilt and not to expose it, so the narrative establishes a pattern of substitutive identifications that play equally on the community of its readers to *fail* to recognize the sublimated incestuous wishes covered by the text. This tension between disclosure and concealment is the narrative corollary to the fetish's function: to mask desire while naming it. Both depend on the intersubjectivity of author, narrator, and reader — an affiliative community that for the readers of *The Scarlet Letter* provokes a certain anxiety.

Therefore, what Dimmesdale witnesses is a mask of deception and a sign that dis-closes, for Hester's frozen calmness belies her passionate conviction that she and Dimmesdale should leave Boston and flee to Europe. As instigator of this plot and in a maternal assumption of responsibility, Hester attempts to direct their mutual future as lovers. That Dimmesdale subverts Hester's intentions by succumbing to his own death speaks to the deeply violative cast of her double role as mother and lover — as well as to the son's desperate psychic need to suppress the incestuous wish and to keep his already violated mother intact. But, although the death mask presages the defeat of Hester's "solution" on one level of the narrative, the A nevertheless holds before Dimmesdale the sign that the worst has already happened; it is the ever-present sign of transgression kept firmly before his and our eyes.

When Dimmesdale, exhausted from having delivered his sermon, moves from the altar and joins the procession of church fathers, he begins his regressive journey back to the maternal, statue-like form: "He still walked onward," Hawthorne writes, "if that movement could be so described, which rather resembled the wavering effort of an infant, with its mother's arms in view, outstretched to tempt him forward" (193). By rejecting the hand of the "venerable John Wilson," Dimmesdale turns away from the powerful fathers and totters toward his greater need, reunion with the long-denied mother. As Dimmesdale finally reaches his literal family and reunites with them, it is with all the weakness of the child in need of support, yet with the moral righteousness of the savior; he is at once the infant Jesus and a sacrificial Christ:

> "Hester Prynne," cried he, with a piercing earnestness, "in the name of Him, so terrible and so merciful, who gives me grace, at this last moment, to do what — for my own heavy sin and miserable agony — I withheld myself from doing seven years ago, come hither now, and twine thy strength about me!" (194)

Hester lends him her physical support as the crowd next beholds "the minister, leaning on Hester's shoulder and supported by her arm around him, approach the scaffold, and ascend its steps; while still the little hand of the sin-born child was clasped in his" (194). It is only when Dimmesdale confesses that he achieves true union with the tainted mother; the comfort of the breast, the reunion with the mother/

lover, robs Chillingworth, the vengeful father, of life, as Dimmesdale turns his eyes from his adversary toward the source of maternal comfort. "He withdrew his dying eyes from the old man, and fixed them on the woman and the child" (196). In his last moments, Dimmesdale, drained by the extraordinary effort his last sermon has cost him, achieves reunion with Hester and fixes his eyes on the double origins of both his pain and his desire. Yet the kiss he gives Pearl, while freeing her to enter the human community, only further ensures his certain death because it reawakens the knowledge that the chain of desire cannot be broken, that the violative incestuous feelings from which he is barred are awakened in the kiss that the father bestows on his daughter. For Dimmesdale, unable to resolve the terrifying involutions of such a Family Romance, death remains the sole escape.

Must a surrender of health, power, and maturity precede the return to the forbidden woman, and must the return lead to death? This question, shadowed as it is by guilt and longing, speaks not solely of Dimmesdale's predicament but, as I have been suggesting, of deep authorial anxieties as well. If the novel takes as one of its concerns the exploration of the extent of language's power, then the recurrent gestures of appeal and failure within the text signal a disturbing and potentially self-defeating judgment on Hawthorne's capacity as author to attain his desires and survive them, a premonitory warning about the nature of fiction writing that may have contributed to his difficulties in completing the novels — and, by the close of his life, his repeated abandonment of them. *The Scarlet Letter,* that most apparently "complete" of Hawthorne's fictions, challenges language to reach beyond the grave, to test the powers of the word in order to discover whether language can carry the writer over the ground of human loss.

In the opening pages of the novel, the prefatory "Custom-House" section, Hawthorne repeatedly plays on this theme of departure, on the need to quit Salem. Invoking the revolutionary image of the guillotine, he ruefully adopts a proleptic, postmortem self that not only escapes the press of the familiar but, with his beheading, the enactment of vulnerability as well. The narrator writes from "beyond the grave"; the "future editor" of *The Scarlet Letter,* at the start of his work, consigns himself to the "realm of quiet" (52). Elaborating on the metaphor of the political guillotine, the narrator assures us that the whole may be considered as the "Posthumous Papers of a Decapitated Surveyor" (52). The beheading acts not only as a device for distancing both text and speaker, but also serves (albeit futilely) as an attempt to dissociate "Hawthorne the editor" from the sexual desires that are the origins of the story he is about to relate. Indeed, as John Irwin has suggested in his *American Hieroglyphics* (1980), the image of the beheading itself may be seen as a symbolic castration. By presencing an absence, the allusion to beheading functions much as does the letter inscribed on Hester's breast, simultaneously marking her incriminating sexuality and gesturing toward its status as forbidden object. However, in the first instance of figural beheading the effect is to displace the fear of castration while preserving the affective charge of punishment; in the second instance, the addition of the sign, of the A, symbolically marks Hester as the object of a desire that must be denied.

In a description that echoes neither the theme of rejection nor a longing for death, Hawthorne recounts the discovery of the cloth letter itself:

> But the object that most drew my attention, in the mysterious package, was a certain affair of fine red cloth, much worn and faded. . . . It had been wrought, as was easy to perceive, with wonderful skill of needlework; and the stitch (as I am assured by ladies conversant with such mysteries) gives evidence of a now forgotten art, not to be recovered even by the process of picking out the threads. (42)

No amount of disentanglement can retrieve the letter's lost secret of composition, and thus Hawthorne makes clear that the A cannot be reconstituted through analysis:

> This rag of scarlet cloth, — for time, and wear, and a sacrilegious moth, had reduced it to little other than a rag, — on careful examination, assumed the shape of a letter. . . . My eyes fastened themselves upon the old scarlet letter, and would not be turned aside. Certainly, there was some deep meaning in it, most worthy of interpretation, and which, as it were, streamed forth from the mystic symbol, subtly communicating itself to my sensibilities, but evading the analysis of my mind. (42–43)

By obscuring the A's origins while intensifying its power, Hawthorne protects the object from scrutiny as he prepares the way for its special status in the text, *its function as a fetishistic object*. Surveyor Hawthorne must uncover in himself the reasons for such an identification/fixation, and this need for self-mastery through understanding becomes the occasion for the story's retelling. Just as Dimmesdale's Election Day sermon affects Hester in the absence of any articulated speech, so the power of the A depends not on linguistic prowess, but on the direct impact of all that cannot be articulated, the power of those unconscious forces that resist our ability either to adumbrate or to censor them.

Consequently, the A acquires power because among its many meanings it represents what cannot be spoken, the inviolate truth of what is most desired and what must be repressed, predominantly, the longing for the mother. Hawthorne's narrative achieves the identification of the mother's power with the A through its treatment of Hester, who demonstrates woman's ability to revise transgression in order to lead a socially constructive, if psychically restricted, life at the same time that she marks, with the wearing of the letter, the barrier against future temptation, or (given her sociocultural milieu) against "sin." Hester's identifying A not only lends her freedom by separating her from the community; it also leads her, in the narrator's view, dangerously close to chaos. For all its apparent freedoms, Hester's marginalization subdues her even as it becomes the source of her strength; even as it bestows compassion on others, motherhood blocks Hester's full intellectual development. In Hester, Hawthorne thus combines a vision of motherhood rendered inviolate with a portrait of the dangerous woman deprived of her full capacity to threaten either the community or contemporary standards of femininity. By making Hester Dimmesdale's contemporary, Hawthorne relaxes the oedipal connection, severing the male from the generational drama of separation anxiety that occurs instead between two females (Hester and *her* daughter, Pearl). Furthermore, by imposing both biological and communal constraints on Hester, Hawthorne reveals her power while he maintains authorial control over her actions and over his own suppressed, unresolved affect toward his biological mother. Narrative displacement serves the authorial "ego" by protecting it from the full force of its unconscious, yet-to-be-resolved conflicts.

When Hester hovers on the edge of a full-blown prophecy, her words are seized from her and an authorial apology is made to stand in their stead: "A tendency to speculation, though it may keep woman quiet," the narrator avers,

> as it does man, yet makes her sad. She discerns, it may be, such a hopeless task before her. As a first step, the whole system of society is to be torn down, and built up anew. Then, the very nature of the opposite sex, or its long hereditary habit, which has become *like* nature, is to be essentially modified, before woman can be allowed to assume what seems a fair and suitable position. (134; emphasis added)

Here one recognizes an equivocation that more generally characterizes Hawthorne's attitude toward Hester, for by describing the "very nature of the opposite sex" as something that may be culturally derived, "which has become *like* nature," Hawthorne introduces a textual mark of his own ambivalence. If it is culture that has determined woman's essential character, then indeed he may, however gently, be calling for a release of woman's nature from her "his-tory"; whereas if biology is destiny, she would perhaps be wise to accept her fate. By such verbal equivocations, Hawthorne marks, though he does not resolve, the conflict that characterizes his problematic understanding of Hester. Is he on her side or is he not? As father and as son, how can he afford to acknowledge her power without violating his own sense of authority, the masculine aspect of the self? By sympathizing with the enormity of the woman's task of transforming society, the narrator has rendered her beyond speech. Not only does all society act as an obstruction to woman's full expression, but also her public character mitigates against any speculative freedom that might culminate in action. So, to efface the discourse of woman while longing for her presence is to assign her a role that could not be equaled were she admitted to the community of social and verbal intercourse. By stripping her of her capacity to act, Hawthorne thus renders her safe: by converting her into myth, he condemns her to silence.

Placing such severe personal and historical restrictions on Hester — curtailing her power while granting Dimmesdale, in the midst of his duplicity, the freedom of speech — Hawthorne, as author, withstands being submerged by female presence. Among the rhetorical attempts to control female power, the most audacious is the metaphorical process whereby Hester Prynne, lover and mother, herself becomes orphaned, isolated, and homeless. Venturing too far in her speculative ruminations, she is lost, wandering "without a clew in the dark labyrinth of mind; now turned aside by an insurmountable precipice; now starting back from a deep chasm. There was wild and ghastly scenery all around her, and a home and comfort nowhere" (134).

Despite the narrative containment of Hester's threatening power, the A will not relinquish its tenacious hold over the narrator's imagination. Discussing the motive that generally informs Hawthorne's narratives, Frederick Crews remarks, "Relief, indeed, is the desired end-point of each romance; not a solution to its thematic issues but oblivion to them" (17). What are the sources of the A's residual power and why will it not fade with the story constructed to release its power? If the A functions as a hieroglyph within the context of the romance, if its meanings accrue through various points of view, then it may be immune (as Hawthorne had stated in the "Preface") to unraveling and hence to analysis. The clue to its power, Hawthorne reveals, is contact with the wearer and the ability of the A to draw all eyes toward it, to *fix* the viewer's gaze. By escaping the boundaries of story, the A achieves status as a sign that draws us back to the origins of Hawthorne's romance, and, as I have argued, back to the scene of the mother's death. Desire for the lost mother and the censoring power of the Custom-House merge in the scarlet A. And it is to a discussion of the A as fetish that I now turn.

According to Freud, the origins of the fetish can be traced to its function as a "substitute for the woman's (the mother's) penis that the little boy once believed in and — for reasons familiar to us — does not want to give up." Freud continues: "What happened, therefore, was that the boy refused to take cognizance of the fact of his having perceived that a woman does not possess a penis," and that "if a woman had been castrated, then his (the boy's) own possession of a penis was in danger" (21: 152–53ff.). As a sign of the history of this fear and longing, which Hawthorne can face only in the disguised form of fictive displacement, the A functions in the narrative both to focus and to dispel such authorial tensions. Whether or not the fetish serves as a textual "symptom" is not really my concern; of interpretive interest here is the way the scarlet letter operates as a narrative means for resolving an otherwise unresolvable conflict within the fiction; in other words, the text functions therapeutically to provide a means for treating material otherwise closed off from literary production.

The A would therefore represent among its meanings the desired Other whose presence in the fiction can only be acknowledged through its absence, the penis displaced by a vagina that becomes a sign of the female genitalia of the mother forever barred from her son. Indeed, the A articulates through its linear geometry the illustration of forbidden desire. Its divergent verticals suggest a schematic drawing of the vagina, viewed at once frontally and from below, and the horizontal bar of the letter signifies the intact hymeneal membrane, the sign that no violation has occurred. Thus the A signifies a double denial: no marriage and no consummation. Scarlet recalls both the blood of the torn hymen (presenting what is in the same symbol denied — that the mother has [not] been violated) and the color of sexual passion. Moreover, in its artful complexity, the embroidered letter converts this potentially threatening vision of blood and pubic hair, the Medusan coils of active sexuality, into a refined and highly elaborated pattern. Constructed by that most domestic of crafts, the female art of needlework, the letter again operates as a fetish by recalling the forbidden sight even as it protects the gazer from the object's symbolic identity.

The relationship between the scarlet letter and its viewers is not, however, restricted to that of a fetishist and his fetish; for there is no *single* character who defines herself or himself solely in these terms. Instead, the scarlet letter becomes a focus that attracts the kinds of sexual ambivalence and tensions that characterize the text in its entirety and that defines itself in relation to each of the primary characters. For Dimmesdale, the A serves as a mirror of the physical torment he suffers — the outward, external elaboration of the stigmatizing desire for the other disguised as a desire for remorse. Consequently, the flagellation he pursues, the simultaneous stimulation and punishment of the self, is a practice that discloses his libidinal energies as it releases them. For Chillingworth, the A functions as the mark of his home; it is what keeps him on the edges of a civilization therefore negatively defined, and what, through his direct and active intervention, reifies his revenge against Dimmesdale, the transgressor, the son. Hester as the mother who is everywhere present but unattainable, who is given a free imagination yet kept from action, who undergoes "rehabilitation" in terms of society yet must suffer the constant torture of shame, receives the kind of ambivalent treatment from the author that Freud would also ascribe to the fetishist. When Dimmesdale, in his dying moments, abjures any hope for Hester's soul, we may sense the anger behind the rhetorical orthodoxy of his rejection of the possibility that her soul, too, might be saved. And the wearer of the fetish herself participates in ambivalence toward the object when she attempts to cast it off, to deny its historicity and return instead to her lover. Out of this matrix of identities, the A emerges not simply as a mark of the forbidden phallic mother, but also as a sign of the complex interdependencies that are at the center of all human relationships.

Furthermore, it is not without significance that Hester wears the A on her breast and that she should first be seen leaving that dark prison with the infant Pearl at her bosom, for the sign of the forbidden transmuted into art — the craft of embroidery — is, throughout the romance, associated with female fecundity. The power of the mother as nurturing artist, albeit severely restricted by the innately conservative narrator's control, stands clear before the reader. Trapped by societal expectations, Dimmesdale, unlike Hester, wins verbal power but is denied all earthly freedom. Oppressed and outwardly punished as she may be, it is the woman who, by the very fact of becoming an outcast, discovers her more "modest" freedom on the margins of community.

This radical, transforming power thus depends on Hester's marginalization; what keeps her from a more austere radicalism are the presence of Pearl and the narrator's convictions concerning the inherently passive nature of woman. However, to the extent that Hester, no matter how tentatively, turns the A into a symbol of compassion, she wins the potential for transmuting guilt into strength. Dimmesdale, unable to do so until his dying hour (itself troubling in its sadistic orthodoxy), spends his postlapsarian years apparently enduring a festering wound that becomes a masochistic sign of the destructive, if supremely eloquent, artist. This somatization of guilt has a double origin in Chillingworth and the minister, as one feeds on the other in a relationship that grotesquely caricatures that of the nursing mother and her infant Pearl.

If, in conclusion, we accept the scarlet letter's resemblance to the fetish, then Hester, rather than Dimmesdale, embodies an alternative prevision to Freudian theories of the fetish. By drawing our eyes to the woman's breast and the art inscribed thereon, Hawthorne not only ensures visibility for the letter, but he also reinforces Hester's roles of nurturer and artist as synonymous and mutually dependent functions. Rather than signifying the fetish as a denial of an unwished-for absence (the way the letter functions for Dimmesdale), for Hester the letter serves to transform the double negative association of the absence of male genitalia and thwarted desire into a sign that represents the combined powers of nursing mother and creative woman. That Pearl is such a difficult child, that through her milk Hester transmits turbulence as well as nourishment, only further underscores the difficulties inherent in the relationship between sexuality and art — an ambivalence toward maternal origins which, in Hawthorne's works, neither man nor woman can evade.

Free to bury, dismiss, or redeem his characters, Hawthorne, at the close of the novel, performs all three gestures, but it is the paradoxical triumph of the A's imaginative life that it will not fade with time, but evades closure to shine with all the initial fervor of the burning desire with which the story began. Vivid as the letter within the narrator's imagination, it shines out past the final moments of the text, but with a telling difference: what we see when we read " 'ON A FIELD, SABLE, THE LETTER A, GULES' " (201) is a verbal substitution for the engraving that is inscribed on a tombstone. The sign is doubly displaced, first by the descriptive sentence that contains the sign and second by the heraldic device that represents, or stands in for, the words bearing the message that identifies the letter. Thus, the fetishistic object undergoes a further distancing as it is associated directly both with death and with the two lovers resting, albeit with a space between them, side by side. Despite the narrator's claim that the inscription serves as a motto for the story that precedes it, the heraldic device, when translated into words, does not so much explain or "sum up" the story as it insists upon the A's abiding presence. In this final description's act of double distancing, Hawthorne reiterates the resilience of what the A symbolizes: the desire for contact and reunion with the forbidden, which must be approached through a language that will protect the very distance the author seeks to traverse.

Theorizing on the character of desire and its relation to denial, Leo Bersani has commented that

> a sense both of the forbidden nature of certain desires and of the incompatibility of reality with our desiring imagination makes the negation of desire inevitable. But to deny desire is not to eliminate it; in fact, such denials multiply the appearances of each desire in the self's history. In denying a desire, we condemn ourselves to finding it everywhere. (6)

In narrative terms, this would suggest that the A, rather than diminishing in force, gathers its own momentum, just as writing provides access to the origins of the scene of repression but cannot, of course, restore the scene with the incestuous wish intact. Although in the opening pages of "The Custom-House," the narrator had announced his desire to depart Salem and escape the "press of the familiar," the romance's close reveals instead a desire to return to the motherland and to speak with a voice that will reach the dead. Like the archives of the unconscious that, as Derrida maintains, "are *always* already transcriptions," so the worn yet still powerfully evocative A-shaped piece of cloth Surveyor Hawthorne discovers *already* represents the transcription of his author's unconscious transgressive desire for the dead mother. As a sign that bars itself, the A operates for Dimmesdale within *The Scarlet Letter* as does the fetish, both to presence the forbidden desire and to keep that forbidden incestuous wish from being brought to consciousness. That the A, on the other hand, empowers rather than defeats Hester, that the experience of mothering affords her the capacity to transmute the stigma of shame into a badge of commitment and charity, suggests the regenerative power of the woman — a fact that she is nevertheless prohibited from displaying in verbal discourse, forbidden as she is from becoming the prophet of a new and more enlightened age. In my judgment, that she is so deprived speaks to the Hawthornian insistence on silencing the mother and thereby of further identifying the deeply troubled but verbally empowered fetishist with the father and the son.

Shadowing the text and shining beyond it, the scarlet A therefore signifies at once the articulated oedipal anxieties and the covert incestuous desires expressed in the fetishistic silence. Yet the A also signifies a breaking of that silence, for it represents a conflict between the desiring authorial son and the yearnings of the phallic mother, the mother who would free herself from his fetishizing imagination to achieve the authority tested, but finally denied her, in *The Scarlet Letter* — the power of the woman's voice. Imprisoned in her maternal identity while protected by it, Hester cannot escape its stigmatization as Pearl can, because the mother is drawn back to the scene of the "crime," as much victimized by the altruism that converts her A into "Angel" as by the adultery for which it ostensibly stands. Similarly, Dimmesdale, the transgressing son, can acknowledge his paternity only at the moment of his death: punishment for the violation that has always already occurred is the price of adulthood. That maternity and paternity are psychically illicit from the point of view of the child only underscores the significance of the primal scene. Finally, when we, as readers, gaze at the scarlet letter, we might imagine the unconscious text Hawthorne recollects in his narrative, witnessing along with him the scar of primal desire, the bleeding yet inviolate wound, the cultural script, or, as Chillingworth would have it, the "dark necessity" that implicates us all in the novel's fatal Family Romance.

WORKS CITED

Baym, Nina. "Nathaniel Hawthorne and His Mother: A Biographical Speculation." *American Literature* 54 (1982): 1–27.

Bersani, Leo. *A Future for Astyanax*. Boston: Little, 1976.

Crews, Frederick C. *The Sins of the Fathers: Hawthorne's Psychological Themes*. New York: Oxford UP, 1966.

Freud, Sigmund. *The Standard Edition of the Complete Psychological Works of Sigmund Freud*. Ed. James Strachey. Vol. 2. London: Hogarth, 1953–74.

Hawthorne, Nathaniel. *The American Notebooks*. Ed. Claude M. Simpson. Columbus: Ohio State UP, 1972.

———. *The English Notebooks*. Ed. Randall Stewart. New York: Russell, 1962.

Irwin, John. *American Hieroglyphics: The Symbol of the Egyptian Hieroglyphics in the American Renaissance*. New Haven: Yale UP, 1980.

Reader-Response Criticism and *The Scarlet Letter*

WHAT IS READER-RESPONSE CRITICISM?

Students are routinely asked in English courses for their reactions to texts they are reading. Sometimes there are so many different reactions that we may wonder whether everyone has read the same text. And some students react so idiosyncratically to what they read that we say their responses are "totally off the wall."

Reader-response critics are interested in the variety of our responses. Reader-response criticism raises theoretical questions about whether our responses to a work are the same as its meanings, whether a work can have as many meanings as we have responses to it, and whether some responses are more valid than, or superior to, others. It asks us to pose the following questions: "What have we internalized that helps us determine what is — and what isn't — 'off the wall'?" In other words, what is the wall, and what standards help us to define it?

Reader-response criticism also provides useful models for answering such questions. Adena Rosmarin has suggested that a literary work can be likened to an incomplete work of sculpture: to see it fully, we *must* complete it imaginatively, taking care to do so in a way that responsibly takes into account what is there. But there are other models and other representatives of reader-response theory. An introduction to several such models will allow you to better understand the reader-oriented essay that follows as well as to see a variety of ways in which, as a reader-response critic, you might respond to *The Scarlet Letter*.

Reader-response criticism, which emerged during the 1970s, focuses on what texts do to — or in — the mind of the reader, rather than regarding a text as something with properties exclusively its own. A "*poem*," Louise M. Rosenblatt wrote as early as 1969, "is what the reader lives through under the guidance of the text and experiences as relevant to the text." Rosenblatt knew her definition would be difficult for many to accept: "The idea that a *poem* presupposes a *reader* actively involved with a *text*," she wrote, "is particularly shocking to those seeking to emphasize the objectivity of their interpretations" (127).

Those readers who Rosenblatt expected would find the idea shocking are the formalists — the old "New Critics." They preferred to discuss "the poem itself," the "concrete work of art," the "real poem." And they refused to describe what a work of literature makes a reader "live through." In fact, in *The Verbal Icon* (1954), William K. Wimsatt and Monroe C. Beardsley defined as fallacious the very notion that a reader's response is part of the meaning of a literary work:

> The Affective Fallacy is a confusion between the poem and its *results* (what it *is* and what it *does*). . . . It begins by trying to derive the standards of criticism from the psychological effects of a poem and ends in impressionism and relativism. The outcome . . . is that the poem itself, as an object of specifically critical judgment, tends to disappear. (21)

Reader-response critics take issue with their formalist predecessors. Stanley Fish, author of a highly influential article entitled "Literature in the Reader: Affective Stylistics" (1970), argues that any school of criticism that would see a work of literature as an object, that would claim to describe what it *is* and never what it *does,* is guilty of misconstruing what literature and reading really are. Literature exists when it is read, Fish suggests, and its force is an affective force. Furthermore, reading is a temporal process. Formalists assume it is a spatial one when they step back and survey the literary work as if it were an object spread out before them. They may find elegant patterns in the texts they examine and reexamine, but they fail to take into account that the work is quite different to a reader who is turning the pages and being moved, or affected, by lines that appear and disappear as the reader reads.

In a discussion of the effect that a sentence penned by the seventeenth-century physician Thomas Browne has on a reader reading,

Fish pauses to say this about his analysis and also, by extension, about the overall critical strategy he has largely developed: "Whatever is persuasive and illuminating about [it] . . . is the result of my substituting for one question — what does this sentence mean? — another, more operational question — what does this sentence do?" He then quotes a line from John Milton's *Paradise Lost,* a line that refers to Satan and the other fallen angels: "Nor did they not perceive their evil plight." Whereas more traditional critics might say that the "meaning" of the line is "They did perceive their evil plight," Fish relates the uncertain movement of the reader's mind *to* that half-satisfying interpretation. Furthermore, he declares that "the reader's inability to tell whether or not 'they' do perceive and his involuntary question . . . are part of the line's *meaning,* even though they take place in the mind, not on the page" (*Text* 26).

This stress on what pages *do* to minds pervades the writings of most, if not all, reader-response critics. Wolfgang Iser, author of *The Implied Reader* (1974) and *The Act of Reading: A Theory of Aesthetic Response* (1976), finds texts to be full of "gaps," and these gaps, or "blanks," as he sometimes calls them, powerfully affect the reader. The reader is forced to explain them, to connect what the gaps separate, literally to create in his or her mind a poem or novel or play that isn't *in* the text but that the text incites. Stephen Booth, who greatly influenced Fish, equally emphasizes what words, sentences, and passages "do." He stresses in his analyses the "reading experience that results" from a "multiplicity of organizations" in, say, a Shakespeare sonnet (*Essay* ix). Sometimes these organizations don't make complete sense, and sometimes they even seem curiously contradictory. But that is precisely what interests reader-response critics, who, unlike formalists, are at least as interested in fragmentary, inconclusive, and even unfinished texts as in polished, unified works. For it is the reader's struggle to *make sense* of a challenging work that reader-response critics seek to describe.

In *Self-Consuming Artifacts: The Experience of Seventeenth-Century Literature* (1972), Fish reveals his preference for literature that makes readers work at making meaning. He contrasts two kinds of literary presentation. By the phrase "rhetorical presentation," he describes literature that reflects and reinforces opinions that readers already hold; by "dialectical presentation," he refers to works that prod and provoke. A dialectical text, rather than presenting an opinion as if it were truth, challenges readers to discover truths on their own. Such a text may not even have the kind of symmetry that formalist critics seek. Instead of offering a "single, sustained argument," a dialectical text, or self-consuming artifact, may be "so arranged that to enter into the spirit and assumptions of any one of [its] . . . units is implicitly to reject the spirit and assumptions of the unit immediately preceding" (*Artifacts* 9). Such a text needs a reader-response critic to elucidate its workings. Another kind of critic is likely to try to explain why the units are unified and coherent, not why such units are contradicting and "consuming" their predecessors. The reader-response critic proceeds by describing the reader's way of dealing with the sudden twists and turns that characterize the dialectical text — that make the reader return to earlier passages and to see them in an entirely new light.

"The value of such a procedure," Fish has written, "is predicated on the idea of meaning as *an event,*" not as something "located (presumed to be imbedded) *in* the utterance" or "verbal object as a thing in itself" (*Text* 28). By redefining meaning as an event, the reader-response critic once again locates meaning in time: the reader's time. A text exists and signifies while it is being read, and what it signifies or means will depend, to no small extent, on *when* it is read. (*Paradise Lost* had some meanings for a seventeenth-century Puritan that it would not have for a twentieth-century atheist.)

With the redefinition of literature as something that only exists meaningfully in the mind of the reader, with the redefinition of the literary work as a catalyst of mental events, comes a concurrent redefinition of the reader. No longer is the reader the passive recipient of those ideas that an author has planted in a text. "The reader is *active,*" Rosenblatt insists (123). Fish begins "Literature in the Reader" with a similar observation: "If at this moment someone were to ask, 'what are you doing,' you might reply, 'I am reading,' and thereby acknowledge that reading is . . . something *you do*" (*Text* 22). In "How to Recognize a Poem When You See One," he is even more provocative: "Interpreters do not decode poems: they make them" (*Text* 327). Iser, in focusing critical interest on the gaps in texts — on what is not expressed — similarly redefines the reader as an active maker. In an essay entitled "Interaction between Text and Reader," he argues that what is missing from a narrative causes the reader to fill in the blanks creatively.

Iser's title implies a cooperation between reader and text that is also implied in Rosenblatt's definition of a poem as "what the reader lives through under the guidance of the text." Indeed, Rosenblatt borrowed the term "transactional" to describe the dynamics of the reading process, which in her view involves interdependent texts and readers interacting. The view that texts and readers make poems together, though, is not shared by *all* interpreters generally thought of as reader-response critics. Steven Mailloux has divided reader-response critics into several categories, one of which he labels "subjective." Subjective critics, like David Bleich (or Norman Holland after his conversion by Bleich), assume what Mailloux calls the "absolute priority of individual selves as creators of texts" (*Conventions* 31). In other words, these critics do not see the reader's response as one "guided" by the text but rather as one motivated by deep-seated, personal, psychological needs. What they find in texts is, in Holland's phrase, their own "identity theme." Holland has argued that as readers we use "the literary work to symbolize and finally to replicate ourselves. We work out through the text our own characteristic patterns of desire" ("UNITY" 816).

Subjective critics, as you may already have guessed, often find themselves confronted with the following question: if all interpretation is a function of private, psychological identity, then why have so many readers interpreted, say, Shakespeare's *Hamlet* in the same way? Different subjective critics have answered the question differently. Holland simply has said that common identity themes exist, such as that involving an oedipal fantasy. Fish, who went through a subjectivist stage, has provided what may be a better answer than Holland's notion of shared fantasies. In "Interpreting the *Variorum,*" he argues that the "stability of interpretation among readers" is a function of shared "interpretive strategies." These strategies, which "exist prior to the act of reading and therefore determine the shape of what is read," are held in common by "interpretive communities," such as the one comprised by American college students reading *The Scarlet Letter* (*Text* 167, 171).

As I have suggested in the paragraph above, reader-response criticism is not a monolithic school of thought, as is assumed by some detractors who like to talk about the "School of Fish." Several of the critics mentioned thus far have adopted over time different versions of reader-response criticism. I have hinted at Holland's growing subjectivism as well as at the evolution of Fish's own thought. Fish, having at first viewed meaning as the cooperative production of readers and texts, went on to become a subjectivist, and very nearly a deconstructor ready to suggest that all criticism is imaginative creation, fiction about literature, or *metafiction*. In developing the notion of interpretive communities, however, Fish has become more of a social, structuralist, reader-response critic; currently, he is engaged in studying reading communities and their interpretive conventions in order to understand the conditions that give rise to a work's intelligibility.

In spite of the gaps between reader-response critics and even between the assumptions that they have held at various stages of their respective careers, all try to answer similar questions and to use similar strategies to describe the reader's response to a given text. One of the common questions these critics tend to be asked has already been discussed: why do individual readers come up with such similar interpretations if meaning is not imbedded *in* the work itself? Other recurring, troubling questions include the following interrelated ones: Just who *is* the reader? (or, to place the emphasis differently, Just who is *the* reader?) Aren't you reader-response critics just talking about your own idiosyncratic responses when you describe what a line from *Paradise Lost* "does" in and to "the reader's" mind? What about my responses? What if they're different? Will you be willing to say that all responses are equally valid?

Fish defines "the reader" in this way: "*the* reader is the *informed* reader." The informed reader is someone who is "sufficiently experienced as a reader to have internalized the properties of literary discourses, including everything from the most local of devices (figures of speech, etc.) to whole genres." And, of course, the informed reader is in full possession of the "semantic knowledge" (knowledge of idioms, for instance) assumed by the text (*Artifacts* 406).

Other reader-response critics use terms besides "the *informed* reader" to define "*the* reader," and these other terms mean slightly different things. Wayne Booth uses the phrase "the implied reader" to mean the reader "created by the work." (Only "by agreeing to play the role of this created audience," Susan Suleiman explains, "can an actual reader correctly understand and appreciate the work" [8].) Gerard Genette and Gerald Prince prefer to speak of "the narratee, . . . the necessary counterpart of a given narrator, that is, the person or figure who receives a narrative" (Suleiman 13). Like Booth, Iser employs the term "the implied reader," but he also uses "the educated reader" when he refers to what Fish calls the "informed" or "intended" reader. Thus, with different terms, each critic denies the claim that reader-response criticism might lead people to think that there are as many correct interpretations of a work as there are readers to read it.

As Mailloux has shown, reader-response critics share not only questions, answers, concepts, and terms for those concepts but also strategies of reading. Two of the basic "moves," as he calls them, are to show that a work gives readers something to do and to describe what the reader does by way of response. And there are more complex moves as well. For instance, a reader-response critic might typically (1) cite direct references to reading in the text, in order to justify the focus on reading and show that the inside of the text is continuous with what the reader is doing; (2) show how other nonreading situations in the text nonetheless mirror the situation the reader is in ("Fish shows how in *Paradise Lost* Michael's teaching of Adam in Book XI resembles Milton's teaching of the reader throughout the poem"); and (3) show, therefore, that the reader's response is, or is perfectly analogous to, the topic of the story. For Stephen Booth, *Hamlet* is the tragic story of "an audience that cannot make up its mind." In the view of Roger Easson, Blake's *Jerusalem* "may be read as a poem about the experience of reading *Jerusalem*" (Mailloux, "Learning" 103).

Richard Brodhead opened the way to a reader-oriented approach to *The Scarlet Letter* in his *Hawthorne, Melville, and the Novel* (1973). He argued that Hawthorne's "concerned yet dispassionate" narrator "implicitly invites us as readers" to exercise a "finely discriminating attention" as we read (50). Occasionally, he suggested, the narrator even invites us to make our own imaginative choices between possible meanings. Making several of the "moves" enumerated by Mailloux, Brodhead went on to show that, at several points, situations described in the text invite this kind of involvement and choice by mirroring the situation the reader is in.

One of these narrative points is that in which a great light appears in the sky above Boston and effectively turns all the characters in the text into readers. Some of the townsfolk, including Arthur Dimmesdale, see in the light a scarlet A. Of those, few read the letter as Dimmesdale does; most see it as a sign that the recently departed Governor Winthrop has been granted status as an angel. As readers, Brodhead points out, we are free to believe the light was simply a meteor (and thus to read the diverse readings of its meanings psychologically) or to see it, as other characters do, as a supernatural event having one or more possible meanings. Calling the chapter a "drama of interpretation," Brodhead continues:

> what is most interesting about this drama is that we are implicated in it. . . . And as we are forced to decide what to make of it the characters' modes of vision become the matter not of detached observation but of our own urgent choice. We are left alone to complete the episode's reality and meaning as we may, and as we do so, Hawthorne's demonstrations of the implications of the available options ensures that we will be highly self-conscious about our own procedure as an imaginative act of a certain sort. (59)

Hawthorne also makes us see how differently the same reality may be read in the scene in which Dimmesdale exposes the stigma on his chest after having confessed. Some townspeople see a red A that Chillingworth has magically wrought; others see a mark that Dimmesdale has inflicted on himself; still others see a mark made by God, and a few "highly respectable witnesses" see nothing at all! Brodhead writes, "Hawthorne releases us from his narrative authority and allows us to choose among these, or to adopt whatever explanation we like" (68).

It is only a short step from Brodhead's approach to that taken by Kenneth Dauber, because both critics stress the reader's active involvement in the meaning-making process. In his book *Rediscovering Hawthorne* (1977), Dauber, like Brodhead, focuses on the way in which the text of *The Scarlet Letter* obliges its readers to choose between different or even *opposite* meanings. At some points we are led to see Pearl as an evil imp; at others, we are persuaded to view her behavior as the natural psychological response to rejection. Similarly, "Chillingworth, described, initially, as the implacable arch-fiend, is demythologized in 'The Leech and His Patient'" (99).

Committing what formalists had called "the affective fallacy," Dauber focuses on the mental activity of the reader who has to make sense of this "fragmented," "dislocated," and "remarkably unhinged" story (97). Adapting the ideas of E. H. Gombrich and modern reading theory, Dauber argues that readers locate individual elements of what they read in structures that they hypothesize *as* they read, fitting them into "patterns" or "schemata" that they "continually project" (98). When "faced with such contradiction" as is found in *The Scarlet Letter,* the reader "may choose to see ambiguity or paradox" *as* meaning, may make sense of the text by "impos[ing] his own world on the world of *The Scarlet Letter,*" or, better yet, may be "drawn into a point 'between' schemata," where "schematizations are never avoided, but they remain potential" (99–100). What Dauber envisions is a reader who learns to see alternative potentialities in each "semi-autonomous" tableau, action, image, or comment that he or she comes across (96).

In the essay that begins on page 263, David Leverenz builds on several ideas about *The Scarlet Letter* advanced by Brodhead and Dauber, while making use of the more general theories of leading reader-response theorists such as Stanley Fish and Jane Tompkins. Like Brodhead, Leverenz sees *The Scarlet Letter* as a novel that dramatizes the act of interpretation and that allows the reader the freedom to choose from among possible meanings. Like Dauber, he sees that the novel contains contradictory elements and invites diverse, even irreconcilable, readings. And, like Fish and Tompkins, he is interested in the way in which "textual meanings are established by readers in any historical moment" — readers whose readings are guided by their "interpretive communities."

But Leverenz avails himself of more of the moves practiced by contemporary reader-response critics than do Brodhead or Dauber. For one thing, he self-consciously alludes to and places himself *vis-à-vis* theorists like Fish and Tompkins, Mailloux and Walter Benn Michaels. For another, he provides a history of readers' responses to the novel, thus discussing the response of the contemporary reader against the background of the novel's reception.

Similarly, Leverenz's essay may be distinguished from those written by contemporary reader-response theorists. Although he alludes to and adapts the theory of interpretive community, he differs from Fish and Tompkins when he suggests that *The Scarlet Letter* seems to have a mind of its own; it "both induces" and resists or "undermines" the "interpretive expectations of its contemporary readers." Thus, Leverenz argues, it is a novel that "posits a more ambivalent relation between text and community than the theory of interpretive community so far allows." Indeed, Leverenz seems willing to admit, formalists may have been right insofar as they granted a measure of authority and independence to the text.

Focusing first on the early chapters of the novel, Leverenz argues that they align our sympathies with Hester and seem to "mandate," certainly for present-day readers, an "aggressive feminist interpretation." But he goes on to show that later chapters encourage other kinds of interpretation. In our attempts to find out truths as yet unrevealed by the narrator, we are aligned with Chillingworth as well as with Hester: "Chillingworth's probing brings out the reader's power of psychological detection," Leverenz writes, "while Hester's character encourages feminist responses." Leverenz's version of reader-response criticism thus verges on being all-inclusive. Like the narratologists, he conceives the reader and the narrator to be interlocked, twin halves of one entity or event, and his interest in past as well as present responses aligns him with reader-reception theory.

But these forays into theoretical territories either at or off the edge of the usual map of reader-response criticism in no way weaken Leverenz's essay as an example of the reader-response approach. After all, reader-response criticism is finally only a name we give to a variety of analyses that share an interest in the reader's reactions. The best of those analyses — whether Norman Holland's in his psychoanalytic mode or

Stanley Fish's in his near-deconstructive phase — resonate with insights developed by any number of theorists that we tend to group separately, just as the best undergraduate essays on *The Scarlet Letter* inevitably provide, through an original response to (or deconstruction of) the text, insights that could be labeled psychological, feminist, or historical.

READER-RESPONSE CRITICISM: A SELECTED BIBLIOGRAPHY

Some Introductions to Reader-Response Criticism

Fish, Stanley E. "Literature in the Reader: Affective Stylistics." *New Literary History* 2 (1970): 123–61. Rpt. in Fish 21–67. Also rpt. in Primeau 154–79.

Holland, Norman N. "UNITY IDENTITY TEXT SELF." *PMLA* 90 (1975): 813–22.

Holub, Robert C. *Reception Theory: A Critical Introduction*. New York: Methuen, 1984.

Mailloux, Steven. "Learning to Read: Interpretation and Reader-Response Criticism." *Studies in the Literary Imagination* 12 (1979): 93–108.

———. "Reader-Response Criticism?" *Genre* 10 (1977): 413–31.

Rosenblatt, Louise M. "Towards a Transactional Theory of Reading." *Journal of Reading Behavior* 1 (1969): 31–47. Rpt. in Primeau 121–46.

Suleiman, Susan R. "Introduction: Varieties of Audience-Oriented Criticism." Suleiman 3–45.

Tompkins, Jane P. "An Introduction to Reader-Response Criticism." Tompkins ix–xxiv.

Reader-Response Criticism in Anthologies and Collections

Fish, Stanley Eugene. *Is There a Text in This Class? The Authority of Interpretive Communities*. Cambridge: Harvard UP, 1980. In this volume are collected most of Fish's most influential essays, including "Literature in the Reader: Affective Stylistics," "What It's Like to Read *L'Allegro* and *Il Penseroso*," "Interpreting the *Variorum*," "Is There a Text in This Class?" "How to Recognize a Poem When You See One," and "What Makes an Interpretation Acceptable?"

Garvin, Harry R., ed. *Theories of Reading, Looking, and Listening*. Lewisburg: Bucknell UP, 1981. See the essays by Cain and Rosenblatt.

Primeau, Ronald, ed. *Influx: Essays on Literary Influence*. Port Washington: Kennikat, 1977. See the essays by Fish, Holland, and Rosenblatt.

Suleiman, Susan R., and Inge Crosman, eds. *The Reader in the Text: Essays on Audience and Interpretation*. Princeton: Princeton UP, 1980. See especially the essays by Culler, Iser, and Todorov.

Tompkins, Jane P., ed. *Reader-Response Criticism: From Formalism to Post-Structuralism*. Baltimore: Johns Hopkins UP, 1980. See especially the essays by Bleich, Fish, Holland, Prince, and Tompkins.

Reader-Response Criticism: Some Major Works

Bleich, David. *Subjective Criticism*. Baltimore: Johns Hopkins UP, 1978.

Booth, Stephen. *An Essay on Shakespeare's Sonnets*. New Haven: Yale UP, 1969.

Eco, Umberto. *The Role of the Reader*. Bloomington: Indiana UP, 1979.

Fish, Stanley Eugene. *Self-Consuming Artifacts: The Experience of Seventeenth-Century Literature*. Berkeley: U of California P, 1972.

———. *Surprised by Sin: The Reader in Paradise Lost*. 2nd ed. Berkeley: U of California P, 1971.

Holland, Norman N. *5 Readers Reading*. New Haven: Yale UP, 1975.

Iser, Wolfgang. *The Act of Reading: A Theory of Aesthetic Response*. Baltimore: Johns Hopkins UP, 1978.

———. *The Implied Reader: Patterns of Communication in Prose Fiction from Bunyan to Beckett*. Baltimore: Johns Hopkins UP, 1974.

Jauss, Hans Robert. *Toward an Aesthetic of Reception*. Trans. Timothy Bahti. Introd. Paul de Man. Brighton, Eng.: Harvester, 1982.

Mailloux, Steven. *Interpretive Conventions: The Reader in the Study of American Fiction*. Ithaca: Cornell UP, 1982.

Prince, Gerald. *Narratology*. New York: Mouton, 1982.

Exemplary Short Readings of Major Texts

Anderson, Howard. "*Tristram Shandy* and the Reader's Imagination." *PMLA* 86 (1971): 966–73.

Berger, Carole. "The Rake and the Reader in Jane Austen's Novels." *Studies in English Literature, 1500–1900* 15 (1975): 531–44.

Booth, Stephen. "On the Value of *Hamlet*." *Reinterpretations of English Drama: Selected Papers from the English Institute*. Ed. Norman Rabkin. New York: Columbia UP, 1969. 137–76.

Easson, Robert R. "William Blake and His Reader in *Jerusalem*." *Blake's Sublime Allegory*. Ed. Stuart Curran and Joseph A. Wittreich. Madison: U of Wisconsin P, 1973. 309–28.

Kirk, Carey H. "*Moby Dick:* The Challenge of Response." *Papers on Language and Literature* 13 (1977): 383–90.

Rosmarin, Adena. "Darkening the Reader: Reader-Response Criticism and *Heart of Darkness*." *Heart of Darkness: A Case Study in Contemporary Criticism*. Ed. Ross C Murfin. New York: Bedford-St. Martin's, 1989. 148–69.

Reader-Response Approaches to Hawthorne

Brodhead, Richard H. *Hawthorne, Melville, and the Novel*. Chicago: U of Chicago P, 1973. See especially chapter 3.

Dauber, Kenneth. *Rediscovering Hawthorne*. Princeton: Princeton UP, 1977. See especially pp. 93–102.

Other Works Referred to in "What Is Reader-Response Criticism?"

Wimsatt, William K., and Monroe C. Beardsley. *The Verbal Icon*. Lexington: UP of Kentucky, 1954. See especially the discussion of "The Affective Fallacy," with which reader-response critics have so sharply disagreed.

A READER-RESPONSE CRITIC AT WORK

DAVID LEVERENZ

Mrs. Hawthorne's Headache: Reading *The Scarlet Letter*

When Hawthorne read the end of *The Scarlet Letter* to his wife, it "broke her heart and sent her to bed with a grievous headache — which I look upon as a triumphant success!" His Chillingworth-like tone belies his own feelings. Ostensibly his "triumphant" sense of professional satisfaction depends on breaking a woman's heart and mind, much as his narrative pacifies the heart and mind of its heroine. But Hawthorne's "success" also depends on evoking great sympathy for female suffering. Several years later he vividly recalled "my emotions when I read the last scene of *The Scarlet Letter* to my wife, just after writing it — tried to read it, rather, for my voice swelled and heaved, as if I were tossed up and down on an ocean, as it subsides after a storm." As Randall Stewart notes, "Hawthorne was not in the habit of breaking down." This scene, and the shaking sobs that overcame him at his dying mother's bedside, "are the only recorded instances of uncontrolled emotion" in Hawthorne's career (95).

Mrs. Hawthorne's headache is a rare moment in the history of American reader responses. It reveals not only a spouse's ambiguously painful reaction but also the author's incompatible accounts of his own first reading. Both responses seem deeply divided: one with a splitting headache, the other with a split self-presentation. If we accept at face value the goal announced by Hawthorne's narrator in the first paragraph of "The Custom-House," to seek a self-completing communion with his readers, his quest to discover "the divided segment of the writer's own nature" (22) ends in frustration. Both Hawthorne and his most intimate sympathizer experience inward turmoil and self-controlled withdrawal. As several first readers commented in print, Hawthorne's romance left them with similarly intense and unresolved feelings — of sadness, pain, annoyance, and almost hypnotic fascination.

The Scarlet Letter's strange power over its contemporary readers derives from its unresolved tensions. What starts as a feminist revolt against punitive patriarchal authority ends in a muddle of sympathetic pity for ambiguous victims. Throughout, a gentlemanly moralist frames the story so curiously as to ally his empathies with his inquisitions. Ostensibly he voices Hawthorne's controlling moral surface, where oscillations of concern both induce and evade interpretive judgments. Yet his characterizations of Hester and Chillingworth bring out Hawthorne's profoundly contradictory affinities with a rebellious, autonomous female psyche and an intrusive male accuser. The narrative's increasing preoccupation with Dimmesdale's guilt both blankets and discovers that fearful inward intercourse. D. H. Lawrence's directive to trust the tale, not the teller, rightly challenges the narrator's inauthentic moral stance (13). But that becomes a complicating insight, not a simplifying dismissal. In learning to see beyond Hawthorne's narrator, readers can see what lies beneath the author's distrust of any coercive authority, especially his own. Though the narrator sometimes seems quite self-consciously fictionalized, he functions less as a character than as a screen for the play of textual energies.

The plot establishes incompatible centers of psychological power: Hester's fierce private passion, at once radically independent and voluptuously loving, and Chillingworth's equally private rage to expose, control, and accuse. These centers have surfaced in modern criticism as feminist or psychoanalytic responses to the text. The narrator's voice acts as a safety valve, releasing and containing feelings in socially acceptable ways. His very self-conscious relation to his readers, whom he frequently appeals to and fictionalizes, both abets, displaces, and conceals his story's unresolved tensions.

The narrator also mirrors the limits of his contemporary American reader's toleration for strong subjectivity, especially anger. As Trollope noted, "there is never a page written by Hawthorne not tinged by satire" (242). The narrator of *The Scarlet Letter* skillfully intermingles earnest appeals for sympathy with mocking exposure of rage, distanced as cruelty. His tolerance for human frailty, his addiction to multiple interpretations, and his veiled hints of self-disgust deflect his fear that anger destroys a lovable self. In claiming that art should veil self-exposure, he invites both sympathy and self-accusation. He is a Dimmesdale who doesn't quite know he is a Chillingworth.

Several nineteenth-century readers sensed Chillingworth's ascendancy in the narrator as well as his narrative. Trollope and Henry James both noted with some surprise that the romance was oddly a hate story, and James speaks of Hawthorne's constant struggle between "his evasive and his inquisitive tendencies (109–10). Anne Abbott felt "cheated into a false regard and interest" by Hester's seeming suffering and Dimmesdale's seeming faith, because Hester's pride destroys her Christian character, while Dimmesdale's suffering becomes "aimless and without effect for purification or blessing to the soul." "A most obstinate and unhuman passion, or a most unwearying conscience it must be," she continues; ". . . such a prolonged application of the scourge." Finally, the man whom Hawthorne considered his most astute critic, E. P. Whipple, concluded that the narrator's tendency to "put his victims on the rack" establishes an uncomfortably compelling despotism. Though the morbid suffering appalls sensible readers, he said, they yield despite themselves to "the guidance of an author who is personally good-natured, but intellectually and morally relentless" (Crowley 166, 344, 346, 160–62).

The narrator is protected by his duplicitous stance from full exposure, as he half admits. The rhetorical strategies that can give his reader a headache preserve his good name. Yet under his interpretive equivocations, unresolved conflicts about anger, authority, and female autonomy continuously impel the contradictions in his voice as well as his story. A close reading of *The Scarlet Letter* along these lines, as I try to offer here, raises the possibility of using formalist methods to explore the text's intimate, ambivalent relationship to the author's own life and the contemporary interpretive community.

In arguing that close reading opens out to questions of social history, present and past, I am of course both using and calling into question the recent thinking of reader-response critics such as Stanley Fish, Walter Benn Michaels, Steven Mailloux, and especially Jane Tompkins. I agree with Tompkins's larger contention that textual meanings are established by readers at any historical moment. But if I am right to say that *The Scarlet Letter* both induces and undermines the interpretive expectations of its contemporary readers, that reading posits a more ambivalent relation between text and community than the theory of interpretive community so far allows. Perhaps my reading is more in line with the wonderful cover of Tompkins's *Reader-Response Criticism,* a cartoon that shows a woman reading a book while standing on a subway. Two men are reading the book with her, over her shoulders. One man is laughing hysterically; the other man is crying his eyes out; the woman's face shows simply a quizzical expression. They are all reading the same page.

I

A surprisingly aggressive feminist interpretation of *The Scarlet Letter* seems self-consciously mandated as the storytelling begins. The narrator's first sentence deflates church and state to "steeple-crowned hats" (53), while the first paragraph associates those hats with the iron spikes on the prison door. As the next paragraph explains, the colony's Puritan fathers have appropriated "the virgin soil" for graves and a prison, while stifling their utopian hopes with a grave distrust of human nature. Hats and "sad-colored garments" blend with the "beetle-browed and gloomy front" of the prison in a shared exterior gloom (53). Inwardness has been shut up and spiked, along with youthful hopes and the virgin land, by a sternly patriarchal, masculine-dominated culture.

The narrator's implicit symbolic advocacy of strong womanhood becomes overt with his presentation of the "wild rose-bush," growing beside "the black flower of civilized society." If the prison is massive, forbidding, even "ugly," the rosebush brings out feminine delicacy and "fragile beauty." It also promises to awaken the body to imaginative life. It "might be imagined" to offer fragrance to a prisoner, "in token that the deep heart of Nature could pity and be kind to him." Perhaps, the narrator muses, this rosebush "survived out of the stern old wilderness, so long after the fall of the gigantic pines and oaks that originally overshadowed it" (53–54). Without pinning himself down, he allegorically intimates that patriarchs will die while tender flowers endure.

Or perhaps, he continues, the rosebush sprang up under the footsteps of "the sainted Ann Hutchinson" (54) — the adjective lets loose his anti-Puritan, even Papist bias — as she walked through the prison door. In either case, his interpretive alternatives evoke a woman's triumphant survival beyond her towering, glowering elders, or at least her stubborn public opposition. As new elders die the natural death of Isaac Johnson, the first dead Puritan patriarch, they will retreat to "the congregated sepulchres"(53) that define their eternity as interchangeably as their gravity defines their lives, while the rose and true womanhood may persevere toward a more naturally blossoming future.

Taking a final swerve from patriarchal authority by abdicating his own, the narrator refuses to "determine" which alternative should hold. Instead he presents the rose to his reader, since it grows "so directly on the threshold of our narrative, which is now about to issue from that inauspicious portal" (54). With a lushly symbolic self-consciousness, the narrator has established a broad array of sympathies joining feminism, nature, youth, the body, and imaginative life. This associational array opposes patriarchal oppression, which doubly oppresses itself. The narrator's rhetorical strategies awaken reader expectations as well as sympathies. When Hester walks through the prison door, she will "issue" as the narrative itself, with all the hopes embodied in what is now the reader's wild red rose.

Yet Hester also walks forth into narrative hopelessness. With a hand even heavier than his heart the narrator suddenly imposes his gloomy end on her brave beginning. He tells us that the rose may "relieve the darkening close of a tale of human frailty and sorrow" (54). That portentous phrase shuts the door on her wild possibilities as massively as the prison door dwarfs the rose. His plot will undercut the hopes his voice has just raised. His other alternative, that the rosebush might symbolize "some sweet moral blossom," seems deliberately anemic beside the contending passions that his introduction promises. The narrator's sudden deflection from the rose's prospects suggests his fatalistic alliance with the prison's "darkening close" (54). His narrative will be both, inextricably. He opens and shuts the door.

What seems here to be only a slight discomfort with the rose's radical implications eventually becomes an ambivalent inquisition into the dangers of Hester's lawless passion. The narrative issues forth as Chillingworth as well as Hester. Chillingworth's probing brings out the reader's powers of psychological detection while Hester's character encourages feminist responses. At once rebel and inquisitor, the narrator falsely joins these poles in a mystifying voice-over. He implies that the law can be transcended by means of Dimmesdale's growth through pain toward spiritual purity or softened through Hester's growth through pain toward maternal sympathy. To the degree that we can also perceive his own voice as an "issue" we can locate the unresolved tensions under his still more mystified "sweet moral blossom" of being true to oneself.

Hester Prynne's first gesture, to repel the beadle's authority, refocuses narrative sympathies. Her radical feminism goes further than Hyatt Waggoner's sense of her as a champion of the oppressed (145) and beyond Nina Baym's various arguments that she champions the private imagination (124–35). In chapter 13 Hester goes so far as to imagine the "hopeless task" of building the whole social system anew, changing sex roles so completely that both womanhood and manhood will become unrecognizable to themselves (134). It seems an extraordinary instance of negative capability that Hawthorne, who forbade his daughter to write because it was unfeminine, could imagine the most radical woman in nineteenth-century New England, even retrospectively. Though his narrator interjects several times that Hester's mind has gone so astray only because her heart "had lost its regular and healthy throb" (134), his abstracted, fitful cavils seem to heighten our sense of her sustained independence.

Hester's private question about the "race" of women can still leap off the page for modern readers: "Was existence worth accepting, even to the happiest among them?" (134). She has long since "decided in the negative" (134) this question for herself. Later, from her radical freedom of fresh perception, she sees all social institutions "with hardly more reverence than the Indian would feel for the clerical band, the judicial robe, the pillory, the gallows, the fireside, or the church" (157). Not even Melville, with his more impulsive extremes of negation, offers such a laconic, liberating list. For Hester the comforts of fireside and church grow from the punitive powers of the clergy and judiciary, as interlocked and equivalent institutions.

Yet Hester's rebellious autonomy shields two very different kinds of loving. Why is it, the narrator asks in chapter 5, that Hester doesn't leave Boston? She could go to Europe, where she could "hide her character and identity under a new exterior," or she could enter the forest, "where the wildness of her nature might assimilate itself with a people whose customs and life were alien from the law that had condemned her." In rejecting both these ways of abandoning herself, whether to a civilized mask or to diffused natural passion, Hester consciously chooses to define her "roots" as her "chain." Her identity is the sin so "galling to her inmost soul." But the clear separation of outer sin from inner soul shows how unrepentant her desire remains. She becomes the jailer of a fearful secret: her dream of "a union, that, unrecognized on earth, would bring them together before the bar of final judgment, and make that their marriage-altar, for a joint futurity of endless retribution." I don't think any commentator has noticed the sacrilegious force of the hope that really impels her: to be united with Dimmesdale forever, in hell. A Dantean fantasy of condemned love "struggled out of her heart, like a serpent from its hole" (75). It terrifies her more consciously self-reliant conceptions of herself.

For the narrator, Hester's passionate loving, like Chillingworth's no less passionate hating, leaves the self wide open to demonic possession. Whether loving or self-reliant, Hester is going to hell. Yet her dream of a love forever framed by patriarchal punishment also allows the narrator to present her more as victim than rebel. She is a woman more sinned against than sinning. Moreover, she is a mother as well as a woman in love. Her daughter's existence providentially prevents her from becoming a radical prophetess like Anne Hutchinson. The narrator observes that mothering, like knitting, fortunately "soothes" Hester's tendency toward conflict. As a solitary, victimized woman Hester can rethink all social relations, but as a mother she has to nurture conventional womanhood, in herself as well as her daughter. As Dimmesdale says to John Wilson in chapter 8, the child "was meant, above all things else, to keep the mother's soul alive" (99). The narrator recurrently echoes the minister's sense of this "softening" charge: "Providence, in the person of this little girl, had assigned to Hester's charge the germ and blossom of womanhood, to be cherished and developed amid a host of difficulties" (134). The narrator veils his ambivalence about Hester's intellectual independence and her passionate desire by reinforcing what Nancy Chodorow has called the "institution" of "mothering" as the cure for all her ills (Chodorow 38).

II

A narrative that begins by challenging patriarchal punishment ends by accepting punishment as a prelude to kindness. From Anthony Trollope to Frederic Carpenter and beyond, the ending has disturbed many readers who like Hester's spirited subjectivity. As one critic noted in 1954, "unlike his judicial ancestor, who consigned a witch to the gallows with an undismayed countenance, Hawthorne would have sprung the trap with a sigh. If one were the witch, one might well wonder wherein lay the vital difference" (Cronin 98).

Though my reading continues that tradition, I question whether the narrator who executes such an about-face represents all of Hawthorne. While he provides a safely overarching frame of moral values to which both Hawthorne and his audience could consciously assent, the narrator's evasive mixture of sympathy and judgment also provides a safe way of going beyond socially responsible norms to investigate dangerously attractive interior states of mind. From the first paragraph of "The Custom-House" Hawthorne presents his "intrusive author" as a solicitous, sensible, yet receptive interpreter whose movement from torpid business surroundings to a romantic sensibility opens the door for Hester's story. His first reaction to the scarlet letter, after all, is hilariously inappropriate: he measures it, and finds that "each limb proved to be precisely three inches and a quarter in length" (43). This habit of precise accounting would seem perfectly natural to the "man of business," the "main-spring" of the Custom-House, who could "make the incomprehensible as clear as daylight," and for whom a "stain on his conscience" would be no more troublesome than an error in his accounts or an ink-blot in his record books (37–38). But the scarlet letter takes the narrator beyond his own more satirical accounts. Its meanings "streamed forth from the mystic symbol, subtly communicating itself to my sensibilities, but evading the analysis of my mind" (43).

This tension between sensibility and analysis persists throughout the narrative. The power of authority to take the shameful measure of vulnerable subjectivity terrifies the narrator. Yet he seems equally terrified of the heart-freezing isolation inherent in aggressive autonomy. Fleeing coercive authority, including his own, he defines himself simply as an imaginative re-creator of Surveyor Pue's manuscript and imagines Hester's rebellious self-reliance with sustained flights of empathy. Fleeing self-reliance, he chastises Hester's pride and relentlessly accuses Chillingworth's self-possessed malice. For him subjectivity always seems vulnerable to alien invasion. Chillingworth's own invasion of Dimmesdale's soul manifests the devil's entry into the scholar-physician. Perpetually oscillating betweeen subjectivity and authority, the narrator dodges being pinned down to one mode or the other. To commit himself either way might expose his fearful cruelty of heart or his equally fearful vulnerability to violation.

His solution, both for himself and his heroine, is the fluidity of sympathetic relationship. He strives to "stand in some true relation with his audience," fictionalizing his reader as "a kind and apprehensive, though not the closest friend." Without such a relation, he says, "thoughts are frozen and utterance benumbed" (22). The metaphor comes close to self-exposure. Seeking a nonthreatening communication that protects him from real intimacy, he indicates his fear of a solidifying self-possession. The audience has to warm the intrinsic coldness of his heart and tongue.

Similarly, the coldness of Hester's radical speculations must be warmed by her mothering heart. "A woman," he concludes, "never overcomes these problems by any exercise of thought"; they can be solved only by letting the heart "come uppermost" (134). Having established Hester's radical potential, the narrator now undercuts her force by dramatizing her transformation back to lovability, not toward public combat. The "magic touch" to bring about her "transfiguration," as he says earlier (133), sets the second half of the narrative in motion. She vows to redeem Dimmesdale from his own weakness and his malevolent tormentor. She will accomplish "the rescue of the victim" from her husband's "power" (135). Meanwhile, like a good mistress, she remains bonded to her child, her duties, her isolation, her marginal status, and her hopeless dreams of union.

The narrator's astonishing corollary to Hester's decline into sympathy unites Chillingworth, Dimmesdale, and himself in a loving ascension. After Dimmesdale spurns Hester to gain an uncontaminated integration for his purified maleness, we are asked to imagine him united in heaven not just with God but with Chillingworth as well. In the middle of the story the narrator oddly interpolates that "hatred, by a gradual and quiet process, will even be transformed to love," if new irritations of hostility do not impede the process (130). At several other points he implies that rage and desire fuse as violent passion. Now the narrator inverts the devil's work. He adopts the ability to transform hate into love as his final test of the reader's tender capacities.

Asking his readers to be merciful to Chillingworth, he wonders "whether hatred and love be not the same thing at bottom." Each supposes "intimacy and heart-knowledge." Each needs dependence. Each dies if the object withdraws.

> Philosophically considered, therefore, the two passions seem essentially the same, except that one happens to be seen in a celestial radiance, and the other in a dusky and lurid glow. In the spiritual world, the old physician and the minister — mutual victims as they have been — may, unawares, have found their earthly stock of hatred and antipathy transmuted into golden love. (199)

The passage still seems to me the strangest in all of Hawthorne. Transforming devilish rage into divine love, it takes Dimmesdale's hierarchy of high and low to its highest extreme. If the narrator hesitates to assert their fanciful union as spiritual fact, he has no qualms about describing them as "mutual victims." Anne Abbott cited this passage as a prime example of Hawthorne's "mistborn ideas" and asked "if there be any firm ground at all" here. Yet she also wondered, in some perplexity, whether Hawthorne might share that "doubt" (Crowley 165). Her reaction is quite right, because the passage substitutes loving victims for strong selves in conflict. Its several levels of meaning bring the reader's contrary responses to their final suspended inversion.

The possibility of spiritual union in heaven joins the two whose intercourse on earth comes to center the story: revengeful father and violated/violating son. The cuckold and the lover rise together to an all-male paradise, while Hester mutely returns to Boston. The narrator's fantasized embrace of father and son gives a more openly oedipal dimension to the classic American fantasy, first described by Leslie Fiedler, of two men in flight from strong women. Moreover, the transmutation suggests an integration of the male self as well, if only in coupling two sides of a self-falsification. Intrusive sadism and guilty vulnerability come together at last, released from any pressure to come to terms with anger, love, or fear.

Most significantly, the union occurs not in the plot but in the narrator's relation to his audience. He sets his readers a last challenge: can you take your sympathy that far? In asking readers to sympathize with Dimmesdale and Chillingworth as "mutual victims" and to imagine hate transmuted into golden love, the narrator brings himself into that embrace, with his reader as witness. All three male voices, ironically at odds on earth, escape together, free from sexuality and emotional conflicts, and free from genuine intimacy.

Yet this narrative flight, like all his extremes, is momentary. Returning to earth, he sympathetically concludes with Hester's solitude, not Dimmesdale's transcendence. Part of the narrator's strategy for reconciling conflicts is to condemn fixity of any kind, physical or spiritual. If rigidity seems fearfully demonic, associated with anger and the lower parts of the soul or body, flexible sympathy becomes the narrator's vague placebo. This tactic allows him to voice his contradictory extremes. But it also establishes multiple authorial interpretations as a shifting medium for the plot. His self-dramatizing ceaselessly pacifies and resurrects his plot's tensions, while deflecting attention from his punitive plotting to the sympathetic puppeteer.

In conforming to his audience's expectations for a morally comfortable narrator, Hawthorne fictionalizes himself so as to partially undermine his own characterization. His fragmenting empathies outstrip the narrator's growing alliances with Dimmesdale's self-centering scrutiny and Chillingworth's intrusive detection. He seems fully aware that his readers will accept Hester only while she suffers for her sin; as no fewer than three reviewers remarked, the narrator avoids the dangers of "the French school" by making his heroine satisfactorily miserable. Yet while silencing Hester with values he and his audience hold dear, he makes his readers uncomfortable with those values (Crowley 163, 156–57, 182).

When he at last offers his "sweet moral blossom," it turns out to be a version of Dimmesdale's anguish over self-display: "Be true! Be true! Be true! Show freely to the world, if not your worst, yet some trait whereby the worst may be inferred!" (198). Like Dimmesdale's public stripping, this is the hesitant exhibitionism of a disembodied Salem Flasher, who encourages his readers to imagine his worst while showing their own. He assumes that his readers share with him not only a self worth hating but also the ambivalent desire to detect, to be detected, and to stay respectably hidden. A mutual revelation of guilty subjectivity constitutes his idea of true sympathy, true community, and true interpretation. As he quietly observes, just after Dimmesdale has seen his A flash across the sky, "another's guilt might have seen another symbol in it" (127). At such moments, while interpretive authority disintegrates, writing and reading converge. They become equivalent, equivocal acts of shared self-exposure and accusation. Uneasy lies the tale that wears that crown.

Finally, however, *The Scarlet Letter* takes readers beyond its narrator and his imagined audience. Dimmesdale's guilt, like the narrator's, conceals a fear of losing approval. But Hawthorne's romance evokes strong subjectivity in opposition to dependence of any kind. Throughout, like an anxious referee, the interpreter's voice strives to rise above the fray. Trying to sympathize, judge, and reconcile, he imposes the masks he wants to lift. Yet while the storyteller oscillates between guilt and decorum, his story brings out a much riskier inwardness, whose unresolved tensions sent Mrs. Hawthorne to bed and Hester to a deeper solitude. Hester's epitaph suitably blazons forth her red strength against her black background. By contrast, the narrator's epitaph could be the remark he addresses to "the minister in a maze": "No man, for any considerable period, can wear one face to himself, and another to the multitude, without finally getting bewildered as to which may be the true" (168). In accommodating his voice to the contradictions of public authority, the narrator joins Boston's congregated sepulchres, while Hester's life continues to speak with embattled vitality.

WORKS CITED

Baym, Nina. *The Shape of Hawthorne's Career*. Ithaca: Cornell UP, 1976.

Chodorow, Nancy. *The Reproduction of Mothering*. Berkeley: U of California P, 1978.

Cronin, Morton. "Hawthorne on Romantic Love and the Status of Women." *PMLA* 69 (1954): 89–98.

Crowley, J. Donald, ed. *Hawthorne: The Critical Heritage*. New York: Barnes, 1970.

James, Henry. *Hawthorne*. Introd. Tony Tanner. London: Macmillan, 1967.

Lawrence, D. H. *Studies in Classic American Literature*. Garden City: Doubleday, 1951.

Stewart, Randall. *Nathaniel Hawthorne: A Biography*. New Haven: Yale UP, 1948.

Trollope, Anthony. "The Genius of Nathaniel Hawthorne." *North American Review*. Spring 1879: 203–22.

Waggoner, Hyatt H. *Hawthorne: A Critical Study*. Rev. ed. Cambridge: Harvard UP, 1963.

Feminist Criticism and *The Scarlet Letter*

WHAT IS FEMINIST CRITICISM?

Feminist criticism comes in many forms, and feminist critics have a variety of goals. Some are interested in rediscovering the works of women writers overlooked by a masculine-dominated culture. Others have revisited books by male authors and reviewed them from a woman's point of view to understand how they both reflect and shape the attitudes that have restricted women.

The Scarlet Letter might seem to be a natural subject for feminist criticism of the latter variety. Its nineteenth-century male author strongly disapproved of Margaret Fuller, an early American feminist, and referred in letters to women writers as "scribbling women." In a biography of Anne Hutchinson he wrote that "Woman's intellect should never give the tone to that of man; and even her morality is not exactly the material for masculine virtue. [It is] a false liberality which mistakes the strong division-lines of Nature for arbitrary distinctions."

And yet Hawthorne created, in Hester Prynne, a powerful woman character, a character that feminist critics cannot help admiring. Carolyn G. Heilbrun regards Hester as the "central female character" in American fiction (63), perhaps in part because Hester at times thinks like a twentieth-century feminist. A "dark question often rose into her mind, with reference to the whole race of womanhood," we are told in the chapter of *The Scarlet Letter* entitled "Another View of Hester." "Was existence worth accepting, even to the happiest [of women]?" For it to become acceptable, Hester decides, "the whole system of society" would have to be "torn down, and built up anew. Then, the very nature of the opposite sex, or its long hereditary habit," would have "to be essentially modified." Only then might women "assume what seems a fair and suitable position" (134).

How can a man like Hawthorne have created a woman like Hester? And how can feminist criticism deepen our understanding of his text? Nina Baym has suggested an answer in an essay provocatively entitled "Thwarted Nature: Nathaniel Hawthorne as Feminist" (1982). "Sophisticated feminist criticism" of Hawthorne, Baym writes, "would be based on the presumption that the question of women is *the* determining motive in Hawthorne's works, driving them as it drives Hawthorne's male characters." Hawthorne's men are said to be "obsessed by . . . fantasies of women," "controlled by" those same fantasies, and "controllers *of* women" *through* their male fantasies (62, emphasis added). In the essay that follows this introduction and "Feminist Criticism: A Selected Bibliography," Shari Benstock bases her analysis of *The Scarlet Letter* on precisely this "presumption," suggesting that Hester is the victim of male fantasies ranging from those that concern "the female body" to the controlling "fantasy of absolute sexual difference" that lies at the very heart of women's repression and exploitation.

During the past twenty years, three strains of feminist criticism have emerged, strains that can be categorized as French, American, and British. These categories should not be allowed to obscure either the global implications of the women's movement or the fact that interests and ideas have been shared by feminists from France, Great Britain, and the United States. British and American feminists have examined similar problems while writing about many of the same writers and works, and American feminists have recently become more receptive to French theories about femininity and writing. Historically speaking, however, French, American, and British feminists have examined similar problems from somewhat different perspectives.

French feminists have tended to focus their attention on language, analyzing the ways in which meaning is produced. They have concluded that language as we commonly think of it is a decidedly male realm. Drawing on the ideas of the psychoanalytic philosopher Jacques Lacan, French feminists remind us that language is a realm of public discourses. A child enters the linguistic realm just as it comes to grasp its separateness from its mother, just about the time that boys — but not girls — identify with their father, the family representative of culture. The language learned reflects a binary logic that opposes such terms as active/passive, masculine/feminine, sun/moon, father/mother, head/heart, son/daughter, intelligent/sensitive, brother/sister, form/matter, phallus/vagina, reason/emotion. Because this logic tends to group with masculinity such qualities as light, thought, and activity, French feminists have said that the structure of language is phallocentric: it privileges the phallus and, more generally, masculinity by associating them with things and values more appreciated by the (masculine-dominated) culture. Moreover, French feminists believe, "masculine desire dominates speech and posits woman as an idealized fantasy-fulfillment for the incurable emotional lack caused by separation from the mother" (Jones 83).

In the view of French feminists, language is associated with separation from the mother, characterized by distinctions that represent the world from the male point of view, and seems systematically to give women one of two choices. Either they can imagine and represent themselves as men imagine and represent them (in which case they may speak, but will speak as men) or they can choose "silence," becoming in the process "the invisible and unheard sex" (Jones 83).

But some influential French feminists have argued that language only *seems* to give women such a narrow range of choices. There is another possibility, namely, that women can develop a *feminine* language. In various ways, early French feminists such as Annie Leclerc, Xavière Gauthier, and Marguerite Duras have suggested that there is something that may be called *l'écriture féminine:* women's writing. Recently, Julia Kristeva has said that feminine language is "semiotic," not "symbolic." Rather than rigidly opposing and ranking elements of reality, rather than symbolizing one thing but not another in terms of a third, feminine language is rhythmic and unifying. If from the male perspective it seems fluid to the point of being chaotic, that is the fault of the male perspective.

According to Kristeva, feminine language is derived from the preoedipal period of fusion between mother and child. Associated with the maternal, feminine language is not only threatening to culture, which is patriarchal, but also a medium through which women may be creative in new ways. But Kristeva has paired her central, liberating claim — that truly feminist innovation in all fields requires an understanding of the relation between maternity and feminine creation — with a warning. A feminist language that refuses to participate in "masculine" discourse, that places its future entirely in a feminine, semiotic discourse, risks being politically marginalized by men. That is to say, it risks being relegated to the outskirts (pun intended) of what is considered socially and politically significant.

Kristeva, who associates feminine writing with the female body, is joined in her views by other leading French feminists. Hélène Cixous, for instance, also posits an essential connection between the woman's body, whose sexual pleasure has been repressed and denied expression, and women's writing. "Write your self. Your body must be heard," Cixous urges; once they learn to write their bodies, women will not only realize their sexuality but enter history and move toward a future based on a "feminine" economy of giving, rather than the "masculine" economy of hoarding (Cixous 250). For Luce Irigaray, women's sexual pleasure (*jouissance*) cannot be expressed by the dominant, ordered, "logical" masculine language. She explores the connection between women's sexuality and women's language through the following analogy: as women's *jouissance* is more multiple than men's unitary, phallic pleasure ("woman has sex organs just about everywhere"), so "feminine" language is more diffusive than its "masculine" counterpart. ("That is undoubtedly the reason . . . her language . . . goes off in all directions and . . . he is unable to discern the coherence," Irigaray writes (101–03).

Cixous's and Irigaray's emphasis on feminine writing as an expression of the female body has drawn criticism from other French feminists. Many argue that an emphasis on the body either reduces "the feminine" to a biological essence or elevates it in a way that shifts the valuation of masculine and feminine but retains the binary categories. For Christine Fauré, Irigaray's celebration of women's difference fails to address the issue of masculine dominance, and a Marxist-feminist, Catherine Clement, has warned that "poetic" descriptions of what constitutes the feminine will not challenge that dominance in the realm of production. In her effort to redefine women as political rather than as sexual beings, Monique Wittig has called for the abolition of sexual categories that Cixous and Irigaray retain and revalue as they celebrate women's writing.

American feminist critics have shared with French critics both an interest in and a cautious distrust of the concept of feminine writing. Annette Kolodny, for instance, has worried that the "richness and variety of women's writing" will be missed if we see in it only its "feminine mode" or "style" ("Some Notes" 78). And yet Kolodny herself proceeds, in the same essay, to point out that women *have* had their own style, which includes reflexive constructions ("she found herself crying") and particular, recurring themes (clothing and self-fashioning are two that Kolodny mentions; other American feminists have focused on madness, disease, and the demonic).

Interested as they have become in the "French" subject of feminine style, American feminist critics began by analyzing literary texts rather than by philosophizing abstractly about language. Many reviewed the great works by male writers, embarking on a revisionist rereading of literary tradition. These critics examined the portrayals of women characters, exposing the patriarchal ideology implicit in such works and showing how clearly this tradition of systematic masculine dominance is inscribed in our literary tradition. Kate Millett, Carolyn G. Heilbrun, and Judith Fetterley, among many others, created this model for American feminist criticism, a model that Elaine Showalter came to call "the feminist critique" of "male-constructed literary history" ("Poetics" 25).

Meanwhile, another group of critics including Sandra Gilbert, Susan Gubar, Patricia Meyer Spacks, and Showalter herself created a somewhat different model, one that Showalter has termed "gynocriticism." Whereas the "feminist critique" has analyzed works by men, practitioners of gynocriticism have studied the writings of those women who, against all odds, produced what Showalter calls "a literature of their own." In *The Female Imagination* (1975), Spacks examines the female literary tradition to find out how great women writers across the ages have felt, perceived themselves, and imagined reality. Gilbert and Gubar, in *The Madwoman in the Attic* (1979), concern themselves with well-known women writers of the nineteenth century, but they too find that general concerns, images, and themes recur, because the authors that they treat wrote "in a culture whose fundamental definitions of literary authority are both overtly and covertly patriarchal" (45).

If one of the purposes of gynocriticism is to (re)study well-known women authors, another is to rediscover women's history and culture, particularly women's communities that have nurtured female creativity. Still another related purpose is to discover neglected or forgotten women writers and thus to forge an alternative literary tradition, a canon that better represents the female perspective by better representing the literary works that have been written by women. Showalter, in *A Literature of Their Own* (1977), admirably began to fulfill this purpose, providing a remarkably comprehensive overview of women's writing through three of its phases. She defines these as the "Feminine, Feminist, and Female" phases, phases during which women first imitated a masculine tradition (1840–80), then protested against its standards and values (1880–1920), and finally advocated their own autonomous, female perspective (1920 to the present).

With the recovery of a body of women's texts, attention has returned to a question raised a decade ago by Lillian Robinson: doesn't American feminist criticism need to formulate a theory of its own practice? Won't reliance on theoretical assumptions, categories, and strategies developed by men and associated with nonfeminist schools of thought prevent feminism from being accepted as equivalent to these other critical discourses? Not all American feminists believe that a special or unifying theory of feminist practice is urgently needed; Showalter's historical approach to women's culture allows a feminist critic to use theories based on nonfeminist disciplines. Kolodny has advocated a "playful pluralism" that encompasses a variety of critical schools and methods. But Jane Marcus and others have responded that if feminists adopt too wide a range of approaches, they may relax the tensions between feminists and the educational establishment necessary for political activism.

The question of whether feminism weakens or fortifies itself by emphasizing its separateness — and by developing unity through separateness — is one of several areas of debate within American feminism. Another area of disagreement touched on earlier, between feminists who stress universal feminine attributes (the feminine imagination, feminine writing) and those who focus on the political conditions experienced by particular groups of women during specific periods in history, parallels a larger distinction between American feminist critics and their British counterparts.

While it has been customary to refer to an Anglo-American tradition of feminist criticism, British feminists tend to distinguish themselves from what they see as an American overemphasis on texts linking women across boundaries and decades and an underemphasis on popular art and culture. They regard their own critical practice as more political than that of American feminists, whom they have often faulted for being uninterested in historical detail. They would join such American critics as Myra Jehlen in suggesting that a continuing preoccupation with women writers might create the danger of placing women's texts outside the history that conditions them.

In the view of British feminists, the American opposition to male stereotypes that denigrate women has often led to counterstereotypes of feminine virtue that ignore real differences of race, class, and culture among women. In addition, they argue that American celebrations of individual heroines falsely suggest that powerful individuals may be immune to repressive conditions and may even imply that *any* individual can go through life unconditioned by the culture and ideology in which she or he lives.

Similarly, the American endeavor to recover women's history — for example, by emphasizing that women developed their own strategies to gain power within their sphere — is seen by British feminists like Judith Newton and Deborah Rosenfelt as an endeavor that "mystifies" male oppression, disguising it as something that has created for women a special world of opportunities. More important from the British standpoint, the universalizing and "essentializing" tendencies in both American practice and French theory disguise women's oppression by highlighting sexual difference, suggesting that a dominant system is impervious to political change. By contrast, British feminist theory emphasizes an engagement with historical process in order to promote social change.

Nina Baym reviews the history of American feminist criticism at the beginning of her essay on Nathaniel Hawthorne (1982). "The initial works of feminist criticism," Baym writes, "analyzed the writings of important male authors . . . in an attempt to uncover the . . . destructive attitudes toward women that they contained." Because Hawthorne's works "presented many problems to the critic who wished to define him as an orthodox espouser of patriarchal attitudes," American feminists ultimately "abandoned him for other writers more suited to their aims." Since then, "feminist criticism has turned away from male authors." As a result, "little work on Hawthorne with a feminist stamp has been produced since 1976" ("Thwarted Nature" 58).

In 1976 Judith Fryer published *The Faces of Eve: Women in the Nineteenth-Century American Novel.* Writing at the end of the era in which feminists critiqued the works of male authors, Fryer revealed patriarchal attitudes in Hawthorne while recognizing other conflicting attitudes — those that in Baym's words had always "presented problems" for early feminists. Using "The Custom-House" to show that Hawthorne believed his own artistic nature "unmanly," Fryer went on to argue that "Hawthorne's ambiguity about Hester" is "an attempt to work out his ambiguity toward himself," both "as artist" and "as man." Fryer recognized something "feminine" and sympathetic with the feminine in Hawthorne, while, at the same time, being skeptical of "twentieth-century readers who would see . . . Hawthorne as a writer with 'feminist sympathies'" (74). Fryer points out that Hester's dark broodings on "the whole race of womanhood" are clearly "bothersome to Hawthorne" (78); they are succeeded by the narrator's observation that "A woman never overcomes these problems by any exercise of thought" (134). Indeed, in life Hawthorne "married a pale maiden" as conventionally feminine as Hester is unconventional (78).

Since Baym started a return-to-Hawthorne movement in 1982, feminists who have written on *The Scarlet Letter* have been much influenced by her — but by Fryer as well. In her book *Women, Ethnics, and Exotics* (1983), Kristin Herzog has perpetuated Fryer's image of Hester as a darkly sensual type of Eve. Arguing that Hester's "'lawless passion' . . . turns her into a kind of white Indian," Herzog concludes her discussion by calling Hawthorne's most memorable heroine "an example of a new American Eve" (15–16).

Other modern American feminists interested in Hawthorne have further analyzed the "ambiguity" or ambivalence detected and discussed by both Fryer and Baym. In *Gender and the Writer's Imagination* (1987), Mary Suzanne Schriber points out that Hester is herself ambivalent, or self-divided. "Assertive, rather than submissive," Hester is nonetheless "conventional" and even "lady-like" (48–49), so much so that "the community eventually comes around, attributing to Hester's *A* the meaning of 'Angel' and 'Able' rather than adulteress" (50). Regarding the novel's ambivalent attitude toward Hester, Schriber suggests that it results from inconsistencies in the mind of the less-than-reliable narrator, as well from differences between the narrator's views and those of the "implied author" (56).

In his *Aesthetic Headaches: Women and a Masculine Poetics in Poe, Melville, and Hawthorne* (1988), a male feminist, Leland S. Person, begins by acknowledging debts to both Fryer and Baym. Not unlike Schriber, he contests their notion that Hester is, in Fryer's words, "'a whole person.'" In doing so, of course, he essentially remakes Fryer's argument that Hawthorne is not really a nineteenth-century feminist and that *The Scarlet Letter* is unsettled and unsettling in its treatment of women. Person admits that Hester may be an artist capable of making the community redefine what the letter A means, but she is also a work of art, someone who has herself been redefined, "the creation not only of the Puritan community (through the medium and signifying power of the letter), but of Arthur Dimmesdale (through his commitment and withdrawal of emotional commitment to her)" (124–25). The "phallic" power to control or "master" women, Person argues, is a favorite subject of Hawthorne's (recall Dimmesdale's temptation to "blight" a young girl's innocence with "a single word" [123]) and one of Hawthorne's own measures of artistic success. Person reminds us that Hawthorne considered *The Scarlet Letter* " 'a triumphant success,' a 'ten-strike' " because it "had such an effect on [his wife] Sophia that it 'broke her heart and sent her to bed with a grievous headache' " (122).

The phallic power to control and master women is very much what the essay that begins on page 288 is about. There, Shari Benstock explains how a patriarchal Puritan society attempts to master one woman, Hester Prynne, in part by marking her with a letter that reduces her to a single, rather simple identity — that of a sinner.

Benstock also shows how Hester subverts such attempts from the moment she steps forth from the prison door and, instead of trying to hide what is meant to stand for her sin, openly reveals the letter on her breast. Through that and other, consequent actions, she identifies herself not as a sinner but as a sexual woman — and more. For, as Benstock points out, Hester proceeds by artfully altering both the letter and other symbols constructed by the Puritan society. Slowly, carefully, sometimes luxuriously, she makes them stand for things unintended by the patriarchs who, by controlling language, have controlled women as well. In fact, Hester ends up by opening "an inexhaustible chain of substitutions," making the scarlet A stand for Angel, Able, Adored — and, finally, "Authority over her own identity."

As Benstock realizes, Hawthorne begins to raise the issue of gender in his introduction to the novel. In "The Custom-House" he associates embroidery, femininity, and storytelling, reinforcing the kind of connections that are part of our culture's masculine-dominated "logic" and forming the kind of connections that Toril Moi refers to as "sexual/textual" in her book, *Sexual/Textual Politics: Feminist Literary Theory* (1985). Ultimately, *The Scarlet Letter* critiques those same kinds of associations — femininity and falsity, truth and masculinity. Like Hester, the novel teaches us to distrust easy, traditional, patriarchal modes of interpretation that would tell us that "A" (or woman) does *not* mean "Able." Moreover, by demonstrating the multiple meanings of a letter and by occasionally dissociating meaning from gender, the novel even manages to undermine or challenge the *idea* of absolute sexual difference.

Benstock's reading of *The Scarlet Letter* has obviously been influenced by French as well as American feminist theory. The French influence shows in local details, such as references to Kristeva's theory. But it is also evident in Benstock's general focus on women and patriarchal or phallocentric language, which associates the feminine with certain words and ideas, the masculine with others. Returning to the Greeks, Benstock explains that early myths linked the earth with the female body, the plow with the penis, and, by extension, with masculinity. Furthermore, she suggests that since civilization has been equated with dominion over the earth, it has also come to imply the domination of women by men. Equally French is Benstock's allusion to a primary bond between Hester and Pearl that precedes language and, therefore, culture.

Benstock's essay, however, does more than critique, or deconstruct, the logic of binary oppositions (male/female, plow/earth, dominant/passive) and associations (male/plow/dominant, female/earth/passive) inherent in masculine-dominated language; it also shows Hawthorne engaged in the same enterprise. As Benstock points out, Hawthorne portrays a New England earth from which wild rosebushes grow but which resists patriarchal, civilizing law; it seems that neither plans nor plows can help the Puritans raise up an ornamental garden from such hard soil. In turning Hawthorne into a precursor of French feminist theory, Benstock again demonstrates what American feminists like Baym and Fryer have long known, namely, that Hawthorne himself is not easily categorized. At once backward- and forward-looking, he is as patriarchal as he is prototypically feminist, as much a part of the answer to "the dark question" concerning "the whole race of womanhood" as he has been part of the problem.

FEMINIST CRITICISM: A SELECTED BIBLIOGRAPHY

French Feminist Theory

Beauvoir, Simone de. *The Second Sex.* 1949. Ed. and trans. H. M. Parshley. New York: Modern Library, 1952.

Cixous, Hélène. "The Laugh of the Medusa." Trans. Keith Cohen and Paula Cohen. *Signs* 1 (1976): 875–94.

French Feminist Theory. Special issue, *Signs* 7 (1981). Essays by Cixous, Fauré, Irigaray, Kristeva.

Gelfand, Elissa D., and Virginia Thorndike Hules, eds. *French Feminist Criticism: Women, Language and Literature. An Annotated Bibliography*. New York: Garland, 1984.

Irigaray, Luce. *This Sex Which Is Not One*. Trans. Catherine Porter. Ithaca: Cornell UP, 1985.

Jones, Ann Rosalind. "Inscribing Femininity: French Theories of the Feminine." *Making a Difference: Feminist Literary Criticism*. Ed. Gayle Greene and Coppélia Kahn. London: Methuen, 1985. 80–112.

Kristeva, Julia. *Desire in Language: A Semiotic Approach to Literature and Art*. Ed. Leon S. Roudiez. Trans. Thomas Gora, Alice Jardine, and Leon S. Roudiez. New York: Columbia UP, 1980.

Marks, Elaine, and Isabelle de Courtivron, eds. *New French Feminism: An Anthology*. Amherst: U of Massachusetts P, 1980.

Moi, Toril. *Sexual/Textual Politics: Feminist Literary Theory*. London: Methuen, 1985.

Wittig, Monique. *Les Guérillères*. 1969. Trans. David Le Vay. New York: Avon, 1973.

British and American Feminist Theory

Benstock, Shari, ed. *Feminist Issues and Literary Scholarship*. Bloomington: Indiana UP, 1987.

Greer, Germaine. *The Female Eunuch*. New York: McGraw, 1971.

Heilbrun, Carolyn G. *Toward a Recognition of Androgyny*. New York: Knopf, 1973.

Kolodny, Annette. "Some Notes on Defining a 'Feminist Literary Criticism.'" *Critical Inquiry* 2 (1975): 75–92.

Millett, Kate. *Sexual Politics*. Garden City: Doubleday, 1970.

Showalter, Elaine. "Towards a Feminist Poetics." Jacobus 22–41.

Woolf, Virginia. *A Room of One's Own*. New York: Harcourt, 1929.

The Feminist Critique

Ellmann, Mary. *Thinking About Women*. London: Macmillan, 1968.

Fetterley, Judith. *The Resisting Reader: A Feminist Approach to American Fiction*. Bloomington: Indiana UP, 1978.

Kolodny, Annette. *The Lay of the Land: Metaphor as Experience in American Life and Letters*. Chapel Hill: U of North Carolina P, 1975.

See also Beauvoir, Greer, Heilbrun, and Millett (cited above).

Gynocriticism: Women's Writing and Creativity

Auerbach, Nina. *Communities of Women: An Idea in Fiction*. Cambridge: Harvard UP, 1978.

Gilbert, Sandra M., and Susan Gubar. *The Madwoman in the Attic: The Woman Writer and the Nineteenth-Century Literary Imagination.* New Haven: Yale UP, 1979.

Jacobus, Mary, ed. *Women Writing and Writing About Women.* New York: Barnes, 1979.

Miller, Nancy K., ed. *The Poetics of Gender.* New York: Columbia UP, 1986.

Poovey, Mary. *The Proper Lady and the Woman Writer: Ideology as Style in the Works of Mary Wollstonecraft, Mary Shelley, and Jane Austen.* Chicago: U of Chicago P, 1984.

Showalter, Elaine. *A Literature of Their Own: British Women Novelists from Brontë to Lessing.* Princeton: Princeton UP, 1977.

———. *The New Feminist Criticism: Essays on Women, Literature, and Theory.* New York: Pantheon, 1985.

Spacks, Patricia Meyer. *The Female Imagination.* New York: Knopf, 1975.

Marxist and Class Analysis

Barrett, Michèle. *Women's Oppression Today: Problems in Marxist Feminist Analysis.* London: Verso, 1980.

Delany, Sheila. *Writing Woman: Women Writers and Women in Literature, Medieval to Modern.* New York: Schocken, 1983.

Keohane, Nannerl O., Michelle Z. Rosaldo, and Barbara C. Gelpi, eds. *Feminist Theory: A Critique of Ideology.* Chicago: U of Chicago P, 1982. See especially the essays by Elshtain, Jehlen, Kristeva, MacKinnon, and Marcus.

Mitchell, Juliet. *Woman's Estate.* New York: Pantheon, 1971.

Monteith, Moira, ed. *Women's Writing: A Challenge to Theory.* Brighton, Eng.: Harvester, 1986. See especially the essays by Monteith and Humm.

Newton, Judith Lowder. *Women, Power and Subversion: Social Strategies and British Fiction, 1778–1860.* Athens: U of Georgia P, 1981.

Newton, Judith, and Deborah Rosenfelt, eds. *Feminist Criticism and Social Change: Sex, Class and Race in Literature and Culture.* New York: Methuen, 1985. See especially the essays by Jones and Smith.

Robinson, Lillian. *Sex, Class, and Culture.* New York: Methuen, 1986.

Women's History/Women's Studies

Bell, Roseann P., et al., eds. *Sturdy Black Bridges: Visions of Black Women in Literature.* New York: Anchor, 1979.

Bridenthal, Renata, and Claudia Koonz, eds. *Becoming Visible: Women in European History*. Boston: Houghton, 1977.

Cott, Nancy F., and Elizabeth H. Pleck, eds. *A Heritage of Her Own: Toward a New Social History of American Women*. New York: Simon-Touchstone, 1977.

Faderman, Lillian. *Surpassing the Love of Men: Romantic Friendship and Love Between Women from the Renaissance to the Present*. New York: Morrow, 1981.

Lesbian Issue, The. Special issue, *Signs* 9 (1984).

Newton, Judith L., Mary P. Ryan, and Judith R. Walkowitz, eds. *Sex and Class in Women's History*. London: Routledge, 1983.

Schipper, Mineke, ed. *Unheard Words: Women and Literature in Africa, the Arab World, Asia, the Caribbean, and Latin America*. London: Allison, 1979.

Feminism and Other Critical Approaches

Armstrong, Nancy, ed. *Literature as Women's History I*. Special issue, *Genre* 19–20 (1986–87), containing feminist/new historicist analyses.

Feminist Studies 14 (1988). Special issue devoted to feminism and deconstruction. See especially Mary Poovey's "Feminism and Deconstruction."

Feminist Criticism of Hawthorne and *The Scarlet Letter*

Baym, Nina. "The Significance of Plot in Hawthorne's Romances." *Ruined Eden of the Present: Hawthorne, Melville, and Poe*. Ed. G. R. Thompson and Virgil Lokke. West Lafayette: Purdue UP, 1981. 49–70.

———. "Thwarted Nature: Nathaniel Hawthorne as Feminist." *American Novelists Revisited: Essays in Feminist Criticism*. Ed. Fritz Fleischmann. Boston: Hall, 1982. 58–77.

Fryer, Judith. *The Faces of Eve: Women in the Nineteenth-Century American Novel*. New York: Oxford UP, 1976.

Herzog, Kristin. *Women, Ethnics, and Exotics: Images of Power in Mid-Nineteenth-Century Fiction*. Knoxville: U of Tennessee P, 1983.

Kamuf, Peggy. "Hawthorne's Genres: The Letter of the Law *Appliquée*." *After Strange Texts: The Role of Theory in the Study of Literature*. Ed. Gregory S. Jay and David L. Miller. University: U of Alabama P, 1985. 69–84.

Person, Leland S. *Aesthetic Headaches: Women and a Masculine Poetics in Poe, Melville, and Hawthorne*. Athens: U of Georgia P, 1988.
Schriber, Mary Suzanne. *Gender and the Writer's Imagination: From Cooper to Wharton*. Lexington: UP of Kentucky, 1987.

A FEMINIST CRITIC AT WORK

SHARI BENSTOCK

The Scarlet Letter (a)dorée, or the Female Body Embroidered

> The word is understood only as an extension of the body which is there in the process of speaking. . . . To the extent that it does not know repression, femininity is the downfall of interpretation.
>
> –MICHELE MONTRELAY, "Inquiry into Femininity"

> As women our relationship to the past has been problematical. We have been every culture's core obsession (and repression).
>
> –ADRIENNE RICH, *Of Woman Born*

When the jail door is "flung open from within" and Hester Prynne "step[s] into the open air, as if by her own free-will," she stands, we are told, "fully revealed before the crowd" (56–57). She denies an initial impulse to cover the token of her shame, the scarlet letter from which the text takes its title, with the body of her infant daughter. Instead, Hester parades her sin, exhibiting baby and letter before the collective gaze of the Puritan community:

> she took the baby on her arm, and, with a burning blush, and yet a haughty smile, and a glance that would not be abashed, looked around at her townspeople and neighbours. On the breast of her gown, in fine red cloth, surrounded with an elaborate embroidery and fantastic flourishes of gold thread, appeared the letter A. (57)

This gesture of revelation, like the exquisitely wrought letter itself, masks self-representation. Offering herself as an object of scrutiny to the crowd, Hester remains obscured to the degree that "her beauty shone out, and made a halo of the misfortune and ignominy in which she was enveloped" (57). As Peggy Kamuf (79) has suggested, the A "so fantastically embroidered and illuminated upon her bosom" (57–58) opens an inexhaustible chain of substitutions (adulteress, angel, able, adored, etc.) that includes Authority over her own identity, an authority that the letter protects.

The opening scene of *The Scarlet Letter* parades before the reader and the assembled Boston public the body of sin, or more accurately, woman's body as (emblem of) sin. The female body is both an agent of human reproduction and a field of representation, emblematized first by the scarlet letter on Hester's slate-gray gown and again at the story's end by the slate tombstone bearing the heraldic legend "ON A FIELD, SABLE, THE LETTER A, GULES" (201). *The Scarlet Letter* exposes a relation between babies and words, between biological reproduction and symbolic representations. Puritan theocracy would suppress one element of this relation, symbolizing the baby as the sign of God's will in the universe ordered by patriarchal religious and civil law. Woman's body serves as the space where social, religious, and cultural values are inscribed (quite literally in Hester's case); moreover, it produces the very terms of that inscription: Pearl *is* the scarlet letter in human form (90).

Hester Prynne, however, subverts the Puritan-patriarchal laws of meaning in two ways. First, she embroiders and embellishes the community's representational codes, thereby confusing them. The letter A, which is to stand as the sign of sexual fall, escapes by way of Hester's needle the interpretive code it would enforce, opening itself to a wholly other logic. It makes a spectacle of femininity, of female sexuality, of all that Puritan law hopes to repress. Second, Hester refuses to name her child's father, thereby placing Pearl — material sign of the mother's sin — outside the bo(u)nds of Puritan ideology. By her birth, which is represented textually as a form of mysterious regeneration, Pearl cannot circulate within the terms of symbolic, communal social-sexual exchange. Missing a father, the guiding term of paternal authority, she remains her "mother's child" (95). Despite all efforts by the Puritan community to bring mother and daughter under the authority of God and man, Hester and Pearl remain resolutely outside patriarchal conventions.

Issues of gender, then, are at the very heart of the story told by *The Scarlet Letter:* the history of the letter, supposedly discovered by Hawthorne in the Custom-House, bears importantly on the questions the tale poses about narrative sources and symbolic powers as well as about the mystery of paternal origins that the story seeks to solve. The scarlet letter is passed from generation to generation by men, and Hawthorne feels burdened by "filial duty" to his "official ancestor," Jonathan Pue, to present again the tale of the letter. "Mr. Surveyor Pue" is the Custom-House official who "authorized and authenticated" the historical events on which the story is based (44).

The tale itself, however, focuses attention on representations of *womanhood,* with special emphasis on Puritan efforts to regulate female sexuality within religious, legal, and economic structures. Puritan thought assigns the powers of naming, owning, and ordering to a paternal theological order, derived linearly (and literally) from the Word of God-the-Father. Divinity transcends biology; God-the-Father is Alpha and Omega, origin of life and its final meaning; the human body is corporeal matter to be transcended. As agents of human reproduction, women are subsumed by this symbolic order, which assigns weight and value to women's work.

Repeating a particularly misogynistic version of paternal ordering, *The Scarlet Letter* draws a relation between mere storytelling and the domestic art of embroidery. In "The Custom-House," the autobiographical introduction to the text, Hawthorne reveals his fear of losing his "imaginative faculty," or "fancy" (45, 46). The text that follows, which he claims to have found and "dress[ed] up" as a romance (44), fashions a tale around the "fantastic" artistry of Hester Prynne's needlework skills (57). By various means, then, Hawthorne suggests that literary genres are marked by gender, displaying forms of sexual-textual difference not only in their subject matter but also in their structures and narrative methods. *The Scarlet Letter* prompts us to ask: does the feminine bear the same relation to storytelling as it does to embroidery or the female body to sin? Following recent developments in feminist theory, I will argue that the feminine, so powerfully at work in Hawthorne's tale, works not to exploit oppositional structures of sexual-textual difference but rather to expose the fictional nature of these modes, revealing absolute sexual difference as a fantasy of patriarchal oppositional and hierarchical logic. I refer to this figure as the "textual feminine," since it reveals itself in language, where it both supports traditional notions of femininity and subverts these powerful representations of woman-in-the-feminine. Fantasies of the feminine undergird classic Western models of narrative, which the textual feminine — represented in Hawthorne's text by the gilded letter A — elaborates, ornaments, embellishes, and seeks to undermine.

The patriarchal construction of femininity, based on masculine fantasies of the female body, is the sign under which sexual difference parades itself in our culture. This spectacle of womanhood, the female body dressed as icon or effigy, wards off patriarchal fears of female sexuality. The Puritan community means to make Hester play such a role, but its efforts fail because she — like all women — embodies an "other" femininity that cannot be fully controlled within the terms of phallic law. As Jacqueline Rose explains, this other feminine, which is not visible to the eye of man, is the place where representation is obscured and where interpretation fails. Refusing to expose itself to public view or to mouth the words it has been culturally assigned, this "other" femininity unsettles orders of patriarchal logic, rendering as nonsense the stories by which culture explains itself to itself. The age-old stories of men's adventures at war and on the high seas (narratives Hawthorne overheard while a customs inspector) and the tales men invent of women — adored as virgins, feared as witches, despised as spinsters, or exploited and abused as wives and prostitutes — assume new meanings according to these "other" terms. The sexual-textual feminine confounds the structures of traditional narratives and circumscribes their limits.

The scarlet letter itself reveals how this double logic works. As Alpha, first letter of the alphabet, it challenges the conventions of meaning and origins of words. For example, if the letter is to mean "Adulteress," all other words beginning with the letter A must be repressed: for the A to signify, it must serve as a sign of *absolute difference*. By not assigning the A to a single word that would inscribe a transcendent meaning, *The Scarlet Letter* opens itself to a profusion of possible meanings that the author and seamstress elaborate. By their silence, Hawthorne and Hester undo traditional methods of interpretation: he refuses to assign the letter to a word (as she refuses to name her baby's father); she embellishes the letter, making it an item of adornment, representation of an extravagant, excessive femininity. Because the letter refuses to call out its name and thereby submit to the law by which meaning (like paternity) can be assigned, the letter comes to signify the fantasy of sexual difference. Some members of the Puritan community interpret it to mean "able" or "angel"; a contemporary feminist might see in its fertile and "gorgeous luxuriance of fancy" (57) an emblem of the female sexual organ itself, a perverse revision of seventeenth-century sexual-textual optics. To the degree that *The Scarlet Letter* is marked by the textual feminine, it makes a fiction of patriarchal, not to say Puritan, modes of interpretation: it is the ador(n)ed emblem of their downfall.

Of Gardens, Gold, and Little Girls

> At some future day, it may be, I shall remember a few scattered fragments and broken paragraphs, and write them down, and find the letters turn to gold upon the page.
>
> —NATHANIEL HAWTHORNE, "The Custom-House"

By the same rhetorical gestures that *The Scarlet Letter* exposes the effects of secret (sexual) sin to the light of noonday sun, it also hides the cultural assumptions that have historically undergirded representations of women. Feminist criticism demonstrates that these assumptions are not "natural" or God-given, as cultures and religions would have us believe, but are socially and economically constructed to further the ends of patriarchy. Patriarchy defines social gender roles for women and men from biological sex functions, thus keeping women within the confines of domesticity and under the husband's power as familial patriarch. Because reproduction of the species takes place through the woman's body, she is seen as closer to "nature," while man is the agent of society and culture, which he creates through symbolic representations of the natural environment. The power of symbols and signs to enforce social order is manifest in Puritan thought, where the spiritual and immaterial is figured by signs and portents and where all natural occurrences (lightning, thunder) take on symbolic meaning. Woman's body, whose sexual organs are hidden internally and whose reproductive operations remain mysterious, becomes a vessel to be filled with symbolic meaning: virgin/adulteress, madonna/mother, whore/witch. Gabriele Schwab suggests that witchcraft was a male invention, born of the fear of sexually powerful or independent women who represented natural forces that needed to be "tamed."

These dichotomous and oppressive representations of woman are the product of the binary structure of Western thought, the earliest forms being those from fifth-century Greek culture, which rewrote earlier agricultural myths. In the most ancient myths, both the land and the female body were inherently fertile, giving birth to seeds and babies by spontaneous generation. The triangular shape of the letter A, for instance, reproduces the sign for the Nile River Delta, an ancient pre-Christian symbol of female fertility and rebirth of the land. Early myths of reproduction linked woman's body to the earth: regeneration of field and family were seen as similar activities associated with female fertility. Later Platonic versions of reproduction, however, imaged the female body as a field in need of ploughing and planting. In these myths, regenerative power was transferred to the male. Penis and plow were instruments of insemination with which man cultivated woman's empty furrow. According to Page duBois, this later metaphor of woman's body as empty field and open furrow underwrites Western notions of sexual difference enforced through cultural symbols, ritual practices, and agricultural methods. Cultivation of the land is equated with civilization, man's dominion over the earth inscribed by field and furrow.

The shift in Greek thought can be accounted for by the social reorganization of the city-states, especially the move away from religious superstitions associated with the ancient gods of earth and environment toward the new written laws of the community, inscripted and enacted by male citizens. The Calvinist religion as examined by *The Scarlet Letter* invokes this world of archaic myth, which gives symbolic power to natural (and inexplicable) occurrences, and also enforces a *communitas* supported by rationality and civility governed by the Puritan selectmen. Ancient notions of female fertility and sexual power provide the (repressed) grounds on which Puritan law constrains sexuality within the bonds of marriage, thereby protecting paternity rights and keeping the "feminine" within the domestic. The question of paternity that the community seeks to answer encompasses both the natural world of forest wilderness and the civilized world of the community. The drama of *The Scarlet Letter* takes place across a dividing line between forest, where the sexual act took place and which shelters the secret of the child's paternity, and village, where the material effects of the sexual union are exposed to communal speculation.

The "untamed forest" of the New World represents a "moral wilderness," a space of sexual and ethnic otherness where Indians roam and the "witch" Mistress Hibbins meets the Black Man. It is a "wild, free atmosphere of an unredeemed, unchristianized, lawless region" (159), a space to be colonized and cultivated by Puritan *communitas*, with its basis in patriarchal and capitalist ideologies. Even within the village limits, however, the landscape resists all but the most primitive efforts at cultivation. Governor Bellingham fails to reproduce in the hard soil his "native English taste for ornamental gardening" (93). Cabbages grow in plain sight of his garden-walk, and a pumpkin vine rooted outside the garden proper "had run across the intervening space, and deposited one of its gigantic products directly beneath the hall-window" (93). A number of symbolic associations attach to this rude image of reproductive excess. Vegetation that overruns its boundaries emblematizes unrestrained female sexuality, which is believed to know no limits or boundaries. In this instance, the cabbages and pumpkin invoke folk mythology of human origins, where babies are found under cabbage leaves. The gigantic pumpkin in the Governor's garden represents not only reproductive excess but capitalist productivity, the ability of gold to reproduce itself: "this great lump of vegetable gold was as rich an ornament as New England earth would offer him" (93). This is one of many places in the text in which capitalist-patriarchal gains are figured as ornament and sumptuary excess. Within the value systems of the story, Hester Prynne's needlework elaborates a gendered relation of economic (re)production to ornament in Puritan society: lacking financial support from her husband or from the father of her child, she produces by her womanly art the gold necessary to support herself and Pearl.

The failure of civilization to bring nature under its control is even more dramatically symbolized by the wild rosebush that blooms in the overgrown grass-plot in front of the prison from which Hester emerges. The rosebush gives rise to various stories about its origins, including speculation that "it had sprung up under the footsteps of the sainted Ann Hutchinson, as she entered the prison-door" (54). Ann Hutchinson, founder of the antinomian sect (which means, literally, "against the law"), figures an alternate history for Hester Prynne, a lost story of female independence and resistance to patriarchal law. Hester's daughter, in response to Pastor Wilson's catechism ("Canst thou tell me, my child, who made thee?" [96]), traces her origins to this rosebush. Rather than attributing her origins to God the father, as church doctrine decrees, Pearl returns to an archaic, preliterate story, substituting roses for cabbages: "the child finally announced that she had not been made at all, but had been plucked by her mother off the bush of wild roses, that grew by the prison-door" (97). In this schema, Pearl is not her mother's daughter but rather a symbolic descendant of Ann Hutchinson.

Pearl is certainly a rarer, more exotic fruit than anything the Governor's garden can produce, and her radiant beauty is intensified by the mystery of her origins: a "lovely and immortal flower," she "had sprung . . . out of the rank luxuriance of a guilty passion" (81). If in the hermeneutics of Hawthorne's romance Hester's gold embroidery signifies spiritual adornment, the "application of a design" on "the fabric of experience" as Evan Carton claims (197–98), then Pearl represents the material sign of Hester's sin, the human matter that invites Puritan speculation. The community imbues her physical features and infant gestures with meaning, but Pearl's beauty (which is described through sets of opposites: pale/radiant, shadow/light, crimson/gold, etc.) and her quixotic personality baffle the citizenry. The name Pearl itself seems inappropriate to a child of ruby or red rose complexion (95). The profound duality that the community imparts to Pearl's character — angel/devil — leads to the scene in the governor's hall when Hester is forced to call on Arthur Dimmesdale in support of her efforts to retain custody of her child. The circumstances of this confrontation between Hester and the community elders bear close scrutiny.

The news of the Boston community's interest in Pearl's relationship to her mother reaches Hester by word of mouth, that is, by gossip: "It had reached her ears, that there was a design on the part of some of the leading inhabitants, cherishing the more rigid order of principles in religion and government, to deprive her of her child" (89). Public attention is drawn to the child by her fantastic dress, the product of Hester's needle, and her untamed and impulsive behavior. The reasons offered for the intervention of civic and religious authorities into a domestic scene, however, are contradictory and constitute a failure of the hermeneutic project that would attach a single meaning to Pearl's presence in Hester's life:

> On the supposition that Pearl, as already hinted, was of demon origin, these good people not unreasonably argued that a Christian interest in *the mother's soul* required them to remove such a stumbling-block from her path. If the child, on the other hand, were really capable of moral and religious growth, and possessed the elements of ultimate salvation, then, surely, it would enjoy all the fairer prospect of these advantages by being transferred to *wiser and better guardianship* than Hester Prynne's. (89, emphasis added)

Without evidence of the child's origin, the community cannot judge her capacity for moral growth. Following the oppositional structure of Puritan thought, the absent paternal signifier can mean one of two things: either Pearl's father is the devil, the "Black Man" who it is rumored impregnated Hester in the woods, or God the Father, in which case her soul is "capable of moral and religious growth" (89). If Pearl belongs to the devil, then it is her *mother's* soul that is in danger; if the daughter belongs to God, then the mother's sinful presence in her life is a stumbling block. That there is no clear material sign of Pearl's spiritual state (or biological paternity), no name-of-the-father to identify her lineage, leaves the community without the means of interpretation.

Pleading before the magistrate and church fathers, Hester claims that Pearl plays a double role in her life: "She is my happiness! — she is my torture, none the less! Pearl keeps me here in life! Pearl punishes me too!" (97–98). When she asks Dimmesdale to support her cause, she asks him to speak from his knowledge of her soul, bringing to bear his pastoral and spiritual authority. In this moment, the double aspect of Pearl's beauty — which is described as both "pale" and "wild" — is divided between the parents, visible evidence of the contrast between Hester and Dimmesdale: she is "provoked . . . to little less than madness" while he is "pale . . . holding his hand over his heart" (98). The child's opposed nature might be reconciled into a single sign had the authorities the means by which to interpret it, knowledge of the paternal signifier. Roger Chillingworth calls on philosophy to answer the question: "It is easy to see the mother's part in her. Would it be beyond a philosopher's research, think ye, gentlemen, to analyze that child's nature, and, from its make and mould, to give a shrewd guess at the father?" (100). The Church fathers reject "profane philosophy," elevating the question to the higher authority of divinity: "leave the mystery as we find it, unless Providence reveal it of its own accord." This gesture does not resolve the mystery but lifts it, unresolved, to higher paternal authority, an authority that gives a "title" to "every good Christian man . . . to show a father's kindness towards the poor, deserted babe" (100).

The scene in the governor's hall reveals a gendered relation between spirit and matter. First, the question of paternity is taken out of the provenance of law (represented by Governor Bellingham) or of philosophy and medicine (Roger Chillingworth) and left to religious authority, which removes it to yet a higher authority. At first glance this decision seems to benefit Hester's rights to custody of her child, returning the question of paternity to the realm of the spiritual, which makes a legal fiction of it. Hester aids the process by remaining silent about her relationship with Dimmesdale, a relationship she claims before the authorities to be solely spiritual. The reasons for her silence are wholly mysterious and never resolved within the text; by keeping silent, however, she exposes herself and her child to possible economic hardship and allows Dimmesdale to ignore the material reality of her situation. Indeed, Dimmesdale never fully recognizes the material existence of Pearl. The riches Pearl later inherits are at the bequest of Roger Chillingworth, Hester's wronged husband. These riches, of course, account for the "very material change in the public estimation" (199) of little Pearl, providing evidentiary proof of her value in God's eyes. That proof comes not through the mother, although Hester is finally deemed by the community an admirable mother, but through an (absent, dead) paternal line, from the man who should have fathered Hester's children but could not. The phallic power that Chillingworth lacked in life, its failure ascribed to the intellectual and ascetic life he led, is transformed in death through the legacy of his properties in England and the New World. Dimmesdale's unacknowledged and illicit legacy is Pearl herself.

Mother as Matter

> We live in a civilization in which the *consecrated* (religious or secular) representation of femininity is subsumed under maternity. Under close examination, however, this maternity turns out to be an adult (male and female) fantasy of a lost continent.
>
> –JULIA KRISTEVA, "Stabat Mater"

Before the authorities in the governor's hall, Hester declares that Dimmesdale has sympathies that other men lack, ascribing to him knowledge of maternal matters: "thou knowest what is in my heart, and what are a mother's rights, and how much the stronger they are, when that mother has but her child and the scarlet letter" (98). Her claim is that maternal ties and mother rights are stronger in the absence of the father, and she charges Dimmesdale to "look to it," that is, to see to it that she not lose her child. Although Dimmesdale's physical weakness feminizes him (he seems hardly able to support the secret phallic signifier he is supposed to bear), he argues forcefully for her in his "sweet, tremulous, but powerful" voice (98). Hester's strength, drawn in no small measure from her maternal role, overshadows her aging husband and her weakened lover, leading many critics (D. H. Lawrence foremost among them) to conclude that she is a witch figure who saps the phallic power invested in these men, unsexing herself in the process. The Puritan code demands that she relinquish her femininity as the price of survival; she assumes a serenity and calm that appear as "marble coldness" (133). The scarlet letter, whose rich embroidery in other circumstances might be read as a sign of feminine adornment, is here the sign that Hester has forfeited her place in the normal exchange of women among men, where fathers hand daughters to husbands. The letter is Hester's "passport into regions where other women dared not tread" (157).

Hester's "lost" sexual nature is transferred to her daughter, whose passionate temperament apparently knows no repression. Indeed, Pearl appears to harbor secret knowledge associated with the scarlet letter, knowledge that Hester both fears and tries to discover in her daughter's regard. Gabriele Schwab argues that the mother makes the child mirror her own fears. Hester tries through her needlework "to create an analogy between the object of her affection [Pearl], and the emblem of her guilt and torture [the letter]" (90). Mother and daughter reflect each other and read each other as signs: Hester searches for evidence of an "original sin," the sin that the mother confers on the daughter through the circumstances of her conception; Pearl searches for the meaning of the scarlet letter, which she sees as the key to her mother's identity and the source of her own origins. In response to Pearl's insistent questions, Hester claims that she wears the scarlet letter "for the sake of its gold thread" (145). This enigmatic response, which the child does not accept, hints that the A is worn for adornment and that the gold embroidery, not the letter, carries meaning. When Hester flings the letter aside in the scene by the brook, Pearl cannot recognize her *as mother* and refuses her insistent demands for recognition. By this time the effects of the scarlet letter are already lodged within the daughter's heart. Hester has succeeded in turning her daughter into a symbol, an image of the mother's (suppressed) sexual nature, by dressing her in the crimson and gold colors of the letter.

If phallic authority and power are handed from father to son along a patriarchal chain of entitlement, mothers hand on to daughters a divided feminine sexuality scored by repressive social and cultural prescriptions. The myth of an unrestrained feminine libido that operates *independently* of cultural codes is a male fantasy-fear whose counterpart is the feminist dream of an idealized primary bond between mother and infant that exists prior to and outside of the social-cultural frame. Society charges fathers with bringing their children — sons and daughters — to conscious awareness of power structures under patriarchal law: boys must learn to uphold the (phallic) law; girls must learn to submit to it. According to psychoanalysts Nicholas Abraham and Maria Torok, the mother's gift (and burden) to her children is the repressed maternal unconscious; although communicated in silence, it becomes part of the child's language and the core to which the child's own repressions will be added. This maternal unconscious becomes the center of the daughter's psychosexual identity, whereas for sons it represents the feminine that the phallic must overcome.

Hawthorne's text dramatizes this psychological passage by way of the scarlet letter, the sign by which Hester passes on to Pearl the patriarchy's double message about sin and seduction. Feminist analysis would see the letter as agent of a *gendered* psychosexual identity. Under its auspices Hester must relinquish her individuality (as woman) to become a generalized symbol of "woman's frailty and sinful passion" (74) — Woman. In a passage that describes Hester's transformation from person to pedagogical tool for Puritan ideology, we learn by oblique reference that the baby we see her holding on the scaffold is a girl: "Thus the young and pure would be taught to look at her, with the scarlet letter flaming on her breast, — at her, the child of honorable parents, — at her, the mother of a babe, that *would hereafter be a woman,* — at her, who had once been innocent, — as *the figure, the body, the reality of sin*" (74–75, emphasis added). The baby is not yet a woman (womanhood in Western culture is attained only through sexual maturity), but the ways in which she will *become* woman make gender an issue in which the community has an interest. By the circumstance of her birth and the stigma of the scarlet letter, Pearl already inhabits a sexual-textual body: the body that gave birth to her and nurtures her, the mother who will instruct her in the ways of womanhood, figure the body and reality of sin.

The relationship of mother to child in *The Scarlet Letter* has been overlooked by traditional critics whose interpretations of the text center on the absent figure of the father and the question of paternity. However, early in the text this relationship is invoked in reference to the most powerful myth of maternity in the West, the Virgin and child, a myth with pagan roots that replaced earlier metaphors of the female body as the spontaneously regenerating earth. The image of virgin mother and holy child that dominates religious iconography is alluded to in the opening scene of *The Scarlet Letter*. At one stroke Hawthorne overlays the Christian myth on its pagan antecedents and supplants Catholic belief with Puritan revisions and purification of Papist excess. A Papist, we are told, might see in the spectacle of Hester and her baby on the scaffold "the image of Divine Maternity" (59). Hester's baby has not yet been assigned gender by the text, but the infant that the Madonna cradles is a male, the son of God.

There is more than mere irony at work in this textual reference to Mary and Jesus, to the circumstances of Immaculate Conception through the Word of the Holy Ghost. All that the child represents in the images of Divine Maternity depends on an invisible, spiritual relationship to God, mankind's origin and final end. The image of maternity that dominates our religious-cultural history is this image of mother and son, repeated in the Pietà. The spiritual transference of power takes place across Mary's body; she is the mat(t)er through which the spirit of God passes into humankind. God's word is the agent of the Immaculate Conception, and, as Julia Kristeva argues, this method of impregnation escapes not only the biological, human condition that Christ must transcend but also avoids the inevitable equation of sex with death (Kristeva 103). Hester and her baby represent a corrupted version of the Virgin Mary–Holy Child icon, of course, but the differences between these sacred and profane visions of motherhood are drawn textually through similar images. The Virgin's halo signifies her special place among women ("alone of all her sex"), while Hester's beauty "made a halo of the misfortune and ignominy in which she was enveloped" (57). Commenting on Hester, a Puritan "goodwife" declares, "This woman has brought shame upon us all, and ought to die" (56). Dressed in blue and white, the Virgin displays the colors of holiness and purity, while Hester is draped in somber gray, appropriate to her status as sinner. Kristeva comments that representations of the virginal body reduce female sexuality to "a mere implication," exposing only "the ear, the tears, and the breasts" (108). Hester reveals even less of herself, her entire body shrouded in gray, her hair covered by a tightfitting cap, her breasts shielded by the scarlet letter. Hester Prynne stands before the crowd not "fully revealed" (57) as the text claims, but fully concealed, her sexual body hidden by the cultural text that inscripts her. Only when she unclasps the scarlet letter from her bosom and removes the cap that confines her hair is the sexual power of her body revealed synecdochically — that is, by mere implication.

These images of maternity inscribe sexual difference around the veiled figure of the mother's body. Daughters read the mother's body as sexual text differently than do sons. Sons, including the Son of God, pass by way of the mother's body into the world of the fathers, whose work they carry on in culture and society. For the son, the mother's body inscribes the myth of sexual difference and the space of an originary otherness: it textualizes alienation and desire. For the daughter, however, the mother's body emblematizes her biological-cultural fate, her place in the reproductive chain. The female body is also the locus of patriarchal fears and sexual longing, its fertile dark continent bound and cloaked. It is a space of shame, of castration. For the daughter, the maternal body maps both her past and future; it is a space of repetition.

Pearl enters this space, however, only to escape seemingly unscathed her own fate as the living emblem of sinful, shameful passion. She slips through the umbilical knot that ties representation to repetition. Made heir to Chillingworth's wealth, she comes to stand in the place of the son, one paternal figure standing in for another, the absent (and unacknowledged) father. The sign of Pearl's altered status is her material wealth, which rewrites the maternal script: she grows up to become "the richest heiress of her day" (199), a circumstance that brings about "a very material change in the public estimation" of her. Material riches controvert notions of Pearl as an "elf-child" or "demon offspring" and open the possibility of her full participation in Puritan life: "had the mother and child remained here, little Pearl, at a marriageable period of life, might have mingled her wild blood with the lineage of the devoutest Puritan among them all" (199). Pearl's future and final end remain matters of speculation among Salem gossips, however. Pearl leaves the Puritan community, and her mother — who returns in old age, still wearing the scarlet letter — remains silent about the circumstances of her daughter's life.

If Pearl insists that the scarlet letter remain with the mother and refuses its message for herself, Hester hands the scarlet letter on to Hawthorne, for whom the "frayed and defaced" cloth calls forth his own repressed sexual anxieties and the feared loss of his storytelling skills. The faded symbol, which Hawthorne finds to hold "some deep meaning . . . most worthy of interpretation" (43), communicates to his "sensibilities" a subtle, subliminal message. The message is never directly stated but remains bound to the "forgotten art" of Hester's cross-stitch that embellishes the letter. Hawthorne, who has felt his imaginative abilities fading the longer he toils in the Custom-House for "Uncle Sam's gold" (which he refers to as "the Devil's wages," 48), finds himself haunted by the "rag of scarlet cloth" (42). Hester's story becomes the subject of his meditations as he paces "to and fro across my room, or traversing, with a hundredfold repetition, the long extent . . . of the Custom-House" (44). Hawthorne's steps retrace the golden cross-stitch that frames the letter.

"The Custom-House" records Hawthorne's hope to transcribe the stories he heard daily there, tales of the sea told by inspectors and sea captains who sat before the fire. Although he muses that "at some future day" these "scattered fragments and broken paragraphs" may "turn to gold upon the page" (47), he rejects the men's stories, claiming that their style and coloring outdistance his weakened faculties (47). These tales of adventures, whose roots extend to the classical epic, defeat

Hawthorne's narrative powers. They are a sign that work in the Custom-House threatens to unman him (47). To take up the woman's story, however, would require quite different storytelling skills and carry certain risks that Hawthorne only dimly perceives in the "tarnished mirror" of his imagination (45). Sexual-textual risk for Hawthorne is always associated with financial gain, with the effort to turn words into gold. His rage against the hoard of "female scribblers" who wrote novels was in no small measure due to their financial success. Thus he transcribes Surveyor Pue's authorized version of Hester's story within the frame of romance, a genre entirely separate from the novel of daily life and a form that elevates the ordinary and domestic nearer to the "imaginative" and mysterious (45). Hawthorne is able to write under the auspices of the textual feminine while carefully distancing himself from the material realities of sexual difference. From the perspective of his Puritan forefathers (William and John Hathorne, for example, who were famous for persecuting witches and heretics), "storytelling" is a "worthless" even "disgraceful" occupation (27). Announcing himself as "editor, or very little more" of Hester's story (23), Hawthorne nonetheless attaches his signature to the text, thus turning her gold embroidery to his financial gain while paying his filial debt to Surveyor Pue and rewriting his relationship to his Puritan forebears. Within the curves and flourishes of that signature, the fantasy of sexual-textual difference is both repeated and reversed, erasing the grounds on which interpretation might stake its claim to any final authority.

WORKS CITED

Abraham, Nicholas, and Maria Torok. *L'ecorce et le noyau*. 2nd ed. Paris: Flammarion, 1987.

Benstock, Shari. *Textualizing the Feminine: Essays on the Limits of Genre*. Norman: U of Oklahoma P. Forthcoming.

Carton, Evan. *The Rhetoric of American Romance*. Baltimore: Johns Hopkins UP, 1985.

DuBois, Page. *Sowing the Body: Psychoanalysis and Ancient Representations of Women*. Chicago: U of Chicago P, 1988.

Kamuf, Peggy. "Hawthorne's Genres: The Letter of the Law *Appliquée*." *After Strange Texts: The Role of Theory in the Study of Literature*. Ed. Gregory S. Jay and David L. Miller. University: U of Alabama P, 1985. 69–84.

Kristeva, Julia. "Stabat Mater." *Tales of Love*. Trans. Leon S. Roudiez. New York: Columbia UP, 1987. 234–63.

Montrelay, Michele. "Inquiry into Femininity." *m/f* 1 (1978): 82–91.
Rich, Adrienne. *Of Woman Born*. New York: Norton, 1986.
Rose, Jacqueline. *Sexuality in the Field of Vision*. London: Verso, 1986.
Schwab, Gabriele. "Seduced by Witches: Nathaniel Hawthorne's *The Scarlet Letter* in the Context of New England Witchcraft Fictions." *Seduction and Theory: Readings of Gender, Representation, and Rhetoric*. Ed. Dianne Hunter. Champaign-Urbana: U of Illinois P, 1989. 170–91.

Deconstruction and *The Scarlet Letter*

WHAT IS DECONSTRUCTION?

Deconstruction has a reputation for being the most complex and forbidding of contemporary critical approaches to literature, but in fact almost all of us have, at one time, either deconstructed a text or badly wanted to deconstruct one. Sometimes when we hear a lecturer effectively marshall evidence to show that a book means primarily one thing, we long to interrupt and ask what he or she would make of other, conveniently overlooked passages, passages that seem to contradict the lecturer's thesis. Sometimes, after reading a provocative critical article that *almost* convinces us that a familiar work means the opposite of what we assumed it meant, we may wish to make an equally convincing case for our former reading of the text. We may not think that the poem or novel in question better supports our interpretation, but we may recognize that the text can be used to support *both* readings. And sometimes we simply want to make that point: texts can be used to support seemingly irreconcilable positions.

To reach this conclusion is to feel the deconstructive itch. J. Hillis Miller, the preeminent American deconstructor, puts it this way: "Deconstruction is not a dismantling of the structure of a text, but a demonstration that it has already dismantled itself. Its apparently solid ground is no rock but thin air" ("Stevens' Rock" 341). To deconstruct a text isn't to show that the high old themes aren't to be found in it. Rather, it is to show that a text — not unlike DNA with its double helix — can have intertwined, opposite "discourses" — strands of narrative, threads of meaning.

Ultimately, of course, deconstruction refers to a larger and more complex enterprise than the practice of demonstrating that a text means contradictory things. The term refers to a way of reading texts practiced by critics who have been influenced by the writings of the French philosopher Jacques Derrida. It is important to gain some understanding of Derrida's project and of the historical backgrounds of his work before reading the deconstruction of *The Scarlet Letter* that follows, let alone attempting to deconstruct a text. But it is important, too, to approach deconstruction with anything but a scholar's sober and almost worshipful respect for knowledge and truth. Deconstruction offers a playful alternative to traditional scholarship, a confidently adversarial alternative, and deserves to be approached in the spirit that animates it.

Derrida, a philosopher of language who coined the term "deconstruction," argues that we tend to think and express our thoughts in terms of opposites. Something is black but not white, masculine and therefore not feminine, a cause rather than an effect, and so forth. These mutually exclusive pairs or dichotomies are too numerous to list, but would include beginning/end, conscious/unconscious, presence/absence, speech/writing, and construction/destruction (the last being the opposition that Derrida's word deconstruction tries to contain and subvert). If we think hard about these dichotomies, Derrida suggests, we will realize that they are not simply oppositions; they are also hierarchies in miniature. In other words, they contain one term that our culture views as being superior and one term viewed as negative or inferior. Sometimes the superior term seems only subtly superior (*speech, masculine, cause*), whereas sometimes we know immediately which term is culturally preferable (*presence* and *beginning* and *consciousness* are easy choices). But the hierarchy always exists.

Of particular interest to Derrida, perhaps because it involves the language in which all the other dichotomies are expressed, is the hierarchical opposition speech/writing. Derrida argues that the "privileging" of speech, that is, the tendency to regard speech in positive terms and writing in negative terms, cannot be disentangled from the privileging of presence. (Postcards are written by absent friends; we read Plato because he cannot speak from beyond the grave.) Furthermore, according to Derrida, the tendency to privilege both speech and presence is part of the Western tradition of *logocentrism,* the belief that in some ideal beginning were creative *spoken* words, words such as "Let there be light," spoken by an ideal, *present* God. According to logocentric tradition, these words can now only be represented in unoriginal speech or writing (such as the written phrase in quotation marks above). Derrida doesn't seek to reverse the hierarchized opposition between speech and writing, or presence and absence, or early and late, for to do so would be to fall into the trap of perpetuating the same forms of thought and expression that he seeks to deconstruct. Rather, his goal is to erase the boundary between oppositions such as speech and writing and to do so in such a way as to throw the order and values implied by the opposition into question.

Returning to the theories of Ferdinand de Saussure, who invented the modern science of linguistics, Derrida reminds us that the association of speech with present, obvious, and ideal meaning and writing with absent, merely pictured, and therefore less reliable meaning is suspect, to say the least. As Saussure demonstrated, words are *not* the things they name and, indeed, they are only arbitrarily associated with those things. Neither spoken nor written words have present, positive, identifiable attributes themselves; they have meaning only by virture of their difference from other words (*red, read, reed*). In a sense, meanings emerge from the gaps or spaces between them. Take *read* as an example. To know whether it is the present or past tense of the verb — whether it rhymes with *red* or *reed* — we need to see it in relation to some other word (e.g., *yesterday*).

Because the meanings of words lie in the differences between them and in the differences between them and the things they name, Derrida suggests that all language is constituted by *différance,* a word he has coined that puns on two French words meaning "to differ" and "to defer": words are the deferred presences of the things they "mean," and their meaning is grounded in difference. Derrida, by the way, changes the *e* in the French word *différence* to an *a* in his neologism *différance*; the change, which can be seen in writing but cannot be heard in spoken French, is itself a playful, witty challenge to the notion that writing is inferior or "fallen" speech.

In *De la grammatologie* [*Of Grammatology*] (1967) and *Dissemination* (1972), Derrida begins to redefine writing by deconstructing some old definitions. In *Dissemination,* he traces logocentrism back to Plato, who in the *Phaedrus* has Socrates condemn writing and who, in all the great dialogues, powerfully postulates that metaphysical longing for origins and ideals that permeates Western thought. "What Derrida does in his reading of Plato," Barbara Johnson points out, "is to unfold dimensions of Plato's *text* that work against the grain of (Plato's own) Platonism" (Johnson xxiv). Remember: that is what deconstruction always does according to Miller; it shows a text dismantling itself.

In *Of Grammatology,* Derrida turns to the *Confessions* of Jean-Jacques Rousseau and exposes a grain running against the grain. Rousseau, another great Western idealist and believer in innocent, noble origins, on one hand condemned writing as mere representation, a corruption of the more natural, childlike, direct, and therefore undevious speech. On the other hand, Rousseau admitted his own tendency to lose self-presence and blurt out exactly the wrong thing in public. He confessed that, by writing at a distance from his audience, he often expressed himself better: "If I were present, one would never know what I was worth," Rousseau admitted (Derrida, *Of Grammatology* 142). Thus, writing is a ***supplement*** to speech that is at the same time ***necessary***. Barbara Johnson, sounding like Derrida, puts it this way: "Recourse to writing . . . is necessary to recapture a presence whose lack has not been preceded by any fullness" (Derrida, *Dissemination* xii). Thus, Derrida shows that one strand of Rousseau's discourse made writing seem a secondary, even treacherous supplement, while another made it seem necessary to communication.

Have Derrida's deconstructions of *Confessions* and the *Phaedrus* explained these texts, interpreted them, opened them up and shown us what they mean? Not in any traditional sense. Derrida would say that anyone attempting to find a single, correct meaning in a text is simply imprisoned by that structure of thought that would oppose two readings and declare one to be right and not wrong, correct rather than incorrect. In fact, any work of literature that we interpret defies the laws of Western logic, the laws of opposition and noncontradiction. In the views of poststructuralist critics, texts don't say "A and not B." They say "A and not-A," as do texts written by literary critics, who are also involved in producing creative writing. But it is the very incompatibility of discourses within literary texts that makes literature mysterious, problematic, worthy of attention. Such incompatibilities will not be found by a reader who believes that construction and destruction are utterly opposed and that the critic must construct an argument showing that a text means one and not the other.

Although its ultimate aim may be to critique Western idealism and logic, deconstruction began as a response to structuralism and to formalism, another structure-oriented theory of reading. (Deconstruction, which is really only one kind of a poststructuralist criticism, is sometimes referred to as poststructuralist criticism, or even as poststructuralism.)

Structuralism, Robert Scholes tells us, may now be seen as a reaction to modernist alienation and despair (3). Using Saussure's theory as Derrida was to do later, European structuralists attempted to create a *semiology,* or science of signs, that would give humankind at once a scientific and a holistic way of studying the world and its human inhabitants. Roland Barthes, a structuralist who later shifted toward poststructuralism, hoped to recover literary language from the isolation in which it had been studied and to show that the laws that govern it govern all signs, from road signs to articles of clothing. Claude Lévi-Strauss, a structural anthropologist who studied everything from village structure to the structure of myths, found in myths what he called *mythemes,* or building blocks, such as basic plot elements. Recognizing that the same mythemes occur in similar myths from different cultures, he suggested that all myths may be elements of one great myth being written by the collective human mind.

Derrida could not accept the notion that structuralist thought might someday explain the laws governing human signification and thus provide the key to understanding the form and meaning of everything from an African village to a Greek myth to Rousseau's *Confessions*. In his view, the scientific search by structural anthropologists for what unifies humankind amounts to a new version of the old search for the lost ideal, whether that ideal be Plato's bright realm of the Idea or the Paradise of Genesis or Rousseau's unspoiled nature. As for the structuralist belief that texts have "centers" of meaning, in Derrida's view that derives from the logocentric belief that there is a reading of the text that accords with "the book as seen by God." Jonathan Culler, who thus translates a difficult phrase from Derrida's *L'Écriture et la difference* [*Writing and Difference*] (1967) in his book *Structuralist Poetics* (1975), goes on to explain what Derrida objects to in structuralist literary criticism:

> [when] one speaks of the structure of a literary work, one does so from a certain vantage point: one starts with notions of the meaning or effects of a poem and tries to identify the structures responsible for those effects. Possible configurations or patterns that make no contribution are rejected as irrelevant. That is to say, an intuitive understanding of the poem functions as the "centre" . . . : it is both a starting point and a limiting principle. (244)

For these reasons, Derrida and his poststructuralist followers reject the very notion of "linguistic competence" introduced by Noam Chomsky, a structural linguist. The idea that there is a competent reading "gives a privileged status to a particular set of rules of reading, . . . granting pre-eminence to certain conventions and excluding from the realm of language all the truly creative and productive violations of those rules" (Culler, *Structuralist Poetics* 241).

Poststructuralism calls into question assumptions made about literature by formalist, as well as by structuralist, critics. Formalism, or the New Criticism as it was once commonly called, assumes a work of literature to be a freestanding, self-contained object, its meanings found in the complex network of relations that constitute its parts (images, sounds, rhythms, allusions, etc.). To be sure, deconstruction is somewhat like formalism in several ways. Both the formalist and the deconstructor focus on the literary text; neither is likely to interpret a poem or a novel by relating it to events in the author's life, letters, historical period, or even culture. And formalists, long before deconstructors, discovered counterpatterns of meaning in the same text. Formalists find ambiguity and irony, deconstructors find contradiction and undecidability.

Here, though, the two groups part ways. Formalists believe a complete understanding of a literary work is possible, an understanding in which even the ambiguities will fulfill a definite, meaningful function. Poststructuralists celebrate the apparently limitless possibilities for the production of meaning that develop when the language of the critic enters the language of the text. Such a view is in direct opposition to the formalist view that a work of literary art has organic unity (therefore, structuralists would say, a "center"), if only we could find it.

Poststructuralists break with formalists, too, over an issue they have debated with structuralists. The issue involves metaphor and metonymy, two terms for different kinds of rhetorical *tropes*, or figures of speech. *Metonymy* refers to a figure that is chosen to stand for something that it is commonly associated with, or with which it happens to be contiguous or juxtaposed. When said to a waitress, "I'll have the cold plate today" is a metonymic figure of speech for "I'll eat the cold food you're serving today." We refer to the food we want as a plate simply because plates are what food happens to be served on and because everyone understands that by "plate" we mean food. A *metaphor,* on the other hand, is a figure of speech that invokes a special, intrinsic, nonarbitrary relationship with what it represents. When you say you are blue, if you believe that there is an intrinsic, timeless likeness between that color and a melancholy feeling — a likeness that just doesn't exist between sadness and yellow — then you are using the word blue metaphorically.

Although both formalists and structuralists make much of the difference between metaphor and metonymy, Derrida, Miller, and Paul de Man have contended with the distinction deconstructively. They have questioned not only the distinction but also, and perhaps especially, the privilege we grant to metaphor, which we tend to view as the positive and superior figure of speech. De Man, in *Allegories of Reading* (1979), analyzes a passage from Proust's *Swann's Way,* arguing that it is about the nondistinction between metaphor and metonymy — and that it makes its claim metonymically. In *Fiction and Repetition: Seven English Novels* (1982), Miller connects the belief in metaphorical correspondences with other metaphysical beliefs, such as those in origins, endings, transcendence, and underlying truths. Isn't it likely, deconstructors keep implicitly asking, that every metaphor was once a metonym, but that we have simply forgotten what arbitrary juxtaposition or contiguity gave rise to the association that now seems mysteriously special?

The hypothesis that what we call metaphors are really old metonyms may perhaps be made clearer by the following example. We used the word *Watergate* as a metonym to refer to a political scandal that began in the Watergate building complex. Recently, we have used part of the building's name (*gate*) to refer to more recent scandals (*Irangate*). However, already there are people who use and "understand" these terms who are unaware that Watergate is the name of a building. In the future, isn't it possible that *gate,* which began as part of a simple metonym, will seem like the perfect metaphor for scandal — a word that suggests corruption and wrongdoing with a strange and inexplicable rightness?

This is how deconstruction works: by showing that what was prior and privileged in the old hierarchy (for instance, metaphor and speech) can just as easily seem secondary, the deconstructor causes the formerly privileged term to exchange properties with the formerly devalued one. Causes become effects and (d)evolutions become origins, but the result is neither the destruction of the old order or hierarchy nor the construction of a new one. It is, rather, *deconstruction*. In Robert Scholes's words, "If either cause or effect can occupy the position of an origin, then origin is no longer originary; it loses its metaphorical privilege" (88).

Once deconstructed, literal and figurative can exchange properties, so that the prioritizing boundary between them is erased: all words, even *dog* and *cat,* are understood to be figures. It's just that we have used some of them so long that we have forgotten how arbitrary and metonymic they are. And, just as literal and figurative can exchange properties, criticism can exchange properties with literature, in the process coming to be seen not merely as a supplement — the second, negative, and inferior term in the binary opposition creative writing/literary criticism — but rather as an equally creative form of work. Would we write if there were no critics — intelligent readers motivated and able to make sense of what is written? Who, then, depends on whom?

"It is not difficult to see the attractions" of deconstructive reading, Jonathan Culler has commented. "Given that there is no ultimate or absolute justification for any system or for the interpretations from it," the critic is free to value "the activity of interpretation itself, . . . rather than any results which might be obtained" (*Structuralist Poetics* 248). Not everyone, however, has so readily seen the attractions of deconstruction. Two eminent critics, M. H. Abrams and Wayne Booth, have observed that a deconstructive reading "is plainly and simply parasitical" on what Abrams calls "the obvious or univocal meaning" (Abrams 457–58). In other words, there would be no deconstructors if critics didn't already exist who can see and show central and definite meanings in texts. Miller responded in an essay entitled "The Critic as Host," in which he not only deconstructed the oppositional hierarchy (host/parasite), but also the two terms themselves, showing that each derives from two definitions meaning nearly opposite things. *Host* means "hospitable welcomer" and "military horde." *Parasite* originally had a positive connotation; in Greek, *parasitos* meant "beside the grain" and referred to a friendly guest. Finally, Miller suggests, the words *parasite* and *host* are inseparable, depending on one another for their meaning in a given work, much as do hosts and parasites, authors and critics, structuralists and poststructuralists.

Miller has written that the purpose of deconstruction is to show "the existence in literature of structures of language which contradict the law of non-contradiction." Why find the grain that runs against the grain? To restore what Miller has called "the strangeness of literature," to reveal the "capacity of each work to surprise the reader," to demonstrate that "literature continually exceeds any formula or theory with which the critic is prepared to encompass it" (*Fiction* 5).

Several poststructuralist critics have exposed the "strangeness" of *The Scarlet Letter* by manifesting its capacity to undercut itself and surprise the reader. In " 'Original Signification': Post-Structuralism and *The Scarlet Letter*" (1984), Paula K. White argues that "language subverts itself" (44). Taking *The Scarlet Letter* as her text, she shows that the narrative, even early on, "asserts and undercuts [its] assertions"; for example, the language of "The Custom-House" "doubles back to negate itself" by presenting Hawthorne as "editor" and "imaginative artist," a recorder of "facts" that are "of [his] own invention." Thus, later "it should come as no surprise . . . when what seems to be the incontrovertible meaning of the 'A,' its 'original signification,' of adultery, expands to include other, sometimes quite opposite meanings — Able, Angel, America, for example; the letter comes to be not the sign of . . . sin, but the 'token of . . . good deeds' " (44–45, 47). The very world represented by *The Scarlet Letter* elicits contradictory interpretations: some of Dimmesdale's friends see Chillingworth as the hand of Providence while others view him as Satan.

John Dolis, in an essay entitled "Hawthorne's Letter" (1984), develops several ideas first articulated by White. For instance, he focuses on Hawthorne's attempt in "The Custom-House" to claim as his own a tale that he first told his readers he *found* on the job. Dolis, however, has been even more influenced by Michael Ragussis, the author of the essay that begins on page 316. Like Ragussis, Dolis connects Hawthorne's desire to establish authority *over* the tale with the "family discourse" to be found *in* the tale: Hawthorne's "problem of nomination" is said to be repeated in the problem Dimmesdale has in admitting "his own paternity to Pearl." But whereas "for Dimmesdale it is a matter of seven years, for Hawthorne it is simply a matter of several pages before he confesses to the lie of editorship and reveals the truth of authorship" (107).

In the essay that follows, Ragussis begins by showing how Hawthorne privileges speech, implying that it is "an act of potency" and associating it with paternity and patriarchy. When the novel opens, Hester's crime is her refusal to "Speak; and give [her] child a father!" (68). As for Pearl, her inability to name that same earthly father seems tied up with an inability to name, and hence claim, a heavenly one; asked to identify either, she simply says, "I am mother's child" (95). Because her father's (and Father's) name is unspoken, Pearl remains to the Puritan community what the scarlet A is to her: a baffling hieroglyph, a sign without the one explanation (of origin) that would identify it and give it meaning.

In Ragussis' view, *The Scarlet Letter* is a text in which meaning and identity are tied to speech and "family discourse" as well as one in which parentage cannot be spoken of convincingly. (Dimmesdale knows that any attempt to confess his paternal identity will be read as something else.) This is a text, then, in which family discourse (like writing itself, a deconstructor might say), continually undercuts itself:

> The titles "parent" and "child," for example, shift both literally (the text carefully shows us both Hester and Dimmesdale as children by showing us their parents) and symbolically (with . . . Hester as Dimmesdale's mother, when he walks with "the wavering effort of an infant, with his mother's arms in view". . . ; with Pearl as the parent of her play-offspring, or an "authority" over Hester and Dimmesdale).

Like the terms "parent" and "child," "truth" and "fiction," "fact" and "falsehood" exchange and reexchange properties in *The Scarlet Letter*. The in-some-ways-fictional preface ends up seeming in some ways more — and in other ways less — true than the truth of the fiction that follows it.

As read by Ragussis, *The Scarlet Letter* is a text in which fact and fiction continually trade properties. Just as Dimmesdale's attempts to confess his identity as Pearl's father are expressed in language that means different things to different people, so Hawthorne's attempts to paternally "determine" the text come out sounding hedged, halfhearted, and uncertain (just as did his earlier claims merely to have found the story of the *Letter*). By the time we are told, at novel's end, that "gossips of that day believed, — and Mr. Surveyor Pue, who made investigations a century later, believed, . . . — that Pearl was not only alive, but married, and happy, and mindful of her mother" (200), we are playing with a text in which "A" means "not-A" and hierarchies have been turned upside down and over again. As John Dolis has suggested, gossip has become the origin of a history that has inspired fiction, and on ad infinitum.

DECONSTRUCTION: A SELECTED BIBLIOGRAPHY

Deconstruction, Poststructuralism, and Structuralism: Introductions, Guides, and Surveys

Arac, Jonathan, Wlad Godzich, and Wallace Martin, eds. *The Yale Critics: Deconstruction in America*. Minneapolis: U of Minnesota P,

1983. See especially essays by Bové, Godzich, Pease, and Corngold.

Cain, William E. "Deconstruction in America: The Recent Literary Criticism of J. Hillis Miller." *College English* 41 (1979): 367–82.

Culler, Jonathan. *On Deconstruction: Theory and Criticism After Structuralism*. Ithaca: Cornell UP, 1982.

———. *Structuralist Poetics: Structuralism, Linguistics and the Study of Literature*. Ithaca: Cornell UP, 1975. See especially chapter 10.

Jefferson, Ann. "Structuralism and Post Structuralism." *Modern Literary Theory: A Comparative Introduction*. Totowa: Barnes, 1982. 84–112.

Leitch, Vincent B. *Deconstructive Criticism: An Advanced Introduction*. New York: Columbia UP, 1983.

Melville, Stephen W. *Philosophy Beside Itself: On Deconstruction and Modernism*. Theory and History of Literature 27. Minneapolis: U of Minnesota P, 1986.

Norris, Christopher. *Deconstruction and the Interests of Theory*. Oklahoma Project for Discourse and Theory 4. Norman: U of Oklahoma P, 1989.

———. *Deconstruction: Theory and Practice*. London: Methuen, 1982.

Raval, Suresh. *Metacriticism*. Athens: U of Georgia P, 1981.

Scholes, Robert. *Structuralism in Literature: An Introduction*. New Haven: Yale UP, 1974.

Selected Works by Jacques Derrida

Derrida, Jacques. *Dissemination*. 1972. Trans. Barbara Johnson. Chicago: U of Chicago P, 1981. See especially the concise, incisive "Translator's Introduction," which provides a useful point of entry into this work and others by Derrida.

———. *Of Grammatology*. Trans. Gayatri Spivak. Baltimore: Johns Hopkins UP, 1974. Trans. of *De la grammatologie*. 1967.

———. *Speech and Phenomena, and Other Essays on Husserl's Theory of Signs*. 1973. Trans. David B. Allison. Evanston: Northwestern UP, 1978.

———. *Writing and Difference*. 1967. Trans. Alan Bass. Chicago: U of Chicago P, 1978.

Poststructuralist Essays on Language and Literature

Barthes, Roland. *S/Z*. Trans. Richard Miller. New York: Hill, 1974. In this influential work, Barthes turns from a structuralist to a poststructuralist approach.

Bloom, Harold, et al., eds. *Deconstruction and Criticism*. New York: Seabury P, 1979. Includes Miller's "The Critic as Host." Also see the essays by Bloom, de Man, Derrida, and Hartman.

de Man, Paul. *Allegories of Reading*. New Haven: Yale UP, 1979. See Part I ("Rhetoric"), especially chapter 1 ("Semiology and Rhetoric").

———. *Blindness and Insight*. New York: Oxford UP, 1971. Minneapolis: U of Minnesota P, 1983. According to Vincent Leitch, the 1983 edition marks "the beginning of deconstruction in America." It contains essays not included in the original edition.

Johnson, Barbara. *The Critical Difference: Essays in the Contemporary Rhetoric of Reading*. Baltimore: Johns Hopkins UP, 1980.

Miller, J. Hillis. "Ariadne's Thread: Repetition and the Narrative Line." *Critical Inquiry* 3 (1976): 57–77.

———. Introduction. *Bleak House*. By Charles Dickens. Ed. Norman Page. Harmondsworth: Penguin, 1971. 11–34.

———. *Fiction and Repetition: Seven English Novels*. Cambridge: Harvard UP, 1982.

———. "Stevens' Rock and Criticism as Cure." *The Georgia Review* 30 (1976): 5–31, 330–48.

Poststructuralist Approaches to Hawthorne

Dolis, John. "Hawthorne's Letter." *Notebooks in Cultural Analysis: An Annual Review*. Ed. Norman F. Catnor. Durham: Duke UP, 1984. 103–23.

Kamuf, Peggy. "Hawthorne's Genres: The Letter of the Law *Appliquée*." *After Strange Texts: The Role of Theory in the Study of Literature*. Ed. Gregory S. Jay and David L. Miller. University: U of Alabama P, 1985. 69–84.

White, Paula K. " 'Original Signification': Post-Structuralism and *The Scarlet Letter*." *Kentucky Philol. Assn. Bull.* (1982): 41–54.

Other Works Referred to in "What Is Deconstruction?"

Abrams, M. H. "Rationality and the Imagination in Cultural History." *Critical Inquiry* 2 (1976): 447–64.

A DECONSTRUCTIVE CRITIC AT WORK

MICHAEL RAGUSSIS

Silence, Family Discourse, and Fiction in *The Scarlet Letter*

"Speak; and give your child a father!" (68)

Hawthorne and his characters imagine speech as an act of potency. But the ban of silence lies on everyone in *The Scarlet Letter*. The act of speech is baffled during the entire course of the tale, suppressed from without and repressed from within, until the confession at the end when the minister comes forth to speak and turns into the father. I must add immediately that the source of what I am calling the ban of silence lies not where we might suppose, with the Puritan censors: in fact, the Puritans issue the command to speak, calling Hester forward to utter the name of her fellow transgressor. The paralyzing silence in *The Scarlet Letter* originates with its four family members, in such acts as Hester's refusal to name Pearl's father, or Chillingworth's command that Hester swear an oath of silence, or Dimmesdale's refusal to name himself as Hester's fellow transgressor, or Hester's refusal to explain to Pearl the meaning of the scarlet letter. With the acts of engendering and speech under lock and key, silence becomes a kind of action potent to obscure, violate, and orphan. The tale's center, then, lies less in the crime of sexual transgression than in the crime of silence: to recognize publicly one's kindred is, after all, the moral concomitant to engendering, the means by which the family is defined not merely biologically but morally.

The dangerous consequences of keeping silent are dramatized when Hester's refusal in the marketplace to name Dimmesdale as her fellow transgressor frustrates her simple desire to protect him, and threatens both her child and herself. In Dimmesdale's description of the pain of hiding a guilty heart through life, we begin to understand the way in which Hester's silence will become a curious punishment more than equal to what the Puritan authorities would require of her lover. Already in the marketplace, Dimmesdale hints at the agony he will suffer as a result of Hester's attempt to protect him: "What can thy silence do for him, except it tempt him — yea, compel him, as it were — to add hypocrisy to sin?" (67). Moreover, in Hester's silence we find an analogue of what we usually take to be the stern Puritan censor, misleading Pearl by obscuring the act of engendering; in the young child's apparently tautological description of herself, "I am mother's child" (95), a half-truth turns out to be a dangerous misunderstanding that means there is no father. Finally, when Hester later wonders where Pearl came from (even to the point of denying that the child is her own), the mother's refusal to name the father grows into self-mystification, robbing her of her motherhood notwithstanding the fact that she has a child. Adultery is a crime against society, but Hester's silence begins to look like a crime against nature. The child engendered by one parent alone and the virgin mother are not members of the human family as we know it.

The ban of silence in *The Scarlet Letter* appropriately begins when all four family members are brought together for the first time. The first act that the reader sees Chillingworth perform is an act that silences another: the physician raises his finger and lays it on his lips, gesturing Hester not to reveal his identity. This gesture of silence precedes, only by moments, Hester's crucial act in the same chapter: "Madam Hester absolutely refuseth to speak" (63). Hester's silence is, of course, meant to protect Dimmesdale, but Hawthorne begins at this point to show us a strange doubling between the two men. At first, Dimmesdale seems Chillingworth's opposite because the minister appears to be asking Hester to reveal his identity, to name him as her fellow criminal. But Dimmesdale's speech is equal to Chillingworth's gesture of silence. The minister calls on Hester to speak, but he delights in her silence: "Wondrous strength and generosity of a woman's heart! She will not speak!" (68). Hester's silence, then, hides the identities of both men, or what amounts to the same thing in this text, their familial relationship to her and her child. At the same time this silence begins a new bond: silence obfuscates the differences between husband and lover. The two men are one in their single desire: each wants the woman to remain silent, each wants her to keep his identity hidden.

The events I have just described occur in the chapter shrewdly entitled "The Recognition." Hawthorne has in mind here the Aristotelian idea of *anagnorisis,* or "the change from ignorance to knowledge of a bond of love or hate."[1] In *The Scarlet Letter* the obfuscated and persistently delayed recognition of enemy and kindred — for both Hawthorne and Aristotle, another way of putting the dichotomy between "hatred and love" (199) — is the source of the prolonged suffer-

[1]See Aristotle, *On Poetry and Style,* trans. G. M. A. Grube (New York: Bobbs, 1958) 21. The editor points out that "bond of love" specifically means " 'dear ones,' by virtue of blood ties."

ing of each of the family members. In this light the entire narrative of *The Scarlet Letter* depends on whatever hinders or hastens the central issue from the start — "Speak out the name!" (68). In "The Recognition" no names are spoken out, no recognitions are made public, and even those recognitions that occur are unrealized in the deepest sense. When Dimmesdale asks Hester to speak the name of Pearl's father, for example, the power of his voice seems to give him away to his child, "for it directed its hitherto vacant gaze towards Mr. Dimmesdale, and held up its little arms" (67). But the blood-bond is not publicly recognized. It is instead painfully pictured in the infant's helpless gesture toward her hidden father. The child unable to speak is at the mercy of adult hypocrisy, false words, and names. In fact, the chapter closes with a silencing of the child that, with Hester's silence over Dimmesdale and Chillingworth, brings all four family members under the same tragic cover of silence: "The infant . . . pierced the air with its wailings and screams; she [Hester] strove to hush it, mechanically, but seemed scarcely to sympathize with its trouble" (68).

"The Recognition" ends with mother and child once again disappearing behind the "iron-clamped portal" (68) of the Puritan jail, but now we understand the way in which the self is incarcerated within the walls of its own silence. In the next chapter, "The Interview," Hawthorne explicitly connects silence and symbolic imprisonment by revealing that Chillingworth possesses "the lock and key of her [Hester's] silence" (101). Hester is now multiply imprisoned, for she takes an "oath" (73) not to speak out the name of her husband or recognize him publicly. In this way she and Chillingworth subvert the power of speech, using it in the service of silence. In his interview with Hester in prison, then, Chillingworth replaces the blood-bond with the "secret bond" not to speak, so that the suffocating prison of silence is reconfigured in Chillingworth's command, "Breathe not" (73). The silence Hester keeps in order to protect her lover now merges with the silence that prevents him from discovering the identity of his worst "enemy" (130). The family drama of *The Scarlet Letter* is played out between the subverted recognitions I have just described and the recognition scene that occurs between child and father at the novel's end. But I will show that because the child is consistently hushed and (mis)educated in speaking out by her silent mother and the repressive Puritan authorities, and because the father, even when he speaks the truth, transforms it into falsehood, the denouement of the tale is delayed.

The crying infant hushed mechanically by its mother becomes, in the course of the tale, the child learning to speak, but in this apparent progression we learn only how the methods of silence are refined. When Mr. Wilson asks Pearl who she is, he seems to be rephrasing, without the sharp edge of command, the earlier declaration that Hester speak. We soon see that the apparently open question is a disguised command to answer by the book. The question of the child's identity is persistently reshaped by an inevitable corollary: Mr. Wilson first asks Pearl "who art thou" and then, "Canst thou tell me, my child, who made thee?" (95, 96). It is essentially the same question asked of Hester, but now the Puritan authorities want a different answer — not the earthly father, but the Heavenly Father. In this way Mr. Wilson inadvertently contributes to Hester's hiding of the father. The child is viewed as the product of a mysterious and contradictory process in which her maker is either spiritual or biological, or — worse — indiscriminately both. In Pearl's case, both answers are incomprehensible; both fathers are absent, invisible, bodiless.

Pearl's refusal to name "the Heavenly Father" as her maker is, stated baldly, a refusal to be complicitous in the crimes of obfuscation that threaten and undermine her identity. In short, she refuses to name Him, the unnameable source of her being, the "Creator of all flesh" (98) who is fleshless himself. The Heavenly Father here seems at once an idealized and ironic double of the nameless father who neglects to name Pearl, and who, after engendering her, disappears from the flesh. She might as well invent her identity, since she already seems an invention, a fanciful unreality: "the child finally announced that she had not been made at all, but had been plucked by her mother off the bush of wild roses, that grew by the prison-door" (97). The fatherless and lawless child appropriately provides her own genealogy according to no law we can understand, as if she were a freak of nature, either plucked from a rosebush or engendered by one parent alone: "I am mother's child" (95).

The mother questions the child's origin by repeating the pattern of Mr. Wilson's questions: "Tell me, then, what thou art, and who sent thee hither?" (88). The mother's puzzlement over who made the child — Pearl's own identity is consistently displaced in the search for another's — reaches its furthest point when Hester questions even the immediate and visible bond that is the child's only certain knowledge: "Child, what art thou? . . . Art thou my child, in very truth?" (87). Hester actually disowns Pearl "half playfully" in what must be a bad joke: "Thou art not my child! Thou art no Pearl of mine!" (88). Both father and mother, then, deny Pearl her source. For these reasons the name the mother bestows, the child's other source of certain identity, becomes the locus of abuse and displacement, even a way of disqualifying Pearl's human nature, for "Hester could not help questioning . . . whether Pearl was a human child" (83). Pearl is identified through a series of "ill name[s]" (189) that place in quarantine the child who is so avoided that she must be considered contagious: she is an "airy sprite" and a "little elf" (83), an "imp of evil" (84) and a "demon offspring" (199). Momentarily we will see that what Pearl suffers — being denied a human name because of her mysterious origin — Chillingworth wills for himself (without realizing the consequences) when "he chose to withdraw his name from the roll of mankind" (101). Finally, unnamed by her father and ill-named by the community, the child is renamed by Mr. Wilson. He objects to the child's answer to his question "who art thou" by arguing with her name: judging by her appearance, Pearl should be named "Ruby" or "Coral" or "Red Rose" (95), more names that deny her human engendering. Such are the liberties taken with an unnamed bastard; Mr. Wilson knows better than the child who made her and knows the child's proper name. Pearl's life is specified far outside herself, and her name seems an ironic tease. Mr. Wilson calls her "my child" (96) (has *he* made her?), but she appears to belong to no one. As a bastard, she is a counterfeit pearl, disowned by father and mother alike — "no Pearl of mine!" (88).

Mr. Wilson's ironic corrections of the child's name, and the persistent questions that both he and Hester direct at Pearl, are part of an educative system that in fact confounds the issue of the child's identity. The social authorities, as I have already implied, "analyze that child's nature" (100) to find the perpetrator of the crime she represents and "put the child to due and stated examination" (99) solely to prove and insure their own beliefs. In such ways the child's life is posited outside itself and questioned from the outside by a catechism whose questions are hypocritical at worst, rhetorical at best. The child-puppet must give another's answers: Pearl's "one baby-voice served a multitude of imaginary personages" (85). The child's attempt to ask her own questions is limited by a system that allows only two kinds of questions: those that have a priori answers ("the Heavenly Father") and those that should not be asked at all ("There are many things in this world that a child must not ask about") (145). Nevertheless, Pearl appears in the text, time and again, as an almost disembodied string of questions that have been prohibited: "[S]he put these searching questions, once, and again, and still a third time. 'What does the letter mean, mother? — and why dost thou wear it? — and why does the minister keep his hand over his heart?' " (144). Such questions are part of the child's native understanding that it is her prerogative to ask and the mother's duty to answer, to explain the scarlet letter: "Tell me, mother! . . . Do thou tell me! . . . It is thou that must tell me!" (88). When Hester answers that she wears the scarlet letter "for the sake of its gold thread," the narrator marks one of those turning points in the text where the ostensible crime (the sexual transgression) shrinks beside a more profound one: "In all the seven bygone years, Hester Prynne had never before been false to the symbol on her bosom. . . . [S]ome new evil had crept into it [her heart], or some old one had never been expelled" (145).

The lie about the letter is so serious because it breaks the bond through which the mother teaches the child the alphabet that articulates her identity and her place in the human community. Hester is, in the educative system I am describing, the teacher of the mother tongue, as Pearl herself acknowledges: "It is the great letter A. Thou hast taught it me in the horn-book" (143). Hester's refusal to inform the child of the letter's greater, or at least special, significance makes the child fail her examination in the simplest of categories, the ABCs of who she is. Hester's final answer to Pearl's questions is no answer at all, but a command to be silent, like the enforced silence under which the mother herself suffers: "Hold thy tongue . . . else I shall shut thee into the dark closet!" (145). Silencing the child is equal to incarcerating her, or returning her to the dark unknown from which she came, denying her here and now, refusing her any existence at all. Not allowed her own questions, kept from the meaning of the letter A, Pearl is reduced either to a perverse silence (self-hushed with a vengeance) or to an incomprehensible language unable to articulate the burden of her pain and rage: a "perversity . . . closed her lips, or impelled her to speak words amiss . . . putting her finger in her mouth" (97); "If spoken to, she would not speak again," or would rush forth "with shrill, incoherent exclamations that made her mother tremble, because they had so much the sound of a witch's anathemas in some unknown tongue" (85). The mother's mystifying language lessons produce a child who is alienated from the community by her inability to speak what Hawthorne calls a "human language" (128).

The mother's lie about the letter teases Pearl to the quick because, as Hawthorne insists, the child is in fact "the scarlet letter endowed with life!" (90). Pearl is a baffling linguistic figure come alive: "She had been offered to the world, these seven years past, as the living hieroglyphic, in which was revealed the secret they so darkly sought to hide, — all written in this symbol, — all plainly manifest, — had there been a prophet or magician skilled to read the character of flame!" (162). The letter shows Pearl as a contradiction, a language whose meaning is at once self-apparent and mystifyingly in need of being read by another. In this light, Pearl is divided from the meaning she is equal to — whether staring at the mirroring brook, experiencing herself as another (as if her identity resides in a mysteriously impalpable image outside herself), or trying to read the letter A, to understand her own identity when it can be deciphered only by another, by some expert reader, some prophet or magician. Moreover, as the letter A endowed with life, the child is conceived as a clue to the reading of another's secret identity: *A* is an abbreviation for *adultery,* even for *Arthur,* while the first two letters of *adultery* are the initials of the father, Arthur Dimmesdale. In short, the child's identity seems foiled simply because it seems to have a representative function, because it seems to point beyond herself. The child, as the first initial of some hidden word or name, is merely an abbreviation. She is an abbreviated form of her father, just as the face she sees in the mirroring brook (as Dimmesdale fears) traces her father's features and threatens to expose him as Hester's fellow transgressor. Finally, Pearl is a living hieroglyphic or abbreviation because she is made out of her parents' linguistic half-truths and deceptions. To deny the facts of Pearl's biological making, to deny that she is their own child, is to transform her into a disembodied linguistic conundrum, as Hester's experience shows: "the mother felt like one who has evoked a spirit, but, by some irregularity in the process of conjuration, has failed to win the master-word that should control this new and incomprehensible intelligence" (84). Hester sees herself as a wizard-scientist who fails to understand the monster-spirit she has conjured, but the mother (like the father) has in her own keeping the master-word that will make Pearl human.

As an unreadable abbreviation, the letter is a sign of Pearl's half-life: a letter or a child is, in isolation, a sign divorced from meaning and in need of definition through others. The letter represents the way in which the child is trapped in a past she is ignorant of, a history of meanings that in turn delimit individual meaning. The mysterious letter A, then, represents the child's dependence on an authorizing context that, in Pearl's case, is hidden. Pearl, like a symbolic letter, becomes a battleground of meaning — among parents, society, and heaven. Once again we see the way in which Pearl has only a representative meaning: she is "meant, above all things else, to keep the mother's soul alive" (99). In fact, Pearl is a prize to be won, a bargain between two beings outside herself, a middle term, even a test case. Pearl is supposed to remind Hester that "if she bring the child to heaven, the child also will bring its parent thither!" (99). For the mother, however, Pearl is also a constant reminder of her sin and shame; just as for the father who fears he will be traced in his child's features, Pearl is the only visible clue that links him to his crime. Because the child — like the scarlet letter — is the public sign of their most private acts, the parents try to obscure its meaning by hushing it or simply denying that it is their own. Such acts become criminal when we realize the way in which signification becomes human, the way in which the child is the letter endowed with life.

Pearl's multiple reflections and her many voices lead the narrator to remark, "in this one child there were many children" (82). I have already suggested one basis for understanding such a remark: the child is divided from herself. Now I wish to suggest that the child, the character at the center of the text, is multiple insofar as she represents a reflection of all the characters in *The Scarlet Letter*. For example, the child, reduced to a mere ghostly symbol of itself (like the image of Pearl in the brook, or the ghostly disembodiments that Dimmesdale and Hester undergo), is a helpless creature in another's control — denied meaning by others, mastered by another's master-words and silences, living in fear of the incomprehensibility of another. At the same time, the process of conjuration, like that of engendering, shows us that the creator's magic backfires, so that the child becomes a figure of frightening power. The control we think we exert over another often produces a new, incomprehensible, and uncontrollable intelligence. Hence Pearl, a "deadly symbol" (165), represents the letter that killeth. Pearl's mere gaze at the letter on her mother's breast, for example, is "like the stroke of sudden death" (87). In the person of the child the letter becomes a vengeful literalism that strikes through guise and deceit. For the child, despite all the methods of parental and societal control exerted over her, represents an alien other to be feared, and one who — though we may deny it — we in fact produce ourselves, but fail to control.

Moving from Pearl's fate to Dimmesdale's, we see the way in which the child owns him as much as he owns her, for the father cannot be himself until he acknowledges his child. Dimmesdale's identity, like Pearl's, rests on a linguistic deadlock that accounts for the duration of the tale. On the one hand, neither Pearl's nor Chillingworth's guesses, nor Hester's betrayal of Dimmesdale's name, will solve the riddle of the father's identity. The father must speak for himself. On the other hand, as I will show, the fluctuation of Dimmesdale's life between two extreme linguistic poles — between asking another to speak for him, and speaking for another — makes solving the riddle impossible. I take this characteristic of Dimmesdale's speech to be the central symptom of a "disorder in his utterance" (171) that recalls his child's linguistic disturbance, her radical shifts between perverse silence and wild incoherence.

By asking another to speak for him and thereby name him, Dimmesdale childishly places his identity outside himself, at the mercy of another. Of course, Hester protects him and refuses his plea to name her fellow transgressor, but even she eventually tries to rename him (the way Mr. Wilson tries to change Pearl to "Ruby"). Hester does not realize that to "[g]ive up this name of Arthur Dimmesdale, and make thyself another . . . thou canst wear" (157) would be to make the minister more lost to himself and one step closer to another "wearer" (101) of false names, Roger Chillingworth. When not asking another to name him, Dimmesdale himself speaks for another; speaking for Hester — she commands him, "Speak thou for me!" (98) — is like speaking for his flock or for his God. In this way Dimmesdale becomes a selfless medium, his own voice in another's body or someone else's voice in his body. Meant to hide his crime, such transgressions only repeat it. As "the mouth-piece of Heaven's messages" (118), the minister is like the puppet-child, a linguistic tool given up to represent another's meaning. In fact, just as Pearl is equal to the scarlet letter, Dimmesdale is equal to his voice, to his utterance. While Dimmesdale rightly wonders "that Heaven should see fit to transmit the grand and solemn music of its oracles through so foul an organ-pipe as he" (175), Hawthorne makes the equation clear. It is not simply mouth, throat, or tongue that Heaven takes over as its conduit, but the whole man, "he." And yet the minister's function as a medium is a useful hiding place that obviates his speaking for himself, being his own person. The father actually courts obfuscation and misrepresentation and turns those acts that endanger the child — being unnamed or misread or silenced — to his own purposes. His utterances are part of a system of counterspeech in which even the truth becomes a hiding place, a deception: "The minister well knew — subtle, but remorseful hypocrite that he was! — the light in which his vague confession would be viewed. . . . He had spoken the very truth, and transformed it into the veriest falsehood" (119–20). To speak double, to intend the opposite of what your words say repeats the strategy behind his request that Hester reveal his identity in the marketplace.

Such speech acts, like his passion, "hurrieth him out of himself" (114), and thereby show his complete confusion over self and other. The minister eventually replaces speaking for another with speaking only to himself, and in so doing he literalizes — and unwittingly parodies — the idea of speaking for himself. He imagines speeches (in "The Minister's Vigil" and "The Minister in a Maze") that are in fact never spoken. The self makes itself an audience and attempts recognition without the aid of another. These speeches, spoken only on the inside, "uttered only within his imagination" (124), completely dispense with other people and divide the self in two, that is, they make Dimmesdale "another" to himself. Such speeches are a narcissistic self-communication, a misconstrued lesson learned from Dimmesdale's sexual transgression, a false antidote to intercourse with another. Speech, like the self it grounds, has become mere hallucination, mere fantasy. The father works himself like a puppet.

The equivocal status of Dimmesdale's identity stems from the fact that he both courts obfuscation and yet suffers from the very acts of speech that make him over into another. This is most sharply expressed when he poses for the entire community the "riddle" (63) of oedipal identity. In the marketplace, Dimmesdale, like Oedipus, calls for the solution of the crime he himself has committed. Knowing that he is the man everyone (himself included) seeks, he is at once a criminal and a hypocrite, a knowing Oedipus. Nonetheless his knowledge of his own identity turns out to be, in substantial ways, incomplete: like the child, he depends on another. Dimmesdale does not realize that the physician is cast, in this complicated family drama, not simply as the cuckolded husband, but as the minister's father, with the old man's feigned "paternal and reverential love for the young pastor" (106) an ironic echo of the true father's refusal to come forth and love Pearl. In the absence of the real father, then, a mock-father seems produced and one who seeks the destruction of the "son" who has displaced him. Dimmesdale's accusation of Chillingworth, the father-substitute — "You speak in riddles" (113) — names the crime he himself commits. What Pearl suffers, the painful riddle of the father's identity, is now turned on him. He has a "nameless horror" (128) of the father-substitute whose namelessness becomes the source of a deadly riddle; "he could not recognize his enemy" (110) in a drama where he withholds recognition from his own kin.

Neither Dimmesdale nor Chillingworth realizes that the self disguised, the self defended from being recognized by another, is the self lost through this very process of self-defense. Dimmesdale's double failure to recognize Pearl and to recognize Chillingworth is part of a single confusion; the deliberate failure to recognize one's kindred merges with the involuntary failure to discover the enemy. When Chillingworth catches in the mirror a grotesquely evil image of himself, "which he could not recognize" (138), he doubly represents Dimmesdale. Neither man can recognize the leech, neither man can recognize himself. The disguise intended to defend oneself against another finally disguises one from oneself: disguise, like false speech acts I have been exploring, alienates one from oneself, turns one into the other. More ominous still, the question asked about the enemy turns out to be the question asked about oneself; in other words, the question Dimmesdale asks about Chillingworth — "Who is he? Who is he?" (128) — merges with the question Chillingworth asks about Dimmesdale, "Who is he?" (72). Each man is confounded in recognizing the other; each man is the subject of the same inquiry; each man is conceived through this anonymous formulation of the third-person pronoun. This question about the identity of the other is the same question asked about the child, and for this reason it is first asked in Hawthorne's autobiographical sketch as the question his forefathers ask about him — "What is he?" (27) — and thereby functions as the motivating force behind Hawthorne's entire project.

What I have been calling Dimmesdale's failure to recognize both Pearl and Chillingworth underscores a profound analogy between these two characters in the text. Both Pearl and Chillingworth seek to expose Dimmesdale's secret; both ask him leading questions, both frighten him, both riddle him. See, for example, Pearl's teasing mock exposure of Chillingworth's identity in an unknown tongue that puzzles her father (128). But who is Chillingworth, and why do his questions often coincide with Pearl's? The man "Chillingworth" comes into being because of Dimmesdale's and Hester's passion: he is as much their child as the unclaimed Pearl. In fact, Chillingworth is the man completely and grotesquely "dependent for the food of his affections and spiritual life upon another" (199), the child entirely dependent on Dimmesdale the father, the leech entirely dependent on the pound of flesh he requires. Or, to put it yet another way: Chillingworth the "devil" (137) is an example of the guilty offspring produced by men who "propagate a hellish breed within them[selves]" (111). The father's refusal to recognize his real child, then, leads to his production of a mock child and to his engendering the enemy in and by himself.

The question that is asked Pearl, "who made thee?" Chillingworth asks himself when he is mystified by the new demonic identity he sees in the mirror: "Who made me so?" (139). But while the text persuasively shows how the self is dependent on another, Chillingworth functions as a limit to this idea: he is responsible for himself (even as he allows himself to become completely dependent on Dimmesdale). One could argue that the two men, "mutual victims" (199), reciprocally produce each other; like Dimmesdale's guilt, Chillingworth's revenge produces the enemy. In this sense, Chillingworth's failure to recognize himself in the mirror as the evil enemy represents Dimmesdale's failure to take responsibility for his own crime. Moreover, such an image suggests the way in which the enemy, conventionally mythologized outside the family and outside the self, in fact resides within the family, within the self; the enemy, in this sense, is produced by the self. So, the attack against the simple and easily identifiable enemy becomes the attack against the family member, and so ultimately self-attack and self-destruction. Finally, insofar as Dimmesdale and Chillingworth produce each other, the real child Pearl is represented as lost among the shadow-children produced in these mock engenderings. But Pearl learns to play the same game. She engenders her own dummy "offspring," "puppets" who are nameless and passive victims held in the child-parent's power. Through mock engendering and through "the hostile feelings with which the child regarded all these offspring of her own heart and mind," the child repeats the way in which she is displaced. In fact, Pearl considers her offspring as "enemies, against whom she rushed to battle" (85–86).

The family member frames and limits one's life, but in what sense the family member assumes the publicly recognized, or even literal, relationship of kindred is another matter. The family member is a sign, like A, with too many significations. Family titles, one could argue, are linguistic shifters,[2] like the pronoun "he" that alternately represents Dimmesdale, Chillingworth, and Hawthorne himself; they relativize the single proper name (which, in this text, is already a ghostly sign, if not a downright lie). The titles "parent" and "child," for example, shift both literally (Hester and Dimmesdale are presented to us as children by showing us their parents) and symbolically (with Chillingworth as the product of Hester and Dimmesdale's passion, or of Dimmesdale's guilt; with Hester as Dimmesdale's mother, when he walks with "the wavering effort of an infant, with its mother's arms in view" [193]; and with

[2]See Roman Jakobson's influential essay "Shifters, Verbal Categories, and the Russian Verb," *Selected Writings*, vol. 2 (The Hague: Mouton, 1971) 130–47. Without using the term "shifter," R. D. Laing suggests how a single member of the family, playing a variety of roles, can be renamed as "granddaughter, daughter, sister, wife, mother, grandmother, niece, cousin, etc. etc." *The Politics of the Family and Other Essays* (New York: Vintage, 1972) 54.

Pearl as the parent of her play-offspring, or as an "authority" over Hester and Dimmesdale [164]). The family's acts of silence unwittingly bring such meanings to the surface and reveal that the deepest family discourse — not the one that the world finds acceptable — casts the family member in every role, including that of enemy. The letter of the law tries to control such meanings, to fix such names as "father" and "husband" and "child," but the scarlet letter, as it exhausts the single meaning the law attaches to it, exhausts such controls generally. It is the badge that every family member wears.

Hawthorne shows the family as the creator of a system of suppression, torture, and violation. In a tale in which the sexual act lies outside the narrative and in which a series of mock engenderments occupy the foreground of the narrative, the deepest meaning of engenderment becomes the violation and death that the family makes for itself. For this reason, in *The Scarlet Letter,* the family sees fall before its own eyes the mythology that divides enemy from kindred, other from self — a mythology that every family makes itself. While the search for the proper name of the father and the child is foiled because of the particular acts of secrecy and deception performed by particular family members, Hawthorne suggests that it is in the nature of families, and the self they define, not to allow such literal, fixed, or single names. In this light the text postpones through its entirety answering the literal questions that the community asks. Who is the father, or for that matter, who the child? What is the crime, and who the criminal? Who is *he?*

A partial answer to this last question comes at the tale's denouement, when Dimmesdale finally confesses in the marketplace. But in *The Scarlet Letter* confession occurs paradoxically through a process of apparent self-alienation. During his public confession, Dimmesdale speaks of himself in the third person: "But there stood one in the midst of you, at whose brand of sin and infamy ye have not shuddered! . . . It was on him! . . . But he hid it cunningly from men, and walked among you. . . . Now, at the death-hour, he stands up before you! He bids you look again at Hester's scarlet letter! He tells you, that, with all its mysterious horror, it is but the shadow of what he bears on his own breast, and that even this, his own red stigma, is no more than the type of what has seared his inmost heart!" (195). Who is the secret man the minister names? The minister's truest moment, when he is most himself, is a moment of self-alienation, of ghostly confession; it shows the self in a mirror, as "he." Appropriately, the man the minister names (or does not name) as "he" answers the question that has echoed through the text: "Who is he?" "He" is the man who walks always beside you, unrecognized. Dimmesdale then becomes the "exemplary man" (168) in an unexpected way — not through his virtue, but through his power of representation. A man dramatizes himself, to himself and others, as another; he makes himself visible, to himself and others, in a reflection, or a representation that is fictional; he/"he" tells the truth.

The fiction of Dimmesdale's confession, as I understand it, is defined in opposition to *The Scarlet Letter*'s view of writing as an attempt at literalization that puts the blame simply and mercilessly on one person, the criminal. The text's powerful example here is the way in which the Puritans use writing to label Hester and her crime. Fiction, on the other hand, is a more generous and complicated form of what Hawthorne in another context sees as "the propensity of human nature to tell the very worst of itself, when embodied in the person of another" (132) — in other words, to confess as "he," like Dimmesdale or the novelist. I am distinguishing between branding and casting out a single victim and accusing an unspecified person, who walks among you; between depersonalization as violent attack (writing's criminal is the Adulteress, the dehumanized Hester) and impersonalization as merciful defense (fiction's criminal is an unnamed "he"). Writing violates, with a sharp-edged instrument, "an iron pen" (147); fiction deflects and defends, with a language that shows that pain and guilt are common to all, that each of us is a member of "the human family" (31). These are the two ways in which the two criminals of adultery are named in *The Scarlet Letter:* Hester is named by another at the beginning of the text, while Dimmesdale is named as another by himself at the end of the text. The first is an object of scorn set apart from all others; the second is an invisible self that we all share but fail to recognize.

The New Historicism and *The Scarlet Letter*

WHAT IS THE NEW HISTORICISM?

If ever a novel cried out for a new historicist analysis, that novel is surely *The Scarlet Letter*. Although a work of fiction, it is based on history, specifically, on Caleb Snow's *History of Boston,* the most credible historical study of the city available to Hawthorne at the time he was writing. At that time, of course, Hawthorne was himself a character in a historical drama; there is reason to wonder, in fact, whether *The Scarlet Letter* would have been written if President Taylor, a Whig, had not defeated President Polk, a Democrat, and caused Hawthorne to be relieved of his political appointment as Surveyor of Customs in Salem, Massachusetts. Hawthorne chose to introduce *The Scarlet Letter* with an essay, "The Custom-House," in which he told *his-story,* i.e., both his personal story of employment and dismissal and the history of political changes that brought about the latter. But, just as he injected fiction with history, so he injected his-story with fiction. The tale of finding a scarlet letter and an accompanying manuscript that relates the tale of its wearer, Hester Prynne, is just that — a tale Hawthorne tells in order to lend to his larger tale an added whiff of historical credibility.

All of these facts make *The Scarlet Letter* a promising candidate for a new historicist analysis because the new historicism is a movement that seeks to destabilize our established conceptions of what history and fiction are. *The Scarlet Letter,* new historicists would have us see, is in itself a historical artifact, not of the Puritan age that the novel describes, but rather of the puritanical nineteenth-century period that Hawthorne lived and wrote in. Conversely, the new historicist argues, the histories of Boston that Hawthorne relied on — early nineteenth-century studies such as Caleb Snow's *History of Boston* — are not without their own fictional dimension, for they reflect the biases of the age and culture in which they were written.

Thus, we might begin to define the new historicism by saying that it is a critical movement interested in providing a "thick description" of the historical contexts of literature. In situating a historical romance like *The Scarlet Letter* historically, the critic needs to be aware of the history of the period in which the novel is set, of the history of the period in which the novel was produced, and even of the historical contexts in which we now read and interpret it, for we are no less without historical biases than were Hawthorne, Caleb Snow, or the Puritan John Wilson — who appears in *The Scarlet Letter* as a character.

To venture beyond the beginning of a definition of the new historicism is to head down a path fraught with difficulties. One of the most recent developments in contemporary theory, the new historicism is still evolving. Enough of its contours have come into focus for us to realize that it exists and deserves a name, but any definition of the new historicism is bound to be somewhat fuzzy, like a partially developed photographic image. Some individual critics that we may label new historicist may also be deconstructors, or feminists, or Marxists. Some would deny that the others are even writing the new kind of historical criticism.

All of them, though, share the conviction that, somewhere along the way, something important was lost from literary studies: historical consciousness. Poems and novels came to be seen in isolation, as urnlike objects of precious beauty. The new historicists, whatever their differences and however defined, want us to see that even the most urnlike poems are caught in a web of historical conditions, relationships, and influences. In an essay on "The Historical Necessity for — and Difficulties with — New Historical Analysis in Introductory Literature Courses" (1987), Brook Thomas suggests that discussions of Keats's "Ode on a Grecian Urn" might begin with questions such as the following: Where would Keats have seen such an urn? How did a Grecian urn end up in a museum in England? Some very important historical and political realities, Thomas suggests, lie behind and inform Keats's definitions of art, truth, beauty, the past, and timelessness. They are realities that psychoanalytic and reader-response critics, formalists and feminists and deconstructors, might conceivably overlook.

Although a number of influential critics working between 1920 and 1950 wrote about literature from a psychoanalytic perspective, the majority of critics took what might generally be referred to as the historical approach. With the advent of the New Criticism, or formalism, however, historically oriented critics almost seemed to disappear from the face of the earth. Jerome McGann writes: "a text-only approach has been so vigorously promoted during the last thirty-five years that most historical critics have been driven from the field, and have raised the flag of their surrender by yielding the title 'critic' to the victor, and accepting the title 'scholar' for themselves" (*Inflections* 17). Of course, the title "victor" has been vied for by a new kind of psychoanalytic critic, by reader-response critics, by so-called deconstructors, and by feminists since the New Critics of the 1950s lost it during the following decade. But historical scholars have not been in the field, seriously competing to become a dominant critical influence.

At least they haven't until now. In his essay "Toward a New History in Literary Study" (1984), Herbert Lindenberger writes: "It comes as something of a surprise to find that history is making a powerful comeback" (16). E. D. Hirsch, Jr., has also predicted a comeback. He suggested in 1984 that various avant-garde positions (such as deconstruction) have been overrated and that it is time to turn back to history and to historical criticism:

> We should not be disconcerted by its imposing claims, or made to think that we are being naive when we try to pursue historical study. Far from being naive, historically based criticism is the newest and most valuable kind . . . for our students (and our culture) at the present time. (Hirsch 197)

McGann obviously agrees. In *Historical Studies and Literary Criticism* (1985), he speaks approvingly of recent attempts to make sociohistorical subjects and methods central to literary studies once again.

As the word *sociohistorical* suggests, the new historicism is not the same as the historical criticism practiced forty years ago. For one thing, it is informed by recent critical theory: by psychoanalytic criticism, reader-response criticism, feminist criticism, and perhaps especially by deconstruction. The new historicist critics are less fact- and event-oriented than historical critics used to be, perhaps because they have come to wonder whether the truth about what really happened can ever be purely and objectively known. They are less likely to see history as linear and progressive, as something developing toward the present.

As the word "sociohistorical" also suggests, the new historicists view history as a social science and the social sciences as being properly historical. McGann most often alludes to sociology when discussing the future of literary studies. "A sociological poetics must be recognized not only as relevant to the analysis of poetry, but in fact as central to the analysis" (*Inflections* 62). Lindenberger cites anthropology as particularly useful in the new historical analysis of literature, especially anthropology as practiced by Victor Turner and Clifford Geertz. Geertz, who has related theatrical traditions in nineteenth-century Bali to forms of political organization that developed during the same period, has influenced some of the most important critics writing the new kind of historical criticism. Due in large part to Geertz's influence, new historicists such as Stephen Greenblatt have asserted that literature is not a sphere apart or distinct from the history that is relevant to it. That is what old historical criticism tended to do, to present history as information you needed to know before you could fully appreciate the separate world of art. Thus the new historicists have discarded old distinctions between literature, history, and the social sciences, while blurring other boundaries. They have erased the line dividing historical and literary materials, showing that the production of one of Shakespeare's plays was a political act and that the coronation of Elizabeth I was carried out with the same care for staging and symbol lavished on a work of dramatic art.

In addition to breaking down barriers that separate literature and history, history and the social sciences, new historicists have reminded us that it is treacherously difficult to reconstruct the past as it really was — rather than as we have been conditioned by our own place and time to believe that it was. And they know that the job is utterly impossible for anyone who is unaware of the difficulty and of the nature of his or her own historical vantage point. "Historical criticism can no longer make any part of [its] sweeping picture unselfconsciously, or treat any of its details in an untheorized way," McGann wrote in 1985 (*Historical Studies* 11). "Unselfconsciously" and "untheorized" are key words here; when the new historicist critics of literature describe a historical change, they are highly conscious of, and even likely to discuss, the *theory* of historical change that informs their account. They know that the changes they happen to see and describe are the ones that their theory of change allows or helps them to see and describe. And they know, too, that their theory of change is historically determined. They seek to minimize the distortion inherent in their perceptions and representations by admitting that they see through preconceived notions; in other words, they learn and reveal the color of the lenses in the glasses that they wear.

All three of the critics whose recent writings on the so-called back-to-history movement have been quoted thus far — Hirsch, Lindenberger, and McGann — mention the name of the late Michel Foucault. As much an archaeologist as a historian and as much a philosopher as either, Foucault in his writings brought together incidents and phenomena from areas of inquiry and orders of life that we normally regard as unconnected. As much as anyone, he encouraged the new historicist critic of literature outwardly to redefine the boundaries of historical inquiry.

Foucault's views of history were influenced by Friedrich Nietzsche's concept of a *wirkliche* ("real" or "true") history that is neither melioristic nor metaphysical. Foucault, like Nietzsche, didn't understand history as development, as a forward movement toward the present. Neither did he view history as an abstraction, idea, or ideal, as something that began "In the beginning" and that will come to THE END, a moment of definite closure, a Day of Judgment. In his own words, Foucault "abandoned [the old history's] attempts to understand events in terms of . . . some great evolutionary process" (*Discipline and Punish* 129). He warned new historians to be aware of the fact that investigators are themselves "situated." It is difficult, he reminded them, to see present cultural practices critically from within them, and on account of the same cultural practices, it is almost impossible to enter bygone ages. In *Discipline and Punish: The Birth of the Prison* (1975), Foucault admitted that his own interest in the past was fueled by a passion to write the history of the present.

Like Marx, Foucault saw history in terms of power, but his view of power owed more perhaps to Nietzsche than to Marx. Foucault seldom viewed power as a repressive force. Certainly, he did not view it as a tool of conspiracy used by one specific individual or institution against another. Rather, power represents a whole complex of forces; it is that which produces what happens. Thus, even a tyrannical aristocrat does not simply wield power, because he is formed and empowered by discourses and practices that constitute power. Viewed by Foucault, power is "positive and productive," not "represssive" and "prohibitive" (Smart 63). Furthermore, no historical event, according to Foucault, has a single cause; rather, it is intricately connected with a vast web of economic, social, and political factors.

A brief sketch of one of Foucault's major works may help clarify some of his ideas. *Discipline and Punish* begins with a shocking but accurate description of the public drawing and quartering of a Frenchman who had botched his attempt to assassinate King Louis XV. Foucault proceeds, then, by describing rules governing the daily life of modern Parisian felons. What happened to torture, to punishment as public spectacle? he asks. What complex network of forces made it disappear? In working toward a picture of this "power," Foucault turns up many interesting puzzle pieces, such as that in the early revolutionary years of the nineteenth century, crowds would sometimes identify with the prisoner and treat the executioner as if *he* were the guilty party. But Foucault sets forth a related reason for keeping prisoners alive, moving punishment indoors, and changing discipline from physical torture into mental rehabilitation: colonization. In this historical period, people were needed to establish colonies and trade, and prisoners could be used for that purpose. Also, because these were politically unsettled times, governments needed infiltrators and informers. Who better to fill those roles than prisoners pardoned or released early for showing a willingness to be rehabilitated? As for rehabilitation itself, Foucault compares it to the old form of punishment, which began with a torturer extracting a confession. In more modern, "reasonable" times, psychologists probe the minds of prisoners with a scientific rigor that Foucault sees as a different kind of torture, a kind that our modern perspective does not allow us to see as such.

Thus, a change took place, but perhaps not so great a change as we generally assume. It may have been for the better or for the worse; the point is that agents of power didn't make the change because mankind is evolving and, therefore, more prone to perform good-hearted deeds. Rather, different objectives arose, including those of a new class of doctors and scientists bent on studying aberrant examples of the human mind.

Foucault's type of analysis has recently been practiced by a number of literary critics at the vanguard of the back-to-history movement. One of these critics, Stephen Greenblatt, has written on Renaissance changes in the development of both literary characters and real people. Like Foucault, he is careful to point out that any one change is connected with a host of others, no one of which may simply be identified as the cause or the effect. Greenblatt, like Foucault, insists on interpreting literary devices as if they were continuous with other representational devices in a culture; he turns, therefore, to scholars in other fields in order to better understand the workings of literature. "We wall off literary symbolism from the symbolic structures operative elsewhere," he writes, "as if art alone were a human creation, as if humans themselves were not, in Clifford Geertz's phrase, cultural artifacts." Following Geertz, Greenblatt sets out to practice what he calls "anthropological or cultural criticism." Anthropological literary criticism, he continues, addresses itself "to the interpretive constructions the members of a society apply to their experience," since a work of literature is itself an interpretive construction, "part of the system of signs that constitutes a given culture." He suggests that criticism must never interpret the past without at least being "conscious of its own status as interpretation" (Greenblatt 4).

Not all of the critics trying to lead students of literature back to history are as "Foucauldian" as Greenblatt. Some of these new historicists owe more to Marx than to Foucault. Others, like Jerome McGann, have followed the lead of Soviet critic M. M. Bakhtin, who was less likely than Marx to emphasize social class as a determining factor. (Bakhtin was more interested in the way that one language or style is the parody of an older one.) Still other new historicists, like Brook Thomas, have clearly been more influenced by Walter Benjamin, best known for essays such as "Theses on the Philosophy of History" and "The Work of Art in the Age of Mechanical Reproduction."

Moreover, there are other reasons not to declare that Foucault has been the central influence on the new historicism. Some new historicist critics would argue that Foucault critiqued old-style historicism to such an extent that he ended up being antihistorical or, at least, nonhistorical. As for his commitment to a radical remapping of relations of power and influence, cause and effect, in the view of some critics, Foucault consequently adopted too cavalier an attitude toward chronology and facts. In the minds of other critics, identifying and labeling a single master or central influence goes against the very grain of the new historicism. Practitioners of the new historicism have sought to decenter the study of literature and move toward the point where literary studies overlap with anthropological and sociological studies. They have also struggled to see history from a decentered perspective, both by recognizing that their own cultural and historical position may not afford the best understanding of other cultures and times and by realizing that events seldom have any single or central cause. At this point, then, it is appropriate to pause and suggest that Foucault shouldn't be seen as *the* cause of the new historicism, but as one of several powerful, interactive influences.

It is equally useful to suggest that the debate over the sources of the movement, the differences of opinion about Foucault, and even my own need to assert his importance may be historically contingent; that is to say, they may all result from the very *newness* of the new historicism itself. New intellectual movements often cannot be summed up or represented by a key figure, any more than they can easily be summed up or represented by an introduction or a single essay. They respond to disparate influences and almost inevitably include thinkers who represent a wide range of backgrounds. Like movements that are disintegrating, new movements embrace a broad spectrum of opinions and positions.

But just as differences within a new school of criticism cannot be overlooked, neither should they be exaggerated, since it is the similarity among a number of different approaches that makes us aware of a new movement under way. Greenblatt, Hirsch, McGann, and Thomas all started with the assumption that works of literature are simultaneously influenced by and influencing reality, broadly defined. Thus, whatever their disagreements, they share a belief in referentiality — a belief that literature refers to and is referred to by things outside itself — that is fainter in the works of formalist, poststructuralist, and even reader-response critics. They believe with Greenblatt that the "central concerns" of criticism "should prevent it from permanently sealing off one type of discourse from another or decisively separating works of art from the minds and lives of their creators and their audiences" (5).

McGann, in his introduction to *Historical Studies and Literary Criticism,* turns referentiality into a rallying cry:

> What will not be found in these essays . . . is the assumption, so common in text-centered studies of every type, that literary works are self-enclosed verbal constructs, or looped intertextual fields of autonomous signifiers and signifieds. In these essays, the question of referentiality is once again brought to the fore. (3)

In "Keats and the Historical Method in Literary Criticism," he outlines a program for those who have rallied to the cry. These procedures, which he claims are "practical derivatives of the Bakhtin school," assume that historicist critics, who must be interested in a work's point of origin and in its point of reception, will understand the former by studying biography and bibliography. (Did Hawthorne begin *The Scarlet Letter* before or after being dismissed as Surveyor of the Salem Custom House? Why did he publish his essay "The Custom-House" as the introduction to *The Scarlet Letter*?) After mastering these details, the critic must then consider the expressed intentions of the author, because, if printed, these intentions have also modified the developing history of the work. Next, the new historicist must learn the history of the work's reception, as that body of opinion has become part of the platform on which we are situated when we study the book. Finally, McGann urges the new historicist critic to point toward the future, toward his or her *own* audience, defining for its members the aims and limits of the critical project and injecting the analysis with a degree of self-consciousness that alone can give it credibility (*Inflections* 62).

Several of the critics who have analyzed *The Scarlet Letter* from a new historicist perspective have focused on "romance," the term Hawthorne applied to *The Scarlet Letter* at what McGann would call its point of origin. In fact, the 1850 edition was subtitled *A Romance.* Michael Davitt Bell, in "Arts of Deception: Hawthorne, 'Romance,' and *The Scarlet Letter,*" takes issue with critics like Perry Miller, Joel Porte, and Richard Chase — critics who in the 1950s and 1960s suggested that by writing a romance, Hawthorne was placing himself in the mainstream of American literary tradition, a tradition in which romance has always figured prominently. First of all, Bell points out, the term "romance" meant something different in Hawthorne's day from what it meant in the mid-twentieth century; it was "less a neutral generic label than a revolutionary, or at least antisocial slogan. To identify oneself as a romancer was . . . to set oneself in opposition to the most basic norms of society: reason, fact, and 'real' business." Thus, a term that meant one thing at the novel's point of origin meant something different at Chase's point of reception. But Bell shows that the problem is even more complex. Hawthorne was himself in the process of surreptitiously redefining romance (even as critics like Bell are doing, openly and self-consciously, today). Before we can analyze *The Scarlet Letter* as a romance, Bell suggests, we first need to provide a thick description of what that term meant, came to mean, and means to us now.

Most of the new historicist analyses of the novel, however, have concentrated not on romance — what it means and meant — but more generally on the historical period during which *The Scarlet Letter* was produced. They have argued that the novel, though set in seventeenth-century America, in fact reflects the concerns and biases — in short, the dominant ideology — of the author's nineteenth-century American culture. The Puritan past in which the novel is set is thus a kind of disguise, or screen, that hides the novel's true agenda. According to Jonathan Arac's essay "The Politics of *The Scarlet Letter*" (1986), that agenda is to warn against the dangers of the abolitionist movement. "Abolitionism," after all, "made the young Henry Adams feel that Boston in 1850 was once again revolutionary," and Hawthorne, cautioning against revolutionary activity, told the tale of an alienated revolutionary thinker, Hester, who gradually comes to see that acceptance plus patient, sympathetic work accomplish more than rebellious thoughts or actions (248). "Students judge *The Scarlet Letter* an intransitive 'work of art,' " Arac writes, "unlike, say, *Uncle Tom's Cabin,* which is 'propaganda' rather than 'art,' for it aims to change your life. If recent revaluation has shown that *Uncle Tom's Cabin* is also art, may it not be equally important to show that *The Scarlet Letter* is also propaganda — not to change your life?" (251).

Arac, who adapts the theories of Marx, Benjamin, and Foucault in his essay, was not the first of the new historicists to discuss the conservative subtext of Hawthorne's text. That subject had been first broached in 1985 by Larry J. Reynolds, in his ground-breaking essay "*The Scarlet Letter* and Revolutions Abroad." Beginning with the observation that the novel was written "in the wake of the revolutions [in France, Austria, and what is now Italy] in 1849," Reynolds argued that Hawthorne, unlike his wife and fellow New England writers, had been less than supportive of European revolutionary activity. Furthermore, he had worried that radical movements in Europe might be imminent or already under way in America. In "The Custom-House," which he at one point refers to as the "POSTHUMOUS PAPERS OF A DECAPITATED SURVEYOR" (52), Hawthorne implicitly compares the victory of the Whigs over the Democrats to revolution gone wrong in France. Even the setting of the novel, remote though it seems from mid-nineteenth-century Europe, has a revolutionary context. "The opening scenes of the novel take place in May 1642 and the closing ones in May 1649. These dates coincide almost exactly with those of the English Civil War fought between King Charles I and his Puritan Parliament," Reynolds pointed out.

> When Hester Prynne is led from the prison by the beadle who cries, "Make way, good people, make way, in the King's name," less than a month has passed since Charles's Puritan Parliament had sent him what amounted to a declaration of war. . . . By the final scenes of the novel, when Arthur is deciding to die as a martyr, Charles I has just been beheaded. (52–53)

Arguing that "a strong reactionary spirit underlies the work," Reynolds proved *The Scarlet Letter* to be an antirevolutionary text: "when Hester or Arthur battle to maintain or regain their rightful place in the social or spiritual order, the narrator sympathizes with them; when they become revolutionary instead and attempt to overthrow an established order, he becomes unsympathetic" (48, 58).

In 1987 Donald E. Pease, following Reynolds' and Arac's lead, suggested that Hawthorne's fear of revolution — revolution that he connected with his own sudden "rotation" out of office — led him to write about America's "*pre*-Revolutionary past," as if to comply with the wish of Puritan ancestors "to get the Revolutionary mythos out of the nation's history" (51). *The Scarlet Letter,* Pease argues, is a novel written against "progress, the belief that every moment exists only, like the displacement of persons in the Custom House, . . . to be superseded by the next. . . . Hawthorne felt called upon to expose both progress and the mythos of the Revolution supporting it as impediments to a vital public life" (52).

In the essay that begins on page 344, Sacvan Bercovitch develops ideas advanced by Arac, Reynolds, and Pease. Like Arac, he sees the novel as a subtle piece of nineteenth-century propaganda — "thick propaganda," as he puts it — as well as a work of art. He extends significantly Arac's argument that Hawthorne was writing against the abolitionists and their radical demands for an immediate end to slavery. Like Pease, he sees in the pre-Revolutionary Americans depicted in the novel a definite political purpose. Hawthorne's steeple-hatted Bostonians are, in Bercovitch's words, "mythic Puritans," an invention by Americans of a later historical period. They are designed, however unconsciously, to look and seem utterly different from their radical English contemporaries, the Puritans who in 1649 decapitated a king and set the stage for later revolutions in America and in Europe.

Most of all, though, Bercovitch develops the seminal ideas of Reynolds, arguing that *The Scarlet Letter* is a nineteenth-century American cultural artifact that contains among its subtexts a warning against the fruitless dangers of European-style radicalism. By describing Hester as emerging from a "moral wilderness" in which she looked at "whatever priests or legislators had established" with "hardly more reverence than the Indian would feel" (157), Hawthorne also pictures her emergence from the "spirit" of speculative radicalism, "then common enough on the other side of the Atlantic," into a spirit of community and compromise (133).

Like Reynolds, Bercovitch recognizes that Hawthorne saw in the Whig victory over the Democrats — the victory that had swept Hawthorne from office, turned him into a "decapitated Surveyor," and *returned* him to his writing desk — a sign that revolutionary activity might be spreading to his own country. But Bercovitch goes beyond Reynolds (and Arac and Pease as well) by suggesting that Hawthorne saw another such sign. That omen was none other than the women's rights movement, a movement that "social commentators" of the day had, as Bercovitch demonstrates, "just designated the first major symptom of the 'red plague.' "

Bercovitch, then, views *The Scarlet Letter* as a historical novel about one age permeated by the biases of another, particularly by its author's historically conditioned concern with three perceived threats to his own culture. By so interpreting the novel, Bercovitch typifies, as much as any critic can, the way in which practitioners of the new historicism see literary works. Equally typical of the new historicism is his final critical "move," which is to suggest that his own — that our own — reading of the novel is also historically determined. Hawthorne doesn't tell us exactly why Hester returns to Boston and reimposes the scarlet A on her breast. In deciding that she did so because she had come to see radical resistance as a dead end and because she had learned the greater value of working within the system, Bercovitch suggests that we "enact the same ideology of liberal consensus" that *The Scarlet Letter* "celebrates and represents."

THE NEW HISTORICISM: A SELECTED BIBLIOGRAPHY

The New Historicism: Further Reading

American Literary History. A journal devoted to new historicist and cultural criticism; the first issue was Spring 1989. New York: Oxford UP.

Dollimore, Jonathan, and Alan Sinfield, eds. *Political Shakespeare: New Essays in Cultural Materialism*. Manchester, Eng.: Manchester UP, 1985. See especially the essays by Dollimore, Greenblatt, and Tennenhouse.

———. *Radical Tragedy: Religion, Ideology and Power in the Drama of Shakespeare and His Contemporaries*. Brighton, Eng.: Harvester, 1984.

Goldberg, Jonathan. *James I and the Politics of Literature*. Baltimore: Johns Hopkins UP, 1983.

Graff, Gerald, and Reginald Gibbons, eds. *Criticism in the University*. Evanston: Northwestern UP, 1985. This volume includes sections devoted to the historical backgrounds of academic criticism; the influence of Marxism, feminism, and critical theory in general on the new historicism; changing pedagogies; and varieties of cultural criticism.

Greenblatt, Stephen. *Renaissance Self-Fashioning from More to Shakespeare*. Chicago: U of Chicago P, 1980. See chapter 1.

Hirsch, E. D., Jr. "Back to History." Graff, 189–97.

Lindenberger, Herbert. "Toward a New History in Literary Study." *Profession: Selected Articles from the Bulletins of the Association of Departments of English and the Association of Departments of Foreign Languages*. New York: MLA, 1984. 16–23.

McGann, Jerome. *The Beauty of Inflections: Literary Investigations in Historical Method and Theory*. Oxford: Clarendon Press-Oxford UP, 1985. See especially the introduction and chapter 1, "Keats and the Historical Method in Literary Criticism."

———. *Historical Studies and Literary Criticism*. Madison: U of Wisconsin P, 1985. See especially the introduction and the essays in the following sections: "Historical Methods and Literary Interpretations" and "Biographical Contexts and the Critical Object."

Morris, Wesley. *Toward a New Historicism*. Princeton: Princeton UP, 1972.

Thomas, Brook. "The Historical Necessity for — and Difficulties with — New Historical Analysis in Introductory Literature Courses." *College English* 49 (1987): 509–22.

Veeser, Harold. *The New Historicism*. New York: Routledge, Chapman & Hall, 1989.

Foucault and His Influence

As is pointed out in the introduction to the new historicism, some new historicists question the "privileging" of Foucault implicit in this section heading ("Foucault and His Influence") and the one following ("Other Writers and Works of Interest . . ."). They might argue for the greater importance of one of these other writers or point out that to cite a central influence or a definitive cause defies the very spirit of the movement.

Foucault, Michel. *Discipline and Punish: The Birth of the Prison*. 1975. Trans. Alan Sheridan. New York: Pantheon, 1978.

———. *The History of Sexuality*. Trans. Robert Hurley. Vol. 1. New York: Pantheon, 1978. 2 vols.

———. *Language, Counter-Memory, Practice*. Ed. Donald F. Bouchard. Trans. Bouchard and Sherry Simon. Ithaca: Cornell UP, 1977. Consists of selected essays and interviews.

Dreyfus, Hubert L., and Paul Rabinow. *Michel Foucault: Beyond Structuralism and Hermeneutics*. Chicago: U of Chicago P, 1983.

Sheridan, Alan. *Michel Foucault: The Will to Truth*. New York: Tavistock, 1980.

Smart, Barry. *Michel Foucault*. New York: Horwood and Tavistock, 1985.

Other Writers and Works of Interest to New Historicist Critics

Bakhtin, M. M. *The Dialogic Imagination: Four Essays*. Ed. Michael Holquist. Trans. Caryl Emerson. Austin: U of Texas P, 1981. Bakhtin authored many influential studies of subjects as varied as Dostoyevski, Rabelais, and formalist criticism. But this book, in part due to Holquist's helpful introduction, is probably the best place to begin reading Bakhtin.

Benjamin, Walter. "The Work of Art in the Age of Mechanical Reproduction." 1936. *Illuminations*. Trans. Harry Zohn. New York: Schocken, 1969.

Fried, Michael. *Absorption and Theatricality: Painting and Beholder in the Works of Diderot*. Berkeley: U of California P, 1980.

Geertz, Clifford. *The Interpretation of Cultures*. New York: Basic, 1973.

———. *Negara: The Theatre State in Nineteenth-Century Bali*. Princeton: Princeton UP, 1980.

Goffman, Erving. *Frame Analysis*. New York: Harper, 1974.

Jameson, Fredric. *The Political Unconscious*. Ithaca: Cornell UP, 1981.

Koselleck, Reinhart. *Futures Past*. Trans. Keith Tribe. Cambridge: MIT P, 1985.

Representations. Published by the University of California Press, this quarterly journal regularly contains new historicist studies and cultural criticism.

New Historicist Studies of *The Scarlet Letter*

Arac, Jonathan. "The Politics of *The Scarlet Letter*." Bercovitch 247–66.

Bell, Michael Davitt. "Arts of Deception: Hawthorne, 'Romance,' and *The Scarlet Letter*." Colacurcio 29–56.

Bercovitch, Sacvan, and Myra Jehlen, eds. *Ideology and Classic American Literature*. Cambridge: Harvard UP, 1986. See especially Jonathan Arac's essay, "The Politics of *The Scarlet Letter*."

Carton, Evan. *The Rhetoric of American Romance: Dialectic and Identity in Emerson, Dickinson, Poe, and Hawthorne*. Baltimore: Johns Hopkins UP, 1985.

Colacurcio, Michael, ed. *New Essays on "The Scarlet Letter."* Cambridge: Cambridge UP, 1985. See especially Colacurcio's essay, " 'The Woman's Own Choice': Sex, Metaphor, and the Puritan 'Sources' of *The Scarlet Letter*" and Michael Davitt Bell's essay, "Arts of Deception: Hawthorne, 'Romance,' and *The Scarlet Letter.*"

Pease, Donald E. *Visionary Compacts: American Renaissance Writings in Cultural Context.* Madison: U of Wisconsin P, 1987. See especially chapter 2, "Hawthorne's Discovery of a Pre-Revolutionary Past."

Reynolds, Larry J. "*The Scarlet Letter* and Revolutions Abroad." *American Literature* 57 (1985): 44–67.

A NEW HISTORICIST CRITIC AT WORK

SACVAN BERCOVITCH

Hawthorne's A-Morality of Compromise

Midway through *The Scarlet Letter,* in the course of a subtle and devastating critique of Hester's radicalism, Hawthorne remarks that "the scarlet letter had not done its office" (134). Hester still has to learn the folly of her wild "freedom of speculation" (133); she has yet to recognize that her love requires, more than a consecration of its own, the consecration of history and community. When in the "Conclusion" she returns to New England, Hester reveals what has been implicit all along, that the office of the A is socialization. She neither reaffirms her adulterous love nor disavows it; or rather she does both by incorporating it into the vision of an age of love to come. It is an act of compromise — bridging memory and hope; self and society; nature and institutions; past, present, and future — that reconciles the novel's various antinomies:

> Women, more especially, . . . came to Hester's cottage, demanding why they were so wretched, and what the remedy! Hester comforted and counselled them, as best she might. She assured them, too, of her firm belief, that, at some brighter period, when the world should have grown ripe for it, in Heaven's own time, a new truth would be revealed, in order to establish the whole relation between man and woman on a surer ground of mutual happiness. Earlier in life, Hester had vainly imagined that she herself might be the destined prophetess, but had long since recognized the impossibility that any mission of divine and mysterious truth

> should be confided to a woman stained with sin, bowed down with shame, or even burdened with a life-long sorrow. The angel and apostle of the coming revelation must be a woman, indeed, but lofty, pure, and beautiful; and wise, moreover, not through dusky grief, but the ethereal medium of joy. (201)

The entire novel tends toward this moment of reconciliation, but the basis for reconciliation, the source of Hester's re-vision, remains entirely unexplained. The problem is not that she returns, which Hawthorne does account for, in his way ("There was a more real life for Hester Prynne, here, in New England," 200). Nor is it that she resumes the A; we might anticipate that return to beginnings, by the principles of narrative closure. What remains problematic, what Hawthorne compels us to explain for ourselves (as well as on Hester's behalf), is her dramatic change of purpose and belief. Throughout her "seven years of outlaw and ignominy," Hester had considered her A a "scorching stigma" and herself "the people's victim and life-long bond-slave" (158, 190, 176). Now she takes up the letter — "of her own free will, for not the sternest magistrate of that iron period would have imposed it" (200) — and reconstitutes herself a counselor of patience and faith. This is not some formulaic Victorian ending. We accept it as inevitable, as readers did from the start, because Hawthorne has prepared us for it. All his strategies of ambiguity and irony *require* Hester's conversion to the letter. And since the magistrates themselves do not impose the A, since the community has long come to regard Hester as an "angel or apostle" in her own right, since we never learn the process of her conversion to the A (her development through the novel tending in exactly the opposite direction), since, in short, neither author nor characters help us, we must meet the requirement ourselves.

"The scarlet letter had not done its office" and when it has, Hester is transformed unaccountably into an agent of social cohesion and continuity. Much the same might be said, earlier, about Dimmesdale's metamorphosis, from secret rebel into prophet of New Israel. Hawthorne specifies the state of despair in which the minister agrees to leave, details the disordered fantasies that follow, and yet leaves it to us to explain his change of mind and heart. In this case, however, the explanation is inherent in the Puritan vision. "The minister," Hawthorne tells us, "had never gone through an experience calculated to lead him beyond the scope of generally received laws; although, in a single instance, he had so fearfully transgressed one of the most sacred of them. But this had been a sin of passion, not of principle, nor even purpose" (158). Accordingly, when he resolves to flee with Hester, he does so only because he believes he is "irrevocably doomed" (158), and we infer on his return that he has made peace at last with the familiar Puritan paradox, and has finally come to terms with the ambiguities of mercy and justice that he had forgotten in the forest. The reasons for Hester's reversal are far more complex. It takes the whole story to work them through. It is the office of *The Scarlet Letter* to teach us why this tragic-romantic heroine, who had turned being compromised into a source of uncompromising resistance, *must* now make compromise the work of culture. In an earlier essay, I discussed that cultural work in terms of Hawthorne's aesthetic techniques (*A-Politics* 629–54). In this essay, I turn the text inside out in order to focus directly on ideological context. My purpose is to explain our complicity in Hester's return by exploring the historical ground and substance of her heroism of compromise.

The most direct connection between text and context is the community to which Hester returns. I refer to the Puritan myth endorsed by mid-nineteenth-century America. For like the letter that they impose, Hawthorne's settlers are a cultural artifact — a very sophisticated one, to be sure, and cunningly embroidered with his personal concerns, broad learning, and elaborate ironies, but woven nonetheless out of the same cultural cloth that produced the legend of the Puritan "founders" (53). It is no accident that Dimmesdale's sermon on the future marks the transition of government from John Winthrop to John Endicott. The unspoken link between the two governors is nothing less than the national tradition that connects Hester to Hawthorne. It represents what by 1850 was the widely celebrated continuity from the New England Way to the American Way — from Winthrop, the *ur*-father, to Endicott, the *ur*-patriot, whose rending of "the Red Cross from New England's banner" was "the first omen of that deliverance which our fathers consummated" in 1776 (Hawthorne, "Endicott" 548).

These mythic Puritans have had a long life in the national consciousness. At mid-century they served above all to provide a crucial contrast between Puritanism in Old and New England. According to general belief, shared by Whigs and Democrats alike — by New York's cultural pundit, Evert Duyckinck (a founder of the Young America Movement and Hawthorne's major advocate in the literary world); by Henry Wadsworth Longfellow (Hawthorne's lifelong friend and his first important reviewer); by the epic historian of the era, George Bancroft (who helped Hawthorne secure his appointment as surveyor at the Salem Custom-House); and by the manifest destinarian John Louis O'Sullivan (Hawthorne's publisher and godfather to his first child, Una) — there were two Puritan revolutions in the early 1600s. One was the Puritan exodus to the New World, a revolution for liberty that offered a model of progress by harnessing the energies of radicalism to the process of settlement, expansion, and consolidation. The Old World counterpart was the Puritan revolution (1642–49) that failed — a revolution prefigured (in Hawthorne's view) by the "mobocracies" of the past and itself a prefiguration of the failed continental upheavals of the next two centuries, including those perpetrated by "the terrorists of France" in 1789, 1830, and 1848 (*The Scarlet Letter* 59).

Hawthorne suggests the reasons for failure in an essay he wrote on Oliver Cromwell. When Oliver was a child, he writes, a "huge ape, which was kept in the family, snatched up little Noll in his fore-paws, and clambered with him to the roof of the house. . . . The event was afterwards considered an omen that Noll would reach a very elevated station in the world" ("Oliver Cromwell" 252). It is a parable for the embittered young radical whose clambering "enthusiasm of thought" (134) Hawthorne details midway through *The Scarlet Letter* (shortly after his reference to the "terrorists of France"):

> [This] was an age in which the human intellect, newly emancipated, had taken a more active and a wider range than for many centuries before. Men of the sword had overthrown nobles and kings. Men bolder than these had overthrown and rearranged — not actually, but within the sphere of theory, which was their most real abode —the whole system of ancient prejudice, wherewith was linked much of ancient principle. Hester Prynne imbibed this spirit. She assumed a freedom of speculation, then common enough on the other side of the Atlantic, but which our forefathers, had they known of it, would have held to be a deadlier crime than that stigmatized by the scarlet letter. In her lonesome cottage, by the sea-shore, thoughts visited her, such as dared to enter no other dwelling in New England; shadowy guests . . . perilous as demons. (133)

The key word is *forefathers,* which carries the entire force of the ideological contrast I mentioned between upheaval in the Old World and progress in the New. And it applies as such directly to what Hawthorne recalled in 1852 as the era of "The Compromise" (Hawthorne, *Pierce* 109–10).[1] His return to Puritan New England in *The Scarlet Letter* joins two historical time frames: first, the fictional time frame,

[1]The most incisive use of the biography in this regard is Jonathan Arac, "The Politics of *The Scarlet Letter,*" *Ideology and Classic American Literature,* ed. Sacvan Bercovitch and Myra Jehlen (Cambridge: Harvard UP, 1986) 247–66. I am much indebted to Arac's essay.

1642–49, with its implied contrast between Cromwell's revolt and the American Puritan venture in "Utopia" (53); second, the authorial time frame, 1848–52, with its ominous explosion of conflict at home and abroad.

The "red year Forty-Eight," as Melville termed it, brought "the portent and the fact of war, / And terror that into hate subsides." He was referring to the series of revolutions from which Europe's kings "fled like the gods" (although by 1852 "even as the gods / . . . return they made; and sate / And fortified their strong abodes") (Melville, *Clarel* 281, 157). But he might have been referring as well to what New England conservatives considered an ominous tendency toward confrontation following the victory of the Whigs. Polk's presidency, 1844–48, was a high point of Jacksonian chauvinism: Mexico had been defeated, the Oregon Territory appropriated (along with Nevada, New Mexico, Colorado, and parts of Utah), gold discovered in California, and Florida, Texas, Iowa, and Wisconsin admitted to the Union. Then, in 1848, the unexpected defeat of Young Hickory called attention to long-festering internal divisions. We can see in retrospect how both tendencies, toward expansion and toward conflict, expressed the same process of ideological consolidation. But for a good many of the disempowered Democrats the tendency toward conflict evoked what newspapers called the "terrors of a European conflagration." It is no accident that Hawthorne connected the revolutions abroad with his loss of tenure at the Salem Custom House. As Larry J. Reynolds has recently demonstrated, Hawthorne links both sets of events in the alternative title that he offers for the novel, "POSTHUMOUS PAPERS OF A DECAPITATED SURVEYOR" (52), and the political innuendos here are expanded throughout "The Custom-House" and the novel at large in recurrent imagery of the 1848–49 revolutions, including allusions to scaffold and guillotine.[2]

Eighteen-forty-eight, then, opens the novel's authorial time frame. Historians have called it the Year of the Red Scare: Chartist agitation in England, the First Paris Commune, *The Communist Manifesto,* and widespread revolt in Belgium, Germany, Poland, Austria, Italy, Czechoslovakia, and Hungary. After a brief period of euphoria, when it seemed events were proving that "our country leads the world," public opinion

[2]Reynolds first explored the relationship between *The Scarlet Letter* and European revolutions in "*The Scarlet Letter* and Revolutions Abroad," an article published in *American Literature* 57 (1985): 44–67. He has recently expanded his research into a valuable book-length study, *European Revolutions and the American Literary Renaissance* (New Haven: Yale UP, 1988).

turned decisively against the radicals. Those who did the turning expressed disillusionment in many ways, but common to all was the contrast between Europe's class warfare and the war for American independence. By fall 1848, Evert Duyckinck reported that New Yorkers associated the "agitation'" with "recollections of Robespierre" (Reynolds 49); shortly after, George Bancroft wrote that Boston was "frightened out of its wits" (White 121); in Paris, Emerson wondered whether the revolution was worth the trees it had cost to build the barricades; by early 1849 American conservatives writing in the *New York Courier and Inquirer* concluded that the European soil was not encouraging to the growth of republics. Worse still, they had already observed the incipient effect in America itself of European conflict — "Communism, Socialism, Pillage, Murder, Anarchy, and the Guillotine vs. Law and Order, Family and Property" (14 July 1848: 1). George Bancroft, who at first tried to calm his frightened Boston friends — who in fact hoped (as he wrote to Secretary of State James Buchanan) that "the echo of American Democracy . . . from France, and Austria, and Prussia and all Old Germany . . . [would] stir up the hearts of the American people to new achievement" — came increasingly to concede that events were tending in just the opposite direction: geographically, from the Old World to the New, and morally, from liberty to license (Bancroft 31, 33).

License took many forms, as these antebellum Jeremiahs detailed its invasion of America. Hawthorne may be said to condense their complaints in his overview of Hester's nihilism, just before her forest meeting with Dimmesdale:

> She had wandered, without rule or guidance, in a moral wilderness . . . [and] looked from this estranged point of view at human institutions, and whatever priests or legislators had established; criticizing all with hardly more reverence than the Indian would feel for the clerical band, the judicial robe, . . . the fireside, . . . or the church. . . . The scarlet letter was her passport into *regions where other women dared not tread.* Shame, Despair, Solitude! These had been her teachers, — stern and wild ones, — and they had made her strong, but taught her much amiss. (157, emphasis added)

The regions to which Hawthorne refers had long been open territory to European radicals: "terrorists of France" as well as England (from Puritan Ranters to the Chartists of 1848). Even there, however, women had characteristically restrained themselves, because (Hawthorne explains) they intuited that to indulge such "tendency to speculation" —

to venture into that "moral wilderness" beyond "Law and Order, Family and Property" — would be to alter their very "natures"; it would drain them of the "ethereal essence, wherein [woman] has her truest life" (134). This explanation is at once essentialist and political. It directly precedes his reminder that "the scarlet letter had not done its office," and there is every reason to assume that he was deliberately evoking what social commentators had just designated the first major symptom of the "red plague of European revolutions . . . on these shores" — the Women's Rights Convention at Seneca Falls in 1848. Reports of "the female 'Reds' of Europe" had already "appalled the American public," and public spokesmen from pulpit, press, and political platform rushed to make the connection:

> This is the age of revolutions. To whatever part of the world the attention is directed, the political and social fabric is crumbling to pieces; and changes which far exceed the wildest dreams of the enthusiastic Utopians of the last generation, are now pursued with ardor and perseverance. The principal agent, however, that has hitherto taken part in these movements has been the rougher sex . . . and though it is asserted that no inconsiderable assistance was contributed by the gentler sex to the late sanguinary carnage at Paris, we are disposed to believe that such a revolting imputation proceeds from base calumniators, and is a libel upon woman.
>
> By the intelligence, however, which we have lately received, the work of revolution is no longer confined to the Old World, nor to the masculine gender. The flag of independence has been hoisted, for the second time, on this side of the Atlantic; and a solemn league and covenant has just been entered into by a Convention of women at Seneca Falls. . . .
>
> [These women] seem to be really in earnest in their aim at revolution, and . . . evince entire confidence that "the day of their deliverance is at hand." (Stanton 805, 804)

Surely Hawthorne means us to hear the strains of this American "Marseillaise" in Hester's "stern and wild" irreverence. And surely, too, his overall critique of her radicalism — from her bitter sense of herself as "martyr" (79) to her self-conscious manipulation of the townspeople (129–35) and her rising scorn for all "human institutions," "whatever priests or legislators had established" (157) — registers the reaction against the rising European "carnage" and its "revolting" influence "on this side of the Atlantic." That reaction included all five major writers of F. O. Matthiessen's *American Renaissance,* in spite of their common devotion to "the possibilities of democracy" (14). Significantly, the most radically American among them was also clearest about ideological parameters. What made "European revolution" unfit for America, according to Emerson, what made it antithetical to "true democracy," was the threat it posed to the tenets of free enterprise. It was not so much the violence that troubled Emerson, though he lamented that "in France, 'fraternity' [and] 'equality' . . . are names for assassination" (*Complete Works* 82). Nor was it the burdens of political engagement, though he noted in April 1848, concerning talk of "a Chartist revolution on Monday next, and an Irish revolution the following week," that the scholar's "kingdom is at once over & under these perturbed regions" (*Journals* 310). Emerson's complaints struck through what he considered "these political masks" to reveal the "metaphysical evils" beyond:

> This tin trumpet of a French Phalanstery [sounds] and the newsboys throw up their caps & cry, Egotism is exploded; now for Communism! But all that is valuable in the Phalanstery comes of individualism. . . . For the matter of Socialism, there are no oracles. The oracle is dumb. When we would pronounce anything truly of man, we retreat instantly on the individual.
>
> We are authorized to say much on the destinies of one, nothing on those of many. In the question of Socialism . . . one has only this guidance. You shall not so arrange property as to remove the motive to industry. If you refuse rent & interest, you make all men idle & immoral. As to the poor, a vast proportion have made themselves so, and in any new arrangement will only prove a burden on the state. . . .
>
> When men feel & say, "Those men occupy my place," the revolution is near. But I never feel that any men occupy my place; but that the reason I do not have what I wish is, that I want the faculty which entitles. All spiritual or real power makes its own place. Revolutions of violence then are scrambles merely. (*Journals* 10: 154, 310, 312, 318).

Even Walt Whitman, Barnburner delegate, Chartist sympathizer, and Free Soiler, joined in elaborating this symbolic opposition between European and American revolutions. In 1847 Whitman had gone so far as to defend the French republican Reign of Terror, but after 1849, when the attack on property and individualism became an American issue, he steadily "recoiled." All that remains in *Leaves of Grass* of the Spirit of '48 (when "like lightning Europe le'pt forth") is

> a Shape,
> Vague as the night, draped interminably, head front and form,
> in scarlet folds,

> Whose face and eyes none may see,
> Out of its robes only this . . . the red robes, lifted,
> by the arm,
> One finger crook'd pointed high over the top, like the head
> of a snake appears. (Whitman 133)

Whitman consoled the "Foil'd European Revolutionaire" by recalling "that defeat [too] is great, / And that death and dismay are great"; and the moral he drew for "comeraderos" at home and abroad was "Educate, Educate, — it is the only true remedy for mobs, wild communistic theories, and red-republican ravings" (Reynolds 51).

Of all of Hawthorne's acquaintances only one, Margaret Fuller, continued to give her full support to the revolutionaries, and it has been argued persuasively that she figures not only in his story of ill-fated Zenobia but, together with her allegedly illegitimate child (the gossip of Brahmin New England in 1849), in his portrait of the tormented radical, Hester Prynne. If so, it might be regarded as a Hawthornesque irony that Fuller returned from Europe "possessed," as she put it, "of a great history" — convinced of the importance of "social struggle" as against the "consolations of prophecy," "fiction," and "the past" — and that she drowned within sight of the lifeboats grounded on the American shore (Douglas 259).

That was in 1850, which I take to be the centerpiece of the novel's authorial time frame. It was the year of the Compromise Resolutions, including the Fugitive Slave Act, and *The Scarlet Letter*. Eighteen-fifty-two marks the close of this period, with the return of Hawthorne's political fortune through the election to the presidency of his friend Franklin Pierce. Hawthorne did his share by writing the official campaign biography, in which he extols Pierce as "the statesman of practical sagacity — who loves his country *as it is,* and evolves good from things *as they exist*" — and he defends Pierce's support of the Fugitive Slave Act by comparing the abolitionists to Europe's "Red Republicans" (*Pierce* 111). The indirection of his comparison suggests a political balancing act, somewhat like the Compromise Bill itself: Hawthorne did not want to alienate those of Pierce's Young America supporters who persisted in identifying European insurrection with the claims of American expansionism. (Besides, Louis Kossuth was then touring the United States, and although Hawthorne himself felt "as enthusiastic [about him] as a lump of frozen mud," he had to acknowledge the "popularity" of the Hungarian revolutionary leader [Reynolds 160].) Still, the comparativist implications in the Pierce biography are unmistakable. Hawthorne charges that (like the "terrorists of France") the abolitionists are hell-bent on chaos: they would tear "to pieces the Constitution" and sever "into distracted fragments that common country which Providence brought into one nation, through a continued miracle of almost two hundred years, from the first settlement of the American wilderness until the Revolution" (*Pierce* 112).

As critics increasingly recognize, the Civil War provides the latent context of the American Renaissance. *Moby-Dick, The Narrative of the Life of Frederick Douglass,* and *Uncle Tom's Cabin* (as well as Cooper's apocalyptic novel of 1849, *The Crater*) all deal more or less directly with loomings of national cataclysm. The visions of transcendent unity in *Walden, Leaves of Grass,* and *Eureka* all depend on a utopianism — utopian nostalgia in Thoreau's case, utopian futurism in Whitman's, dystopian metaphysics in Poe's — that circumvents or submerges the actual divisions of the time. Considered together with the popular sentimental and Gothic novels of the period, these works provide a multivocal narrative of American liberal ideology during a crucial period of its formation. The special position of *The Scarlet Letter* in this narrative may be inferred from its centrist strategy: it employs sentimental themes and Gothic techniques in order to mediate between utopian and dystopian resolutions, and its return to cultural origins speaks to the threat of cataclysm while evading the prospects of conflict.

No doubt the overall tendency is toward evasion. Indeed, we might almost read Hester's counsel (after the letter has done its office) as a preview of Hawthorne's answer to the abolitionists. Slavery, he explains in the Pierce biography, is "one of those evils which divine Providence does not leave to be remedied by human contrivances, but which, in its own good time, by some means impossible to be anticipated, but of the simplest and easiest operation, when all its uses shall have been fulfilled, it causes to vanish like a dream" (*Pierce* 111–12). Only the security of commonplace could allow for this daring inversion in logic, whereby slavery is represented, symbolically, as part of the "continued miracle" of America's progress. Like the scarlet letter, Hawthorne's argument has the power of a long-preserved cultural artifact.

But of course the two artifacts are different in kind. The argument in the biography reflects a certain tactic of the culture; its power derives from a system of ideas connecting racism and progress. The power of the scarlet letter derives from its capacities for mediation. It reveals the variety of tactics available to the culture at a certain historical moment. As I have noted, antebellum culture was particularly volatile, not in the sense of transition but of consolidation: volatility redirected into channels of social growth. It was a culture feeding on change; nourished by technological innovation, territorial expansion, shifts of power centers, and waves of immigration; and, as a symptom of its increasing confidence, accommodating itself to new conditions by moving toward a resolution by violence of its major internal conflict. To call Hawthorne's racism a cultural tactic is not to excuse it but to distinguish the biography from the novel. Considered as part of an intracultural debate, Hawthorne's response to the Fugitive Slave Act differs dramatically from that of abolitionists like Emerson and Stowe. But if we step outside that context the difference reflects something else entirely: a series of no longer avoidable contradictions within a system whose values and biases (including racism and American exceptionalism) they all shared. The *Life of Pierce* advances what turned out to be an inadequate mode of resolving a social crisis. *The Scarlet Letter* expresses a particular culture's mode of resolving crisis. It is not that the novel transcends propaganda. It is that its imaginative forms reveal the complexity of beliefs implicit but submerged in any single-minded doctrine that we commonly associate with propaganda. The biography presents a certain choice; the novel represents a metaphysics of choosing. It advocates not a particular course of action, but a world view within which that course of action makes sense and takes effect.

We might call the novel thick propaganda. Its range of possibilities includes virtually every form of resolution generated by the antebellum North. To repeat the logic of Hester's vision (insofar as it prefigures the Pierce biography), injustice is to be removed by some "divine operation" that has not yet done its office. This representation of contradiction as an ambiguity in the process of resolving itself is not substantially different from the Liberian solution proposed by Harriet Beecher Stowe and enacted in the happy ending to *Uncle Tom's Cabin* by her mulatto hero George Harris. Nor is it different in substance from the expansionist argument that to repeal the Fugitive Slave Act would revitalize the national errand, or, in John Greenleaf Whittier's words, inspire children of Puritans, North and South, to cross "the prairie as of old / Our fathers sailed the sea" and thereby ("Upbearing like the Ark of old, / The Bible in our van") "make the West, as they the East, / The homestead of the free!" (Whittier 317). Nor again is Hawthorne's solution different in substance from that proposed a decade later by those who believed *they* were the divine operation, providence incarnate, moving irresistibly toward the Armageddon of the Republic. In his debates with Stephen A. Douglas, Lincoln effectually reversed Hawthorne's argument — it was the antiabolitionists, he charged, who were fragmenting the Union and subverting the fathers' legacy — and in his Second Inaugural Address of 1865, reviewing the causes of the Civil War, he described "American slavery" as "one of those offenses which, in the providence of God, must needs come, but which, having continued through His appointed time, He now wills to remove" (Lincoln 8: 333).

The difference between Lincoln's counsel for reconciliation and Hester's for patience is the turn of a certain circular symbolic logic. The Northern rhetoric of the Civil War represents negation as affirmation, the destined union made manifest in violence. Hawthorne's rhetoric builds on affirmation by negation — manifest inaction justified by national destiny. From this perspective, it is worth recalling the enormous force of the negative imperative in *The Scarlet Letter*. Negation is far more than a form of moral, political, and aesthetic control; it is the very ground of Hawthorne's strategy of process as gradualism, the antidialectic through which he absorbs the radical energies of history into the polar oppositions of symbolic interpretation. "The scarlet letter had not done its office": negation leads us forward toward that deeper significance which Hawthorne promises at the start — that comprehensive "deep meaning . . . most worthy of interpretation" (43) — precisely by evoking the fear of process run amuck, pluralism fragmenting into diversity, disharmony, discontinuity, chaos.

That is the overt purpose of Hawthorne's imperative. But the effect goes further than that. Hawthorne's mode of negation may almost be said to take on a counterdynamic of its own, as though in equal and opposite reaction to the fear of uncontrolled process. Negation gathers such momentum in the course of the novel that it threatens the very process it is designed to guide. *Not* doing its office nearly comes to define the function of the symbol. When after "seven miserable years" (176) Hester at last finds the strength to discard the A, it takes all of Hawthorne's resources (providence, Pearl, Dimmesdale, nature itself) to have her restore it against her will. And even so the restoration serves at first to highlight the letter's negative effects. As she awaits her moment of flight with Dimmesdale, Hester stands alone in the marketplace with a "frozen calmness" (176), her face a death mask, ***and because of that*** with all the radical vitality for which we have come to admire her:

> After sustaining the gaze of the multitude through seven miserable years as a necessity, a penance, and something which it was a stern religion to endure, she now, for one last time more, encountered it freely and voluntarily, in order to convert what had so long been agony into a kind of triumph. "Look your last on the scarlet

> letter and its wearer!" — the people's victim and life-long bond-slave, as they fancied her, might say to them. "Yet a little while, and she will be beyond your reach! A few hours longer, and the deep, mysterious ocean will quench and hide for ever the symbol which ye have caused to burn upon her bosom!" (176)

That is why Hawthorne must not only bring her back but also force her to resume that A "freely and voluntarily." It is as though, under pressure of her resistance, the letter were slipping out of his grasp, losing its efficacy as an agent of reconciliation. In terms of what I have called the novel's latent context, the impending Civil War, the antinomies in this passage ("people" and "victim," "freely" and "bond-slave") assume an explosive force, an almost irrepressible tendency toward confrontation that endangers both symbolic process and narrative closure. That tendency may be seen as the political aftereffect of the rhetoric of liberty, in which "slavery" served ambiguously to denote all forms of bondage, "private or public, civil or political" (Bailyn 232–33). More directly, it is the rhetorical counterpart to what Edmund Morgan, describing the tensions in antebellum politics, termed "American freedom/American slavery" (passim). It is a testament to Hawthorne's sensitivity to those rhetorical-political tensions that he allowed the danger to surface, that indeed he played it out almost to the point of no return. It is a testament to the resilience of the ideology that it drew on that he could nonetheless resume process and as it were rescue the symbol from the ocean's depths, by simply, sweepingly, *assuming* an interpretive consensus.

The silence surrounding Hester's final conversion to the letter is clearly deliberate on Hawthorne's part. It mystifies Hester's choice by forcing us to represent it through the act of interpretation. Having given us ample directives about how to understand the ways in which the letter had not done its office, Hawthorne now depends on us to recognize — freely and voluntarily, for his method depends on his seeming *not* to impose meaning (as in his remark that "the scarlet letter had not done its office") — the need for Hester's return. In effect, he invites us to participate in a free enterprise democracy of symbol making. Its cultural model is the ambiguity universalized in the Declaration of Independence: "*We* hold these truths to be *self*-evident." The silent problematic of "we" may be inferred from Pip's revelation of the plural meanings of the doubloon in *Moby Dick* — "I look, you look, he looks, we look, ye look, they look" — especially if we remember, as Pip seems not to, that the grammatical declension masks a social hierarchy, *descending* from the captain's *I* to the shipstokers' *they*. The silenced problematic of "self-evident" may be inferred from the voluntaristic terms of Ahab's covenant: "I do not order ye; ye will it" (Melville, *Moby-Dick* 969, 1258).

Hawthorne, too, may be said to elicit these problematics, but unlike Melville he does so in order to guide us toward accommodation. When, in the most carefully prepared-for reversal in classic American literature, Hester herself imposes the symbol, she signals her recognition that what had seemed a basic problem — basic enough to have made her want to overturn society — is really a question of point of view; and Hawthorne so veils this epiphany that our multiple perspectives enact the same ideology of liberal consensus that his novel celebrates and represents.

WORKS CITED

Bailyn, Bernard. *The Ideological Origins of the American Revolution.* Cambridge: Belknap-Harvard UP, 1967.

Bancroft, George. *Life and Letters.* Ed. Mark A. DeWolfe Howe. Vol. 2. New York: Scribner's, 1908. 2 vols.

Bercovitch, Sacvan. "The A-Politics of Ambiguity in *The Scarlet Letter.*" *New Literary History* 19 (1988): 629–54.

Douglas, Ann. *The Feminization of American Culture.* New York: Knopf, 1977.

Emerson, Ralph Waldo. *Complete Works.* Ed. Edward Waldo Emerson. Vol. 5. Boston: Houghton, 1903–04. 12 vols.

———. *Journals and Miscellaneous Notebooks.* Ed. Merton M. Sealts, Jr. Vol. 10. Cambridge: Belknap-Harvard UP, 1973. 16 vols.

Hawthorne, Nathaniel. "Endicott and the Red Cross." *Tales and Sketches.* Ed. Roy Harvey Pearce. New York: Library of America, 1982. 542–48.

———. *Life of Franklin Pierce.* Boston: Ticknor, Reed and Fields, 1852.

———. "Oliver Cromwell." *True Stories from History and Biography.* Ed. William Charvat et al. Vol. 6 of the Centenary Edition. Columbus: Ohio State UP, 1972. 251–60.

Lincoln, Abraham. "Second Inaugural Address." *Collected Works.* Ed. Roy P. Basler. Vol. 8. New Brunswick: Rutgers UP, 1953. 20 vols.

Matthiessen, F. O. *American Renaissance: Art and Expression in the Age of Emerson and Whitman.* New York: Oxford UP, 1941.

Melville, Herman. *Clarel: A Poem and Pilgrimage in the Holy Land.* Ed. Walter E. Bezanson. New York: Hendricks, 1960.

———. *Moby-Dick: or, The Whale. Redburn, White-Jacket, Moby-Dick.* Ed. Thomas Tanselle. New York: Library of America, 1983.

Morgan, Edmund. *American Freedom/American Slavery: The Ordeal of Colonial Virginia.* New York: Norton, 1975.

Reynolds, Larry J. *European Revolutions Abroad and the American Renaissance.* New Haven: Yale UP, 1988.

Stanton, Elizabeth Cady, Susan B. Anthony, and Matilda Joslyn Gage, eds. *History of Woman Suffrage.* Vol. 1. New York: Arno, 1969. 6 vols.

White, Elizabeth Belt. *American Opinion of France.* New York: Knopf, 1927.

Whitman, Walt. *The Complete Poetry and Collected Prose.* Ed. Justin Kaplan. New York: Library of America, 1982.

Whittier, John Greenleaf. "The Kansas Emigrants." *Complete Poetical Works.* Boston: Houghton, 1894. 317.

Glossary of Critical and Theoretical Terms

Most terms have been glossed parenthetically where they first appear in the text. Mainly, the glossary lists terms that are too complex to define in a phrase or a sentence or two. A few of the terms listed are discussed at greater length elsewhere ("deconstruction," for instance); these terms are defined succinctly and a page reference to the longer discussion is provided.

AFFECTIVE FALLACY First used by William K. Wimsatt and Monroe C. Beardsley to refer to what they regarded as the erroneous practice of interpreting texts according to the psychological responses of readers. "The Affective Fallacy," they wrote in a 1946 essay later republished in the *Verbal Icon* (1954), "is a confusion between the poem and its *results* (what it *is* and what it *does*). . . . It begins by trying to derive the standards of criticism from the psychological effects of a poem and ends in impressionism and relativism." The affective fallacy, like the intentional fallacy (confusing the meaning of a work with the author's expressly intended meaning), was one of the main tenets of the New Criticism, or formalism. The affective fallacy has recently been contested by reader-response critics, who have deliberately dedicated their efforts to describing the way individual readers and "interpretive communities" go about "making sense" of texts.

See also: Authorial Intention, Formalism, Reader-Response Criticism.

AUTHORIAL INTENTION Defined narrowly, an author's intention in writing a work, as expressed in letters, diaries, interviews, and conversations. Defined more broadly, "intentionality" involves unexpressed motivations, designs, and purposes, some of which may have remained unconscious.

The debate over whether critics should try to discern an author's intentions (conscious or otherwise) is an old one. William K. Wimsatt and Monroe C. Beardsley, in an essay first published in the 1940s, coined the term "intentional fallacy" to refer to the practice of basing interpretations on the expressed or implied intentions of authors, a practice they judged to be erroneous. As proponents of the New Criticism, or formalism, they argued that a work of literature is an object in itself and should be studied as such. They believed that it is sometimes helpful to learn what an author intended, but the critic's real purpose is to show what is actually in the text, not what an author intended to put there.

See also: Affective Fallacy, Formalism.

BINARY OPPOSITIONS *See* Oppositions.

BLANKS *See* Gaps.

DECONSTRUCTION A poststructuralist approach to literature strongly influenced by the writings of the philosopher Jacques Derrida. Deconstruction, partly in response to structuralism and formalism, posits the undecidability of meaning for all texts. In fact, as the deconstructive critic J. Hillis Miller points out, "deconstruction is not a dismantling of the structure of a text but a demonstration that it has already dismantled itself." See "What Is Deconstruction?" page 304.

DISCOURSE Used specifically, this term can refer to (1) spoken or written discussion of a subject or area of knowledge; (2) the words in, or text of, a narrative, as opposed to its story line; or (3) a strand within a given narrative that argues a certain point or defends a certain value system.

More generally, discourse refers to the language in which a subject or area of knowledge is discussed or a certain kind of business is transacted. Human knowledge is collected and structured in discourses. Theology and medicine are defined by their discourses, as are politics, sexuality, and literary criticism.

A society is made up of a number of different discourses or "discourse communities," one or more of which may be dominant or serve the dominant ideology. Each discourse has its own vocabulary, concepts, and rules, knowledge of which constitutes power. Feminist and new historicist critics tend to see literary works in terms of discourses that inform or compete with their discourses. The psychoanalyst and psychoanalytic critic Jacques Lacan has treated the unconscious as a form of discourse, the patterns of which are repeated in literature.

See also: Feminist Criticism, Ideology, Narrative, New Historicism, Psychoanalytic Criticism.

FEMINIST CRITICISM An aspect of the feminist movement whose primary goals include critiquing masculine-dominated language and literature by showing how they reflect a masculine ideology; writing the history of unknown or undervalued women writers, thereby earning them their rightful place in the literary canon; and helping create a climate in which women's creativity may be fully realized and appreciated. See "What Is Feminist Criticism?" page 275.

FIGURE *See* Metaphor, Metonymy, Symbol.

FORMALISM Also referred to as the New Criticism, formalism reached its height during the 1940s and 1950s but it is still practiced today. Formalists treat a work of literary art as if it were a self-contained, self-referential object. Rather than basing their interpretations of a text on the reader's response, the author's stated intentions, or parallels between the text and historical contexts (such as the author's life), formalists concentrate on the relationships *within* the text that give it its own distinctive character or form. Special attention is paid to repetition, particularly of images or symbols, but also of sound effects and rhythms in poetry.

Because of the importance placed on close analysis and the stress on the text as a carefully crafted, orderly object containing observable formal patterns, formalism has often been seen as an attack on Romanticism and impressionism, particularly impressionistic criticism. It has sometimes even been called an "objective" approach to literature. Formalists are more likely than certain other critics to believe and say that the meaning of a text can be known objectively. For instance, reader-response critics see meaning as a function either of each reader's experience or of the norms that govern a particular "interpretive community" and deconstructors argue that texts mean opposite things at the same time.

Formalism was originally based on essays written during the 1920s and 1930s by T. S. Eliot, I. A. Richards, and William Empson. It was significantly developed later by a group of American poets and critics, including R. P. Blackmur, Cleanth Brooks, John Crowe Ransom, Allen Tate, Robert Penn Warren, and William K. Wimsatt. Although we associate formalism with certain principles and terms (such as the "Affective Fallacy" and the "Intentional Fallacy" as defined by Wimsatt and Monroe C. Beardsley), formalists were trying to make a cultural statement rather than establish a critical dogma. Generally Southern, religious, and culturally conservative, they advocated the inherent value of literary works (particularly of literary works regarded as beautiful art objects) because they were sick of the growing ugliness of modern life and contemporary events. Some recent theorists even suggested that the rising popularity of formalism after World War II was a feature of American isolationism, the formalist tendency to isolate literature from biography and history being a manifestation of the American fatigue with wider involvements.

See also: Affective Fallacy, Authorial Intention, Deconstruction, Reader-Response Criticism, Symbol.

GAPS This term, used mainly by reader-response critics familiar with the theories of Wolfgang Iser, refers to "blanks" in texts that must be filled in by readers. A gap may be said to exist whenever a reader perceives something to be missing between words, sentences, paragraphs, stanzas, or chapters. Readers respond to gaps actively and creatively, explaining apparent inconsistencies in point of view, accounting for jumps in chronology, speculatively supplying information missing from plots, and resolving problems or issues left ambiguous or "indeterminate" in the text.

Critics sometimes speak as if a gap exists in a text; a gap is, of course, to some extent a product of the reader's perceptions. Different readers may find gaps in different texts and different gaps in the same text. Furthermore, they may fill these gaps in different ways, which is why, a reader-response critic might argue, works are interpreted in different ways.

Although the concept of the gap has been used mainly by reader-response critics to explain what makes reading an active, interactive process, it has also been used by critics who, though taking other theoretical approaches, are conversant with the vocabulary and practices of reader-response criticism. A deconstructor, for instance, might use gap when speaking of the radical self-contradictoriness of a text.

See also: Deconstruction, Reader-Response Criticism.

GENRE A French word referring to a kind or type of literature. Individual works within a genre may exhibit a distinctive form, be governed by certain conventions, and/or represent characteristic subjects. Tragedy, epic, and romance are all genres.

Perhaps inevitably, the term "genre" is used loosely. Lyric poetry is a genre, but so are characteristic *types* of the lyric, such as the sonnet, the ode, and the elegy. Fiction is a genre, as are detective fiction and science fiction. The list of genres grows constantly as critics establish new lines of connection between individual works and discern new categories of works with common characteristics. Moreover, some writers form hybrid genres by combining the characteristics of several in a single work.

Knowledge of genres helps critics to understand and explain what is conventional and unconventional, borrowed and original, in a work.

IDEOLOGY A system of beliefs underlying the customs, habits, and practices common to a given social group. To members of that group, the beliefs will seem obviously true, natural, and even universally applicable. They may seem just as obviously arbitrary, idiosyncratic, and even false to members of a group who adhere to another ideology. Within a society, there may be several ideologies, one or more of which may be dominant.

Ideologies may be forcefully imposed or willingly accepted. Their component beliefs may be consciously or unconsciously held. In either case, they come to form what Johanna M. Smith has called "the unexamined ground of our experience." Ideology governs our perceptions, judgments, and prejudices, our sense of what is acceptable, normal, and deviant. Ideology may cause a revolution; it may also allow discrimination and even exploitation.

Ideologies are of special interest to sociologically oriented critics of literature because of the way authors reflect or resist ideologies in their texts. Feminist critics, for instance, have sought to expose, and thereby call into question, the patriarchal ideology mirrored or inscribed in works written by men — even men who have sought to counter sexism and break down sexual stereotypes. New historicists are interested in demonstrating the ideological underpinnings not only of literary representations but also of our interpretations of them.

See also: Feminist Criticism, New Historicism.

INTENTIONAL FALLACY *See* Authorial Intention.

INTENTIONALITY *See* Authorial Intention.

INTERTEXTUALITY The condition of interconnectedness among texts. Every author has been influenced by others, and every work contains explicit and implicit references to other works. Writers may consciously or unconsciously echo a predecessor or precursor; they may also consciously or unconsciously disguise their indebtedness, making intertextual relationships difficult for the critic to trace.

Reacting against the formalist tendency to view each work as a free-standing object, some poststructuralist critics suggested that the meaning of a work only emerges intertextually, that is, within the context provided by other works. But there has been a reaction, too, against this type of intertextual criticism. Some new historicist critics suggested that literary history is itself too narrow a context and that works should be interpreted in light of a larger set of cultural contexts.

There is, however, a broader definition of intertextuality, one that refers to the relationship between works of literature and a wide range of narratives and discourses that we don't usually consider literary. Thus defined, intertextuality could be used by a new historicist to refer to the significant interconnectedness between a literary text and nonliterary discussions of or discourses about contemporary culture. Or it could be used by a poststructuralist to suggest that a work can only be recognized and read within a vast field of signs and tropes that is *like* a text and that makes any single text self-contradictory and "undecidable."

See also: Discourse, Formalism, Narrative, New Historicism, Poststructuralism, Trope.

METAPHOR The representation of one thing by another related or similar thing. The image (or activity or concept) used to represent or "figure" something else is known as the "vehicle" of the metaphor; the thing represented is called the "tenor." In other words, the vehicle is what we substitute for the tenor. The relationship between vehicle and tenor can provide much additional meaning. Thus, instead of saying, "Last night I read a book," we might say, "Last night I plowed through a book." "Plowed through" (or the activity of plowing) is the vehicle of our metaphor; "read" (or the act of reading) is the tenor, the thing being figured. The increment in meaning through metaphor is fairly obvious. Our audience knows not only *that* we read but also *how* we read, because to read a book in the way that a plow rips through earth is surely to read in a relentless, unreflective way. Note that in the sentence above a new metaphor — "rips through" — has been used to explain an old one. This serves (which is a metaphor) as an example of just how thick (another metaphor) language is with metaphors!

Metaphor is a kind of "trope" (literally, a "turning," i.e., a figure that alters or "turns" the meaning of a word or phrase). Other tropes include allegory, conceit, metonymy, personification, simile, symbol, and synecdoche. Traditionally, metaphor and symbol have been viewed as the principal tropes; minor tropes have been categorized as *types* of these two major ones. Similes, for instance, are usually defined as simple metaphors that usually employ "like" or "as" and state the tenor outright, as in "My love is like a red, red rose." Synecdoche involves a vehicle that is a *part* of the tenor, as in "I see a sail" meaning "I see a boat." Metonymy is viewed as a metaphor involving two terms commonly if arbitrarily associated with (but not fundamentally or intrinsically related to) each other. Recently, however, deconstructors such as Paul de Man and J. Hillis Miller have questioned the "privilege" granted to metaphor and the metaphor/metonymy distinction or "opposition." They have suggested that all metaphors are really metonyms and that all figuration is arbitrary.

See also: Deconstruction, Metonymy, Oppositions, Symbol.

METONYMY The representation of one thing by another that is commonly and often physically associated with it. To refer to a writer's handwriting as his or her "hand" is to use a metonymic "figure" or "trope." The image or thing used to represent something else is known as the "vehicle" of the metonym; the thing represented is called the "tenor."

Like other tropes (such as metaphor), metonymy involves the replacement of one word or phrase by another. Liquor may be referred to as "the bottle," a monarch as "the crown." Narrowly defined, the vehicle of a metonym is arbitrarily, not intrinsically, associated with the tenor. In other words, the bottle just happens to be what liquor is stored in and poured from in our culture. The hand may be involved in the production of handwriting, but so are the brain and the pen. There is no special, intrinsic likeness between a crown and a monarch; it's just that crowns traditionally sit on monarchs' heads and not on the heads of university professors. More broadly, "metonym" and "metonymy" have been used by recent critics to refer to a wide range of figures and tropes. Deconstructors have questioned the distinction between metaphor and metonymy.

See also: Deconstruction, Metaphor, Trope.

NARRATIVE A story or a telling of a story, or an account of a situation or of events. A novel and a biography of a novelist are both narratives, as are Freud's case histories.

Some critics use the word "narrative" even more generally; Brook Thomas, a new historicist, has critiqued "narratives of human history that neglect the role human labor has played."

NEW CRITICISM *See* Formalism.

NEW HISTORICISM One of the most recent developments in contemporary critical theory, its practitioners share certain convictions, the major ones being that literary critics need to develop a high degree of historical consciousness and that literature should not be viewed apart from other human creations, artistic or otherwise. See "What Is the New Historicism?" page 330.

OPPOSITIONS A concept highly relevant to linguistics, since linguists maintain that words (such as "black" and "death") have meaning not in themselves, but in relation to other words ("white" and "life"). Jacques Derrida, a poststructuralist philosopher of language, has suggested that in the West we think in terms of these "binary oppositions" or dichotomies, which on examination turn out to be evaluative hierarchies. In other words, each opposition — beginning/end, presence/absence, or consciousness/unconsciousness — contains one term that our culture views as superior and one term that we view as negative or inferior.

Derrida has "deconstructed" a number of these binary oppositions, including two — speech/writing and signifier/signified — that he believes to be central to linguistics in particular and Western culture in general. He has concurrently critiqued the "law" of noncontradiction, which is fundamental to Western logic. He and other deconstructors have argued that a text can contain opposed strands of discourse and, therefore, mean opposite things: reason *and* passion, life *and* death, hope *and* despair, black *and* white. Traditionally, criticism has involved choosing between opposed or contradictory meanings and arguing that one is present in the text and the other absent.

French feminists have adopted the ideas of Derrida and other deconstructors, showing that we not only think in terms of such binary oppositions as male/female, reason/emotion, and active/passive, but that we also associate reason and activity with masculinity and emotion and passivity with femininity. Because of this, they have concluded that language is "phallocentric," or masculine-dominated.

See also: Deconstruction, Discourse, Feminist Criticism, Poststructuralism.

POSTSTRUCTURALISM The general attempt to contest and subvert structuralism initiated by deconstructors and certain other critics associated with psychoanalytic, Marxist, and feminist theory. Structuralists, using linguistics as a model and employing semiotic (sign) theory, posit the possibility of knowing a text systematically and revealing the "grammar" behind its form and meaning. Poststructuralists argue against the possibility of such knowledge and description. They counter that texts can be shown to contradict not only structuralist accounts of them but also themselves. In making their adversarial claims, they rely on close readings of texts and on the work of theorists such as Jacques Derrida and Jacques Lacan.

Poststructuralists have suggested that structuralism rests on distinctions between "signifier" and "signified" (signs and the things they point toward), "self" and "language" (or "text"), texts and other texts, and text and world that are overly simplistic, if not patently inaccurate. Poststructuralists have shown how all signifieds are also signifiers, and they have treated texts as "intertexts." They have viewed the world as if it *were* a text (we desire a certain car because it *symbolizes* achievement) and the self as the subject, as well as the user, of language; for example, we may shape and speak through language, but it also shapes and speaks through us.

See also: Deconstruction, Feminist Criticism, Intertextuality, Psychoanalytic Criticism, Semiotics, Structuralism.

PSYCHOANALYTIC CRITICISM Grounded in the psychoanalytic theories of Sigmund Freud, it is one of the oldest critical methodologies still in use. Freud's view that works of literature, like dreams, express secret, unconscious desires led to criticism that interpreted literary works as manifestations of the author's neuroses. More recently, psychoanalytic critics have come to see literary works as skillfully crafted artifacts that may appeal to *our* neuroses by tapping into our repressed wishes and fantasies. Other forms of psychological criticism that diverge from Freud, though they ultimately derive from his insights, include those based on the theories of Carl Jung and Jacques Lacan. See "What Is Psychoanalytic Criticism?" page 223.

READER-RESPONSE CRITICISM An approach to literature that, as its name implies, considers the way readers respond to texts, as they read. Stanley Fish describes the method by saying that it substitutes for one question, "What does this sentence mean?" a more operational question, "What does this sentence do?" Reader-response criticism shares with deconstruction a strong textual orientation and a reluctance to define *the* meaning of a work. Along with psychoanalytic criticism, it shares an interest in the dynamics of mental response to textual cues. See "What Is Reader-Response Criticism?" page 252.

SEMIOLOGY, SEMIOTIC *See* Semiotics.

SEMIOTICS The study of signs and sign systems and the way meaning is derived from them. Structuralist anthropologists, psychoanalysts, and literary critics developed semiotics during the decades following 1950, but much of the pioneering work had been done at the turn of the century by the founder of modern linguistics, Ferdinand de Saussure, and the American philosopher Charles Sanders Peirce.

Semiotics is based on several important distinctions, including the distinction between "signifier" and "signified" (the sign and what it points toward) and the distinction between "langue" and "parole." Langue refers to the entire system within which individual utterances or usages of language have meaning; parole refers to the particular utterances or usages. A principal tenet of semiotics is that signs, like words, are not significant in themselves, but instead have meaning only in relation to other signs and the entire system of signs, or langue.

The affinity between semiotics and structuralist literary criticism derives from this emphasis placed on langue, or system. Structuralist critics, after all, were reacting against formalists and their procedure of focusing on individual works as if meanings didn't depend on anything external to the text.

Poststructuralists have used semiotics but questioned some of its underlying assumptions, including the opposition between signifier and signified. The feminist poststructuralist Julia Kristeva, for instance, has used the word "semiotic" to describe feminine language, a highly figurative, fluid form of discourse that she sets in opposition to rigid, symbolic masculine language.

See also: Deconstruction, Feminist Criticism, Formalism, Poststructuralism, Oppositions, Structuralism, Symbol.

SIMILE *See* Metaphor.

SOCIOHISTORICAL CRITICISM *See* New Historicism.

STRUCTURALISM A science of humankind whose proponents attempted to show that all elements of human culture, including literature, may be understood as parts of a system of signs. Structuralism, according to Robert Scholes, was a reaction to " 'modernist' alienation and despair."

Using Ferdinand de Saussure's linguistic theory, European structuralists such as Roman Jakobson, Claude Lévi-Strauss, and Roland Barthes (before his shift toward poststructuralism) attempted to develop a "semiology" or "semiotics" (science of signs). Barthes, among others, sought to recover literature and even language from the isolation in which they had been studied and to show that the laws that govern them govern all signs, from road signs to articles of clothing.

Particularly useful to structuralists were two of Saussure's concepts: the idea of "phoneme" in language and the idea that phonemes exist in two kinds of relationships: "synchronic" and "diachronic." A phoneme is the smallest consistently significant unit in language; thus, both "a" and "an" are phonemes, but "n" is not. A diachronic relationship is that which a phoneme has with those that have preceded it in time and those that will follow it. These "horizontal" relationships produce what we might call discourse or narrative and what Saussure called "parole." The synchronic relationship is the "vertical" one that a word has in a given instant with the entire system of language ("langue") in which it may generate meaning. "An" means what it means in English because those of us who speak the language are using it in the same way at a given time.

Following Saussure, Lévi-Strauss studied hundreds of myths, breaking them into their smallest meaningful units, which he called "mythemes."

Removing each from its diachronic relations with other mythemes in a single myth (such as the myth of Oedipus and his mother), he vertically aligned those mythemes that he found to be homologous (structurally correspondent). He then studied the relationships within as well as between vertically aligned columns, in an attempt to understand scientifically, through ratios and proportions, those thoughts and processes that humankind has shared, both at one particular time and across time. One could say, then, that structuralists followed Saussure in preferring to think about the overriding langue or language of myth, in which each mytheme and mytheme-constituted myth fits meaningfully, rather than about isolated individual paroles or narratives. Structuralists followed Saussure's lead in believing what the poststructuralist Jacques Derrida later decided he could not subscribe to — that sign systems must be understood in terms of binary oppositions. In analyzing myths and texts to find basic structures, structuralists tended to find that opposite terms modulate until they are finally resolved or reconciled by some intermediary third term. Thus, a structuralist reading of *Paradise Lost* would show that the war between God and the bad angels becomes a rift between God and sinful, fallen man, the rift then being healed by the Son of God, the mediating third term.

See also: Deconstruction, Discourse, Narrative, Poststructuralism, Semiotics.

SYMBOL A thing, image, or action that, though it is of interest in its own right, stands for or suggests something larger and more complex — often an idea or a whole range of interrelated ideas, attitudes, and practices.

Within a given culture, some things are understood to be symbols: the flag of the United States is an obvious example. More subtle cultural symbols might be the river as a symbol of time and the journey as a symbol of life and its manifold experiences.

Instead of appropriating symbols generally used and understood within their culture, writers often create symbols by setting up, in their works, a complex but identifiable web of associations. As a result, one object, image, or action suggests others, and often, ultimately, a range of ideas.

A symbol may thus be defined as a metaphor in which the "vehicle," the thing, image, or action used to represent something else, represents many related things (or "tenors") or is broadly suggestive. The urn in Keats's "Ode on a Grecian Urn" suggests many interrelated concepts, including art, truth, beauty, and timelessness.

Symbols have been of particular interest to formalists, who study how meanings emerge from the complex, patterned relationships between images in a work, and psychoanalytic critics, who are interested in how individual authors and the larger culture both disguise and reveal unconscious fears and desires through symbols. Recently, French feminists have also focused on the symbolic. They have suggested that, as wide-ranging as it seems, symbolic language is ultimately rigid and restrictive. They favor semiotic language and writing, which, they contend, is at once more rhythmic, unifying, and feminine.

See also: Feminist Criticism, Metaphor, Psychoanalytic Criticism, Trope.

SYNECDOCHE *See* Metaphor, Metonymy.

TENOR *See* Metaphor, Metonymy, Symbol.

TROPE A figure, as in "figure of speech." Literally a "turning," i.e., a turning or twisting of a word or phrase to make it mean something else. Principal tropes include metaphor, metonymy, simile, personification, and synecdoche.

See also: Metaphor, Metonymy.

VEHICLE *See* Metaphor, Metonymy, Symbol.

About the Contributors

THE EDITOR

Ross C Murfin, general editor of the Case Studies in Contemporary Criticism and volume editor of Joseph Conrad's *Heart of Darkness* and Nathaniel Hawthorne's *The Scarlet Letter* in the series, is provost and vice president for academic affairs at Southern Methodist University. He has taught at the University of Miami, Yale University, and the University of Virginia, and has published scholarly studies of Joseph Conrad, Thomas Hardy, and D. H. Lawrence.

THE CRITICS

Shari Benstock is professor of English at the University of Miami, where she has served as director of the Women's Studies Program. She is editor of a series on feminist criticism, *Reading Women Writing,* published by Cornell University Press. Her books include *Women of the Left Bank: Paris, 1900–1940* (1987) and *Textualizing the Feminine: On the Limits of Genre* (1991). She is at work on a biography of Edith Wharton.

Sacvan Bercovitch is Charles H. Carswell Professor of English at Harvard University, where he teaches courses in American literature. A leading scholar of the Puritan tradition, his renowned studies include *The Puritan Origins of the American Self* (1975) and *The American Jeremiad* (1978). He has edited *Reconstructing American Literary History* (1986) and *Ideology and Classic American Literature* (1986), and is general editor of the forthcoming *Cambridge History of American Literature*.

Joanne Feit Diehl is Pierce Professor of English at Bowdoin College, where she teaches literary theory and American literature. Author of *Dickinson and the Romantic Imagination* (1981) and *Women Poets and the American Sublime* (forthcoming), she is currently doing research on the poet Elizabeth Bishop.

David Leverenz is professor of English at the University of Florida. His publications include *The Language of Puritan Feeling* (1980) and *Manhood in the American Renaissance* (1989).

Michael Ragussis is professor of English at Georgetown University. His books include *The Subterfuge of Art: Language and the Romantic Tradition* (1978) and *Acts of Naming: The Family Plot in Fiction* (1986). He is at work on a book-length study of Jewish identity in British fiction.

(Continued from page iv)

"Re-Reading *The Letter:* Hawthorne, the Fetish, and the (Family) Romance" by Joanne Feit Diehl is a newly revised version of the essay that appeared in *New Literary History* 19 (1988).

"Mrs. Hawthorne's Headache: Reading *The Scarlet Letter*" by David Leverenz is a newly revised version of the essay that appeared in *Nineteenth-Century Fiction* 37 (1983).

"Silence, Family Discourse, and Fiction in *The Scarlet Letter*" by Michael Ragussis is a newly revised version of the essay that appeared in *ELH* 49 (1980).

"Hawthorne's A-Morality of Compromise" by Sacvan Bercovitch is a newly revised version of the essay that appeared in *Representations* 24 (1988).